"HONOR and DUTY and DIGNITY REVEAL THEMSELVES MOST PROUDLY WHEN WRITTEN IN BLOOD . . ."

They met in the middle of the wide field late in the afternoon, while the sun was dying. Purple shadows . . . red stares . . . and thousands upon thousands of horsemen in battle array waited resolutely.

The wind flapped the heavy stretched walls of the tent. From far off, cawing birds seemed intent upon communicating to the connivers some message they did not care to interpret.

Each felt that he possessed the secret of victory.

"Take what I offer you," Thameron insisted, "and be done with this treachery. You will only bring yourself to harm and all these men with you."

"Dog! I should submit to you?" growled Kurus. "You give me nothing! *You* remain king! *You* hold Lasura! *You* command the army! I submit to nothing! Emaria needs a *man* upon its throne, not an imposter! *Boy!* I fight for *Emaria*, damn you! For my country! And against *you!*"

The Fall of the First World by David C. Smith

Published by Pinnacle Books
Book I: THE MASTER OF EVIL
Book II: SORROWING VENGEANCE
Book III: THE PASSING OF THE GODS

THE FALL of the FIRST WORLD

The Passing of the Gods

David C. Smith

PINNACLE BOOKS NEW YORK

For
TOMMY, TARA, JOSHUA,
LORI and BRIAN—
carry on.

The verse by Michael Fantina appears in this book through permission of its author.

THE FALL OF THE FIRST WORLD BOOK III:
THE PASSING OF THE GODS

An original Pinnacle Books edition, published for the first time anywhere.

First printing, December 1983

ISBN: 0-523-41740-3

Can. ISBN: 0-523-43073-6

Cover illustration by Kevin Johnson

Printed in the United States of America

PINNACLE BOOKS, INC.
1430 Broadway
New York, New York 10018

9   8   7   6   5   4   3   2   1

Major Characters in *The Passing of the Gods*

In Athadia, the Western Empire, and its Territories:

King ELAD I
Queen SALIA, his wife
Lady ORAIN, widow of the executed Prince Cyrodian
Prince GALVUS, her son, regent to the throne
Count ADRED, a young Athadian aristocrat and rebel
OGODIS, the Imbur of Gaegosh and father of Queen Salia
OMOS, friend to Galvus
SOTOS, the palace physician
RHIA, a Suloskai rebel in Sulos
Lord General THOMO, envoy to Salukadian-held Erusabad
Major THYTAGORAS, once a Captain of Athadian troops
  in Erusabad, now serving in the Gaegoshan Army
Lord SIROM, an Athadian official in Erusabad
Lord Colonel VARDORIAN, Acting-Governor of Sulos in
  Kendia
Captain UVARS of the Athadian Imperial Army, Cavalry
Lord UTHIS, Governor of Bessara
Lord RHIN, a Councilor on the Congress of Nobility in
  Athad
Lord FALEN, a Councilor on the Congress of Nobility in
  Athad
Governor SULEN, of Abustad
Captain MANDOUM, Chief of the Khamari, the Athadian
  palace guard

Others:

ASSIA, a prostitute and businesswoman
ASAWAS, a wandering *ikbusa*
SALLUS, Captain of the *Doron*
LATHEN, Captain of the *Wing*
THARS, Captain of the *Jewel*
SOSSIAN, a poet
KEDROM, a Khamar

In Emaria:

THAMERON, a sorcerer and usurper of the throne of Emaria

Sir JORS, once an adviser to the Emarian court

In Erusabad, in the eastern empire of Salukadia:

AGORS *ko-Ghen*, Chief of Salukadia

NIHIM, his brother

bin-SUTUS, a court *aihman* to Agors *ko-Ghen*

UTTO-sen-gar, *hetmuk* of Erusabad

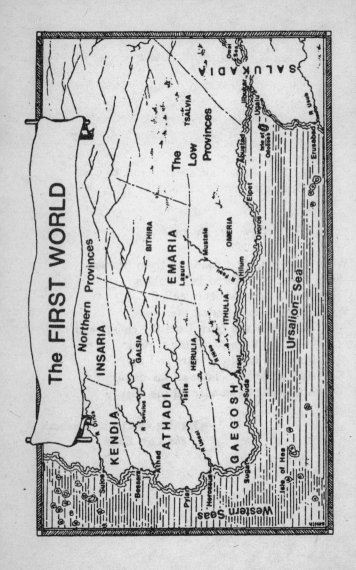

The FIRST WORLD

Es Atu

When earth was first sundered from heaven,
When God first rejoiced in the skies,
When evil announced its intention
With death to imprison all life:
    Then man was born from the clouds and rain,
    Man was born for limitless pain,
    Man was born for tears and lies,
    And made to wonder all his days,
    And made to wonder all the days.

—Opening chorus of Sossian's
Of the Lost Earth

The Events of *The Fall of the First World*: Book I—
THE MASTER OF EVIL

Part I: *A Throne of Blood*

Following the death of his father, King Evarris of Athadia, Prince Elad plots to usurp the throne from his mother, Queen Yta. He does this with the tacit approval of powerful members of the High Council and the elder of his two brothers, Prince General Cyrodian—all of whom feel that Elad will prove accommodating to their special interests once he is enthroned. Queen Yta, undecided whether or not to yield the crown to Elad, decides to query the Oracle at Mount Teplis; learning of her intention, Elad and Cyrodian, accompanied by the youngest prince, Dursoris, visit the Oracle before Yta can arrive there. When Elad fails to understand what the Oracle tells him, he forces her at swordpoint to speak more clearly. "You will rule to see everything precious destroyed," she warns him, "every hope ruined. You will rule Athadia and see the world die in anguish." Terrified by the implications of this, Elad is overcome and slays the Oracle; when he and his brothers escape from the holy mountain, Dursoris vows to bring the facts to light in court. Cyrodian therefore murders him. Yta, learning from the Oracle's spirit what has occurred, returns to the capital at Athad, orders Cyrodian imprisoned pursuant to his execution, and commands that Elad take the throne he desires so much: "No greater punishment can I offer."

Part II: *A Lamp in a Storm*

In Erusabad, a city considered holy by both the western Athadian and the eastern Salukadian empires, a young priest named Thameron runs into conflict with the bureaucracy of his temple. The Church of Bithitu is the religious foundation of the Athadian empire; but it has long ceased to embody the wisdom of its Prophet Bithitu and has, over the course of two thousand years, become a reactionary, stagnant anachronism. Thameron, believing unconditionally in the words of the Prophet, fights hypocrisy in the Church and soon finds himself expelled. Crushed and embittered, he decides to escape Erusabad and takes leave of the only true friend he has—Hapad, a fellow novitiate—and says farewell to the only woman he has ever loved—a young prostitute named Assia.

Part III: *End Without Mercy*

Elad takes the throne and kingship of the empire as his mother leaves to live out her years on Hea Isle, a religious retreat. Unknown to Elad, the angry Cyrodian has plotted with schemers loyal to him to assassinate Yta; meanwhile the Imperial Army, which holds Cyrodian in great respect as one of its own, threatens dissension unless Elad overrules the death sentence and allows his brother exile. The intimidated neophyte king orders Cyrodian removed in chains beyond Athadia's border. Conspirators loyal to Cyrodian chase down Yta's galley and murder her and her crew, then return home to plot the assassination of Elad. They are, however, discovered and executed; but when Elad orders a patrol to return the dismissed Cyrodian home to stand trial for his new crimes, he learns that his brother cannot be found.

Part IV: *The Dispossessed*

Thameron in his journeys experiences life at its most depraved and unspiritual. In despair, and still seeking enlightenment, he turns to a misanthropic sorcerer, Guburus, who promises to help guide Thameron on his mystical quest. But the impatient Thameron, dissatisfied with the lessons Guburus insists he must learn, gives up his spirit to a demonic force he scarcely comprehends. When Guburus realizes what his pupil has done he tries to fight him, and Thameron slays the elder. Too late,

Thameron realizes that he has allowed himself to become the vessel of Evil on earth—the Master of the Hell of Men.

In Athad, a humiliated but wiser Elad sincerely tries to repent for his past errors and applies himself to the task of becoming a good king. But the atmosphere of crime, death and vengeance in the palace lingers. Count Adred, a friend of the slain Dursoris, offers to take Lady Orain, Cyrodian's wife (and secret lover of the good Dursoris) and her son Prince Galvus, on a vacation to the uplands, to Sulos in the Province of Kendia. Mother and son readily assent; in Sulos, the three pass a pleasant month and prepare for the holiday weeks (it is the time of the Church's great celebrations) in the home of Adred's friend Count Mantho, a wealthy aristocrat. There is, however, a storm growing in Sulos—indeed, a storm is growing throughout the Athadian empire: for the economy, long mismanaged by wealthy businessmen and high-seated plutocrats, has created a situation of rising unemployment, rampant inflation and increasing public anger. Attempts by the working people to change government and business policies have been met with deaf ears; riots and disturbances designed to publicize the working people's plight have been put down by force. Now, in Sulos, the first mass revolt by the workers leads to the assassination of the city governor and many aristocrats (Mantho among them) and several nights of bloodshed and violence.

Part V: *The West is Dying*

Three generations of expansion by the eastern Salukadian peoples have brought them to the shores of the great Ursalion Sea—and to the doorstep of the wide Athadian empire. Huagrim *ko-Ghen*, Chief of the Salukads, lives in his capital at Ilbukar, where he resides in splendor. But Huagrim is old and realizes that he will die soon; therefore he decides to climax the ever-westward movement of his empire by taking complete control of the east-west shared city of Erusabad. Huagrim's elder son, Agors, supports this move, but the chief's younger son, Nihim, is against it.

Adred, who had left Sulos during the holidays but before the

3

outbreak of violence, is in Mirukad and now hears of the rebellion. Frightened that his friends may be in danger, he tries to board any ship sailing south but learns that the harbor of Sulos is closed until further notice. King Elad, meanwhile, concluding that force must be resisted by even greater force, orders two legions north to the city, where those revolutionaries still alive are executed, their corpses beheaded and their heads piled onto a war galley. The war galley is towed to the capital, where it is displayed and burned as a warning against any further violence on the part of insurrectionists within Athadia. It is a strong-willed but wrong-headed move by a king still uncertain of his crown.

Adred, at last able to get a ship to Sulos, discovers Galvus and Orain still alive and living on the docks. They tell him that Mantho was killed and that they have decided to live incognito and to help the oppressed and the dispossessed as Sulos starts to rebuild. Adred, now definitely sympathetic towards the rebels, takes up their fight and sails on to the capital, where he intends to make King Elad face these matters squarely.

Part VI: *Far Paths, Other Shadows*

Cyrodian has taken refuge with King Nutatharis of Emaria, a land-locked nation situated between Athadia and the Lowlands. Nutatharis wishes to expand into the Lowlands, a breadbasket area bordering Salukadia; Huagrim agrees not to interfere with Emarian military movements while at the same time gaining guarantees from Nutatharis that should Salukadia's takeover of Erusabad lead to war with the west, Nutatharis will side with the east.

Count Adred, in the capital, engages in a hot-tempered argument with King Elad, promising him that the revolution will sweep across the empire unless Elad quickly agrees to look into matters of reform. Caught in webs of political intrigue, Elad procrastinates; meanwhile, his marriage to Princess Salia, daughter of the Imbur of Gaegosh, approaches. Salia is renowned as the most beautiful woman in the world.

Adred leaves the capital and returns northward; during a stopover in Bessara, he becomes involved with the revolutionary movement there and meets Rhia, the estranged wife of Lord

4

Solok, an aristocratic liberal and rebel sympathizer. Following a demonstration in the city, Solok and many others are arrested, but Adred and Rhia escape and go into hiding.

Part VII: *New Chains*

General Kustos of Emaria, together with his new military adviser, Cyrodian, leads the expedition into the Lowlands. The farmers and villagers of the territory fight fiercely against the sophisticated Emarians and take a heavy toll, while the invading troops are victimized by winter storms. Kustos is severely wounded during one engagement; and when it becomes apparent to Nutatharis that his advance into the Lowlands has stagnated, he orders his army to hold its ground until spring and commands Kustos and Cyrodian back to the capital at Lasura. There, Nutatharis informs Cyrodian that his brother Elad has demanded Cyrodian's return to Athad; but in return for Nutatharis's refusing to submit to Elad's capias, Cyrodian binds himself to the Emarian king by a warrior's pledge—the oldest of oaths. Cyrodian hungers to become general of the Emarian army now that Kustos is dying of his wounds. When he looks in on the ill man one night, he finds the bed-ridden Kustos being harassed by one of Nutatharis's courtiers, Eromedeus. To his shock, Cyrodian learns that Eromedeus is not a man at all, but an undying creature who wishes Kustos to give up his soul for him so that Eromedeus may make his peace with the gods. Kustos dies without agreeing, and Cyrodian wrathfully stabs Eromedeus—and discovers that the man cannot be killed.

The Emarian military maneuvers in the Lowlands create apprehension in the rulers of the Athadian-controlled Province of Omeria. In response, Elad sanctions the disbursement of troops from Elpet to Abustad to guard Omeria's northern border. Among the camp followers is Assia, who left Erusabad after Thameron's departure. Ill, she had traveled with her father to Elpet, where he continued to use her as a prostitute until he was killed in a tavern brawl.

While the Emarians are attacking the Lowlands, Huagrim's soldiers occupy the northern, western-controlled section of Erusabad—an overt act of war. In Athad, members of Council

5

demand that Elad answer this provocation with armed force; but the king, fearful of the Oracle's warning, refuses. So long as trade and pilgrimage rights for Athadian citizens are respected, Elad (who realizes that he had overreacted to the riots in Sulos) decides not to go to war with Salukadia. In Erusabad, Huagrim *ko-Ghen* orders the Temple of Bithitu to be partially dismantled and redone as an eastern pantheon.

Thameron returns to Erusabad intending to confront his mentors in the Temple and finds the city occupied by the eastern military forces. He learns that the Church elders, disgraced, had committed suicide, but finds his old friend Hapad, now living in a ghetto apartment, dying of a fever. When Hapad discovers what Thameron has done, he condemns his friend with his last breath and bemoans the fact that he did not die before learning of Thameron's everlasting damnation.

King Elad, on a winter's day, marries Lady Salia of Gaegosh. As the couple exit the state palace following the ceremony, a revolutionary disguised as one of the Khamar palace guards attacks Elad and stabs him several times before he is overpowered and slain by the king's soldiers.

The Events of
The Fall of the First World:
Book II—
SORROWING VENGEANCE

Part I: *An Attack of Conscience*

From their small apartment in Sulos, Galvus and Orain operate a clandestine enterprise by which they secure food and necessities for the jobless and poor of the city. Galvus has made friends with a young man named Omos, an outcast of the streets; they have become lovers. Learning that Elad was the target of a murder attempt, but not knowing the outcome of it, Galvus and Orain both feel uncomfortable and are undecided as to whether or not return to Athad.

Adred and Rhia, revolutionaries in Bessara, witness more deaths caused by the execution of Rhia's estranged husband and fellow rebel, Lord Solok.

Elad, in Athad, is recuperating from his wounds. He has what he calls an "attack of conscience" and one evening talks with Abgarthis about philosophical matters. An intelligent man but not a wise one, a sincere yet not decisive king, Elad has nevertheless sought to come to grips with the issues of the working people, and he determines to look into the matter of the *sirots* or workers' democratic assemblies. Abgarthis is quite pleased with this change in attitude.

Lord General Thomo, the king's envoy to Erusabad, arrives in the Holy City to take power over Acting-Governor Lord Sirom and maintain peace and security in the Salukadian-held metropolis. He and Captain Thytagoras, the angry pessimist and racist, disagree on how this should be done. Meanwhile, Huagrim *ko-Ghen* and his sons have established a palace for themselves and their court in Erusabad by renovating a spacious villa abandoned by a wealthy Athadian family.

Thameron is living a life of means in Erusabad and searching for Assia, whom he feels he still loves. He entertains prostitutes who are unable to arouse in him the emotions he had shared with Assia; he decides to leave Erusabad and travel, in hopes that he might sense his old love in some other place. Assia, meanwhile, is with the Athadian troops in their camp on the border of the Lowlands. A soldier named Urwus, who mistreats her but claims to care for her, convinces Assia to return with him to Abustad when his unit is recalled from the border.

Part II: *Coals Beneath the Ashes*

In Emaria, King Nutatharis intends to make Cyrodian his General of the Army; before doing so, however, he wishes to dispense with their warriors' vow and so asks Cyrodian to slay Eromedeus, whom Nutatharis has come to mistrust. Despite his knowledge of the immortal wanderer's true nature, Cyrodian makes the attempt and fails. Disgraced, he is arrested on Nutatharis's orders so that the king—finally answering appeals from Elad of Athadia—can return him to Athad for his crimes. And now that Nutatharis understands just what Eromedeus is, he becomes most apprehensive and banishes the wanderer to the mountains north of Lasura.

Elad publishes his announcement concerning imperial consideration of reforms and the formation of the people's *sirots*. In Bessara, Rhia and Adred learn of this announcement just before they are arrested by Lord Uthis's police. Under the new circumstances they are imprisoned, but they cannot be executed.

In Sulos, which has known peace for several months under the lenient hand of its new city governor, Lord Colonel Vardorian, disgruntled workers in the fields outside the city occupy graneries as a form of protest; they demand economic reforms and a voice in controlling their own lives. Vardorian, not wanting another bloodbath, stalls for time and contacts King Elad. Lord Abgarthis intercepts this message as well as the official reports from Bessara concerning the arrest of Count Adred and devises a plan which Elad sanctions: to send Adred to Sulos where he can contact

Galvus and Orain, and have Galvus, with his liberal reformist proclivities, act on behalf of the throne to gain promises of restraint from the rebellious workers in return for a fair hearing later from the throne. This frees the well-intentioned gadfly Count Adred (as well as Rhia, whom he insists on taking with him to Sulos), and gets Elad's nephew and sister-in-law back to the capital where he feels they truly belong. Galvus agrees: his system of distributing necessities to the underprivileged and the victimized can be left in the hands of others, and if he can come to terms with the workers he can return to Athad and present his uncle Elad with solid proposals for reform. Rhia, however, decides to remain in Sulos and work with Galvus's friends there. She is committed to her ideals and has come to recognize that Adred's deepest feelings are reserved for Orain—something that Adred himself had not fully realized until seeing her again after their prolonged separation.

Part III: *The Wound and the Scar*

In Erusabad, Huagrim *ko-Ghen* dies. Thomo writes of this to King Elad, suggesting that it might be politic for Athadia to send a high-ranking diplomat to the east to assure the new Salukadian government—Huagrim's successor, his son Agors—that Athadia wishes to continue its policy of amity and parity with the east.

In the farming regions of Omeria a new prophet has made his appearance—a farmer who has taken the name Asawas ("seeing one") because of a mystical experience and wanders the countryside preaching the vision of the one true god, On, and foretelling a great destruction for the world. In a small town just south of the Emarian border Asawas meets Cyrodian, who is chained, caged and being escorted to a waiting Athadian troop to be conducted home. Cyrodian is contemptuous of this prophet, but what Asawas tells the exiled prince so astonishes and frightens Cyrodian that the prince's hair turns white.

Thameron journeys to Ugalu where he does not find Assia and so moves on to Abustad where he discovers her living with the brutal Urwus. Assia wishes to go with Thameron, but when Urwus attempts to kill him the sorcerer is forced to slay Urwus. Thameron and Assia then escape and live together for several days, recalling what they have each suffered since both left Erusabad. Thameron confesses everything to Assia; she declares that she still loves him, but the sorcerer—who now feels mystically called to the north—knows that she cannot stay with him. He ends their profoundly emotional reunion by filling her purse with gold coins transformed from rose petals so that Assia may have all she might need to take care of herself.

Part IV: *The Return*

Adred, Galvus, Orain and Omos return to Athad, appalled by the obvious poverty, joblessness and decay in the capital that have resulted from the eroding economy. They meet with Elad (who introduces them to Queen Salia). Adred discovers that his arrest as a revolutionary has had a bad effect: though freed through imperial intervention, much of his property has been confiscated and a certain percentage of his financial holdings cannot be returned to him. Brooding, he takes a carriage ride around the capital; Orain goes with him and both are disturbed by the obvious corrosion of the social structure—poor men and women living hand-to-mouth, and the socially prominent hidden in expensive mansions behind high gates and stone walls.

Adred and Galvus present to Elad their plan for restructuring the economy—a redistribution of all wealth, ownership of all businesses by the workers, the freedom of a pluralistic economy and the establishment of the *sirots* as representative of the people in the Athadian High Council. Galvus declares that he is purchasing a large tract of land in the Diruvian Valley outside Sulos—where the workers have rebelled—so he can begin the process of this new economy. Elad is both surprised and impressed; he tells both men that two members of Council, Lords Rhin and Falen (who are not sympathetic to the revolutionary ideals), are investigating the most plausible methods of instituting the *sirots*, and in a few weeks the matter will be opened to debate in the Council Chamber.

Thameron, traveling north, crosses paths with Asawas. They recognize one another's spirits—the universal elements of harmony and discord which they personify. Thameron performs an act of sorcery which terrifies the people nearby, but Asawas quietly reverses the effects of it; he begs Thameron to give up his intention: it is still not too late for the young man to cast out that spirit which possesses him and moves him in the course of mankind's destruction. But Thameron, believing his mystical insights are far more truthful than this prophet's reminders of love, honesty and justice, scorns Asawas and continues traveling north.

Elad learns that Cyrodian is being returned to him by King Nutatharis of Emaria and orders preparations made in the palace dungeon. He also receives Lord Thomo's letter from Erusabad suggesting that a diplomat be sent as an emissary of goodwill to the Salukadian court. Considering this, Elad realizes that the sole individual of estimable rank in his palace whom he might free for such a mission is his own wife. Salia, uncomfortable because her father the Imbur has stayed in Athad following the assassination attempt and distressed because no one seems to respect her, is greatly excited at the opportunity of journeying to the other side of the world in an imperial capacity.

Part V: *The Prisoning Heart*

Nutatharis sends his troops into the Lowlands in a second attempt at the conquest which failed so disastrously the previous winter. But tremendous spring floods wipe out whole legions of his army and at the same time destroy all croplands in the Lowlands and in wide stretches of Emaria. Within mere weeks the unprecedented floods have reduced the Emarian army to a band of killers ravenous for food and are responsible for widespread death and starvation throughout the farmlands and peasants' villages. Armed Emarian squadrons cross the border into Athadia, attack villages and steal stores—a direct provocation to war. Nutatharis's economy, already unstable and on the brink of bankruptcy, is pushed beyond its limits by the king's attempts to buy food and weapons on credit from any source he can find. Into this arena of national devastation comes Thameron the sorcerer, demanding an audience with Nutatharis and then demanding from Nutatharis knowledge of the "man of shadows" Thameron feels is near, for it is his destiny to meet this creature. Nutatharis, suspecting that the gods hate him, tells Thameron where Eromedeus has gone; in

11

return, Thameron with his sorcery causes grain to multiply, thus buying Nutatharis time to remain in control of his throne.

In Abustad, Assia uses the gold Thameron gave her to go into business for herself: she buys a boat, has it outfitted as a pleasure barge and hires prostitutes to entertain the wealthy clientele to whom she will cater. Without Thameron, Assia is a woman lacking any sense of self-purpose, and so she cynically determines to make the most practical use of her talents and fortune—by going into business.

Cyrodian is returned to Athad and is placed in the dungeon beneath the palace; Elad refuses to speak with him and in Council gains guarantees from the Imperial Army that it will not interfere with the death sentence. Orain and Galvus visit Cyrodian who is contemptuous of them both; but when Orain asks him if he did what he did because he truly believed it to be the best for the empire, Cyrodian tells her, "Yes." Seeing that Orain is very upset, Adred secretly visits the prisoner, sneaking a bottle of wine down to the cell. Both he and Cyrodian drink and become tipsy; Cyrodian bares his soul enough to admit to Adred why his hair turned white and mentions Asawas's name.

Elad announces to his High Council that he is sending Salia to Erusabad; he cannot be overruled in this, but Ogodis causes a disturbance and palace guards escort him from the hall.

That afternoon, the public execution of Prince Cyrodian takes place.

Part IV: *Stormtide*

In the mountains north of Lasura Thameron meets Eromedeus, the undying wanderer. Their encounter, Eromedeus explains, signifies the beginning of the end of this world of men, for he knows himself to be the fulcrum in the shifting of cosmic elements on earth. Thameron is destined to gain great power, but even as he strives to create what he feels is the destiny of humankind, the prophet of goodness—Asawas—will come with a light to Thameron, and their confrontation will coincide with the beginning of the end. Mankind has waited long for this; mankind wills this to happen; deep in its shadowed heart humanity is purging itself.

In the city of Hilum Asawas announces the signs that portend the end of the world. Lord Abadon of Hilum has him arrested for inciting public disorder; the powerful Inquisitor of the Temple of Bithitu in Hilum, Seraficos, interviews Asawas, thinking that he claims to be Bithitu returned to this world. Seraficos, smug, proud and hypocritical, demands that Asawas show him the power of God if he is truly the prophet he claims to be. He commands him to turn a stone into bread, offers to give him the world and demands that Asawas jump from a height to test his claimed powers. Asawas refuses and charges Seraficos, "Where is your faith?" knowing that this spiritual leader is utterly without faith. The astounded and angry Seraficos orders Asawas sent in chains to Athad, to be brought before the throne of the empire on charges of treason.

Salia leaves for Erusabad. Elad convenes the Council for debate on the matter of instituting the *sirots*. Galvus, surprising the assembly, presents working men from the Diruvian fields to offer testimony regarding the corruption and injustices of the businessmen who own them and argue for a free voice by the working people. Lord Rhin, a wealthy businessman himself and autocratic, fiercely denounces their accusations. The Councilors are indecisive. Elad feels despondent, trapped between his duties to the hereditary nobility and his yearning for justice for all of his citizens.

In Erusabad, Thytagoras resigns from the army because he cannot abide King Elad's "appeasement policy" toward the east; he leaves for Athad to protest this in the capital. Lord Thomo meanwhile meets with bin-Sutus of the Salukadian court to explain that the emissary King Elad is sending is his wife. This could be taken as an offensive gesture, for women are held in low regard in the east. bin-Sutus assures Thomo that Agors *ko-Ghen* will understand.

In Lasura, the army and the professional soldiers of the capital plot to overthrow Nutatharis. When Thameron returns to the city from the mountains they enlist him and offer to sponsor him if he will usurp the throne, for they know he is a powerful man.

In a transparent power play in Council, Lord Rhin, realizing that Elad is moving toward liberalizing the government, argues for the establishment of a coalition ministry to take effect as soon as the *sirots* are instituted. Galvus and Adred are outraged; this coalition, the Khilu, to be composed of workers', public administration and aristocratic representatives, is obviously a device intended to undermine the power of the people before they even have it.

Part VII: *The Fall*

Salia arrives in Erusabad; she is feted by Agors and the eastern government and charms all of them. Agors finds himself attracted to the western queen and at an evening's entertainment determines that Salia is happy to be free of the restrictions that held her captive to duty and protocol in Athad. The days progress, and as the visiting nobles, ministers and lawyers hammer out agreements and accords with the lawyers of the Salukadian empire, Agors deliberately plays upon the girl-queen's apprehensions, romantic notions and self-delusions. They enter into a romance.

Thameron murders Nutatharis and takes the throne of Emaria, backed by the palace guard and the strongest voices in the home army. He learns that a rebel officer, a survivor of the disastrous floods in the east, is gathering men to him and marching to Lasura to take the throne for himself. Meanwhile Eromedeus, trying to alter the course of destiny, secretly enters Lasura and attempts to assassinate Thameron. He fails, and the sorcerer laughs at him and does not harm him in turn but banishes him from his borders: "I am now as deathless as you, undying one, until the hour of mercy comes down."

Although she knows that it means the possible loss of all that the two empires have come to terms on, Salia determines to give up her crown and remain in Erusabad with Agors until he tires of her, then live her own life, free of her father, her husband and the chains of her caste. Thomo fears that her decision will cause a war between west and east; Lord Sirom of Erusabad denies this possibility. Thomo leaves the Holy City to report what has happened to King Elad. A strange wind (the third of Asawas's signs) hastens his ship's journey. In Athad, the Lord General explains what has happened to his king, then reviews the incident before a special session of Council. Ogodis, the Imbur, is certain that his daughter is being held against her will; he hires Thytagoras—who knows Erusabad well—to sail with him and his army against the eastern empire to make war if Salia is not released. Elad, angry but despairing, rallies and decides that Athadia, too, must send an armed flotilla to Erusabad so that if his wife is not returned to him he can commence military action against the Salukadian empire.

PROLOGUE

The Master of Hell

The fire had burned all night.

From where he stood on a balcony, Thameron watched black columns of smoke rise in the west to spread a haze against the dull whites and grays of the dawn sky. The loud chorus of cries that had carried through the night from that end of the city had dwindled and disappeared; the crowds had departed and returned to their homes. The mighty pandemonium of horses and soldiers and wagons, too, had fallen silent. All that remained, from what Thameron could observe, was the lifting black smoke, with no further hint of flames.

Behind him, across the chamber, there came a truculent pounding on the door, followed by the creak of old hinges. Thameron turned. Into the dimness of the room came Sir Jors. He made his way toward the sorcerer, and as he did the gray light of the new day filled his features. Sir Jors's face was streaked with lines of exhaustion and worry; indeed, his entire frame betrayed weariness, as though his corpulence had somehow reduced itself during the agonies of the night.

Not meeting Thameron's gaze, Jors handed him a rolled parchment, then brusquely turned and went to a wide table. There he took up a decanter and poured himself a liberal quantity of white wine. As he lifted the goblet to his bearded lips, Sir Jors's hand quietly shivered.

Saying nothing, Thameron opened the parchment, held it out to the light and scanned the double columns of names that had been penned very neatly by a court scribe. Satisfied, he rolled it up again and, approaching Sir Jors, dropped the parchment on the table.

Their eyes met.

"All of these?" Thameron asked quietly.

Jors ducked his head. "All . . . of them." He swallowed, betraying his discomfort, sipped wine, then turned and moved half-way across the floor. It seemed as though he wished to keep some amount of distance between himself and the usurper.

Staring into some shadowed recess, Jors admitted lowly, "*You* didn't have to listen to them scream . . . *you* didn't have to smell the—flesh . . . cooking. . . ."

"You're a soldier. Surely you—"

". . . all night long," Jors said, in his tense whisper. "All . . . night . . . long."

"I assume," Thameron commented, "that we made every possible attempt to force open doors and windows, to break in and allow at least some of them an avenue to safety?"

"A thousand soldiers out there," Sir Jors replied. He turned now and faced the sorcerer. "A thousand soldiers—two thousand—with swords and bars, chains and weapons and tools—and they couldn't pry open a single door! They couldn't force open one single window!"

"How peculiar. The heat of the flames must have affected the entire structure in some strange way."

"The access doors to the roof opened easily enough," his minister reminded him. "Some of them were able to make it onto the roof. Some of them were on fire, but they made it to the roof. We had no way to save them. They hurled themselves to their deaths."

Thameron shook his head as though deploring such a tragedy.

Jors asked him coldly, "Why didn't you just banish them to the frontier?"

"Explain yourself."

"Did you have to trap all your political enemies in the Diet Hall and let them burn alive that way? Did you?"

Thameron did not respond.

"You are foul, Lord Usurper. You are evil!"

"At your behest I slew your own king, Jors. You asked me to do that. Now I destroy his enemies! How can you in honesty stand there and—"

"We are *civilized!*" was the angry retort. "Nutatharis had ample time to make his decision. He might have escaped . . . gone into hiding, chosen self-exile in the east. He chose to *allow* himself to be slain by you!"

"Civilized," Thameron smiled. "I chopped off Nutatharis's head with a sword. The blood poured onto the floor in a flood. Your own guards mounted it on the entranceway to this very palace, so that every citizen in Lasura might know that the madman was truly dead. And they cheered. The crowds came and the soldiers, and they cheered. You yourself announced me to them, and they bowed to me, Jors. They bowed to me! No one rebuked me on that day! I was their savior and a hero! And what have I done for you in these scant weeks since that blood flowed? Your people *believe* again, Sir Jors! Your soldiers *believe* again!"

"In you."

"In me and in themselves. In their nation. In a purpose, a destiny!"

Sir Jors stared for a prolonged moment into the usurper's eyes. "And because whatever nobles and aristocrats and businessmen who still lived sought to petition you for redress—because their crops were lost or their homes ruined, because they wished—"

"Because they wished to overthrow me, Jors. They wished to use me as a tool to defy your king, and once I had accomplished that they assumed they had no further use for me."

"You don't know that."

"But I do."

"They called for a peaceful assembly in the Diet. They requested *your* presence. You even agreed that you would attend!"

19

"How fortunate for me that I was detained, so that I too was not trapped in that conflagration."

Sir Jors, glaring at him, trembled anew. No remorse . . . no apologies . . . not even an admission of his crime. The minister glanced toward the table at the wine, made one quick step in that direction, then furiously hurled his empty goblet against a wall. Frowning and grunting, he moved to an ornate chair and slumped in its pillows. One hand pressed to his head, he told Thameron again: "You are foul! And you are more than a mere usurper. Do you cause flames to happen the same way you cause grain to grow? Are you truly a sorcerer?"

Thameron laughed. "Who tells you that I am a sorcerer?"

"Men speak of it. We . . . know."

"I command forces of Nature as you command troops of men; some are born to such gyrations of the stars. It is not profound." Thameron stepped toward Jors, read his pale looks, his posture. "You reproach me because you fear me, Jors."

"I fear you mightily. The gods will damn me for ever having invited you into this palace! Here is my reward! I have damned my nation through you!"

"Don't speak like a fool! It took your Nutatharis years to bring Emaria to ruin. In just a few weeks, I have already begun to rebuild it and to rebuild its spirit! Your citizens are proud and pleased to wear their badges of the Emarian League! Your guards are eager to serve as my police! Your soldiers are happy to hear the trumpets call again, so that they can defend their country against anarchists and aggressors! I have given them meaning and purpose and hope!"

Sir Jors replied in a very low, very cold, deliberate voice: "I sense there is some mighty secret to you, sorcerer, that goes beyond even these powers you claim for yourself. I truly believe you are evil. I have known angry men and deluded men, frightened men and murderers and madmen, but I never considered any of them to be evil. But you—there is some atmosphere about you . . . almost as though a shadow covered you . . . I can almost smell it!"

Thameron's eyes brightened. "Shall I tell you what it is, Jors? Shall I tell you what this is that you sense? Not so long ago I was a priest serving the Prophet in his Temple. I was eager and wished to do good; yet I saw that those men who served the Prophet in

20

positions of great power were greedy and corrupt and had totally savaged all that was honest and open and promising in the Prophet's words. I left that temple; I wandered; and I met a man who claimed to be a magus, and I delved into mysteries with this man. Others spoke of him in awe and fear, certain that he was evil; yet he was not: he simply saw that which others were too blind to perceive. He taught me many mighty truths, Jors. And now you say that *I* am evil. Well . . . I am not. I bring solace and meaning, authority and direction to the multitudes, yield answers to their questions, remind them that they do not live in vain. Do I lie? I merely interpret for them what they desire. Where then is the evil? What can your answer possibly be to someone like myself? I merely reflect the soul of humanity."

Sir Jors said nothing to this.

Thameron smiled. "If I were so evil and so powerful a sorcerer, then why do I not silence you? Slay you? Force you to my will? I have no interest in that. I want you to be what you are, minister. Have your doubts; have your fears; you will learn, soon enough. If you do not care to serve me, then I shall ask you to step down, and I will find another to replace you."

Sir Jors shook his head. The anger and ill will that held him had passed, or he had suppressed it. Perhaps he thought that now was not the time or place for him to give vent to what he felt; or perhaps he had not yet had enough time to put into perspective what he sensed or to plan. He rose from his chair, indicating that he meant to leave.

Thameron asked, "Our troops are prepared to march east today?"

"At your command, Lord Thameron."

"What news of this rebel chief?"

"Captain Kurus's latest messenger, last night, claimed that he owns an army of five legions, all survivors of that . . . debacle in the Lowlands."

Thameron nodded.

"He has taken control of the city of Ilrukad, thirty leagues east of here, and his messenger issued you a summons to meet Kurus's troops there within five days or face a siege against Lasura."

Thameron sighed and showed an awkward smile.

"With the Fifth, Eighth and Tenth Legions sitting on our

western border, we have only two here with which to defend ourselves."

"I am aware of that, Sir Jors. Only I do not intend that we will defend ourselves."

Jors was astonished. "Not *defend* ourselves?"

"We ride today to meet Kurus in the field outside Ilrukad."

"But we have only two legions!"

"We will take the offensive, Jors—and we will triumph."

"But how can you possibly—"

"A quick defeat—and the survivors among the rebels will be happy to return to their true master."

Abashed, Jors reminded him, "But . . . on the west? What of the Athadian forces?"

"Athadia does not attack us. Athadia is presently interested only in containing the raiding parties that have crossed her border for food. Our troops now have food. The Athadians don't wish a war, and we don't want war with Athadia."

After a moment's indecisiveness Sir Jors—gravely troubled, uncertain and eager to be quit of that room and Thameron's presence—saluted and turned to go.

"You will ride beside me," Thameron told him, "this afternoon, when we head out to Ilrukad."

"Certainly, my lord." His minister lent him another long, dark look, said nothing more but went out.

And as soon as the chamber door was closed Thameron crossed the room, reopened it and looked out. Two palace guards stood there at attention, fully armed and both wearing black armbands embroidered with the white seven-pointed star, inverted—which Thameron had made into his symbol of state.

He nodded to one of them. "Enter."

The man did so, closing the door behind him and saluting with great formality.

"Find me a soldier," Thameron ordered this guard, "whom I can take into my confidence, who will readily accept the proposal that he act as retainer and bodyguard to Sir Jors."

The soldier smiled. "My lord, I know of a man already."

"Who is this?"

"Myself, Lord Thameron."

The usurper chuckled. "I suspect," he allowed, "that you may indeed be that man. Come over here and take a seat. Take a glass of wine. I wish to ask you some questions. . . ."

"Time hurries, Nutatharis. We live in days of consequence; the incidents come more and faster, roadmarks on the path to our conclusion. Do you not hear the storms at night? Don't you see it in the stars, feel it in the twilight at the end of every day? If you listen closely, in the silence of the dawn, you can feel it eating away at the soul of every man and woman in this nation. The fear. The knowing. The understanding. We live at the end of time. It is the end of time that you feel, pulling at you, pressing on you. Do you really suppose that mornings now are as innocent as they were when you were a child? We live in the shadow of a mighty Wheel, Nutatharis. Time tests man as much as man tests time. And now we live in an age when the mysteries happen fast, visit us with cause—and so many that men don't believe what they see and feel. The Shadow has descended upon me, and it possesses me. I quicken with this comprehension. . . ."

He knew that there was now no way to halt the revolution of the Wheel, to alter the course of destiny which the storm of humankind had chosen in its heart—no turning away from what had been begun. Why then did he indulge in this pretense? This mockery of leadership and the assumption of power? The rescuing of this nation that had allowed itself to be brought low? Why did he pretend that he led this nation to a destiny, when its destiny had already been reckoned?

Did it mean something in and of itself to him, to perform this farce? Or was it only the pantomime of a man who could do as he wished, so long as he did not interfere with the Shadow?—the pantomime of a man who was no longer a man, but a thing reborn which understood that all of history is meaningless, except when seen as blind pantomime? That humanity, resourceful to the last, plots its own demise even as it presumes to inherit the wisdom of years and the progress of evolving time. A humanity hungry for delusions that do not explain life but hold life away at a safe distance, where it cannot interfere with the comfortable illusions.

Emarian legions, cavalry and infantry, horses and chariots, gathered in rank and file in the streets of Lasura, preparing to march to war.

Thameron, reborn, dressed himself in bronze and leather and steel, strapped weapons to himself, wore upon his head a brilliant crested helmet, and on horseback reviewed his troops, then signalled for the notes to sound that trumpeted the headlong rush of an entire nation into an abyss of its own choosing.

Five days later they met in the middle of the wide field late in the afternoon, while the sun was dying. Purple shadows . . . red stares . . . and while thousands upon thousands of horsemen in battle array waited resolutely, these agents of dark immutable vision flung their ambitions at one another as challenges. Captain Kurus of the Emarian Cavalry, in his wide tent, supported by armed retainers who betrayed gaunt, unhappy faces, the hungry staring eyes of men brought to their reckoning. And Lord Thameron the usurper, dressed too in Emarian armor and plumed helm, the palms of his hands scarred with strange hieroglyphic burns, supported by Sir Jors, Sir Jors's personal bodyguard Thamu, and a handful of others who—like Kurus's men—were gaunt and unhappy, restless and provoked.

The wind flapped the heavy stretched walls of the tent.

From far off, cawing birds seemed intent upon communicating to the connivers some message they did not care to interpret.

While each one felt that he possessed the secret of victory.

"Take what I offer you," Thameron insisted, "and be done with this treachery. You will only bring yourself to harm and all these men with you."

"Dog! I should submit to you?" growled Kurus. "You give me nothing! *You* remain king! *You* hold Lasura! *You* command the army! I submit to nothing! Emaria needs a *man* upon its throne, not an imposter! *Boy*! I fight for *Emaria*, damn you! For my country! And against *you*!"

And so papers were rolled up, chairs were pushed away, weapons clattered and jangled on their chains. Lord Thameron withdrew with his retainers, and rode back to his campsite on the eastern end of the long field. Kurus returned to the head of his lines and ordered his men to prepare themselves for the advance in the morning.

For such is the commitment to conflict that generals always see it as the final persuasion of a long series of failed alternatives: conflict planned as the final alternative, and not as something to be

24

avoided like a disease or a catastrophe. War, think the generals, is always a solution. War, they believe, is ever inevitable. War, they presume, grows in men's hearts as a desire as naturally as does the need for wife and family, prosperity and comfort. War, they hold, is only one of many things that men have continued to inherit from their forebears, and will always inherit. And to resort to war is never to resort to weakness and pride and anarchy, but rather to rise to a challenge of honor and duty and dignity.

As though honor and duty and dignity reveal themselves most proudly when written in blood.

Thus have the mothers of all nations ever given birth to generations of sons whose ultimate destiny is to soak the earth with their running blood, offer their burned and broken and festering flesh to the maggots and the vultures, so that generals and all engineers of war may honorably and dutifully rise to their challenges with dignity.

As night came down the thousands in Thameron's two legions spoke among themselves with apprehension, fear and doubt. They were too few, and their lord was no field commander: how could they hope to defeat this Kurus with his many more trained horsemen?

Worried retainers took this concern to Lord Thameron, in his tent on a height overlooking tomorrow's battlefield. Thameron told his retainers and especially reminded Sir Jors: "We will not enter the field until the fog has lifted."

They did not understand. "The sky is too clear," objected Sir Jors. "There will be no fog."

Thameron told him again, "We will not enter the field until the fog has lifted."

When Jors and the others had gone, Thameron mounted his horse and, ordering none to follow him, rode off into the darkness in the direction of the low hills that skirted the battlefield to the north.

He was not seen for the remainder of the night; and when his sentries saw him return in the morning, Thameron entered the camp not from the north but the south. He seemed an apparition when he returned, for during the night the air had become heavy and cold and a wide, low, thick fog had settled in.

Sir Jors, who had slept fitfully, sat by his orange campfire, watched as Lord Thameron dismounted and strode into his tent and suspected that the sorcerer had been born to strange stars indeed. . . .

Despite the sudden treachery of the weather, Captain Kurus's temper was such that he assumed he could take advantage of the fog and so double the effectiveness of his columns and lines. The trumpets sounded; his men mounted their horses and chariots. So heavy was the weather that not one soldier could see his comrades a short arm-length away. Several commanders suggested to Kurus that he wait until the fog had lifted before beginning the advance; Kurus's reply was to signal the trumpets to sound their call.

The advance began.

Slowly and uncertainly . . . with whispering voices . . . the hollow sounds of clanking weapons, muffled. . . . When they reached the middle of the field, Kurus's men reacted to the sudden sounds of thunder in the air. An earth tremor shook the very ground beneath their feet. The trumpets blared, calling for arms to be lifted and shields raised.

Abruptly, a wild army of horsemen—ghost riders dressed in shimmering armor and weaponed with lengths of steel, maces, swords and lances—swarmed upon the rebel legions from both sides of the field. They thundered down from the north, they crashed in from the south. Bursting through the clouds of fog, appearing and swiftly disappearing again, their horses kicking up clods of earth and mud. Thousands of horsemen.

Thousands of them.

Kurus's men, in their uncertainty and panic, lost their formations but heaved against the attack with all the spirit and steel they could muster.

The screams of soldiers pierced the swirling thickness. Toppled bodies were thrown and pulled through the restless clouds of fog. Blood erupted in all directions, spattering in explosions, arching in jets. Metal ripped metal. Curved spikes and pointed ends caught on flesh and bone. Animals fell, neighing and shaking their heads, breaking their legs in the crush. Eyes were punched out, hands severed, legs smashed. Lengths of gore were pulled across the mud by frantic horses. Confounded Emarians thrown from their saddles tried to scramble away and were cut down by weapons that leapt from the fog and vanished again in the same

moment. The soggy ground turned into a thick marsh, so flooded
was it with blood. Corpses and pieces of corpses began to pile up
in small hills, which quickly became slippery, crowded mountains
of gore. The trumpets fell silent and after a long while the horses
fell silent, and all that could then be heard of the few survivors
were moans and sobs of anguish.

The fog began to lift; the late morning sun shined through,
glowing in the dust.

The battlefield sounded like a pasture in springtime, whispering
and trickling with countless wet noises.

Kurus, bleeding but still atop his horse, stared upon a landscape
that brought revulsion even to his tempered soul: the wide plain
was filled from north to south with tall heaps of the dead and
dying. The blood sprawled in lakes, steaming in the sun; vultures
and kites and buzzards had already descended at the far edges of
the plain to rip the fresh meat from the fallen. And so loud was the
chorus of the dying that Kurus thought he had somehow raced off
the earth in the fog and taken a trail straight down into Hell. For
surely he was in Hell. Save for the handful close by him, every
man of his command—five full legions—had been slaughtered as
though they had been defenseless, as though they had been
unarmed children pretending to play at war, totally at the mercy
of—

Tears of wrath poured down Captain Kurus's face.

"*Thameron!*"

He stared across the field to where the usurper's camp sat upon
the low hills to the west. Not one man there had entered the field.
All stood mounted and prepared, pennants flapping in the morning
breeze, horses unmoving upon the slope.

This was madness.

"*Thameron!*"

Where had these reinforcements come from? *Where* had these
thousands upon thousands of expert horsemen come from, to slay
his own soldiers so effortlessly? And not one of the ghost riders
had fallen dead himself? It was unnatural. It was beyond possi—

"*Thameronnnn!* Dog! *Usurper!* What have you done to my
men?"

And from where he sat on his mount: "Praise the gods," Lord
Thameron blasphemed, as he looked down upon the field of red
carnage, "for delivering this miracle into our hands."

Sir Jors, watching him, went white.

Thameron lifted a gloved hand and waved his retainers forward; he led the way down into the wide blood-filled and breeze-swept plain, making a path through the chopped, heaped corpses already thick with flies and insects. Behind him came Sir Jors and Thamu and forty companions.

When Thameron was yet some distance from the panting, crimson-spattered Kurus, he halted and called back, "Notch your bows!"

His retainers did so, lifting their weapons and aiming them at Kurus and those few rebels still alive alongside him.

Heaped field . . . red stares . . . two proud warriors staring at one another in the quiet of the morning, in a brown and scarlet field at the end of the world.

"Praise the gods," Thameron whispered, "that these traitors and rebels have met their just reckoning."

"What . . . have you done?" Kurus asked him, eyes wide and staring, stunned by the enormity of it. "What . . . have . . . you . . . done. . . . ?"

Thameron shook his head, did not answer.

He lowered his hand.

Bowstrings snapped, humming, and forty bolts hissed as they shot across the field.

When they returned to Lasura, the men of Lord Thameron's legions had another wonder to share with their brethren and communicate in the taverns and the city barracks. This same leader who had come to fallen Emaria, taken control of the tyrant's throne and filled the tables with bread, had gone to battle against the rebel chief and had defeated him without one sword being lifted. Without one soldier moving into the field! Surely he stood in great favor of the gods! Surely Emaria was blessed in having so fortunate a deliverer seated upon its throne! None had believed that a fog would come, but indeed the fog had appeared to confound Kurus's troops and condemn the rebellious soldiers into slaying one another! What new miracles might come to pass? What greater events awaited their people with such a man commanding the nation?

The military destruction of Captain Kurus and his forces was touted as a great triumph, a successful turning back of the forces of anarchy and self-defeat which had seemed to hold Emaria in a strangling grip for so long. Harmful forces within the nation were being exposed and expelled; belligerent enemies were being repulsed; after years of suffering under the mismanagement and instabilities of King Nutatharis's rule, Lord Thameron was at last bringing self-sufficiency to the people. The common citizens and peasants and many of the soldiers began to think of him in terms of awe. The fiery destruction of the Diet and the deaths of the Councilors who had been trapped in that inferno was made out to be less an unfortunate accident than it was an intervention by the all-seeing gods for mysterious but profound purposes. In the same way had this providence seen fit to aid Thameron's outnumbered but patriotic legions with the unnatural morning of fog at the Battle of Ilrukad.

In the days that followed, the symbol of the seven-pointed star began to appear more and more prominently throughout Lasura. The state flag of Emaria was removed from many locations, while the black star on its white background replaced it. The Emarian League swelled in numbers, as more and more citizens, soldiers and merchants joined political rallies to add their confidence to the growing expression of nationalism. The offices of the cavalry and infantry commanders became crowded with volunteers eager to serve the new order. And in the humid summer nights great bonfires were built in the streets, fueled by old reminders of the displaced regime: legal documents from the offices of Nutatharis's government; Emarian state flags; books and scrolls issued by Nutatharis's printing offices—all thrown into roaring flames by chanting, cheering citizens caught in the excitement of new-found pride and patriotism.

It seemed that only Sir Jors held reservations concerning this new king—this stranger who within weeks had taken command not only of the crown and throne, but of the very hearts and minds of everyone in the country. A few incidents—a mysterious fire, a skirmish touted as a great battle, loads of grain carted into the farmlands, and this brooding, disturbing and sinister young man was lord of Emaria in more than name. But Jors found it inadvisable, indeed he found it dangerous, to voice his opinions of Lord Thameron publicly, for his lone voice of dissent in a crowd of rabid support could only earn him harm.

Intriguingly, it was none other than Thameron himself to whom Jors could speak of his grave doubts and disillusion. And while he was repelled by and mistrustful of this new lord of the imperial seat, Jors was also fascinated by him, in the way a man might be fascinated by exotic poisons or foreign weapons which he knows might be turned against him at any time. The special lure or enchantment new dangers hold, perhaps as a test of one's own abilities.

Thameron understood such things; indeed, he understood far more than Sir Jors credited him with. For as they sat one night looking down at the streets from a er of the palace, the two of them alone and sipping wine and sharing whatever attraction or companionship there had developed between them, the sorcerer remarked to his minister:

"You do not fear me, Jors—you fear the meaning of me."

"And what are you suggesting by saying that?"

The line of a smile, obscurely lit by the flames from the street far below, moved within the shadows of his face. "We cannot now alter what will come," Thameron spoke. "All that we might have done before to change the future—those opportunities are lost to us, now. All we can do for the present is sit and watch and wait for the future to unfold, for those things we have set in motion to accomplish themselves. And how effortless it is, and how it galls men to realize that all their actions will prove fruitless, that indeed their actions now forestall nothing, but only hasten the coming of events which their actions have provoked. Think of it. For that is man's fate: that he directs his own destiny without fully comprehending that he does so. He sows the seeds of his own destruction and does not understand it until it is too late; if only he had taken more care with those seeds, he might have understood. But he did not take care, and thus he brings about his own doom. And even as his fate befalls him, man will refuse to recognize what it is that makes it come about. What a fool man is; what a liar, a blind savage, an ignorant giant. His destruction will come, and he will call it the work of God, or evil, or misfortune. Call it rather by its proper name, o humanity, and look into your mirror."

Sir Jors did not reply, but only stared at the sorcerer who had mouthed these disturbing thoughts.

Thameron was not looking at him; however, he was staring into the street, with the pale shimmering brightness of the bonfires coloring his face, while the chanting choruses of the multitudes below lifted up in praise to his name.

The world is a battlefield, the world is at war; but it is not a war of soldiers, and there is no battlefield of blood. It is a war of hearts that men are joined in, a battlefield of thoughts and great purposes upon which they clash—men striving to gain a balance and hold it. The rebirth of men is the cycle of their wisdom, and men die and are reborn just as the earth dies and is reborn. The outcome of the earth is to be reborn with the heart of a child.
O prophets and wanderers, lovers and kings, men and women of all kinds!
O humanity, o lost, born in a storm and wandering in a storm! These things that come, they come with cause.

PART I

The King Without a Crown, the Warrior Without a Sword

1.

To my lord King Elad of Athadia on this day 24 Shom 1879 DP, in the Year of the Dragon, thus: From the city of Isita in the Province of Herulia from your servant Lord Governor Amalcar. *Kale im Porvo Athadis.* My lord, I say:

I must request immediate aid for my city of Isita. We are in a dire emergency and cannot much longer sustain ourselves, or deplete our treasury any further. . . .

To my lord King Elad of Athadia on this day 29 Shom 1879 DP, in the Year of the Dragon, from the city of Herossus from your honored servant, Lord Governor Osellos. *Kale im Porvo Athadis.* My lord, I beseech you most expressly:

Due to the troublous circumstances of local rebellion and the additional onset of requests for the summoning of military and naval personnel received recently from your office, I must beg to give you notice that the allotted interest due on our loans from the Imperial Treasury cannot be met by the date agreed to in our contract, and we are therefore forwarding you transcripts of our latest reports from the city treasury. . . .

To my lord King Elad of Athadia on this day 21 Shom 1879, thus: From the city of Pylar from your honored servant, Lord Governor Imet. *Kale im Porvo Athadis.* My lord: Due to the extreme difficulty we have recently incurred. . . .

Shaking his head, Adred dropped this letter on top of the many others which lay in a loosely scattered pile on the table.

"They all say the same thing," Galvus complained, watching his friend from where he sat. "Every city and territory is caught in a storm."

Adred frowned. "And you're inheriting them." He threw his hands behind his back and crossed the floor, sat down in a chair near the prince.

They were in one of the small offices off the main hallway on the first floor of the palace. The door was open, and to them came the ceaseless hurry and noise of clicking boots, urgent voices, harsh commands. With a bored expression Galvus glanced into the outer hall, while idly fingering the golden tassels that decorated his collared tunic.

"Are you ready for this?" Adred asked him. Dressed as he was in new clothes purchased only days before, he felt as uncomfortable as Galvus obviously did.

"Have I had any time to *be* ready?"

On the other side of the office Omos made a slight sound and stood up. Galvus looked at him, tenderness in his eyes. He asked if anything was wrong.

Omos shook his head, walked to a window and looked out. Below, in the garden, two servants were walking Queen Salia's puppies. Omos turned away and sat down again.

"Nervous," Adred interpreted.

Young Omos smiled weakly and nodded Yes. "I *am* nervous; but I'm worried, too."

"Well, there's plenty to be worried about," Galvus remarked, "but don't let my taking the throne cause you to lose sleep."

"But you have enemies," Omos reminded him.

"Name me the man who can get through his life without gaining a few enemies," Galvus smiled.

"But," Omos persisted, "powerful . . . enemies. . . ."

Galvus chuckled. "The more powerful the man, the more powerful his enemies. But enemies betray their weaknesses by taking themselves very seriously, Omos; laugh in their faces. They never know what to do when you laugh at them."

Adred was watching him; laugh at them, indeed. He knew that Galvus spoke more to strengthen his own resolve than he did out of experience. What if Bors and the other workers in the Diruvian Valley had laughed? What if all the dispossessed working people and the unemployed began to laugh at the iron fist that was strangling them? Laugh, indeed. They'd still be dead, all of them. . . .

Adred was becoming impatient and irritated with the loud comings and goings in the hall. Restless, his eyes fell on the table of papers and correspondence.

"What?" Galvus asked him, noticing.

"Nothing from Vardorian? No more from Sulos?"

Galvus quietly shook his head and looked away. "And I'm not sure yet what I can do about it," he admitted. "Perhaps now I'll find out why Uncle Elad has done some of the things he's done with the crown of the empire on his head."

Adred swallowed a deep breath; he realized that he was worried by what that statement might anticipate. The strength and the power and the responsibility that would very soon rest in those young, pale hands. . . .

A slight tapping sounded on the open door, and Abgarthis strode in. Adred, reacting out of habit, took to his feet, but Galvus and Omos remained seated.

Abgarthis wore a false smile and exuded artificial enthusiasm. "Well," he asked, "is the lord regent prepared to take up his office?"

"As prepared, my friend, as I'll ever be. What's the reason for the delay, Abgarthis?"

Cautiously: "I believe . . . your mother and King Elad have been in conversation."

"Indeed?" Galvus wiped his hands together. "Well, I hope she gave him a piece of my mind."

Abgarthis chuckled lowly.

Came the trumpeting sounds of horns; quickly the noises in the hallway faded away. The trumpets blared again, this time with a renewed vigor and a new melody. Abgarthis cleared his throat, looked around the room and said, "Well."

Galvus stood up; Omos walked over to him and helped him straighten his clothes. Then the prince-regent stepped up beside Lord Abgarthis. They passed into the outer hall but waited at the office door; a coterie of Khamars shouldered them, erect and dignified. The newly-scrubbed marble floors gleamed; festooned flowers and giant wreaths filled the spaciousness below the high ceiling. From where they stood, Galvus could see long lines of aristocrats and military leaders slowly making their way up wide staircases to the galleries overlooking the throne hall, to witness this ceremony of succession.

"I want you to know," Abgarthis whispered to Prince Galvus in those few moments that remained, "that I feel very good about this."

"Do you, Abgarthis?"

"I swear it on the soul of the Prophet. I believe our fortunes will turn, now. I feel almost as if . . . your grandfather had returned."

Galvus swallowed thickly and looked the old man in the eyes; tears rimmed Abgarthis's lashes. "Thank you," the prince-regent told him. "Thank you. Nothing else you could have said, Abgarthis, could make me feel as good about this."

"I say it because I mean it." Though he stared now across the hall, the old minister reached out with a hand and gripped one of Galvus's arms, held it firmly to emphasize what he had said.

Then, as the last of the spectators disappeared on the landing above, trumpets blared, the Khamars in the hallway slapped their chests, and Galvus and Abgarthis fell into step with them and moved across the hallway, down to the main entrance doors of the throne hall.

Adred and Omos, smiling to one another, watched them go, followed a bit, then quickly ran up the staircase to find seats so that they, too, could watch.

It proceeded quickly.

King Elad, dressed in his armor and state colors (to further impress upon the audience in the throne hall his reason for taking leave of the capital) wasted no time in reading the official pronouncement of Galvus's ascension to the throne of the empire. And although the hall was filled with hundreds upon hundreds of guests and government representatives and official witnesses, still, when Elad made his address and began the formal ceremony of succession, his loud voice seemed to ring hollow and to echo in the spacious, crowded chamber.

". . . by the power vested in me, Elad, King of Athadia, I hereby declare Prince-Regent Galvus of the blood of the House of Evarris, Acting Authority of this throne and final arbiter of all processes of jurisdiction, interpreter and administrator of all imperial offices of this empire, executive authority of the Imperial Athadian High Council and its Coalition Ministry and all administrative and legal offices. . . . ."

From where he stood on the gallery, Adred saw Orain standing on the steps of the throne dais only a short distance from her son. Pride emanated from her like a glow; Adred felt his love for her fill his imagination. The delicate fine beauty of her, the tilt of her head and the slight smile on her lips. . . .

"I'm the mother of the man who will one day be the lord of the empire," Orain had told Adred once, on that long-ago day last winter, when he'd found them living ignominiously on the docks of Sulos, aiding the revolution, helping those people whom the empire had chosen to forget. *"He is strong—terribly strong . . . wise. . . . Can you imagine the kind of king he'll make?"*

". . . and until such time as I, Elad, King of Athadia, return to this throne to personally sit in direction once more of the seal and scepter of imperial government, Prince-Regent Galvus of the House of Evarris is hereby discharged. . . ."

And a cruel smile broke on Adred's lips, as he watched how Lords Rhin and Falen and some other aristocrats stood, visibly shivering in the presence of this succession. Yes, Adred could imagine the kind of king Galvus would make—the kind of king who would certainly and swiftly make even greater enemies of the nobles and the businessmen than he'd already made of reptiles like Rhin and Falen.

". . . here and now offer this crown and scepter to Galvus, Prince-Regent of the House of Evarris. . . ."

And it was done.

Elad placed the imperial crown on Galvus's head; the young man knelt before his uncle and kissed the outstretched hand. Rising to his feet, Galvus accepted the scepter of state, then positioned himself in the throne.

Elad nodded to trumpeters in the hall; they sounded several loud notes in a proclamation. Stepping up onto the dais, Elad positioned himself at Galvus's right hand and silently and respectfully watched as all present began to make their way forward in a slow, single file, bowing and saluting the prince-regent, and offering Galvus their flattering and somewhat sincere congratulations.

There might have been a celebratory feast that evening, done in Galvus's honor, but the succession had not been accomplished in that spirit. The overriding concern of the moment was for Elad to take command immediately of his armed forces and order the flotilla to begin its journey across the world for the military confrontation with the *Ghen* of the Salukadian empire. Galvus, nevertheless, spent that evening in a private session with the members of his High Council, and so it was left to the many aristocrats and nobles and courtiers who had attended the ceremony to observe the change of government in their own fashion. This they did in various chambers of the palace itself and in their villas or in rented apartments. The general tone of these revels (as Adred noticed when he passed through the palace halls) seemed less one of satisfaction than it was of doubt and puzzlement. Everyone at court had become familiar with the prince-regent's radical views in regards to economy and society and imperial rule: what now did it portend, to have a boy-king on the throne who possessed all the powers of Elad himself, and of such a mentality? And what if this military expedition—the gods forfend!—did not see Elad's return?

Adred himself was not so concerned with this; he knew Galvus better than did any of these asps and sycophants, and his own private feelings toward the acting-king were the same as Orain's, the same as Abgarthis's—Galvus might, in fact, prove himself to be a better monarch in a month than had Elad in a year.

But he knew he couldn't very well express this optimism to the companies of worried aristocrats and unctuous businessmen gathered in the palace without inviting dispute and resentment and bitterness. So after moving from one loud, crowded chamber to another, Adred finally made his ways upstairs to his room. As he came down the hall he was surprised to find Orain's chamber door open: he thought certainly that, tonight of all nights, she'd be someplace other than her own private room. Adred stepped in, knocked, passed through the antechamber and glanced into the sitting room.

Orain was sitting alone, her back to him, in a small divan facing her open balcony.

Adred tapped a fist on the door and called her name.

She turned suddenly and looked at him; he saw that she had tears in her eyes.

That made him smile with surprise. "What are you *crying* about?" he chuckled, hurrying to Orain. He sat beside her on the pillows, reached for her with gentle hands. But when Orain faced him, Adred wasn't sure from her expression whether she was weeping out of sadness or anger.

"What is it?" he asked her more seriously.

She shook her head and caught her breath, nodding; Adred waited.

"Before the ceremony—" she sat up straight, worked her hands together nervously "—Elad and I . . . talked. He feels very alone and I truly believe, Adred, that he's afraid. He needed to talk with a woman. But he's very afraid because all he talked about, over and over, was what happened with the Oracle at Mount Teplis. And I know he'd give his soul up seven times over, if he could only go back and live that moment again, not—do what he did."

Adred watched her carefully.

"That . . . was the beginning of everything. It changed him. He did it, and he didn't realize what he was doing, and it caused everything else to happen. Elad, at least, believes that." Orain quickly wiped one hand across her cheeks, smudging her make-up; but she'd stopped crying, although she still sounded frustrated, resentful. "Ever since then, no matter what he's tried to do, everything's gone wrong. Elad feels alone and frightened and not in control; he told me he feels like he's an imposter pretending to be king. So he's going away and he's leaving it all in Galvus's hands."

Adred swallowed heavily but still said nothing.

Orain looked at him with meanness in her eyes. "I suppose he does love the woman, as much as he *can* love, for a man who thinks he's alone all the time and doomed. But Elad feels that no matter what he does he can't stop time, and in time what the Oracle prophesied will come to pass."

"Does he—" Adred's voice cracked; he coughed slightly. "Does he think that sending this armada east will lead to war with Salukadia? It doesn't have to."

Orain shrugged. "He knows that; but he seems to feel that it doesn't matter any longer what he does or what happens. And that's what makes me so *angry*!" She stood up and crossed the room, fidgeted with some knickknacks on a table, turned toward Adred. "Nothing has meaning for him anymore. Cyrodian . . . the revolution . . . all these businessmen on Council fighting him simply out of greed . . . the Imbur, who's a fool. . . . He—he told me, Adred, that he doesn't know what holds it all together anymore; those were his words. He's been looking at the world for the last several months and he doesn't feel as though he's truly part of it; he doesn't understand what holds it together. He sat there and whispered it, as if he expected the world to fall apart right there, right under his feet. He doesn't have any convictions or any reasons, he's not doing what he's doing because he *believes* anything anymore! He simply—" Orain was very upset; she worked her hands together some more, shook her head and growled low in her throat.

"Come over here," Adred told her. "Sit down. Here—I'll get you some wine."

"I don't want any wine. Don't you *see*?" she asked him sharply. "Council says, Build an armada and we'll launch a crusade to save the Athadian queen—and so Elad's doing it! This isn't a *crusade*! There's no glory attached to this. Salia is a stupid, ignorant girl! Her father is a fool! Elad's doing it because whether he does it or not, he still expects the world to fall apart! And the businessmen all want to make as much money as they can, and they don't care how they do it! Adred! The world is too important, people are too *important*, to leave in the hands of leaders like these!"

He laughed—too loudly, but he laughed in surprise at the honesty of her remark.

Orain glowered at him; she'd worked herself into a true fury and stood there trembling with rage. To Adred she seemed to be an emotional punch waiting to be thrown. He got to his feet, moved toward her but walked past Orain and stopped beside the table.

He unstoppered a decanter of wine, poured some into two goblets. "Here."

Orain came up to him, her mouth frowning, but she took one and sipped to calm herself. "*I* didn't have any answers for him!" she complained.

"No one's going to have any answers for him," Adred assured her, "unless Elad comes up with some for himself."

"But . . . the situation is so unstable."

"The situation has always been unstable. If there were only two people in the world the situation would be—unstable. . . ."

She regarded him with deep eyes and a puzzled frown, then looked away, sipped her wine, listened to footsteps come nearer then recede, outside in the hall. "I want to believe in something . . . anything," she confessed to Adred, "even if it's evil, if it helps to explain what's happened . . . if it can explain even a little why all this is happening. I want to believe in something again. I want to trust the world again. . . ." She faced him. "That's not stupid of me, is it? That doesn't mean I'm being naive, does it, Adred?"

2.

In Erusabad Nihim, brother of the *Ghen* of all the east, sat at his desk and by the light of his oil lamp wrote a letter which he had been planning for some time.

> To Elad, King of the Athadian People: this from the brother of your enemy, Agors *ko-Ghen* of Salukadia: Greetings.
> I write to you to explain why that which has happened has

41

come to be. I write to you, Elad King, to tell you why it is that the follies of men lead to their ruin. I write to tell you of your wife, Queen Salia of the Athadians, and of what has occurred here since her arrival in this city. I believe that, in the eyes of all gods that watch the earth, it is most important for men to speak with one another and not raise arms: to recognize one another as men first and not assume to be evil those things which are in fact dictated by fear or misunderstanding or deception. Men create evil out of ignorance; but where there is pain, misunderstanding or prejudice there is only ignorance and not evil. I hope you will believe me when I tell you these things, for I do not believe that warfare or the decision to raise weapons is the answer we seek. If evil could be destroyed by the sword then it would have been vanquished long ago: so I say that our two governments are involved in a situation not of evil but of pride and weakness and misunderstanding. To speak as men with open hearts will eradicate the evil. We are men, my brother is a man, and the gods (whatever you or I might call them privately) have breathed life into both of us, into all of us, and I think it would be better to trust to that breath of life, rather than to assumptions which might poison our appreciation of that fact. . . .

He continued to write, sometimes rambling, but explaining as best he could his feelings on this matter of Salia's "defection" to the east, her troubled personality and her search for truth, and the pain that people cause when they feel pain themselves. And when he was done, Nihim sealed his letter and ordered a palace courier sent to him, and indicated to that man that he must deliver this package immediately—tonight—to Lord Sirom of the Athadian government in his Authority Building in the city.

Nihim felt assured that this courier, whom he knew by name, would do as he had requested. As soon as the man had gone, Nihim poured himself a cup of tea, sat down in a crouch on his woven mat in the center of his chamber floor and stared at the endless circular maze of the *loht* tapestry which hung on the opposite wall.

His courier, however, did not leave the building. The man moved through the halls of the palace and, in accordance with proscriptions recently set down by Agors *ko-Ghen*, placed Nihim's package into the hands of an official stationed outside the *Ghen*'s office. It was the duty of this official to censor or clear any message or delivery emanating from the Salukadian palace.

Therefore, he opened this letter and read it, ordered a soldier to guard his closet and desk while he approached the *Ghen*.

Agors, as had become his habit late in the evening, was eating a solitary supper and drinking wine in one of the large rooms on the third floor. Several courtiers were with him; Salia, however, was not present. She had tended to isolation within the past few weeks. Agors and his ministers were refreshing themselves with food and idle talk and listening to musicians. When the official entered, he was given leave to approach the *Ghen*; moving across the floor, he held his arms open wide in a gesture of subservience and peace, bowed before his master and placed the letter upon Agors's table.

Agors nodded and the man exited.

The *Ghen* proceeded to finish a leg of roast fowl before deciding to read what had been brought; when he took it up, his fingers left grease stains on the paper. Agors read the letter without any show of emotion.

From several tables down bin-Sutus watched him with a careful stare.

Agors finished reading the letter, refolded it, turned his attention once again to the musicians and idly dropped the parchment into a burning incense brazier close by him on his table.

The letter fanned into flames, produced several long puffs of smoke and was reduced to charred flakes.

While Agors *ko-Ghen* reached for another leg of fowl.

Feeling restless and frustrated, Adred could not stay in his room; too much of what Orain had said to him had driven too deeply, caused him to reimagine many scenes and episodes. His mind was working as busily as a furious swarm of flies, and he could not calm himself. Irritated, he decided to go out.

What holds it all together? And why? Why?

The night was quite warm, and so he did not even consider putting on his light coat when he left the palace. Sentries in the foyer saluted him as he exited, but Adred was so preoccupied with his thoughts that he didn't even hear them. He went out into the

43

west gardens but found no calm in the quiet solitude; and so he followed one walkway out toward the pedestrian gate and left the palace grounds.

He headed west until he came to the Odasian Square, turned south and strolled briskly past the still open shops and stalls and taverns. Even this far from the docks he spotted numerous gatherings of soldiers and sailors sporting badges from all the major ports and cities of the empire. Their voices carried in guffaws and friendly yells, some melodious and others thickly inflected and accented. And as he continued south, walking toward the docks on the River Sevulus, Adred noticed larger groups of military personnel seated on the verandahs of restaurants or crowded inside taverns whose doors and windows were open to the warm night.

Tomorrow. . . . Tomorrow they'd all be shipping out, sailing for Erusabad and—what? War? Could this pretentiousness lead to war? Or was it all a bluff or a desperate blunder? Even if Elad didn't intend for this to lead to war, couldn't he be setting in motion events that might unpredictably rage out of control?

He took a table on the patio of a restaurant and ordered a cup of beer, sipped it slowly and tried to order the memories that gripped him so strongly—the compounding of events and effects and deliberate actions that must somehow have led to this grim imbalance, this dance with chaos.

"Adred, I see your heart. Do not mourn. Do not look behind. May I entrust you with a philosophy?" "I would be honored, Queen Yta." "Strive. Aspire. We enter a dark age. I have seen the future, and it is dark, but there is a light."

"The common people of this nation are screaming for dignity and respect. King Elad, if you do not take measures to help them—if you do not assure the people of this empire that you are their king, as well as the king of the wealthy and the aristocratic— then they will turn against you! They want their lives! They want the future!"

"Oh, she's all right. She gets into trouble because she wants to do the right thing." "Everybody wants to do the right thing. But the world's still in trouble."

"They had me in a cage, like an animal. I don't know where. This little village. And there was this priest. Telling stories. He looks at me, he's watching me, all these people around, and he

44

starts talking about this and that—I'm an evil man and I cause pain to everybody . . . all this ass shit. I spit in his eye . . . and then he starts talking about. . . . I don't know."

"Let's face reality, gentlemen. None of us is naive; we all know how the world operates, so let's dispense with this charade of brotherhood and community and equality."

"I want to believe in something : . . anything, even if it's evil, if it helps to explain what's happened . . . if it can explain even a little why all this is happening. I want to believe in something again . . . I want to trust the world again."

As he began walking back toward the palace, the tension of the day's events and the weariness of his worries quickly began to tire Adred. He considered hiring a carriage but, for some obscure, self-demanding reason, refrained. In the Odasian Square most of the stalls were now closed, and only a few taverns yet echoed with lingering, brawling, heroic sounds.

What holds it all together? What?

Thoroughly exhausted (and glad of it) he at last reached the palace grounds and passed through a gate in the southern wall. Ahead of him Adred noticed a squadron of troops collected before the south entrance portico; intrigued, he hastened his pace. But the troop had already begun to disperse by the time he reached the steps.

Adred noticed that they had delivered a prisoner to two Khamars, who were escorting the chained man toward the doors of the palace prison, off the eastern wing. When he came into the entrance foyer, Adred paused and nodded to one of the sentries on duty and walked over to him.

"Good evening, Count Adred."

"Good evening. Could I ask you something? Who was that prisoner I saw those Khamars with just now?"

"Oh, him. Just arrived from Hilum tonight. Some priest."

"A priest?" Adred rubbed his forehead, remembering something. "A priest from Hilum. . . ." Looking up suddenly: "What's his name? Do you know his name?"

The sentry shrugged and motioned to a companion seated at a desk near the doors. "What's the name of that robe they just brought in? Did you hear?"

The Khamar made a noncommittal gesture—who paid attention

45

to such things?—but then guessed, "As—wasas? Asa—wasas. Something like that."

Adred, raising a hand to his lips, whispered quickly, "Gods . . . it's him. He's the one!"

The sentry overheard. "What'd you say, sir?"

They had me in a cage, like an animal. And there was this priest. He looks at me, he's watching me, all these people all around, and he starts talking about this and that—I'm an evil man and I cause pain to everybody . . . I spit in his eye. . . ."

The priest who'd put such fear into Cyrodian that the giant's hair had turned white.

The one Seraficos had had arrested on charges of sedition and treason.

The one all the people were claiming was a miracle worker and a doom-sayer, even saying that he was Bithitu himself returned to earth.

Asawas. . . .

And though the candles and the lamps burned low, still Nihim and Salia sat in her room and sipped tea and spoke occasionally when their stray glances met. Nihim in his plain robe, unadorned by any jewelry or fashionable device. Salia, beautiful yellow rose of the west, in her poverty of spirit and with that unquelled rage against herself unquiet in her heart, barely clothed in her sandals and her brief skirt and her ornaments and shining pendants.

She was sitting on a divan. It was a wide divan, long, and desolate of pillows or cushions. Salia might have stretched herself upon the length of it and been as free as though she were upon a beach; but she did not. She sat huddled in one corner of it, as though the empty space about her were pressing upon her intolerably.

Nihim was seated in a wooden chair across the room, watching her in the silence of the night, more aware of her than Salia was of him.

A stark hollow noise erupted briefly in the hall outside, beyond the hanging curtains. Salia reacted tautly, turning her head like a startled cat.

Nihim hardly moved. "It is not him," he said quietly.

Salia lent him a cruel look, then intently studied her white arms,

46

began picking at her skin and some of the scabs that had formed on scratches she had done to herself. "I know that," she admitted. "He never comes here anymore. It's just as well. I don't want him to come here anymore. I don't want him to—" She looked up and stared into a corner, giving great thought to what she wished to say, how she might phrase it. "I don't want him to . . . come here—anymore. . . ."

Nihim, after a long while, rose to his feet, clasped his hands behind him and slippered across the floor to the queen. Salia followed him slyly out of the corners of her eyes, but did not move her head: feline and uncertain.

Nihim said to her, "My master Toshin said that it is a good thing to understand others, but true awareness comes only from knowing oneself. I think, Queen Salia, that you do not know others, yet you have suffered from their actions toward you; you have allowed them to make of you something—someone—whom you do not understand. Now, you try to understand yourself, you look for yourself, but no one has given you the light, they have taken the light away. Your search is confusing and fruitless. You do not know where to begin.

Now she looked at him. It was not scorn on her face, nor mistrust in her expression, but a relief mixed with questioning—a quivering hopefulness. "Your master . . . Toshin . . . is a very wise man."

"He is indeed."

"Perhaps you can help me, Nihim, to find myself."

He shook his head. "How could I succeed where others have failed you? *You* must do this. But you must forget everything you have been taught. You must look into a mirror and not see yourself as you appear; you must force that image out of the mirror. Then you must concentrate on what remains."

Her brows knitted. "Is this a puzzle, Nihim? If I force the picture of myself—the reflection of myself—from my mirror, I will not be there. What will remain?"

"Light," he replied. "Light."

Salia stared at him for some moments; dissatisfied, then, she looked away. "I cannot do that. I can't do. . . ." She shrugged.

Nihim sighed. He began to walk away, to leave her. "If ever you wish to speak with me again or see me, you need only ask."

47

Salia waited until he had nearly left the room, then called after him, "*Ghen-usu.*"

He turned, making a whispering sound.

"Tell me . . . there are rumors that my husband prepares a navy to come here and make war upon your brother. Is this true?"

"It is."

"He does this for me?"

"He does this because of you."

"And do you think he will actually make war upon this city? Will Agors answer him with war? Will we go to war, Nihim?"

Standing behind her and speaking from where she could not see him, his might have been a voice from the beyond, presenting her with words and ideas as though from a young god or a demon or from some secret sense of Salia herself. A voice. Nihim said:

"War, as sad a thing as it is, is not so difficult to understand. It is merely the last resort of societies that feel their self-interests threatened; and those societies are merely composed of people who have sworn allegiance to some common idea. The ideas go to war, ideas born of fear or ignorance or prejudice. It seems to me that when you ask me, queen, will your husband and my brother go to war because of you, you see yourself as a fulcrum between two conflicting opposites. Such is not the case.

"Wars are often committed for excuses, not reasons: and those excuses are rooted in fear and ignorance and prejudice, while the reasons are otherwhere, hidden like the sword in its scabbard or the gold in its purse. Consider this: every living thing in the world is intent first of all upon preserving itself; this is a truth. Yet all things too are born to die, and all their powers to preserve themselves cannot prevail against this natural law. So what is to be done? In the matter of humankind, most of us deny this ultimate fact and make excuses, entertain ideas that ignore the reality around us. We rely upon token concepts that do not explain but seem to. So . . . though a man loses his life, still he assumes that he has insured the purpose of his life by helping to preserve what gave his life meaning. Doing this, he feels he has conquered death, conquered meaninglessness.

"Animals, Toshin teaches us, preserve their essence by protecting their brood. Man, Toshin teaches us, preserves his essence not only by protecting his brood but by endowing his societies with purposes that seem as profound as Nature's purposes. Men institute their ideas, beliefs and passions into the fabric of their societies. When new life is born it is welcomed with celebration; yet when new ideas are born, old ideas are seldom relinquished or left to die: and this is because men seldom test the ideas upon which they have based their societies. People do not seek the truth that will challenge them, but desire only comfort that will sustain them: old, familiar ideas—like old, familiar habits—are the most comfortable. Thus, we may commit ourselves to actions which permit of unfairness or duplicity or evil and still believe these things to be right and correct, for we remain comfortable in a place that is an old habit, and truth must bow to custom, not custom to new truths.

"So, Queen Salia . . . you ask me if your husband and my brother will go to war. I ask you to reflect on these things I have just told you: that men will preserve themselves or preserve what they identify with themselves, at any cost, and that they will be comforted with lies they have trusted out of habit rather than take responsibility for the truth. Old customs and new ideas will go to war. I remind you that Toshin teaches us that there are three parts to a man which he must bring into balance within himself. If a man cannot do this—and societies are composed of men—then we may judge that man as being one of three kinds. It is not the different kinds that are important: it is the balance or imbalance which is important. Now, I answer your question with another question, Queen Salia. And I ask you to consider ideas, and customs, and self-preservation. Would you say that your husband is an intellectual man?"

"No," she replied in a dry voice, "he is not an intellectual man."

"Would you say that he is a passionate man?"

"No more so than other men, I suppose. No . . . not so passionate."

"Would you say that he is a moral man?"

Salia replied, "Yes. I suppose he considers himself to be a moral man."

"I see. Do you consider my brother to be a moral man, in his outlook?"

"No, not in the way we in the west regard morality."

"Do you consider him to be an intellectual man?"

"No, not Agors."

"Is he, then, a passionate man?"

"Yes," Salia answered with conviction. "A passionate man."

"One a moral man, the other a passionate man. I leave you, Queen Salia, to decide whether or not we will go to war."

Late that night, unable to resolve these words to her satisfaction, seeing them as separate and not as pieces of a whole, Salia tried to fit them together mentally as she would physically a puzzle, but she became exasperated and gave it up. Nervous and agitated as she was, however, as the night neared dawn she stepped before one of her mirrors and stared into it, pressed her fingertips to her reflection, tried by an act of willpower to eradicate the image of herself that was so plainly and distinctly to be seen in the polished silver.

But when she could not, after repeated attempts, focus her mind to accomplish this, she went to her bed, where she wept until she fell asleep, biting on her fingers.

And the only light to be seen in her mirror was the hazy reflection of dawnlight, as it slipped through the shutters of her windows. . . .

3.

Four hundred ships in the harbor of the capital city.

War galleys and trading galleys stripped and prepared for combat service, large merchanters filled with supplies and biremes and triremes.

They flew the pennants of Sulos and Bessara and Athad, Pylar and Herossus and Isita, Adkar and Imusad, Himosis and Belara. And above their pennants flapped the rectangular state flag of the empire: the lion and sun and crown.

Onto their wide decks marched the lines of soldiers calling out songs and tramping dust as they made their way down the overcrowded quays and filed up the gangplanks. Thousands upon thousands of men trimmed and dressed in their bronze and leather and steel. The Sixth West Legion out of Pylar, under Major Dever, and the Ninth West under Major Undas. The Tenth West from Athad under Major Ostorian, and the Sixteenth West under Major

Hadad. The Third Company, Fourth West out of Athad under Captain Sadir. And joining them, when they made port at the Isle of Odossos in three weeks' time, would be the First Legion Red out of Abustad under Major Tor, as well as seventy-five vessels from Sugat commanded by the Imbur Ogodis and filled with another three Gaegoshan legions and four companies of warriors and seamen.

Fifty thousand men, armed and trained and prepared to accomplish war, learned in the lessons of war.

For who in the capital this morning could look from rooftop or window or balcony and see crowds upon crowds of soldiers filling up the docks and filling up the ships that sailed out to take formation beyond the broad mouth of the Sevulus, and suppose that King Elad did *not* mean to make war? Too many men . . . too many ships . . . too many supplies, for the king not to mean this sincerely.

The pick of the armed might of the empire, simply to bluff a savage chieftain on the other side of the world? Veterans and observers and those who had survived other campaigns looked from rooftop and window and balcony and whispered to one another and shared earnest expressions. Too many men, too many ships. . . .

On the decorated roof of the southern wing of the palace, Adred and Abgarthis stood with other fascinated spectators, staring southwest across the capital. The docks could not be seen from this direction, but as each vessel made its way down river and joined the formation of the armada, the watchers had a clear view of hundreds of colorful little ships dotting the endless expanse of the blue western seas.

Occasionally someone there would make an exclamation or comment, but neither Lord Abgarthis nor Count Adred said much. They were simply too overwhelmed. And through Abgarthis's mind hurried the deadly, unrepentant and brazen words his king had spoken to him weeks earlier, when the necessity for this martial exercise had become clear:

"*We live in a cemetery, Abgarthis. Look around. It's all dead. It's all in the process of dying, and if you look carefully enough, you can see all the dead things beneath the living things. Everything is built upon the death of everything else. I must tell you that . . . I am no longer afraid of the Oracle's words.*"

51

Footsteps, behind. A Khamar, apparently just off duty, approached the low wall and stood beside Abgarthis, nodded to Adred and stared out at the sea, rapt. He said nothing, and all was quiet for some time on the rooftop, the other spectators intimidated by the palace guard's presence.

But after a moment Abgarthis remarked in a quiet voice, "Does it ever bother them?"

The Khamar glanced at him. "My lord?"

"These generals and commanders . . . does it ever bother them to order all these young men into battle, knowing that they will not return? That they are simply being used? As though they were so much . . . meat beneath the knife?"

The Khamar did not answer.

Adred, however, stared at the old minister, tears beginning in his eyes.

Abgarthis's wrinkled hands trembled on the low wall and he whispered: "I have lived too long. Born in days of peace . . . I will die in days of war. . . . What good does it accomplish for anyone to pretend that beauty and love and compassion and tolerance are meaningful, when the will of one man can do—this? We should dig us a large trench and every human being in the world should leap into it, and then we could be done with it all and leave Nature to grow in peace. Lies . . . lies . . . all the lies. . . ."

Galvus was not in the least interested in the preparations for war; he did not care to partake of the hurrying and the random disorder that filled the noisy palace, nor did he wish to stand on a rooftop and observe what many years of zealous plotting and armament hoarding had wrought. Instead, he spent the afternoon in Elad's office, in the company of Omos and a few friendly persons on the Council and read through piles of papers and notes and files, concentrating mainly on the most recent developments in the major cities.

Early in the afternoon a servant delivered to him the box containing the day's correspondence, and as Galvus perused these letters and lists, his worst suspicions were confirmed.

When Adred, himself in a grim mood, stopped in just before the evening bells, he found his friend in a depressed state of mind.

Save for Omos, who sat in a chair in a corner, silent and frowning, they were alone.

"If there was ever any sense or order to our . . . revolution," Galvus sighed to Adred, "it's gone now, I'm afraid. Read these. They're a roll call of defeat. You can see these people falling against themselves like stacks of coins."

Frowning, Adred glanced at some of the letters; his cursory scanning told him everything pertinent.

Galvus slumped in his chair, propped his elbows on the arms of it and rested his chin on clasped hands. His stomach growled, but he ignored it. "Vardorian and Sulos are both in serious trouble," he explained to Adred. "The Loduli have moved back into the Diruvian Valley and taken command of their graineries again. Look at that list of names! And every one of them is dead. Those are the men I promised, last winter, to help. And Rhin and his pet vermin are behind it; look at that letter from Vardorian. He wants to know when it was that King Elad sanctioned the use of secret police in terrorizing the workers and the protestors! Secret police! He's arrested one of them already but can't do anything until he hears from me. The Khilu! The people in Sulos know the name already, and it doesn't mean the Coalition Ministry to them—the Khilu means *secret police*!"

Adred was reading the letter. "Rhin and his . . . boot-lickers have been bribing unemployed brutes and giving them badges and swords—sending them into the streets?"

Galvus sneered. "And what are the revolutionaries doing? That one—look at that one. *Those* people were killed by the *Suloskai*! Now revolutionaries are killing revolutionaries! Sulos . . . Bessara . . . Pylar . . . Isita—every city, Adred, is part of it. And if it's not for jobs or money or food, then they're rebelling against the army. They're afraid we'll institute a draft to force people into the imperial army."

Adred dropped the letter atop the others, shot a pained glance at Omos.

"And food shortages," Galvus continued. "We've got a drought in the midlands, did you know that, did you hear about that yet? And the merchants are destroying anything they have left because of the losses they've already suffered; people are stealing food and the businessmen are destroying whatever they can get their hands on, just so they'll get a better price on what's left!

They don't trust the throne to prop up the economy any longer. I wonder why! We're in debt up to our necks, and we don't have enough columns on a page to record the deficits we've sold ourselves into!"

Adred said nothing, only looked at him. Galvus was livid.

"And what does the king do about it?" he fumed, hammering a fist on the arm of his chair. "What's Elad doing about it? He decides to run away! He runs off to—"

"You know that isn't—"

"Oh, yes, it is!" Galvus yelled, losing his temper completely. "Four hundred ships and hundreds of thousands of men and for what? For *what*? For some *stupid woman*? So we can go to *war*? Why doesn't he just turn his soldiers loose on the *people*? That'll save him the trouble of sailing all the way across the world to have it done *for* us!"

Cursing, Galvus turned his head away; then, still very angry, he leaned forward and grabbed a handful of papers, nearly crumpled them, but slapped them down on the desk again.

"Damn! *Damn* him! All this . . . *nonsense* from a man who hasn't even—"

"Galvus, please," Adred reminded him quietly.

The prince-regent gave him a hot-eyed stare, but then let out a long breath and slumped back in his chair.

From his corner, Omos let out a squeaking cough.

"I could change it all in a day," Galvus complained, "if I had the power. But I don't have that power, and I don't believe that anyone *should* have that power, even if he were a very good man. But if we give that power to the people now, Adred, they'll kill each other in the streets. If we let the plutocrats have the power, they'll simply kill the people first and fight it out amongst themselves later. If we go to war—" He shook his head. "Hell, we *are* in a war!"

"Not with Salukadia. We haven't even—"

"We are with Emaria. Elad signed all the documents just before he left; the only thing that remains is for me to date them, whenever I feel it necessary to formally call up our troops. I can mobilize them in an hour. But we're already in it. Whoever this fool is who's on the Emarian throne now—some maniac; they've chosen some insane priest or something—he's got everyone so excited that they're joining the Emarian army in droves and hurrying to the borders as fast as their horse carts'll carry them.

Somewhere in here is a letter from Uvars's border patrol. . . . He's got one company of five hundred men somewhere close to the mountains, they've been up there for six months without encountering any trouble whatsoever, and now he says he's spotting Emarian legions moving into Athadian territory and taking control of land and livestock and entire villages. He wants men immediately; Major Hurs and the rest of them say the same thing. They want a minimum of three legions out there to buttress what they've got; and they want a declaration of war so they can run against these Emarians before things get even more out of control." Exhausted, Galvus wiped a shivering hand through his long hair. "I don't like war . . . I don't believe in war . . . I refuse to declare a war. And yet—I'm going to have to do that."

Adred stared at him for a long time, not knowing what to say.

Omos finally got out of his chair and walked over to Galvus, held his shoulders and reminded him that it was time for supper.

"Yes, yes, yes. . . ."

Omos gave Adred a look full of meaning, although Adred wasn't sure what to make of it. He got to his feet, tapped his fingers on the table and said quietly, "Well, anyway . . . the reason I came in here was for something else entirely."

"And what was that?"

"It seems absurd, now. But do you remember me telling you about that priest your father met in Omeria? The one that turned his hair white?"

"Yes, I remember."

"The Church in Hilum had him arrested and ordered him shipped here to stand trial for sedition."

"That's absurd."

"Of course it is. But Abgarthis got Elad to sanction the order, because he and I both knew that this priest was the man who'd put such a scare into Cyrodian. He arrived last night."

"Did he? Where is he? Down in the prison?"

"That's right."

"It certainly ought to prove interesting to talk to him; you're right. I hate to keep him in the prison if he hasn't really done anything, but it's going to have to wait a while."

"I know that. But you ought to have Abgarthis look into it, perhaps. Just to make sure that this priest isn't processed as a criminal."

55

Galvus nodded. "Yes, yes. . . ." He stood up, stretched. "What was he doing in Hilum, anyway? To be arrested for sedition?"

Adred smiled wryly. "The impression Abgarthis and I got was that he was doing the same thing the rest of us were—telling the truth."

Galvus pursed his lips and chuckled.

While Orain sat on a divan, repairing some of her clothes and decorating them with stitching, Omos crouched on the floor beside her, nervously plucking loose threads from the carpet.

Sounding remorseful, somewhat anxious, he murmured, "I think . . . I want to go back."

Orain set down her thread and dress. "What do you mean? Go back where? You don't mean to Sulos?"

"I do, my lady."

"Oh, Omos. . . ."

He didn't look at her as he spoke, but continued plucking at the carpet more noisily. "I . . . I don't feel comfortable here anymore. But with everything I've seen and read since I've been here, all the people I've met . . . I've learned a lot . . . perhaps I could help in Sulos. Like we used to."

"But, Omos, it's very dangerous, it's much too dangerous to—"

Lifting his head abruptly, he stared at her with wet eyes. "I don't like it here anymore! Everyone's been very good to me, but I . . . I have nothing to *do*! I want to do something to *help*."

Orain smiled a little, nodding. "I can understand that. I can."

The boy looked back to the carpet, examined the frayed threads. "It bothers me, my lady, that Galvus is changing."

"What do you mean, he's 'changing'?"

"He's just— It's not bad, I don't mean that. But he's a king now, he has been ever since King Elad decided to go to war, and I don't really have anything to do with that. I'm not part of that. He's just becoming . . . more like a king. He needs to do that, I understand, but—"

"Omos—don't you love Galvus any longer?"

Shocked, he stared at her with wide eyes, trembling lips. "Lady Orain, of course I still love him! And I know he loves me! But he

56

can't . . . he can't afford the time to be himself, the way he used to be. He can't be as personal as he used to be, he has to spend more time with ideas than he can with people and—"

Orain swallowed heavily.

"—and I really think, although it frightens me to admit it . . . but with everything I've learned, with everything he's done for me—and you, too—and Count Adred . . . everyone . . . well, maybe I don't need Galvus as much as I used to. Or not in the ways I used to. I've become more independent, just like he has."

He seemed almost ashamed to admit it, this frightened young boy they'd rescued from the docks and taverns. Orain moved from the divan, sat down on the floor beside Omos and hugged him strongly. "I think that's wonderful," she said to him.

"Do you?"

"Yes, I do. I think it's wonderful," she whispered.

"And, anyway," Omos told her, leaning against her, "I could go back, help, stay with—what was that woman's name?"

"Rhia?"

"Rhia. I could help her. . . ."

And so it was decided among them—Galvus, Adred, Abgarthis and three Councilors from the *Priton* Nobility, three from the *Priton* Public Administration.

They would never have enough agreement with the aristocracy and the nobility, that was certain, but—yes, enough agreement amongst the untitled members of the Public Table. And Galvus . . . as dangerous as it was, Galvus must be very careful to act as boldly as he could and with as much responsibility as the action warranted. But the boldness was as necessary as the action.

"The time for real change is long overdue," Lord Osudu assured Galvus. "Many on the *Priton* Nobility want to side with you, but there's no denying that Rhin and Falen and their special friends intimidate and threaten. They've become truly powerful; they're eroding the power of the throne itself."

"It's a very difficult business," allowed Lord Ellu. "You're walking a very narrow path, my lord. But I feel you must do as we've decided."

Galvus nodded absently, frowned as he thought, followed the design on his goblet with a finger.

Across from him, old Count Raphal leaned forward, settled his fists on the table. "This moment will not come again," he warned everyone there. "You have the distinct advantage now, Lord Galvus. But if you prolong your indecisiveness, the moment will pass. Their king will hold your queen ransom; their soldiers will surround your king."

Galvus looked up slowly, something in his eyes. "Are you referring to *usto*, Count, or . . . the world situation?"

Raphal grumbled a low laugh.

Galvus saw that Sion kad Sios of the Public Administration, informally seated next to Raphal, seemed eager to speak his mind. Galvus nodded to him.

But all the young bureaucrat said was, "I agree. This must be done."

Adred was sitting farther down the table, listening; he hadn't yet said anything in regards to their problem, but now he felt Galvus's eyes on him.

"You're worried about justice, essentially, aren't you?" Adred asked his friend. "About doing the right thing to achieve the right ends? Well, you and I both agree about what's right and what's just: it's immoral and unjust for some of us to have more than we need while others of us—the people in the streets, the workers, the old people—don't have as much as they need. They're hungry, they need clothes, they have to be able to spend money, they need *dignity*—correct? And since the means we've both been fighting for to achieve this justice, this redistribution, is in the hands of people who intend to keep what they have—well, then, our problem is actually quite simple: do we have the right to take from those who have—even under emergency conditions—to give to those who don't have, using the methods the 'haves' used to take in the first place? Do our ends justify our intentions? Or are we no better than Rhin and Falen if we steal from them to give back to the people they stole from in the first place?"

Galvus was scratching his head. "We've decided that what was allowable in the past is no longer fair. So can I use unjust means to correct injustice? Or should we simply institute a policy that will rid us of injustice as time goes by?"

Raphal was grumbling with impatience; when Galvus glanced

at him, the old aristocrat showed the prince-regent a fist which he moved through the air in a twisting motion. Galvus smiled.

"It undermines all our principles," Adred said, "to use unjust means to gain just ends. It'd be using pitch to clean ivory. But the other answer is this: times have changed, awarenesses have changed, society has changed. Let me quote Radulis: *'When a house has grown so wracked and weathered that it no longer serves the purpose for which it was constructed, that house is torn down, and a new one of better material and workmanship is erected in its place.'* So you're tearing down that old house—the comfort and security a few have now—and replacing it with a new house—comfort and security for the many. *'From the few to the many in quantity, from the many to the few in quality'*—at least, if we still plan on keeping authority figures at the top of society."

Abgarthis interjected: "I commend the discussion and Lord Galvus and Count Adred for adhering to moral motives and argument. However, it might be best to keep in mind that while you deal with knowledge, the plutocrats and the aristocrats fighting this redistribution will use propaganda, and while you are using reason to settle your difficulties, they will resort to violence. I speak from experience."

"Absolutely!" Raphal agreed loudly. "Absolutely, Lord Abgarthis! You are correct!"

Galvus shook his head sadly, resigned to placing duty before ideals. "As I said earlier, Adred, about Emaria. . . ."

Adred nodded. "It's the same old problem," he sympathized. "Can a roomful of just people live in a household of unjust people? What can we do, practically, in an unjust world?"

Count Raphal intruded with: "The practicality of the matter, gentlemen, is this: Rhin and his lapdogs now have the upper hand. I've heard this kind of talk before, about nonviolence, about answering cruelty with kindness and so forth. Well, you're right, Count Adred, we do live in a houseful—a *worldful*—of unjust people; and besides being unjust they're scheming maggots, they're brutal and selfish, they're cruel and greedy thieves, they think only of themselves and they'll use whatever they have to make sure they *hold onto* what they have, and everyone else be damned. Well, I say to that, if they want to live in a society with their fellow men, then the time has come for these vultures to live by the *rules* their fellow men *make*! Does that answer your problem? *Take* it from them, Galvus! Do it! Because if you allow them to continue with what they're doing now, you'll never be able to correct anything! They'll make sure of it!"

Silence prevailed for many long, thoughtful moments.

Galvus rubbed his forehead, profoundly thoughtful. He stood up, pushed back his chair, threw his hands behind his back and paced a few steps. When he paused, he regarded Lord Abgarthis, who was seated like a wise gray specter at the opposite end of the table.

"What have you to say to this?" the prince asked him.

The old man's voice was very quiet, yet powerfully effective because of that. "Your grandfather, Galvus, was a man who believed in justice. And the changes and reforms he made in his government were accomplished because King Evarris felt that they would insure justice and freedom for most of his people. In some ways they did; in other ways they were not so successful. Evarris could not change the world in one lifetime, although he could alter its course; he could not command entirely all that his empire had become, but he did what he could, with foresight and industry. But, as I say, some of those programs which he initiated have led to excesses which now demand correction and reform. And Evarris would have been the first to make those corrections and reforms, boldly, decisively." Then Abgarthis reminded him, "You are, Galvus, lord of the kitchen, after all."

The prince-regent didn't understand. "Lord of the kitchen? What does that mean, Abgarthis?"

Adred watched, trying to recall when the high minister might have used the phrase before.

But Abgarthis only shook his head and replied, "It is something . . . Elad and I once discussed. . . ."

4.

All was quiet to his ears. He did not sleep but lay with eyes open, hands upon his breast, stretched upon his cot and covered only by a thin blanket. Attentive. Aware. He did not sleep and he did not listen—but he heard.

Heard, from deep within him, the sounds of the earth as if they were his own body's sounds . . . felt, from deep within him, the

60

feelings of the earth . . . was aware, as though it were his own mind and senses, of the god of humanity moving toward the great convulsion, the seizure it sought to bring upon itself.

From far away, from the other end of the corridor, he heard the only other prisoner in this hallway call to him, the voice loud and heavy but indistinct, blurred by the silence and the walls and thickened by the darkness, the shadows.

"Hey, old man! You ain't asleep, are you?"

He lay with eyes open, hands upon his breast, feeling, aware.

"Talk to me, old man. I want to know who you are."

Silence. . . .

"Tell me who you are, old man. I been down here . . . I don't know how long. . . . Nobody to talk to. What'd you see out there, old man? What's happening out there? You know anybody named Lemus the Skinner? Do you? Tell me!"

Deep within him, the feelings of the earth.

"Hey, old man . . . you dead?"

The god of humanity moving toward the great convulsion.

"Hey, old man, I know you ain't asleep. Wake up, old man! Talk to me, damn it! They can't hear us!"

He saw, through the silence, an Oracle woman beheaded by a decorated sword; he saw plagues sweeping across rivers and over mountains; he saw drought dusty and windswept upon the plains; he saw a great war; he saw an evil creature, contorted but burning brightly, hidden by skins of shadows, whispering and posturing upon a throne; and he saw walls topple; he saw cities smashed; he saw fires touch the stars; and he saw blood everywhere, heard screams—everywhere.

"Hey, old man! Old man!"

He lay with open eyes, hands upon his breast, feeling, aware.

"Stupid . . . old man. . . ."

Part of him wanted to reject this false manhood embodied by his uncle Elad and by his father; part of him wanted to escape again into the warm affection and the curiosity and the stubborn reality of womanhood—taught him by his mother and by Queen Yta—who were unpretentious and full of desolation but filled, too, with remarkable humor and honesty. Part of him wanted to escape, yes, into the truth of a community and the willingness and the

61

goodness of masses of people helping and serving one another despite the clouds and shadows and flames of life. Part of Galvus wanted all this.

Wanted to abdicate this throne that was still cold to his touch, as though it were an unclean thing. Wanted to give the world to the people who lived in it; wanted to forgo asking any more questions or deciding upon issues or resolving problems that were not his to resolve, but were the common property of humanity.

And yet. . . .

Another part of him hungered to accept this responsibility which destiny had given him. Part of him wanted to leap ahead and with the strength of a man deny the foolishness of patience and tolerance. That part wanted to take up the scepter and charge headlong into the fray and do what obviously was meant to be done. *Too many ideas!* had his father complained? *What does it all mean!* Elad had asked?

For now he understood this phantom that was power, that was responsibility, and why honest toil was good because it earned one results that could be felt and held and accepted by others. Now he understood what the burden was that had hung so heavily on his father and on Elad, on Yta and Evarris and all of them. Were there actually decisions to be made? Were there actually laws to be decided? Were there actually limits to be drawn, profundities to be propounded, clear choices to be made? Or were there no choices and, thus, no decisions? Were there simply actions to be taken, simply things to be done?

Galvus, alone in his room, stood at a window and looked out toward the ocean. The lights of the ships of the armada were still visible, far upon the dark horizon. He shook his head, turned and crossed the room, sat down at his desk once more. He took up his pen, moved to dip it into his ink gourd—when his eyes fell upon that memento Queen Yta had given him. The locket his uncle Dursoris had had made—Dursoris who, more than his own father, had loved his mother.

Galvus stared at that locket—then turned to his papers and began writing.

And all the while he was aware that what he himself sought, in his doubt, was guidance. He, the authority, did not desire any authority above him, but only a Voice to tell him or remind him that what he must decide was what needed to be decided. Yet the only voice he could rely upon was his own—the beating of his own heart, the judgements of his own temperament, the memories of his own mind.

"... and I don't believe that anyone should have that power, even if he were a very good man. ..."

Galvus set aside his pen and read what he had written.

He knew what would come of it. Rhin and Falen and their allies, deliberately claiming martyrdom, would find power shifting to them even as other power and authority moved toward Galvus: for he was bringing into the daylight things which had remained secret, and so he would openly force men to choose. And the war. ...

Many, he knew, would take advantage of the new situation, this war with Emaria, to enlist in the armed forces, thus to better their stations—for why wait for society to resolve its problems (it hadn't so far!) when a man could move up the ranks in a war and reenter society as a champion? And those left behind would find in the war a way in which to brutalize their fellow men and so profit in their own manner. Galvus pictured them as gnomelike creatures waiting under rocks, ready to scamper out at the first whine of anguish to grasp and claim, to increase their incomes and tally their profits, snarl over the spoils—while the remainder of the empire's citizens suffered from lack of food and clothing and shelter. And the economy? Instantly Galvus saw the falsely growing economy which would benefit the unscrupulous but cause an inflation that would offset or even destroy any of those redistributive measures that he was fighting so hard to institute.

Decisions to be made? Choices to be made? If he did not speak up soon, decisions and choices would inevitably *be* made.

He felt totally isolated—cut off from even his closest friends and his family, cut off even from history and precedent. He felt no kinship with those men who, in this chair and at this desk, had had to decide similar things in the past. *Was* there no progress? *Was* there no sense to the endless repetition of humanity's self-hatred?

With a heart full of doubt and conflict, Galvus rose from his chair, crossed the room and opened his door. He ordered one of the guards outside to alert the Captain of the Khamars that the prince-regent wished words with him. Then Galvus poured himself a fresh cup of tea and pondered what he had done, until his man appeared.

"My lord!" Captain Mandoum saluted when he entered, then stood rigidly at attention.

Galvus lent him a sad smile and said, "Please . . . I am uncomfortable with formality, Captain Mandoum. Take a chair, pour yourself some tea—yes."

"As my lord wishes." The Galsian moved to the table where tea was set out.

"I apologize for asking for you so late at night."

"Think nothing of it, Lord Galvus." Mandoum sat.

"I've asked you here because the throne has always tried to maintain the best of relations with the palace guard—the throne generally and myself specifically."

"We appreciate that, Lord Galvus. Rest assured that every soldier in the regiment thinks just as highly of you."

"It's good to hear that, Captain, because—" he paused briefly to form his thought "—tomorrow I intend to take actions which may result in grave consequences, and I want you to understand what I'm doing and why. It goes beyond what is ordinarily required of the palace police, and I'm afraid I've had to wrestle with my conscience a bit in coming to terms with it."

Mandoum, a practical but not unsympathetic badge, who was as aware of court intrigues as anyone residing in the palace might choose to be, was interested in what this disclosure suggested. He set aside his tea and spoke frankly:

"If I might, my lord, may I tell you not to hesitate in making plain your intentions. You can trust myself and the Guard to do our utmost for your benefit."

Galvus drew in a breath, tapped his foot nervously on the floor, then leaned forward and explained his plans to Captain Mandoum and everything of concern to the Khamars.

When he was done, Mandoum reassured him: "Might I say, Lord Galvus, that I personally don't consider your intentions to be either unethical or impractical. Morality I can't judge but, as the saying goes, a bold opening move outdoes two countermoves. Indeed, I honestly believe that if your uncle, King Elad, had taken just such precautions last year, the capital would not now be in the predicament it's in. I pledge you my faith, and that of the Guard. It's best, after all, to keep savage dogs leashed, true? They may guard your house . . . or they may turn against you. Keep them leashed, I say."

64

The ships with their torches and lanterns like a confusion of
comets caught in a dark whirlpool, distant and drawing away,
parting an unseen curtain that opened before them and fell closed
behind—the all-inclusive dark. . . .

Like bits of life, a city of people, surrounded by the darkness of
Time, Time before birth and the long Time after death. . . .

"He won't come back, will he?" Orain whispered.

Adred looked up.

She was watching from her window as the last small lights of
the armada vanished around her outside wall.

"Elad, you mean?"

"Elad. Yes. . . ."

Adred stood up and went to her, placed his hands on Orain's
shoulders, kissed the back of her head. "Of course he'll be back."

"He's afraid of so many things . . . so many things. . . ."

"Perhaps it's wise, sometimes, to be afraid. Orain. . . ."
Adred's voice revealed his worry; he turned her around so that she
could look at him, but she refused to meet his stare. Her gaze
lingered on the tile floor. "What are you so afraid of? Tell me."

"Galvus. . . . Now he'll learn to be afraid of many things,
too."

"You're tired, my heart. Lie down; it's time you got some
sleep."

"I'm much too nervous to sleep."

"I'll make you some tea."

"I don't want any tea, Adred."

He was becoming frustrated with her; Orain sensed it, moved
from him and walked quietly as a slipping shadow across the
room, dropped onto a divan. Her face was full of tension and
worry and doubt, circles and lines.

"Tell me," she asked, "what's Galvus decided? I know it must
be something."

Adred nodded.

"He's being forced to act against his will, isn't he? By those
politicians on the Council. Rhin and those others—I knew they
wouldn't wait long."

"They haven't been here this evening," Adred told her, "and
they haven't tried to communicate with Galvus at all."

"Omos is worried . . . I'm worried. . . ."

"Galvus is forcing *himself* to act in a manner he never anticipated, Orain. I'm afraid that's the truth of it. If he's going to salvage anything of what he believes in, then he's got to sacrifice some of it. That's what he's doing tonight."

Shock lit her eyes. "What do you mean? What are you saying?"

He looked at her.

"Adred? Tell me! What's Galvus planning?"

Now he crossed the floor and sat down beside her, held her hands—

Told her.

The following morning, just after sunrise, as Lord Rhin was sitting up in his bed and coming awake, he was surprised to hear the low rumble of horses' hoofs outside. Scowling, he pulled himself from his bed and went to a window, yanked back the shutters and stared across his verandah. Only lifting clouds of dust upon the road leading to his home gave evidence that the riders he'd heard were not a figment of his sleepy imagination.

In the next moment, Rhin was startled by loud footsteps clattering within his villa, by the calling of servants to one another, and then the pounding of fists on his doors. Astonished, and now fully awake, the plutocrat hastily dressed and exited his sleeping room, just as a number of servants tumbled down the hallway toward him to report breathlessly:

"My lord! Palace guards! And they demand to speak with you at once!"

Lord Falen was seated at breakfast in his own home, some leagues away from Rhin's villa, and he himself was the first to notice the approaching troop of Khamars that came through his gate (opened without his command only to nobility or messengers obviously dispatched from the palace). They dismounted in his courtyard and deliberately took the steps to his front door. Falen trembled at the sound of their demands for entry, suspecting that their arrival was not due to anything he and Rhin had set in motion.

Lord Edar was bathing when his servants brought him word of Khamars coming up the walkway to his manor.

While Count Domaris was feeding the birds that collected habitually outside his windows every morning at dawn.

Lord Avarru was on his way to his stables; he had made plans to enter the capital earlier than usual this morning to meet with some informants on matters of business.

While Lord Sinnu was engaged in some erotic play with one of his house servants, the thunder of many horses interrupted his attention and spoiled his mood.

All of them, and a few others besides, reacted to this gross incursion on their privacy and property by the elite Khamar guards with the same apoplectic anger that Lord Rhin vented when he heard their purpose for coming:

". . . to be detained indefinitely upon these premises under house arrest," read the leader of the guards in his villa, "under direct order from the throne. The command is signed by Lord Galvus and affixed with the seal of the empire, Lord Rhin."

"This is outrageous! This is against the law! There are civil—"

"This is pursuant to criminal indictment against you, my lord—"

"So I'm guilty already, am I?"

"—and Prince Galvus is wholly within his office to order us to hold you here."

"He has no reason to charge me with anything!" Rhin roared. *"He's* the *criminal*! *He's* the *revolutionary*! *He's* as bad as his *uncle*! Who in the name of the gods does he think he is? He has *no right* to—"

"And if you seek by any means to vacate these premises or escape from this villa, Lord Rhin, my men and I are under strict orders to treat you as we would a prisoner in the cells."

"This is absolutely the most preposterous—"

As they made their way in unhurried pairs and trios into the Council Chamber later that morning, and began taking their accustomed seats, the palace advisers and Councilors discovered that Prince-Regent Galvus was not seated upon his throne. This seemed peculiar, for they had all been issued summonses earlier in the day signed by his hand requesting their immediate presence at a special assembly, and they had answered his apparent impatience with promptness. There was a ceaseless rise and roll of conversation and speculative gossip in the Chamber. Then more as the last of the lords and bureaucrats straggled in, and it became apparent that quite a number of seats were to remain vacant.

What did this portend? What did Galvus suppose he was doing? Why this sudden—?

Their earnest apprehensions were interrupted by Lord Abgarthis, who made his way up the steps of the throne dais to read the roll call of those present. When he had finished, Abgarthis pounded the gavel upon the arm of the throne. This was a device only rarely employed: the king himself always sounded the gavel to begin proceedings.

But immediately upon the command for attention, still another shock awaited the convened Councilors, as the great doors of the Chamber were swung open and into the stunned silence of the great hall strode a troop of palace guards—Khamars all dressed and outfitted in their regalia, advancing two abreast in a fashion usually reserved for imperial processions. In formation they parted when they reached the congress area in the center of the hall, one wing of Khamars advancing up the stairs of the dais and around the tall throne to form a guarding hemisphere, and the other wing taking the same position around the collected membership of the *Priton* Nobility and the *Priton* Public Administration.

Every man in the room was thoroughly astonished—save for Lord Abgarthis, who viewed the event with a cool, detached complacency.

When the last Khamar had stamped his boot upon the floor—as the echo of it still lingered in the air—Prince-Regent Galvus entered the Chamber through the main door, unannounced by any horns. He was dressed unspectacularly in a simple tunic and plain belted trousers, which too was something unexpected, for it gave him the informal air of a man too preoccupied with his business to bother with his appearance.

Galvus made his way to the throne amidst the awed quiet, beneath dozens of stares, and took his seat, placed his crown upon his head and lifted his scepter and placed it upon his lap. He then undid one of two wound scrolls he had brought in with him and read it to his assembled lords and ministers.

"This document, dated by me on this day, the second of Elru in the Year of the Prophet 1879, was dictated by King Elad and endorsed by him, and carries his signature. It is, gentlemen,

68

a declaration of war against the nation-state of Emaria. I will read—"

Spontaneous cheers and outbursts created a sudden din which drowned out the exasperated voices of those in the hall who were obviously disappointed with this bold move made by their new lord.

"*I will read it*—" Galvus's voice lifted "—and when I have done so, I will issue my own commands and orders, to be initiated immediately throughout the empire in accordance with the War Law under which this empire is now controlled, due to our enterprise recently launched against the peoples of Salukadia."

Chairs shifted, voices continued to murmur lowly, and Galvus read his uncle's proclamation:

"'On this day I, Elad I, Emperor and Lord King of Imperial Athadia, due to repeated international discord fostered by the nation-state of Emaria, and due to that government's unwillingness to negotiate a settlement in any peaceful manner with, or by any amicable means admit to acts of hostility directed against the empire of Athadia, or redress those acts of spoilage, murder, criminality and provocation against the empire of Athadia, do by the power invested in me declare a state of war to exist between the empire of Athadia and the nation-state of Emaria. By me, Elad I, 2 Elru 1879 DP.'"

Silence in the Council Chamber.

Galvus set aside this declaration and took up the second. He cleared his throat and began, "Gentlemen—" and read:

"'On this day I, Prince-Regent Galvus of the House of Evarris, in accordance with that authority invested in me as Acting-Authority of the imperial throne of the empire of Athadia, hereby declare the following measures to take effect immediately, under the provisions of the War Law and Hostilities Act *T.R.*: No armed force shall be convened or summoned to be convened, save for those lawful assemblies expressly granted approval by the throne and acting in accordance with the direction of this throne— explicitly, the Imperial Army of the Empire of Athadia; the Khamar Guard of the Imperial Palace in Athad; those policing and law enforcement city guards employed by the territorial governors and city mayors operating under the jurisdiction of the Athadian high throne; and any units or regiments of combat personnel inducted or by other means accepted into the service of the

Imperial Army of the Athadian Empire, should the necessity for such be invoked; further, the Imperial Treasury of the Empire of Athadia shall be the sole purchaser and distributor of arms, rations, supplies or other provisions or essentials necessary for the maintenance of armed forces serving the direction of this throne, and for the maintenance of the civilian population and any and all noncombatants; further—' "

A profound sense of unease gripped the men in that room: surely this had much to do with the absence of Lords Rhin, Falen and others of their compatriots.

" '—this throne hereby places a War Tax upon any and all property within the empire, the legal possessors of this property to pay the sum of two percent of its latest assessed value into the Imperial Treasury as a War Tribute, in accordance with the tables and estimates given below, to maintain and—' "

Yes, surely . . . certainly, this had everything to do with the absence of those men who for too long had taken advantage of a lax government and an impolitic economy to advantage themselves at the expense of everyone else. Yes, surely . . . Lord Galvus the "revolutionary" was moving swiftly and boldly to curtail any further erosion of government standards or business practices—curtail them before they had even the first slim opportunity to—

He finished his proclamation and rolled it up, eyed every minister and nobleman and bureaucrat seated before him.

Yes, surely. . . .

"Gentlemen . . . in accordance with this statement and our War Law, I have acted already to detain a number of businessmen and government officials against whom I have the strongest evidence and proof of criminal activity. You will notice the empty chairs and benches, if you haven't already."

A few wry chuckles sounded hollow in the Chamber.

"I am going to war against Emaria, not because I consider it to be in the best interests of this empire, but because I consider it to be the most logical and expedient course for this empire to follow, in view of the precipitating circumstances. And I am abrogating certain privileges and enforcing the law against certain high-seated individuals, not vindictively, but rationally, to ensure that no one in this government and that no citizen of this empire, during this time of crisis, is victimized by any other citizen or

70

government servant. I would appreciate your support in this. I think we would all be in agreement, my lords and officers, that the people of Athadia should go to war against their *enemies*, and not against themselves. And this is all I have to say to you this morning, and so if you will excuse me, the Council servants will deliver to your offices copies of all that I've read to you during this meeting. . . ."

5.

"I think," Orain said, looked intently at her son, "that you've done the right thing."

But Galvus was doubtful. "I'm not so sure. . . . We must do more than simply treat foolish men like Rhin the way they treat us. It's a moral problem, mother. I'm afraid it's a moral problem."

They were sitting in a pergola in the western garden. The afternoon was growing late, but still Galvus was not in the mood to force himself to return to his office and his paperwork.

In his glum frame of mind, he continued: "Everything must change. We run our businesses and our government as we do our military—from the top down. We don't cooperate with people because they *are* people; we take advantage of their numbers because it's easier to deal with numbers than it is people. This ordering of commands, this efficient way of accomplishing things . . . we only damn ourselves because it's so *in*efficient, it's so short-sighted. It fails to deal with *people*. Life is a human enterprise, it's not a . . . *business* enterprise."

Orain watched him, marveling at him. Why did it take something evil, like a war, to place so moral a man on the throne of government? She remembered Dursoris, she thought back to Galvus and herself living on the docks in Sulos, she thought of Queen Yta's grave concerns for the empire—

As if overhearing her thoughts, Galvus faced her. The ivy and the bunched flowers that clung to the trelliswork behind him shadowed his face in a moving pattern—perhaps an outward show of the many tangled thoughts working in his mind.

Footsteps came to their ears and they looked up.

Adred, hands behind his back, was wearing a half-smile, uncertain whether or not to intrude.

71

"It's all right," Orain told him. "We're just talking."

"Abgarthis sent me to tell you that the prisoner's being brought up. Whenever it's convenient."

A smudge of worry clouded Orain's features. "Prisoner?" She looked to Galvus.

"The priest," he told her. "That priest from Hilum. The one Seraficos had arrested for sedition."

Orain's eyes went wide.

The jailer woke him with his loud jangling of the key ring. The cell door grated and squeaked as it was pulled open.

"The prince-regent wishes to speak with you."

Asawas sat up on the edge of his cot, swung his legs to the floor. "This is . . . the king?"

"That's right. Please come along."

Asawas stood, moved toward the open door. In the corridor outside stood two tall, gleaming Khamars, the same sort who had brought him down here some nights before. Asawas walked to them; they asked him to head down toward the door that was opened at the end of the corridor.

"Am I being brought to trial now?" he asked.

"This is merely an interview. Prince-Regent Galvus wants to hear what you have to say about the charges brought against you. Step along now, please."

As he moved toward the door, the prisoner farther down the corridor yelled out: "Hey, old man! Tell him about *me*! *I* don't belong in here, neither! Be sure to tell him about what they did to *me*! *I'm* innocent, too!"

The door slammed on his echoing voice.

Galvus was surprised, first of all, by the size of the man. He hadn't formed any preconception of what this priest might look like, but now he realized that he'd vaguely expected the fellow to be of small stature, or perhaps simply less dominating in his appearance because of all that he had suffered. But this Asawas was a large man, quite obviously the farmer from the plains of Omeria that his records indicated; and he exuded strength and vitality, presence—purposefulness. Galvus felt he also exuded

72

honesty and integrity. Those things seemed as much a part of him as were his rough worn robe, his battered sandals, his weathered walking staff.

His Khamar escort led Asawas to the foot of the short dais upon which Galvus sat in a decorated chair. The prophet saw that there were only a few others in the room: a young bearded man who might be an aristocrat, a blonde woman whose features indicated that she must be the prince-regent's mother, and a very old man who wore the robes of a state minister and a long beard that attested to years of service in the imperial halls.

The Khamars, at a nod from Galvus, unshackled their prisoner and stepped back—but remained near enough that they might take action, should that prove warranted.

And so here, in this small audience chamber, with only a few witnesses, Galvus spoke with the man who had managed to strike such fear into Prince General Cyrodian that the man had gone to his death scared—arrogantly and proudly, but changed.

Galvus looked into the farmer's eyes and read something deep there; but maintaining his composure, he turned his attention to the documents in his hands and reviewed them as he said to the prisoner:

"Your name is Asawas."

"That is so."

"You are an Omerian—a farmer."

He bowed his head. "Yes."

"This report from the official in Hilum who had you arrested— he indicates that you caused public disturbances in Hilum and refused to cooperate with the Inquisitor of the Church, Seraficos."

"Do you wish me to tell you what happened?"

"Yes, I'd like to hear your side of it."

"I was coming toward Hilum, preaching the word of God, when a red rain fell on the countryside, inspiring fear in the people. I told the people that the red rain was a sign from God and that if they had faith, the rain would turn clear again, would become water again. I put my hand into the water of a fountain, and I touched the red rain that many people brought me, and it became clear because I have faith in God."

Galvus stared at him.

"This is what caused the disturbance in the streets of Hilum."

"I . . . see." Galvus emitted a low cough. "And the reason

73

why Seraficos charges that you refused to cooperate with him, and Lord Abadon?"

Asawas replied, "Seraficos the Inquisitor charged me with claiming to be the Prophet Bithitu returned to the earth. He asked me to perform miracles, to condemn myself and to betray God. I refused to do this, which infuriated him. Furthermore, I told Seraficos that while he was a man of high position in his Church, I felt that he was not a man of faith, and that he was a hypocrite for claiming to be a man of faith and holding his position in the Church."

Abgarthis let out a chuckle, but quickly raised a hand to his mouth. Asawas lent him a look; Galvus did the same. Lord Abgarthis composed himself.

"The Inquisitor Seraficos," Galvus agreed, "is a proud man."

"The world, sir, is full of proud men, and they cause only harm. They must overcome their pride."

Galvus lifted an eyebrow. "Is this the nature of what you told Seraficos?"

"It is."

"I see. . . . You say that he charged you with being the Prophet returned. This is sacrilegious, is it not? Do you claim to be Bithitu come back?'

"No."

"What, then, do you claim?"

"I am only a man who has been filled with the spirit of God, and God has asked me to speak to the people and administer to them his word, and to give warning to all people that the world will soon die, so that it may be reborn."

Orain uttered a gasp and quickly moved forward; she gripped one arm of Galvus's throne and stared at Asawas. "What did you say? What do you mean—that the world is going to die?"

"The world is humanity; God is humanity; God is the world. This world that is full of pain and anger, tumult and grief—it will soon end. It will heave and split and cause a great destruction, and many lives will be lost, many cities will fall, all that we know and depend upon will be brought low. God makes this happen through the world, so that men may know themselves and do the truth."

Galvus was astounded by this bold statement. "You say that God—the god above all the other gods, I presume?—will make this happen?"

"There is only one god."

"There is?"

Asawas nodded.

"Who is this one god?"

"I call him On, but he is not a person or a thing; he is all persons and all things. You and I and all the world, we are God."

"Mother Hea!" Orain breathed, lifting a hand to her mouth. "Who *are* you, *who*?"

Galvus turned to her. "Mother, please. . . ." He was himself visibly shaken. "You say . . . you said these things to our officials in Hilum, and so they had you arrested?"

"Is it not the destiny of those who bring Truth into the world to suffer for it?"

Galvus watched him, now. "It is indeed, my friend," he replied quietly. "It is indeed." And then: "You say—what? That we're going to experience a great destruction of the lands, the cities, the—"

"The world, Prince. The signs of its coming have already begun."

"And what are these signs?"

Asawas told him, "The first was a seeming madness that possessed animals and all wild creatures. Cattle and dogs, wildlife and birds—".

Adred exclaimed suddenly, "The birds!" and reminded Abgarthis: "Do you remember? The birds I told you about, when I came here last year for Evarris' funeral!" He looked at Orain. "And . . . the dogs in the street, remember? when we left for Sulos." Astonished, he stared at Asawas at length—

"We enter a dark age. I have seen the future, and it is dark, but there is a light. . . ."

—and then asked in a quieter voice: "What . . . else?"

"The second sign was the red rain that fell in the countryside. The third was a great wind that caused destruction—"

"I remember that," Galvus interrupted him. "Adred? Abgarthis? When Thomo came from Erusabad with—with his news."

Abgarthis solemnly nodded his head.

"The fourth sign," Asawas explained, "occurs even now, with me. I, who bring the word of God, come before the highest court in the world to be judged by the king of the world."

Galvus leaned forward. "And what do you suppose my judgment to be, priest?"

"You and I know that already, because we are good men; God has touched both of us, though we live in a world of pain and hatred, and those elements seek to do us harm. You and I seek . . . balance and harmony."

"Oh, Galvus. . . ." Orain held his arm.

"The fifth sign," Asawas continued, "will be a day and a night of plague. This is the sign that the true end has begun, that it approaches quickly. Many will fall and scream out in terror and fear, not trusting to God, not believing in the everlasting truth of the All. Then I will meet an old enemy, *ro kil-su*, the Spirit of Discord and proud of the evil it has caused, who even now sits as a potentate on a throne."

"Agors!" Adred exclaimed—and immediately regretted his outburst.

But Asawas told him, "No, not that one. There are many kings in the world, but only one who knows who I am and expects me."

Galvus silently considered this. "And the seventh sign?"

"The seventh sign is no sign, but the last act of this humanity and its world. The end will come."

"And what will that be?"

"You will know it when it happens. Only you must not fear it."

Galvus took a deep breath, deliberated upon these things, and spoke slowly: "You say all this . . . I suspect that you believe it to be the truth. And yet—"

"Do not think with your mind, Prince—feel with your heart."

Galvus asked him then: "Suppose we wish to prevent this . . . 'great destruction.' What can we—"

"You cannot prevent it, Prince. It has already begun. You must understand and believe that deep within its soul, humanity wishes this to be. One man here, one woman there—they are terrified, they are afraid, they no longer know what to believe, they clutch at any safety, they breathe prayers, they do not want to know that what they hold and what they believe and what they desire will all be done away with. Yet the whole of humanity—deep within its soul—has hungered for this thing; it has reached out for God, and God is only the answer to all that is in our hearts and has been in our hearts for generation upon generation. What comes to happen, we have made to happen—not because we sit at a table and decide what to do, but because our souls know more than we allow ourselves to admit. This is why it comes. We know that we must die to be reborn, whether we admit this or not in our conversation. Just so, the world must die to be reborn. Should we fear death when it comes? We know that it is only another kind of life that awaits us, and that it is a channel again to this life, where we strive and work and grow with knowledge. Just so with the world. There is no death; there is no life; there are simply many expressions of God, which is the unity of the All, the completeness, the whole."

Galvus was affected profoundly by these words; for a very long time he stared at Asawas. Then, when he spoke up at last, it was to order one of the Khamars to fetch a number of servants, and when they were brought in the prince-regent ordered food and drink and extra lamps delivered into the hall. He came down from his dais and sat at one of the tables in the center of the chamber, invited Asawas to sit across from him and indicated that his mother and Adred and Abgarthis, too, should be seated. They would eat a meal and listen to what this priest, this—prophet— had to tell them.

The lamps began to burn low . . . at the table questions were asked and insights given and argued over, voices listened to . . . while Asawas told these people that which he had been reborn to tell.

"All persons are different," Asawas proclaimed, "but the differences are meant only to enhance our sameness and to provide avenues by which each may share in the experiences and pains and rewards of all. Yet see what men do when they acknowledge these differences. We can blame only ourselves for the griefs that grip our world, because we have acted foolishly and selfishly, because we have not acted when others were foolish and selfish, and so we allowed them to do as they pleased with us. Here is a truth: When men gathered behind walls and begin to fear what is outside those walls, then they become sick animals afraid of any voice or sound that is foreign to them. These men listen only to one another, and so they become afraid of other sounds and other voices, they begin to fear those who do not speak as they do or look as they do or dress as they do, they fear opinions and other experiences. They have contrived a false world. But they suppose that the real world is now against them, merely because they will not go out into the world. They feel they are powerless because the true world is not within their walls, and so they want to harm the real world, spitefully, out of ignorance."

And Asawas continued: "Men build weapons because they fear that they are weak. Yet what is stronger than the heart, the mind, the hand that builds, the love that binds? Yet these are not obvious strengths, and they are strengths that are built upon honesty and truth. Of what use are they to dishonest men and false men, liars and perpetrators? These men will desire other strengths, obvious strengths: they take steel and make it into weapons that can break hearts and destroy minds, and claim that they have a strong weapon, a weapon stronger than the hearts and minds all around them. Yet we have had weapons for as long as there have been men, and still the hearts and minds come and the swords cannot kill all of them, the strength of the weak and the frightened cannot defeat the strength of the hearts and minds and working hands of the others. Yet while the weak persist, there is no balance, there is discord, and like the fever which begins in one man and can, unless that man is isolated, spread to all other men, so this fever of steel and mistrust, dishonesty and hate spreads and infects—until only a few remain who begin to doubt truth and honesty, who begin to think that the men of swords and hate are right, because the world they see around them is a world that sits in the shadow of swords and hate. And one ray of sunlight in such a world seems false, an illusion or a dream, a figment of the imagination. We should all distrust men of swords and hate and violence: yet when the world is a thing of swords and hate and violence, men of love and charity are mistrusted. And all is then lost."

Galvus told Asawas of the revolution which gripped the cities of the empire; Asawas was familiar with the anger and the conflict this revolution had caused. Galvus told the prophet that he had helped the revolutionaries in Sulos, because he believed their struggle to be a worthy one: yet he disliked what was happening now, because ideals were being lost, ideals were being smothered and confounded by the anger and the violence. It seemed that what the people were fighting for and what they were fighting against, had become the same thing. Galvus himself had tried rigorously to maintain his beliefs; now, however, his uncle the king had gone forth to make war (Asawas knew of this, as well) and Galvus, as the acting king, had had to make decisions which compromised his beliefs. What of this?

"Any decision you have made," Asawas assured him, "is the correct decision."

"But how can you say that? How can you possibly say that?"

"Because *all* that happens is correct. Who are you to determine that your acts predispose anything to happen outside the province of God, or despite God? You cannot claim that your acts are determined and brought into being without being part of the All. You misjudge the apparent for the actual: you deem that thing to be real which you can hold in your hand, weigh or judge or even discuss. Surely all of existence cannot be reduced to such a level: men's thoughts discover new wonders and mysteries constantly and rediscover others that have been lost; and when this happens you and men like you alter how you consider the world. Yet one who has experienced God, the All, the whole, knows that all discoveries which await men, and all the thoughts which can be considered by men, are yet but a small portion of the All."

Galvus shook his head, intrigued by this. "Suppose I were to order murders . . . outrages . . . executions . . . pogroms and wars and devastations?"

To each enormity which he listed, Asawas nodded his head in agreement and answered, "All of these are one with the God. Why do you think that a wonderful love between two people or a feeling of calm when it possesses you or your own happiness at hearing music, is a celebration of God, and yet murder and destruction, violence and ugliness are not? You have been prejudiced by men who have made decisions in the name of God and have taught these prejudices to their fellows—but they are only men, after all."

"Surely murder and . . . rape . . . destruction . . . the willful harming of one person by another . . . all manner of intolerance—these are not good things?" Galvus protested.

"They are not good; who cares for such things, if one is indeed a caring, thoughtful individual? But how can a thing which offends you or disgusts be found reprehensible by God, who is much more than the offensive thing and you and your reaction to it? You judge these things because you live in a society with your fellow men where such things occur, and so you must deal with them and their effects. You experience existence one life at a time;

God is all lives at all times, however—the unity of the All. Life," Asawas said, holding up a goblet, "is such a thing as this: it seems real to the touch, but it grows old and it changes and passes away. The spirit, however, is all around—it seems never to change, it seems as if it is not there, that it is there all around only so that we may see the goblet. Yet could it not be, perhaps, just the opposite—the goblet, or life, is here so that we may realize that the spirit is here, as well? And may it not be that both—dissimilar as they are—exist together, in different ways, and for different purposes that are still mutually beneficial?"

Orain had a very important personal question to ask Asawas. "My husband," she confessed, "was a murderer, a soldier, a cruel man, very strong. He was banned from this empire by King Elad but he was caught and put in chains, and he was returned here to meet his execution. We know that you met him—Cyrodian—he was my husband—we know that you met him somewhere in your travels, when he was held in a cage, a prisoner of the Emarian government."

"I remember," Asawas told her. "Yes, this is so."

"You told him something which terrified him. It . . . made his hair turn white."

Asawas thought for a moment; his features wrinkled, then opened with brightness. "Yes, I remember."

"What . . . if we may ask—what did you tell him?"

"I merely looked into his heart, read his soul. What he appeared to be to others did not interest me; the soul inside him, that is what I saw, and it was to his soul that I spoke. I told him only that his mother yet watched him and loved him, and forgave him."

Orain was very moved; her taut hands gripped together and trembled. "But . . . his mother—Queen Yta—by that time she was dead. . . ."

"Her body no longer housed her spirit, yes."

Orain was staring at him deeply. "Yes. She . . . was dead."

Asawas smiled complexly. "Look around you," he urged Orain. "*Feel*. All things exist and are, forever. That which was born can never die, for it has always been."

Orain began to sob at the beauty and wonder and the stark simplicity of this and moved her hands to her face. Adred drew an arm about her shoulders and showed Asawas an expression concerned and grave, yet again wondering.

Lord Abgarthis, cynical though he was after his many years of imperial service, was nevertheless impressed by this quietly forceful farmer-turned-*ikbusa*. So that he himself could take measure of Asawas, Abgarthis turned the conversation toward the coming conflict in the east. "Even now," he stated, "as we sit here speaking, my lord King Elad hastens with his flotilla toward the Holy City to challenge the *Ghen* in the name of his wife, whom this eastern king has stolen. Will you tell me why this should be? Will you tell me that this war must come to pass? It is foolish and stupid, yet pride is involved, arrogance and the wills and passions of two strong men."

"It comes to be," Asawas told him.

"Then there will be a war?" Abgarthis persisted.

"It will happen as it happens," was his reply.

But Abgarthis was dissatisfied with this. "Don't dissemble with me, please. Tell me if you know: shall our empire be plunged into a war with the empire of the Salukadians? We are already at war in Emaria."

"What do you wish me to say?" Asawas asked. "The hate is already in their hearts; the damage is done. If the hate is there so strong and deep, so rooted, does it matter then if it takes form or not? It is not the war you should fear: it is the hate and the mistrust, the war of hearts that you should fear. Why should you grieve over a war, and not grieve over the hate that was there all along, sowing the seeds of war? What is a war compared to the never ending hate and mistrust, the greed and the deception that will always cause wars to come? How can you claim to be concerned with life, and not deal with the *fear* all around you that is the enemy of life?"

The hours continued to pass, the discussions and arguments and ideas moved around and around the table, until at last Orain, exhausted by the emotional excitement, began to fall asleep. Adred offered to lead her upstairs to her room. Galvus suggested then that it was time they all retire, and he asked Asawas if the prophet wouldn't care to spend a few more days with them—and not in a cell (for which the prince-regent apologized), but in a room of the palace, so that all who might wish to could speak with Asawas and gain of his wisdom.

The prophet declared that he would be happy to spend a few days in the palace, and to speak with all that might care to visit him. But he warned against speaking publicly or addressing Galvus's assembled Council. "I will speak from my heart to other hearts," were his words, "but I cannot stand and speak to many different minds at once in a hall reserved for politics and law and business. My voice there would sound as hollow as the hearts of many of the men who might witness me. Let me speak from heart to heart, rather than from voice to mind."

Galvus was amenable to this. And so Adred at last led Orain from the hall. Abgarthis and Galvus stood up and stretched and thanked the prophet mightily before leading the way out and directing Asawas to a room upstairs.

And as the prince showed the prophet a room and made his good night to him, he spoke informally and from his heart, full of misery and doubt as he was. "All the people," Galvus said, ". . . and all their hopes and ambitions . . . all that they strive for. . . . The people *are* good," he insisted, as though it were necessary to reiterate such an obvious fact. "The people *do* desire peace and goodwill and . . . brotherhood."

"This is true," Asawas nodded.

"Their faith should be in themselves; but they raise so many false things into a faith. Faith in money . . . faith in other men. . . . Why are we so weak? Why are we so eager to find others to tell us what to do? What is our fear? All men could decide amongst themselves; the truth is known—falsehood was created by men, it wasn't found growing in the trees or in the fields. There is no great secret to gaining peacefulness and brotherhood and generosity; and yet we constantly give power to those who foster just the opposite. We constantly allow a few greedy, selfish, fearful and brutal men to cajole us and cheat us, and we allow them to make us into men like them! Why? *Why*? Where *is* our faith? Where *is* our hope?" Galvus turned to Asawas and, in a voice full of emotion, told him: "I have gone sometimes into the temples and joined in services, and I have been so deeply moved at times that I wondered, What can be more powerful than the faith of a whole people? It seems like all the world and the stars might join in harmony, at moments like those. And yet, it remains a dream, an illusion. It seems false."

"It is not false," Asawas replied, and then paused as a maid

82

servant walked past him and the prince-regent, heading down the corridor toward the servants' quarters carrying a baby in her arms. Asawas bowed to the young woman, smiled and told Galvus: "What is more powerful than the faith of an entire people? Only the cry of a newborn child, Prince Galvus—which sounds purer and more true, open and honest, than all the hymns of belief of any faith anywhere."

PART II

Sowing the Tares

1.

On the sixth day of Elru, the month of the Lion, King Elad ordered his armada to drop anchor just off the coast at Arsol, an important port city which sat at the mouth of the Hiso River. Major Undas of the Ninth Legion West had taken ill, and it was deemed advisable that he be replaced by a man of similar rank, temperament and ability. Therefore, on this very warm late summer day, Elad ordered a longboat lowered and Major Undas ferried ashore, so that he could be cared for by the military medical services. Then the king had immediate orders delivered to Major Hamaro of the Twentieth Legion West, stationed in Arsol, to replace Undas's command.

In the hour or two needed for these actions to take place, Elad was able to invite aboard his flagship the *Crown* his governor in Arsol, Lord Mendar, and so learn from that man what news was current in the city and the countryside.

What Mendar told his king did nothing to improve Elad's already grim mood. Strikes, demonstrations and insurrections were occurring throughout the city and in the surrounding areas; perhaps a full third day of the city workers and the laborers of the major industries and businesses in Arsol had refused to cooperate with the austerity programs Elad had called for. There were demonstrations occurring outside the military barracks in Arsol, as well as at the offices where young men were being recruited for imperial service. This had led to violence on numerous occasions, for many men, out of work and unable to support themselves, were turning to the military for employment, work and shelter. Food shortages were also a problem: the drought that had begun in midsummer had not let up, and farmers to the north reported that their croplands and their livestock's grazing pastures were parched and being burnt up. Lord Mendar appealed to King Elad to intervene and see that food was sent to his city for distribution to the needy. Conflicts had arisen on the docks between fishermen employed by the seafood concerns who were selling at excessive prices and the jobless and homeless poor who had no money with which to buy, yet were warned away from the fishing areas reserved for businessmen. To Elad's suggestion that Mendar contact the governors of nearby cities and territories for loans of food and other necessities, the lord of Arsol replied that all of them were in the same predicament.

"I fear that our system has broken down," were Mendar's words. "We need your authority, my lord, to impose strictures, to show us how to return to prosperity. I fear that the longer we deter making substantial decisions, the worse our predicament will become and the more dire the solutions the people might resort to."

Elad, on his way to make war in the east, could offer Lord Mendar little hope and even less promise of action. He told him to contact the prince-regent in Athad and apply for extra grants from the imperial treasury. Mendar told Elad that he had already done so twice, but had heard no reply.

When Major Hamaro boarded his flagship of command, Lord Mendar left the *Crown*, taking a skiff back into his city, dissatisfied and bitter. Elad watched him from the rail and saw that crowds had sprung up all along the docks, shouting and yelling and waving signs and banners. Military police rode amongst them, trying to maintain order, attempting to protect Mendar as the governor moved to his carriage. It appeared to Elad that the military police were not being as forceful or severe in their control of the crowds as they should be.

It came to him then that perhaps the situation truly was as serious as Mendar had insisted. Perhaps these troops, too, had empty bellies? Perhaps the system was failing for them, as well as for those who were temporarily out of work?

Elad ordered the crew of the *Crown* to lift anchor and continue down the coast.

And as Arsol receded from his view, the king allowed himself to consider all the events that had happened to him in the past year. These memories caused him much heartache and anguish. Elad suffered a true ache in his body when he recalled that almost exactly one year ago to the day the death of his father had occurred. One year ago, the death of Evarris . . . and one year ago, Elad's own mad scheme to take the throne from his mother . . . his journey to the Oracle at Mount Teplis . . . the beginning of this chain of circumtances, this weaving of actions and people that had led him, as though predetermined, to—

To this.

Himself, the king, standing on the boards of a war galley, carrying the sword of vengeance to the eastern empire, and all to rescue—what? To defend—what? His wife? His empire? His economy? Or only to fulfull a destiny in which he was as trapped as was everyone else on earth? To make of the world the funeral place it seemed now to be to his somber eye and disillusioned heart?

Elad had wanted to be king, and now he was king, and he did not wish to be king.

He had hungered to marry Salia, but now that he was married to her he no longer felt himself to be her husband or she his wife, and he no longer wished to be married to her.

He did not want to make a war, yet he was on his way to create war. He was dressed in armor, his crown replaced by a helmet and a sword hung at his side—yet he was no soldier, he was no warrior, he did not want to perpetrate a war.

Had any man in the history of the world ever begun so many things that must be fulfilled, been so responsible for so much, and yet not understood how they had come about, not understood what he had done to make them happen? How could it be that a man in his heart did not want something to happen, and yet everything he did worked to make that very thing come to be?

What madness was it that took the world men had made, ripped it from their hands, fashioned it and caused it to work against men—and all the while lie to men that they themselves were yet in control?

What explanation could anyone give him that he was doing a thing which he did not wish to do, and yet which circumstance forced him to do?

And how on earth could anyone dare to look upon him, point a finger at him—Elad, himself—and declare that he, because he was a king, was responsible for all this madness? That was unfair, and it was a lie.

It was a lie.

Surely it must be . . . a lie. . . .

The word from the Twenty-ninth Legion's rider had been succinct: five thousand men trapped in a steep gulley three leagues west of the Emarian border, engaged by hostile forces and in desperate need of reinforcements. Major Ensoris agreed to do what he could, but as Emarian cavalry had been sighted all along the border, and raids demanding attention were known to have taken place in the farmlands, all he could spare was Captain Uvars's Second Company. And that reduced his command by half, for Ensoris's Third Company had been dispatched three days earlier to escort refugees west to the river towns.

For three days Uvars's troop had cautiously advanced over the hilly terrain and the plains, following the Twenty-ninth's rider to the scene of the battle. Unspoken, but silently acknowledged, were his fears and his men's that no unit, not even the Athadian Twenty-ninth, could possibly be expected to defend itself for six days in the midst of enemy territory.

And this dismal prospect was confirmed when Uvars and his men made their way up the steepness of a ridge that overlooked the wide gulley. Down there, beneath the hot sun and in the shadows of rocks, lay five thousand corpses, their stretched and torn, disfigured forms already stripped of weapons by scavenging Emarians, and the bodies themselves already partially denuded by the gliding carrion eaters that cawed and floated and ripped the meat from the bones.

Several of Uvars's men, youngsters recently taken into the service and without much experience, hurriedly dismounted and ran for the underbrush to retch and vomit. Battle, they had been taught, was a path to glory; but the remnants of battle—the acres of corpses and the mountains of bodies and the stink of flesh and the sounds of beaks ripping and the bones drying and breaking and the swarms of insects—these realities had not figured much in their adolescent fantasies.

Uvars himself stared down upon the scene of devastation and, in the age-old manner of all warriors everywhere, determined to answer the death of comrades with vengeance. Ensoris's directive had been logical: if the Twenty-ninth is beyond need of reinforcements, continue into Emarian territory, and take the enemy's ground wherever possible, with as little risk to yourself as is practicable. "We are now in a state of war, Captain," he had said to Uvars. "My notice from the prince-regent was just delivered. We are at war with the Emarians—and now we may do some honest soldiering."

Captain Uvars ordered his horns blown, and he led his troop back down the steepside and into the more shallow terrain surrounding it. Upon a suggestion from the Twenty-ninth's messenger—the only man still alive from the slaughtered five thousand—Uvars ordered his riders around to the southeast, where the last information gathered indicated a barricade manned by at least one full Emarian legion.

Uvars had no intention of throwing away the lives of his men in a futile offensive against an entire Emarian legion: but he could reconnoiter, his men could perhaps engage in guerilla tactics, and he could relay what information he would learn in regards to positions and numbers to Ensoris or (even better) to Major Temeth's Thirtieth on the Ithulian border.

Some honest soldiering. . . .

The company's expectations of combat were, however, interrupted that night in a most singular manner. Encamped upon a rise overlooking the western Emarian plains, Uvars's men were engrossed in conversation and speculation regarding their inevitable clash with enemy forces, when an abrupt miracle took place in the skies and turned everyone's attention toward the stars. Far away to the northeast, the sky was lit with a glow that spread and throbbed, filling the black emptiness of night with a red-orange haze. Very soon after this display came another, and then another, beginning a series of apparent fires in the sky. Thunder and rumbling, too, reached the ears of Uvars's men, while the ground beneath them quavered. Their horses began to react energetically, neighing and bucking and whinnying; several broke their tethers and galloped away and had to be chased down by soldiers who feared that the wild noise and yells would draw the attention of any enemy scouts in the vicinity.

To his captain, Uvars's lieutenant bespoke his wonder at what this night's turmoil in the sky foreshadowed. The younger officer, betraying religious convictions, declared that he had heard talk of the end of the world from people calling themselves Doom-Soulers and Reborn Witnesses to Bithitu and The Followers of On. Then again, he had heard that there were sorcerers and mystics in the world who, through demonic bargainings, had gained the powers of gods and were sometimes prone to open portals into recesses and pits where humanity could only suffer most abominably.

Uvars, however, was too disciplined to believe in sorcery, and he gave little credence to the notion that the world was in imminent peril of an apocalypse. He was a practical man, and he'd had some education in his youth. So it seemed to him that what they were all witnessing was not some supernatural performance, but a devastating natural occurrence.

"A volcano," he declared it to be.

"A volcano?" His lieutenant was awed.

"Haven't you ever heard of them? They're a mountain and an earthquake and a river of fire combined. Whether or not the gods have a hand in them, a volcano is a mountain whose tops break off, and it discharges hot rivers of sludge. Read your history. It could cover a city in a day. Burn everything in its path."

This comment inspired some grave worries in the young lieutenant. "Is this one going to—does this one seem close enough to *us* to . . . to bury *us*?"

Uvars chuckled. "I don't think so. No. . . . If it had done that—" a nod "—close enough to us, I imagine all this land you see would be covered with smoke or on fire. We'd be in a lake of fire. But that one's so far away . . . no, it won't hurt anybody."

* * *

The earth stretched before him, scaled and cracked and broken deep, dried like the hide of some enlarged animal. Dust and dead chaff and brown grass blew in small whirlpools around him. Farther away, to the north, where the parched earth gave way to huge fields of dead grass and gnarled decaying trees, flies and gnats swarmed in the heat of fallen animals. Many birds . . . a dog . . . the carcass of what had been a horse. . . .

Sem, the son of Omul, licked his parched lips and stared in all directions, trying to measure the distance he had come. He surveyed the landscape, but it was very difficult to tell if this was the same area he had stood in with his father last spring, when all had been green and moist and growing. He took a few steps and decided that, yes, this was where he and his father had been. Lifting his spade from his shoulder, Sem spat into his bruised and calloused hands, took up his spade and began to dig.

He was a young man, by the standards of people in the cities; but as he stood there working, Sem seemed many years older than he was. His frame was bent to his task; his body was thin from lack of nourishment; his clothes hung worn and tattered, and his long hair and beard were in disarray. Flecks of dead grass and dust clung to his hair, his beard, the back of his neck.

Occasionally, as the morning passed, Sem paused in his work to rest. Often he would glance toward the north, where last night the sky had been lit with that fire from the gods. Then, after catching his breath, he would begin digging again, calmly and unhurriedly so as not to deplete his strength.

"Sem . . . toward the end of summer, when all this is nearly lost in the drought, you will find water here."

"A drought?"

"It comes. Do not fear it, but prepare for it. On provides. But when the drought is nearly over and you fear that all will be lost, come here, to this place and dig down until you find water."

When the day was more than half gone Sem began to worry that either he had remembered the location incorrectly or that his father had been mistaken in his sense that water was here. Pausing to catch his breath, he leaned on his spade and watched as his youngest brother Amral came across the dead field, carrying another spade and some food.

They sat and ate what little they had—some old bread and dried fruit—and sipped only a little of what water was left in the village. They spoke but little. Sem asked Amral how the day was going with the others; his brother reported that two old men, a woman and a child had passed on, and that their sister's newborn was very sick, feverish, and had stopped crying so much—a bad sign.

Together, the brothers continued digging. Soon they were waist deep in the hole Sem had excavated; they kept up their digging until their shoulders were level with the ground and great hills of raw earth were heaped around them. They continued until the sun began to set.

Any doubts Amral had had about his brother's doing as their father had asked, he had held in silence until now; but it was apparent that no water was to be found—at least not here, at this location. They might exhaust themselves and fall dead before finding any water.

"I think," Amral said in a quiet, gasping voice, "that we should return to—"

"Amral."

"What is it?"

"Perhaps . . . I am falling ill. I think I've hurt my foot. Reach down, feel—"

His brother did so, pushing his fingers upon Sem's sandals. They were wet.

Amral brought up his hand; he sniffed his fingers, lifted his hand above him so that, despite the falling darkness and the shadows of the heaped earth, he might see what had dampened his hand.

It was not dark or thick, like blood.

"Sem. . . ."

"It's water, isn't it?"

"Oh, name of On, Sem! It's water! It's water!"

They began digging furiously. In only a short while the earth beneath them, which had been as dry and hard as slate, turned muddy and soggy. And then the water gushed freely and poured through the floor of their hole. The brothers helped one another out, exclaimed their thanks to whatever gods or god might be listening, ducked their heads in the rising water and wetted their arms and faces and yelled and howled for joy.

They returned to their village long after dark; and all through the night the many families moved back and forth in a dusty path, visiting Sem's well of life-nourishing water with buckets and pitchers, old clay pots and sturdy jars. And in the morning they sent men to the other villages in the area to alert them that Sem, Omul's son—the son of Asawas, the visionary of On—had done as his father had said, had gained life for the families and villages of the dead plains.

2.

"It frightens me," Omos confessed, watching the sky from his window.

For the second night in a row the heavens were filled with that strange, silent fire, far to the north.

"It means . . . it means everything is really going to die, doesn't it?" he said in a low and sad voice.

"No, not everything." Asawas, alone with him in the room, walked to the young man. "How can everything die," he asked, "when everything is God, and God lives?" Of all those in this palace who had to do with the court and the nobility, this young man, this . . . splinter of the great soul, caused in Asawas the most profound and deepest of sentiments. Nor did he doubt the cause of this.

"You remind me," he told Omos, "of my oldest grandson."

The youth turned and faced him. "I do? You . . . you have a grandson? You have children?"

The prophet nodded.

"But . . . I thought priests— I mean—"

"That priests are celibate?" Asawas chuckled. "True, I suppose, for priests who serve in the temples. But I was called to God late in my life, when I already had my family."

"Is—" Omos was very intrigued. "Is your family still alive? Do they know you're here?"

Asawas shook his head. "When On spoke to me, I knew that he wished me to journey the world and tell of his truth and wonders, and so I had to leave my wife and my family behind. I love them very dearly, and I know that On, in his purpose, loves them as well, and protects them. But I had to make this journey alone."

"Will you ever see them again?" Omos asked.

Asawas answered him in a very low tone. "No. No, I will never see them again—not in this life."

Omos swallowed, disturbed by the words. "Doesn't that make you sad?"

"Yes. But think of it—consider it in this way. Sometimes, when we see a beautiful flower growing in a patch by the road, don't we uproot that flower and bring it home? We bring it home so that it might give us some of its beauty and life and quality. But the flower will never again be rooted with the others in the patch by the road; never again will it die and be reborn with the other flowers. I, like that flower, was plucked from my roots and sent by On to other places, to shed truth and beauty and share life."

Omos felt his eyes misting; he turned from Asawas, looked out the window again. "Me . . . too," he said. "I . . . I was not born here, in Athad. I am from Sulos. That's a city to the north."

"So Lord Galvus told me."

"I have no family. I never had any roots. I lived wherever I could, and I had to do bad things in order to live—"

"There are no bad things, Omos."

The youth smiled sadly but continued to stare out the window. "Galvus—he was my only friend. We love one another very much. Some people . . . they think we're wicked, because we love one another."

"On sees all and he rejoices in your love, Omos. He sees your souls and celebrates the happiness you share."

Now Omos looked behind him and smiled at Asawas. "Really?"

The prophet blinked slowly.

"The priests in the temples . . . they don't think it's right."

"They are mistaken. Love is what is important."

"Anyway. . . ." Omos scratched his hair, leaned on the window. "I'm afraid, now. Not just because of—of what you said, but. . . . I think it's time for me to leave Athad, and to leave Galvus. I don't want to, but since I've been here I've learned a great deal, I've *listened*, and now I want to help people. I want to go back to Sulos—I was born there—and I want to help the people. I don't care if God wants to see the the world die or not. I want to go back there and help the people—*hope*. . . ."

"Omos."

"Yes?" He moved, looked up into this tall, strong man's face, his immense sad eyes beneath the brows, his features that seemed to mirror all the pain and anguish, the fears and wonders of every person whom he had ever touched.

Behind them, then, the sky lit once more with that great orange wave of dry fire, and though Omos could not see the sky, he saw the brilliance of it reflected in Asawas's eyes, saw it color the prophet's face and clothes for a glowing moment.

That affected him. That . . . fire in the sky, and the face of the prophet, and the awareness in him that he was alone and that he must try to help people—*hope*. . . .

"I'm so afraid," Omos whispered. "I feel something inside me . . . but I'm so *afraid*!"

Tears began to flow down his cheeks.

Asawas opened his arms, inviting Omos to shelter himself there.

And the youth did so, closing his eyes, falling forward, hugging the prophet with all his strength. He felt as if he were a child again, terrified by the very presence of life itself. He feared that he had become a small animal or a leaf, battered by a storm, astonished at its own fragile awareness of its own existence.

But as he hugged the prophet, Omos sobbed and shivered and gradually felt these fears and tremblings release him, to be replaced by great strength which almost physically seeped from Asawas into himself.

Sniffling, Omos pulled his wet cheek from the prophet's robe and looked up into his face once more—the wrinkled eyes, the bearded face, the tousled hair.

Asawas raised a large hand and pressed Omos's hair with it. "It is well," he promised the young man. "It is well. You are well. On sees you, and you will live. You will live to bring hope to the people, Omos. On sees you, and it is well."

How mysterious and profound was the grandeur of God, who chose the slightest and least remarkable of his creatures, the merest fragments of his glory, in which to deposit the mightiest of truths, to fulfill the most refined of his blessings. . . .

Mirhu said, "We shouldn't stay here any longer. We're not going to be safe here anymore. Not with—"

Rhia, at the window, glanced at her.

"Not with all kinds of—city guards and police and the Khilu out there."

"You think they know we're here? For certain?"

"Don't you think it's *safest* to think that way?"

Rhia faced the window again. "I don't know. I'm not sure."

Mirhu moved across the silent room, poured herself a cup of tea, carried it to a chair. She sat down; she was so tall and slim that she seemed out of place in the small chair. "People don't depend on us like they used to."

"They're too frightened."

"There's no way to get out of Sulos, is there? Have you—"

"Not now, Mirhu." Rhia sighed strongly, shuddered, thought a moment. "I don't *want* to leave here. I think we should—" She stopped, lifted her arms to her belly.

Mirhu leaned forward, watching her carefully. "Are you all right?"

Rhia nodded, but Mirhu didn't believe her. Setting aside her tea she crossed the floor and took hold of Rhia's shoulders, gently massaged her neck. "You're not strong enough to have a baby."

"I'm fine."

"You're weak. You're not eating enough."

"No one's eating enough. I'm fine."

"Rhia. . . ." Mirhu stopped massaging, stared down at her friend.

Rhia gripped one of her hands. "It's—a good baby. It will be a boy, it will be *his* baby. And I *want* it to be strong enough to—really fight back."

"I understand what you're saying but—" Oh, what did it matter? Mirhu went back to her chair, feeling tired.

Two months pregnant and not well enough to be certain of her own health, let alone the health of a—

"He's coming."

"All right."

Rhia watched until Endric, in the street below, disappeared from her view; she heard his footsteps coming up the stairs, then his light tapping on the door. No one else was in the street. No one had seen him.

Mirhu let him in; Endric, tall and clean shaven, dark haired, dressed in deceptively good clothes, seemed out of place in this squalid room, out of place beside his poorly-dressed wife and the thin, pale Rhia. When he came in he walked straight to a table and deposited there what he was carrying; it was a satchel, and Endric opened it, set out the contents. As he did, he muttered:

"All we need is a little more time. Let them make war wherever they want to. Soon enough, once they get a taste of that, the military will be on *our* side. They'll join us . . . and the revolution will finish what these fools have started!" He looked up, noticing Mirhu watching him. "I found some milk for Rhia."

"*Found* it?" his wife smiled.

"Oh, it was just sitting there. Right inside the shop. Right behind the counter. Had her name on it. . . ."

Rhia thanked him but didn't move from the window. She asked Endric, "What's it like out there?"

"Quiet. Very quiet. Odd sort of quiet. No one around the military offices . . . very few people in the streets or in the squares. Very—quiet. What with half the men gone off to the front and digging ditches and signs of wonder in the sky. . . ."

"Mirhu thinks we should move."

"From here?" He looked at his wife.

Mirhu shrugged.

Endric shook his head. "We're safe here," he insisted. "I know you think we've been here too long, but we're safe here. It's quieted down. They seem more concerned with something happening uptown or on the east end. Not down here. There's nothing *down* here."

Mirhu made some comment and went back to her chair and her tea.

"The best thing we can do," Endric said to both of them, "is to sit and wait. A month—two months—three or four—wait for something to develop that we can take advantage of."

Rhia continued to stare out the window; it was all she seemed to do these days. Abruptly she lifted her hands to her belly, wondering if what she felt inside her was the stirring of life, or merely an upset stomach. No way to be certain, at the moment; she'd never been pregnant before.

A man appeared in the street, farther up; he turned a corner, crossed the bricks, vanished behind another building. And oddly, Rhia then found herself thinking of Adred. Perhaps that stroller had reminded her of him. It had been so long since she's seen Adred, and things had changed so much. She wondered where he was now—back in the capital with Galvus and with—Orain. Well, Rhia knew that he'd been in love with Orain. Was he still? Was he even still alive?

She found herself wondering what it would be like, were this Adred's child inside her.

And then she found herself—on this cool, late summer's day, as she stared into the desolate and quiet streets of Sulos, as she listened to the vacant hollow noises that Endric and Mirhu made behind her—Rhia found herself wondering what it must be like to die.

To die. . . .

As her husband had, and as Bors had, as—as all of them had died.

"Rhia?" Mirhu was concerned because she'd become so quiet.

"I'm—" She stood up and moved across the floor toward a door. "I think I'm going to lie down for a while."

"Are you all right?" Mirhu asked.

Beyond her, Endric showed grave concern on his face.

Rhia smiled. "Yes, yes, I'm all right. Just—tired. And thinking. I want to take a nap. That's all. . . ."

Out from deep winds of Time comes the Voice of a destiny.

A Voice that is humanity's voice, the voice of a god that is humanity's God.

Events that seem to return to the pools of blood and the shadows of fire from which humanity birthed itself: the pool is deep, the shadows are old, the fire burns with flames that burn forever.

O humanity born in a storm and wandering in a storm, why do you turn from the future and return to your past? O lost and disbelieving, you wander in your search for belief and you dream that there is only one sun, one road, one destiny.

Small animal spirits, seeking and learning, ignorant of our true purpose and caught in cages of clay, trapped on an earth of seasons and storms, manacled to events which seem to doom us since the hour of our birth.

O souls in solitude, o angers visiting us with self-righteousness, o damnable pride that confuses itself with purpose and ambition—

O humanity, unproven, truculent, born to die and become

reborn, ever reaching to grasp beyond you that which is hidden in your own heart—

Die, o humanity.

These things that come, they come with cause.

He took his leave of them early in the morning, and they let him go without wishing for him to depart.

"Do you think," Asawas asked them, smiling sadly, "that if I stay here these things born to happen will not come to be? Do not resist the storm, as would an aged tree which has grown old in calm seclusion, for the storm will break that tree. Remain pliant, bend where the storm blows you, like the young sapling which will not break: and then when the storm ceases you, like the sapling, will remain to continue growing."

Abgarthis, old and experienced in the ways of men's politics, and grown so aged only because he had learned to remain pliant when imperial storms had arisen—

Count Adred, who held so much in him, and who in another time might have been acclaimed by his generation, but now was as trapped as the others by the onrush of confusion—

The Lady Orain, princess and mother of the monarch, in her features the uncertainty of her heart, the strength and the givingness of her spirit—

Young Omos, in whom a spark of the One God had housed itself, yet in doubt and because of this doubt, capable of believing—

Prince-Regent Galvus, whose old soul recognized truths and values as ancient as humanity, whose youth seemed a prison containing these truths unfairly—

Asawas bowed before each of them and thanked them all for what they had done for him. His talks with Lord Abgarthis had permitted Asawas to see immediately how the simple truths of life can be perverted and choked and mismanaged by men in power. And his hours with Count Adred had warned the prophet how the best in men can be thwarted by the stupidities of others' greed and anger. And his afternoons with Lady Orain had reminded him that in the heart of Woman there reposed and would forever repose that timeless flame of rationality and awareness that was so different from Man's dependence upon outward things, customs and structures. And from Galvus Asawas had seen—had been reminded of—the new hope that can come from the strongest of the new.

"You have taught us more than we might ever have expected," Galvus declared to Asawas. "I thank you for it. Many doubts that were in me . . . they are reconciled. And come what may, I will persevere. I hope that you yourself, wise one, will find the peace you so deserve, when you have fulfilled all that God has called upon you to accomplish."

Asawas bowed his head low and thanked the prince-regent again, and reminded him and all of them of this above all else:

"Do not fear. All of this must come to be, because men for too long have feared when they should have trusted, feared when they should have believed, feared when they should have been humble. Do not fear. Mankind will live forever, for mankind is God. Trust and believe in this, and be humbled when you think on it."

Then he left them. They had pressed upon him new robes and sandals, and had insisted that Asawas take with him all that he might carry—food, extra blankets and so on. He had taken food and an extra cover but had refused any money, and he kept with him his walking staff that had served him all his years, from his days as a farmer in Omeria through his wandering the paths of the empire.

They watched him move down the wide steps of the palace and through the gates, out into the square. They watched as he disappeared into the street and was obscured by the great moving crowds of the capital.

"I wish," Orain whispered, "that I could call him back, that he *would* come back."

"Mother," Galvus said quietly to her.

She looked at him.

He shook his head slightly and smiled a bit, meaningfully.

And everything they had ever suffered together came to her in that moment, as Orain looked into Galvus's eyes and realized that what Asawas had said to them was indeed there—in her son's eyes, and alive between them.

But while the others returned inside, Orain, agitated and feeling forlorn, made a suggestion to Adred; together they took a carriage to the eastern wall of the city and, under the guidance of the guards stationed there, mounted to the highest ramparts of Athad and stared toward the east.

"Is it, Adred? Is that him, do you think?"

"I believe it must be. . . ."

The prophet, alone on a long thin ribbon of road, leaning on his staff and walking with a tireless stride up into the hills that must carry him, day after night after day, into the farmlands, into the valleys of the Sevulus, into Galsia and then into Herulia, and finally into—

Emaria.

The land of the resurrected deliverer of darkness, *ro kil-su*, the Evil One.

There to face him, so that mankind itself might die to be reborn.

3.

On the tenth of Elru, when she returned to Port Abustad, Assia discovered city government officials waiting to speak with her. This alarmed her; immediately she tried to consider some method by which to deceive them or plot some way to stall them, for she was sure that they meant to arrest her on some exaggerated charge (bribery of city officials, breaking some law concerning morality, or some such thing). It was no secret that her pleasure barge enterprise was most successful and that she had a long list of aristocrats and government servants waiting their turn upon her Abustad-to-Aparu route. Assia had deposited quite a few large sums at her bank in the city, and she was certain that no one, especially an ex-prostitute, could for long keep so estimable a means of profit to herself. Hers had become the most popular barge in the city. So now, obviously, some toad in the city authority wanted to begin helping himself to a slice of Assia's loaf.

She bade farewell to the last of her customers, paid her employees with gold from her own purse and told them to report back to the barge in three days' time, when it would be ready to begin its next cruise. As her young women and boys pranced off, Assia reluctantly approached the two city officials who stood waiting for her on the quay.

"Shall we step aboard," she offered, "and conduct our

business over a glass of wine?'' She knew that these two were not stupid enough to place themselves in such a compromising position, but then—they would no doubt have thought less of her had she not made the suggestion.

"Thank you, no," replied the tall one, who was overdressed and reeked of perfume.

"We are here," continued his shorter companion, "to inform you that the city of Abustad is confiscating your boat for imperial business, because of the war emergency."

"*War* emergency? *What* 'war emergency'?" Assia snarled.

"Even as we speak," answered the tall one, "King Elad's flotilla approaches Erusabad, and the entire empire is in imminent peril of war. Governor Sulen has ordered all nonessential trade craft and luxury vessel operations suspended indefinitely, and made available for military transport use, if and when that should become a necessity."

"This is outrageous!" Assia complained. "How many other owners have had to put up with this nonsense?"

The city officials were completely prepared to answer her. The tall one unrolled a document that he carried in a bag, quickly scanned it, and read to her: "Three hundred and sixteen have complied; forty-two have failed to comply; and forty-two writs for arrest have been issued." As he rerolled his document, he smiled in a vaguely obscene way. "You're number forty-three. Or three hundred and seventeen. Whichever you prefer."

Muttering and grumbling, Assia asked him: "I assume I'm allowed to remove my personal things from the boat before your soldiers go aboard to fight this damned war?"

"Oh, it's yours, it's yours," the short one reassured her. "The boat's still yours. And the empire will be very happy to reimburse you for any damage or loss incurred, if and when that should occur."

"That sounds too good to be true," Assia said coolly. "What about my lost profit? What about that? Are you going to reimburse me for that?"

The tall official lent her a grave expression. "All of us," he pronounced dolorously, "must make sacrifices in this time of national emergency. Certainly we can't reimburse you for any profits you might or might not realize. We *are* permitted, however, to issue you a credit voucher for the value of your craft. Surely this is agreeable to you."

"More agreeable than having a warrant issued for my arrest. Are we talking about cash, now?"

"The empire cannot spare cash for such indulgences," the short official explained. "We're only *borrowing* your boat; we're not *buying* it from you! We're prepared to deliver you a credit voucher in the amount of the assessed value of your craft, upon your signing the release form giving us temporary rights to—"

"Who assesses what, here? And temporary for how long?"

"For as long as necessary. But wars don't last forever, do they?"

"Neither do boats. Who assesses the value? Not me, certainly."

"Oh, no, we couldn't allow that. Officials from the Abustad Office of Revenue and Imperial Taxation decide that matter."

"That is just wonderful," Assia smirked. "No wonder business is prospering! You people know more tricks than any of the girls I have working on that—"

"Careful, now," the tall one warned her.

"Yes, careful what you say," echoed the short one. "We're not here to single you out. Everyone must make sacrifices in a time of—"

"Yes, in a time of national emergency. Right, right. Gods!" Assia clenched and unclenched her fists. "How long before I have to turn over my papers to you?"

"Well, there's certainly no rush about it," the tall one promised her. "It's still morning. Anytime this afternoon will do."

"Anytime this . . . *afternoon*?" Assia exclaimed, aghast. "This *afternoon*?"

"As we said, there's no rush. Appear in our offices this afternoon, and we'll be more than happy to issue you your credit voucher."

Assia sneered at them. Furious, she eyed them venomously as they bade her a good day, and she made an obscene gesture after them when they turned their backs and moved on down the quay to accost the next ship coming in to drop anchor.

He stood proudly, regarding his audience through narrowed eyes. A tall man, nobly made, perhaps in his late forties or early fifties, the gray entering his hair and beard, but the eyes still bright and brilliant.

"I am an illusionist," he announced to those gathered in the tavern. "Allow me a few moments to charm and entertain you. My name is Eromedeus and my games, while very ancient, always seem new. Watch, and I will astonish you."

Eyes turned toward him, conversations rumbled low, and a few whistles and hand slaps sounded as Eromedeus opened the satchel he had placed on the table before him and began removing objects by which to work his illusions.

And he thought, *I am weary of this. It is time I moved on from Mustala.*

"For my first trick, let me show you—"

Weary . . . as weary as the world. . . .

What did it matter any longer, keeping up this pretense? He didn't do it for others, but only for himself. There were no more lies to be conjured, no more dreams to enact, no further nightmares to consider: he had seen all and experienced all, and with all that he had done and seen and experienced, even he—the most ancient of men, an undying shadow that wandered over all the face of the earth—even he could not destroy this evil that grew and spread like a quickening disease.

"The man in me is gone," Thameron had warned him. *"Who was that mortal child? Listen— Yes, time hastens; it hastens with the pull of its own tidal end. There are not many dawns left for you to travel, wandering one. Do you feel the footsteps of humanity hurrying . . . hurrying?"*

"I feel them. . . . They may yet pause in their tread and step away from the chasm, away from the abyss that lures them."

"Then go, and warn them if you can, for the things of men outstrip men themselve. Humanity will not listen to you, Eromedeus. Go—find the soul that will free you at last. And as you are freed, listen to the thunder of the Night, as it comes down for Man. . . ."

He stared upon the crowd in the tavern—impatient, all eyes and arms and faces, mistrustful: a crowd of strangers, though deep within them burned a common soul. How could they remain so blind? What stopped them from simply looking into one another's hearts and realizing the truth?

"Warn them if you can. . . . Humanity will not listen to you, Eromedeus. . . ."

Why did everyone live just long enough to understand the truth as they died, yet forget that truth when they were reborn?

"Come on!" someone called. "Show us your tricks!"

"Yes, show us your tricks!"

"Do something or get out of the way! Let the girls dance!"

"Yes, get those girls out here to dance!"

He stared upon them . . . and at last lifted his hands, turned them this way and that to indicate that he held no device or contrivance—

"To astonish you, then," Eromedeus reminded the crowd. "To astonish you and alarm you and make you question yourselves— let me show you how I turn a piece of cloth into a flame. . . ."

Assia decided to leave Abustad. Too many people in the city either knew her or knew of her, and she couldn't trust any of them. She didn't actually believe that she'd ever get her ship back, either. And aside from the fact that she felt she'd outworn her welcome in the city, she had finally accumulated enough money to do as she pleased. The wisest course seemed to be for her to travel elsewhere. She could return "home"—but if war was on the horizon, then obviously there was no sense in trying to return to Erusabad.

She'd learned to speak Athadian fairly well, and the dialect indigenous to this section of the world was more difficult than the "classical" Athadian farther west, so Assia wasn't deterred by apprehensions of moving farther into the empire. She considered going on down the coast to Elpet or even to Ovoros. The farther away from Abustad, the farther from the effects of war the better. But even then, any of the major seaports could offer her only insecure havens. Assia had spent too much of her life wandering aimlessly to begin wandering aimlessly again. Perhaps she should go north. Not into the Low Provinces—she knew far too much about life there—but northwest. Into the farmlands, into the country. She'd never been in the country, and as strange as the promise of calm and quiet and wide vistas seemed to her, they seemed to her a lure, as well.

Besides, hadn't Thameron told her when he'd left her that he, too, intended to head north. That "something" had called to him from the north?

Perhaps, by some miracle or mischance, Thameron would intrude upon her life again. Assia felt that she wanted that to happen, if it were meant to.

So she withdrew all her money from her bank, hid some in her boots and some inside various articles of clothing, pinned some inside her hair, then bought herself a horse and left Abustad late one evening. She rode northwest into the hills and surrounding farmland.

Unfamiliar with life outside cities, she had guessed that there must be numerous hostels and inns along the road for the convenience of travelers. Yet as night came down and Abustad's walls disappeared behind her, Assia became somewhat alarmed to notice ahead of her only continuing farmland and wide forests darkening in the dusk. No lights shined, and no homes or farms or inns appeared in the distance.

This worried her.

Yet she pressed her horse on. No other travelers came by her on the road, and when at last the night became very dark and her horse seemed in need of rest, there was nothing for Assia to do except dismount, walk her animal into a small stretch of woodland just off the road and let the animal sleep. She tied it to a tree, took down one of her rolled blankets and lay it on the ground. She wasn't sure how to go about building a fire, nor did she have anything with which to make a fire, should she want one. Assia was thankful that it was still mid-Elru and warm enough for her to sleep in the open.

When she awoke in the morning she made herself a cold breakfast out of some food she had brought, rolled up her blanket and mounted her horse and continued following the road. Just over the first hill she noticed a small inn, and laughed at herself for being so impatient the night before. Assia stopped at this inn and bought a good meal, purchased a sack of wine and a small bit of fresh bread and asked about any other possible lodgings to the west. The man who ran the hostel couldn't tell her for certain where there was another inn; he seemed to recall one from years ago but doubted that it was still in existence. Assia rode on.

The day was warm and sunny, and as she traveled she found

herself thinking about her life, all that she had suffered and experienced, and what it all might mean. Images and emotions, memories and desires, fears and doubts came flooding back to her; she dwelt at length on Thameron and her father, her life as a prostitute in Erusabad. In just the past few months she seemed to have aged five or ten years: grown older and wiser and more experienced through her discomforts and tribulations. Now she felt dependent upon no one, in charge of her own life, and this realization frightened her but emboldened her as well.

Late that evening Assia did indeed find another inn, and she passed a very pleasant evening in the company of the rustic couple who operated the enterprise. They had three daughters who served meals and helped with the farming and gardening. They were enthralled by the stories Assia related to them concerning life in the city. She was careful (as she spoke under the watchful eyes of the parents) not to divulge too much of her own history. She also skirted some of the more dangerous and compromising facts of life regarding cities in general and Abustad in particular. But Assia admitted to the three daughters that, yes, she had been born in the east, she was proud to be an Athadian—if not by birth then by custom—that she had never before been into the countryside but loved it here, and that she entertained hopes of one day living in the farmlands permanently.

When the young women retired for the night, Assia had a franker but still pleasant conversation with the mother. The only jarring moment occurred when she inquired about a man named Thameron. She said she had once known a young man by that name whom she had loved very much; but she had been separated from him and knew only that he'd intended to travel north after leaving Abustad.

The old woman answered Assia's inquiry in a grave, nervous voice, saying: "There is a man in Emaria—far from here—he is a king. I believe his name is Thameron or a name like that. I hope—"

"I doubt that it's him. My friend was a priest, not a king or a prince."

"Well, I hope for your sake that it isn't the same man, for this King Thameron in Emaria is a very evil person."

"Evil?"

The old woman leaned close. "He has caused wars to happen

107

and earthquakes and volcanoes—who knows what else? I may be only a farmwife and a poor woman, but I hear that the king of Emaria is evil, and I believe it."

Shaken by the possibility of this being her own Thameron from Erusabad, Assia had difficulty sleeping that night. But the following morning the innkeeper's wife was as friendly as ever, and even made Assia a special bag of meats and bread to take with her on her trip. Assia thanked her profusely, gave her husband some extra money in gratitude for the care he'd taken with her horse, then set out.

The day grew cloudy, overcast, as Assia continued westward. The forest all around became sparser, opened more and more into wide long hills of grain and grass. In some places the ground was parched and dead from prolonged sun; Assia wondered when this part of the world had last seen rain. She thought that even if it had been quite awhile, it might nonetheless rain today, for a downpour certainly seemed to be gathering in those heavy clouds above.

Yet by late afternoon the ominous clouds had passed on, moving slowly toward the east, and the brilliant sun returned, as if to mock the lands below, devastate them ceaselessly.

By early evening, when she stopped to let her horse rest and graze and water at a thin stream, Assia heard from another traveler—an old farmer who passed by in a cart—that she had entered the province of Omeria. Part of the Athadian empire, to be sure; but she was now in Omeria. The farmer warned her that there would be no place for her to find shelter that night, no inns or lodgings, so if she had brought protection with her, she had best plan on making use of it.

Assia decided to spend the night where she was. She unrolled her blanket again and lay it out under some trees by the road; she tethered her horse, ate some fruit, relaxed and began imagining the sort of life she might someday live. Without realizing that she'd done so, Assia drifted into sleep. When she awoke she thought at first that she had stayed awake. Then it occurred to her that it must be just before dawn, and that the noises she'd heard had come from her horse.

But they hadn't.

Startled, Assia sat up in her blanket.

Someone growled at her and slapped her on the head, forcing her back down.

In the dimness, and because of their noise, she made out three of them in the forest beside her—three men dressed in armor. Their horses made sounds farther back in the trees.

Assia, trying to maintain her composure, asked them who they were.

They told her they were mercenaries and in need of food and money.

Assia assured them that she had only a little food and no money at all.

The three men suggested that she was a liar. They told her that she must be punished for not having any money. When Assia tried to stand up the three men slapped her again, then began beating her; they held her down, ripped her clothes and brutalized and raped her, there in the night in the forest.

Assia never even screamed; she was too astonished and too frightened. All she could think of, as the men used her again and again, hurting her and twisting her, was that she had done something wrong and that the gods were using these men to punish her. For some reason the gods had made fun of her; they had allowed her to earn a little money, they had allowed her to think that the sordidness and the cruelty she had experienced was behind her, they had allowed her to think that her illness was past, that she might somehow improve her life or better herself, or plan on a future without pain.

She watched herself being mauled and beaten, torn and forced, and listened to the gruff men make rude comments about her body, as if she were someone else observing the torment of an utter stranger.

The mercenaries left her naked and bleeding, torn and stained and bruised, there on the ground of the forest. They left her only her blanket and torn clothes and took her horse and all the belongings Assia had bundled on its saddle.

For the rest of the night she lay there, still feeling like a stranger, barely able to breathe, not able to cry, not able even to think.

When morning came, with sunlight and the sounds of birds, Assia was still lying in the same position. She moved slightly and agony ripped through her. Slowly, shivering, she sat up, touched her face and felt the bumps and the raw bruises and scratches, felt her body and touched places where the blood had dried or where the injuries were so sore that they seemed to hurt her very bones.

And when the sun rose fully, she heard the sounds of a horse's hoofs and a cart on the road, coming from the east. Instantly she understood that the men had not gone far, that they had remained nearby, and that they were going to assault her again.

Dully, mutely, with tears dripping from her puffed eyes, she stared down the road.

Beyond a hill there gradually appeared the horse and cart—and the farmer—of the day before. Casks and boxes jostled in his wagon. As he came nearer, he saw Assia naked and bleeding in the shadows of the trees.

Instantly the farmer stopped his horse and jumped from his wagon and ran to her.

"Oh, God, oh, God, oh, *God*!" he breathed, kneeling beside her and looking at her, wanting to touch Assia, wanting to help her, but uncertain what to do.

Assia only stared at him, sniffling, trembling. She began to draw in great gulps of air.

"Young woman . . . young woman . . . who did this to you? Who? *Who*?"

She tried to tell him, but she could not.

"Oh, God, oh, *God*!" he continued to whisper, in a suffering voice. "Can you stand up? Should I help you stand up? Young woman . . . young woman, answer me, look at me. Oh . . . God!"

Finally Assia began to cry; the tears poured down her face, then she screamed and fell forward. The old farmer caught her in his arms and hugged her shivering body close to him. He said what he could and did what he could to comfort her, but he seemed as hurt and frightened by what had happened to her as Assia was for having suffered it.

At long last, however, she let him help her to her feet. He wrapped her in her blanket, led her to his cart and helped her up on to it. He fetched her torn clothes and threw them into his wagon, made sure that she was covered up well and promised her, "We'll take care of you . . . listen to me, I'm your friend. My wife and I, we have a farm just farther up the road. Do you hear me? What's your name? Young woman? All right . . . all right, you just sit there and hold on, we'll take care of you, we'll take care of you. . . ."

4.

On the fifteenth of Elru, after sailing for several days under good conditions, Elad's armada dropped anchor off the western shore of the Isle of Odossos; the king was lowered in a longboat and rowed ashore, where he met with Major Tor, commander of the First Legion Red out of Abustad, and his father-in-law Ogodis, the Imbur of Gaegosh, whose seven legions were waiting impatiently ashore in beach houses and lean-tos they themselves had hastily erected.

Elad's first concern was that Odossos, ostensibly as much a part of the Athadian empire as had been the nothern portion of Erusabad, might have been occupied by Salukadian soldiers. Ogodis assured him that such was not the case; under his command Gaegoshan patrols, acting in the name of the Athadian throne, had reconnoitered the island and discovered only a few fishing villages inhabited by rustics whose alarm revealed their ignorance of any recent contact with soldiers. No eastern warriors, and no hint of any on the sea that could be discerned from the eastern shores of Odossos. Elad was satisfied of his troops' security.

That evening he met with his commanders—General Thomo, Majors Tor, Dever, Hamaro, Ostorian and Hadd and Captain Sadir—and with Ogodis, on the open western beach beneath the warm late summer twilight. Elad produced maps indicating his plans for deploying warships and ground combat units, should the necessity for conflict become apparent. The only voice sounding in dissent of the plan (which Elad had conceived and fashioned en route, with advice from his military advisers) came from Major Commander Thytagoras of Gaegosh—that one who had stormily vacated his post in the Athadian army in protest of General Thomo's appeasement policies in Erusabad. Thytagoras was in favor of attacking the Holy City immediately upon arriving at its shores; but he was unanimously outvoted. His presence there, however, presented another difficulty, which Elad broached privately to Ogodis, later that evening.

"From this moment on I want one thing understood between you and I, Imbur."

Ogodis knew what he intended to say already.

"I am in command of all the forces here assembled. We are not two armies under two leaders fighting the same battle. We are one leader, and I am the chief general in command of the Gaegoshan as well as the Athadian troops. Is that understood?"

Somewhat to his surprise, his father-in-law replied: "Yes, of course. I will relay to my men your orders, and they will follow them expressly."

"I think it regrettable that you acted so hastily in accepting Thytagoras into your ranks—or, even more, promoting him. But that's your decision. I will not, however—and mark me on this, Imbur!—I will *not* have 'Major' Thytagoras of the Gaegoshan army dictating orders to anyone of lesser rank in the Athadian legions. Is that understood?"

"Entirely, my son-in-law."

Elad stared at him for a long moment, not trusting him. He allowed: "Major Thytagoras will be accorded all the respect due his station—but I must remain the word and the law here, and no one else."

"Say no more, Elad. I understand your concern—that what you need now is absolute and unquestioned authority and unity. I give you allowance to do as you wish, provided only that you return my daughter to me safely and unharmed." He paused, then added: "Reprisals against this barbarian animal we can decide later."

Elad left him then and went outside to walk in the cooling night, alone on the beach. Behind him, his men of rank and his retainers were enjoying a late meal and lifting cups in toasts to anticipated victory, calling the Salukadians every vile epithet they could collectively cull from their assorted vocabularies. And out before Elad, stretching like a net of yellow stars caught upon the black sea, sat his lighted warships and biremes and triremes.

The king stood silently, watching, thinking, so self-involved that he did not feel the sea-scented breezes that laved him.

Shortly General Thomo approached, boots crunching on the ground, calling out in a friendly voice; when he reached Elad he offered him a cup of common soldier's ale. The king, who had not

112

drunk ale in quite a long time, nevertheless took and sipped the brew. Yet he did not say much to Thomo.

Thomo, however, seemed in a mood to converse. "Well, we're on their doorstep now," he commented. "Tomorrow this time we'll be in the harbor."

Elad grunted.

"Does it feel more . . . alarming to you, now, my lord? Now that we're on the edge of it?"

Elad looked at him. "Alarming, General?"

Thomo instantly feared that he had overstepped the bounds of protocol; he apologized with: "Excuse me . . . I did not mean to—"

"I don't know that it's so alarming, Thomo, no," Elad said. "I really can't think of any word to describe it. It . . . doesn't matter though, does it? It doesn't matter, actually, how we feel about it. About whatever will happen. Does it?"

Thomo was silent, uncertain what his king might mean by this.

"Here," Elad told him, handing him the cup of ale. "I've had enough."

General Thomo took it and held onto it and watched as his king continued down the beach, hands behind his back, solitary, walking quietly in the night.

Orain awoke to the fluttering sounds of loose paper. She rolled onto her side, lay her head on her pillow and looked across the room where Adred, completely naked, was standing by a table, sorting through a pile of documents. She was amused; it was as though she were invading his privacy in some way, simply because he no doubt thought her still asleep. Contented, Orain watched as Adred unfolded something, read it, scratched his beard and, setting the paper aside, went on to something else.

As though overhearing her silent mind, suddenly aware that she was awake, Adred glanced toward the bed and saw Orain looking at him. He smiled in that uncertain, boyish way he had—one of those small, silly things that Orain truly loved about him.

"Sleep well?"

She grinned. "Yes, thanks to you. What're you doing over there?"

"Oh, just going through all this. I guess I'm nervous; I just like

113

looking through these once in a while. My father's letters
. . . the things I've saved. That letter from Rhia."

"Oh, yes . . . *Rhia*," Orain chuckled.

Adred picked up one well-worn and very creased square of
paper and carried it with him to the bed. He sat down, leaned to
kiss Orain good morning, showed it to her. "Remember this?"

Her grin faded a little as she looked at it. It was that manifesto
she'd given him in Sulos last winter—the declaration of the
working people and the underprivileged, their call for equality and
justice.

*It is the privilege and the duty of men and women in a civilized
society to create a cooperative community of common good for
all.* . . .

"Sad," she remarked, letting Adred take it back. "Sad
. . . because what's come of it? The revolution and the anger and
the real fight to accomplish all this . . . and what's come of it?"
She shook her head. "Maybe it's better to just leave people alone.
We can't say that our revolution has done anything."

"Oh, I think it has," Adred disagreed. "I think it has. Give it
time. This war scare will be over in a few months, Elad will come
back, and then we'll have to get back to business. And don't
forget, Galvus has put the fear in Rhin and Falen and the rest of
those characters. Give it time."

"Time. . . ." Orain said it in a low voice, almost dismissing it
with her tone, as though it were a word or a concept foreign to her.

"But when I look at this," Adred said to her "—you know,
hold this in my hands—it's so funny, but I almost feel like I'm
back in Sulos . . . as if you and I are still sitting there on that
bench in the snow. . . ."

"I remember." She looked at him intently, stared deeply into his
eyes.

"Gods," Adred whispered, "I love you."

Orain answered with a sound in her throat and sat up; she drew
her arms around Adred and held him close, kissed him strongly.
Adred let the manifesto drop to the floor, and he lay down beside
her, held her, kissed her—looked at her.

It was so perfect, what they had. So reasonable, so friendly, so
simply good. Sometimes, when Adred was with Orain, he felt as
he did now: that they would be like this forever. But at other

114

times—in moments when he felt that the entire world might suddenly lurch, or stop, or skew like a wheel in a track—

"Gods, I love you."

"And I love you. So much. . . ."

In moments like that, he secretly feared that their love might be stolen from them as quickly and completely as some half-formed thought might vanish before it had even been uttered.

For if ideas and purposes could be purged so easily, then what of something as fragile as love?

Their conversation fell quiet again for a moment; Galvus sighed and reached to pour himself a fresh cup of tea. He fumbled, nearly knocking the porcelain pot from its small burner—and that made him realize how tired he truly was. He glanced across his room to the windows; sunlight was shining through from behind the shutters in dusty streaks of brightness.

"Gods," he smiled, "we've been up all night!"

"I know," Omos replied, getting up from the chair opposite Galvus's divan; the cushions were nearly flattened from his sitting on them. He stretched, walked to the table beside Galvus, took hold of the pot and poured them both another cup of tea.

"After this," he said, "It's time we both caught some sleep."

"Yes. . . ." Galvus sat forward, rubbed his face with his hands. He smiled as his friend handed him his tea.

Omos crossed to one of the windows, unlatched the shutters and pushed up the sash to let in the early morning breeze.

"So . . . all ready to sail out this afternoon?" Galvus asked him.

Omos turned. "Yes, I suppose so. I'm . . . almost having doubts, now."

"Don't."

"I'm going to miss you."

Glavus grinned honestly. "I'm going to miss you, too—but it's not like you're going to disappear forever! Trust me; I fully intend to stay in touch with you. You'll be getting letters from me often."

"I'm going back to *help*."

"Yes, and I'm going to need your help." Galvus nodded to the wooden box that sat on a table across the room, by his desk. "My first concern is getting representatives of the people into this government. I'm not going to let the *sirots* die out just because everyone's excited about a war. I've got all sorts of contradictory reports in there, but they all come down to one thing: *maybe* we have representatives coming from seven cities. That's not good . . . that's not good, at all. So whatever else happens, I want delegates from the *sirots* in every city here, in the capital, by the thirtieth of the month. If, when you get to Sulos, things seem too fractioned, then I want you to come back here yourself. We've already got four different organizations calling themselves the true *sirotsi* in Sulos, and that's nonsense. There are soldiers out there, and secret police, and the gods only know what else!"

"It'll be fine," Omos assured him. "People are using the possibility of a war to take advantage of the situation."

"I know that." Galvus shook his head. "I refuse to believe that the whole idea was born to die in just a few months!"

"The people won't let you down," Omos told him. "Give them a little time. The best thing we can do is to get the first delegates here, even if they only come from a few cities, so that it's understood that real progress *is* being made. Once that happens, you'll have a floodtide on your hands."

"I hope so. I hope you're right."

Omos smiled. "Perhaps things don't seem as certain, or as obvious, from the point of view of a throne."

Galvus looked at him.

"It's not your fault. But I still sit on regular benches and chairs, and I feel absolutely confident about all this." Omos smiled.

But the suggestiveness of the remark disturbed Galvus. He sipped his tea, sat back wearily and rubbed his head, exhaled a heavy breath. "Tell me something frankly, please."

"Certainly."

"Omos . . . have I—changed? Have I?"

"No! You've done fine. You've done remarkably well. Galvus, you're still the same man you were when you took the throne. It's only been a few weeks!"

"But there's so much. . . . You're right about the 'perspective,' the 'point of view.' It becomes difficult. . . ."

"You're doing splendidly. Only *you* would worry that you're becoming too kinglike as king! Oh, Galvus . . . the thing for you to do now is to find that handful of people here, in the palace, on the *Pritons*, who are loyal to you, and give them the support

116

and whatever they need to accomplish things. Look where things might be a year from now, or two years from now."

Galvus smirked. "But the world isn't going to last that long, is it?"

"What do you— Oh, Asawas."

"Yes."

Omos returned to his friend and sat down beside him. "Asawas, I think, would be the first to tell you that you must act as though life will go on forever. Just because we know we'll die someday doesn't mean we let ourselves become preoccupied with the idea every day. If we did that, then life wouldn't be worth living at all; we might as *well* be dead! You must do what you believe and work for what you believe, whether the world might die tomorrow or at the end of time. Besides . . . the death of the world—whatever Asawas truly meant by that—doesn't mean the end of us. People."

Galvus stared at him, stared into the young man's eyes and felt again the deepness of him, the truth and honesty in him. "You're right. You're very right."

Omos leaned to him and kissed Galvus quickly, almost shyly, on the cheek. "I love you very much. I know you know that, but—I'm part of you. I've always leaned on you for strength when I've needed to, and I want you to lean on me when you have to. We have to start thinking that way—as if all of us in the world are just parts of one extended person, one complete person who happens to be fragmented into many smaller persons."

"Yes . . . we *do* have to think that way."

Omos reached for Galvus's hands. "If the gods, tomorrow, took everyone on earth except for just a handful of people, then humanity would still be alive. And so . . . we must plan for tomorrow as if we ourselves were just as strong as the gods, ourselves."

There, in the quiet early sunlight of Galvus's chambers, with the passing of the night, with the passing of the long hours of conversation and debate, confusion and doubt, planning and thinking—

Galvus felt profoundly just what it was that Omos was telling him.

Just as Omos had learned it from Asawas himself.

". . . we must plan for tomorrow as if we were just as strong as the gods, ourselves."

Early afternoon, and the prophet was somewhere in central Athadia. He did not know precisely where he was; he did not know if the road which he traveled had a name. This morning a farmer and his son had taken Asawas as far as a small village; there he had been given a meal and had carefully examined the ill child of an important woman in the village. The child had a fever and was suffering terribly; Asawas had felt her face and neck and chest, had muttered: "So many come back now . . . so many, to help with what is coming. . . ." and then had prayed for the child's recovery. When he was certain that On had answered him, Asawas had told the woman what to do to insure the girl's health, had refused any money, and had continued on his way.

Now, as the afternoon began to darken, Asawas felt the earth beneath him begin to tremble, as though with anger. He paused, leaning on his staff. All around him were dry fields and brown grass; trees dotted the landscape and low hills curved away in all directions. Asawas looked up at the sky. It was blue, sunlit, white. Suddenly the sky jumped away from him, then pulled quickly toward him. With the shock of it Asawas was thrown to his knees, pushed onto his side as though by a large, invisible hand.

Ahead of him, farther down the road, three clustered trees, old oaks, danced as the sky jumped, as the earth moved. Screaming and groaning, the trees twisted and pivoted and crashed across the road. Dust erupted from many places along the road and in the fields all around.

Followed by silence.

It had lasted for only a heartbeat. A sudden change in the earth, and with it renewed quiet and calm. Asawas, standing up, looked around and saw only those few signs of damage. But he realized the devastation this must have caused farther away, in cities, in towns.

Facing the east—facing the direction in which he traveled—the prophet held his head low and prayed to On for strength and guidance and hurried on with quickening steps.

* * *

118

In Athad, Galvus was just dismissing his Council for the afternoon when the earthquake struck. He was just rising from his throne as the abrupt tremors pushed him back into his seat. The great chair slid to one side and nearly tipped from the long stone dais. Below him, the heavy tables and chairs of both *Pritons* creaked and rocked. Two Councilors, grabbing onto tables before them, were thrown forward when they broke in half and smashed to the floor, shattering.

Throughout the hall the walls and immense pillars trembled and grated—for the space of a heartbeat. The huge oil lamps and chandeliers suspended at the height of the great ceiling rocked and swayed; the chains of one of them snapped and the iron-and-wood chandelier dropped free, sped to the floor and crashed in a far corner where, fortunately, no one was seated. A Khamar who had been standing there only a moment earlier had run to the aid of two frightened ministers.

Upstairs, Adred was reading when the sudden trembling of the capital palace sent his chair skidding across the floor and through the open doors of his balcony. It nearly toppled over the low protective wall. Astonished, Adred grabbed hold of the shaking wall. Loud cracking and rupturing sounds below him caused him an instant's breathlessness; he feared that his entire balcony was giving way. But as the rumbling ceased he looked down into the gardens: several stone pillars and benches had collapsed in a pile, and part of the garden wall was twisted into a skewed position. Shrieks and screams from somewhere downstairs lifted in a belated chorus of terror.

Orain, bathing in her own chamber across the hall from Adred, screamed in alarm at the first jostling of the tiled floor. One of her windows shattered and part of the sill creaked and broke; mortar in the wall crumbled free and spat dust. But other than that, the moment's quake—that abrupt interruption in the heartbeat of the earth—was come and gone in the space of a whisper.

Adred hurled himself across his room, ran outside into the corridor. Khamars were already scurrying up and down the halls, looking for damage and injury. Some columns were twisted on their bases, walls had cracked, there were wide seams in the marble and stone of the floor, and torches and draperies had been ripped from their supports—but in all, the huge old imperial palace had withstood the moment remarkably well.

Adred burst into Orain's room and frantically called for her. "I'm here, Adred! I'm *here*, and I'm *all right*!"

In the city itself, damage was widespread but minimal, due to the minor shock of the concussion and its brevity. Facades had broken from buildings; a few loosely-built structures had partially collapsed or been twisted on their foundations; carts and stalls had been tipped over; fountains had broken and burst; wooden scaffoldings and pier pilings had torn loose. Crowds had been thrown against one another, resulting in injury but no deaths.

Still, throngs in the streets screamed and howled in sorrow and anguish. Dogs barked, children cried, horses broke free and birds shrieked and flapped from their cages in the squares. A few fires erupted in the backs of taverns and restaurants and metalworking shops. Immediately the city patrol charged into the avenues from all directions, causing great confusion as they attempted to restore order.

But as the moment passed and the people began to calm themselves, it seemed the startling intrusion it had made into the ordinariness of the day bespoke something profound. This came too closely after that mighty wind of a few months before. It was as though, people decided—as they helped one another to their feet, as they fought to extinguish fires or examined wounds or tried to recapture escaped animals—it was as though the gods for some reason were issuing warnings or beginning a series of disruptions and calamities.

But if for some reason—then what reason could it be?

5.

Erusabad, on the other side of the world, across the wide Ursalion Sea, far from Athad, where West becomes East.

A great city, Erusabad, a crossroads, a port and a wharf, a city of paths, of businesses, of merchants; city of men and animals; city of windows and lights, city of taverns and halls, of prayers and curses; and city of a thousand crowds, of voices, of clothes and robes and sandals and rings and jewelry, of perfumes; city of faces, hands and feet; city of arts; city of loneliness amidst plenty.

Holy City—elusive and real. City of many cities. City piled to the edge of the waves, city pushed into the fields and land. Maker of turbulence, owner of souls, dealer in lives. City between two empires, sharing both, clashing with both, groaning beneath the weight of both. City of east and west, city of west and east. Holy City—uncertain. . . . City of a two-edged sword, city of no repose, city of destiny. . . .

Erusabad, the Holy City, on the late summer evening of the sixteenth day of the month of Elru the Lion, as the people of the west kept their calendar.

Erusabad, with its pleasure barges and fishing boats and transport galleys and house rafts slowly swimming into and away from its hundreds of wharves and quays on both sides of the brilliantly-lighted, dusk-darkened, gently flowing River Usub. And just beyond its brilliant lights and its pleasure barges and its hundreds of wharves and quays—

Four hundred warships flying the colors and pennants of the Athadian lion and sun and crown. Battle-ready galleys. Biremes. Triremes. War ships. Bristling with steel and bronze, filled with armored men whose weapons, thrust into the shadowed sky and lit by torches and lamps, might have been a hundred thousand fangs and teeth—the fangs and teeth of open angry jaws, ready to clamp upon the arteries and muscles and bones of the city of destiny, the Holy City, Erusabad. . . .

The *ghen's* unarmed messenger returned from the harbor that night with his communication from Elad, King of the Athadians. No parchment or scroll, no message written on a document or order, but only a single sentence:

"Return the Queen of Athadia to her king and her people, or prepare yourselves for war."

Agors's initial reaction was to laugh at the sheer effrontery of this. The king of the west going to these great lengths, merely to force the return of his wife? Merely to impress the *ghen* with the importance in which this foolish woman was held? Yet he did not laugh: for the madness of this exploit bespoke its own resoluteness, and the madness of it did not suggest any real shallowness or duplicity. Men, Agors knew, will work patiently and until the end of time over matters of grave import; yet it is

121

from matters seemingly trivial that great events most often grow, like monsters breeding in the forgotten dung of some imaginary beast. The *ghen* of the Salukads therefore determined to meet this challenge with the directness and solemnity it demanded. Whereupon he ordered a scribe to him and addressed this message to his foreign intruders:

"From Agors, *Ghen* of Salukadia, to Elad, dog of the Athadians, greetings. You presume much in supposing that Queen Salia is held here as a hostage against her will, or in a manner meant to aggravate the tensions between our thrones. You may take her as you wish. Come to me tomorrow morning at dawn, and I will deliver her to you. Come with your retainers and, if such is your desire, bearing sheathed weapons: but know that I do not draw weapons upon you and that the hospitality of my home is yours."

This dictated, Agors ordered it delivered immediately to the flagship in his harbor. He then bade to him his brother Nihim, and awaited him in a private chamber of the palace.

When Agors's message was delivered to him, Elad's initial reaction was to laugh at the sheer effrontery of it. Himself addressed as a dog? Salia not held a hostage? Yet he did not laugh, for the blandness of the writer's style told him much.

Lord General Thomo was greatly relieved to hear the contents of this letter and he assured Elad that, so far as he could determine from the succinctness of it, it must indeed have originated from the *ghen* himself.

Major Thytagoras was not so certain. And the Imbur Ogodis, predictably, was as outraged by the snide tone of it as he was with the insinuation it contained that his daughter was not the victim of some barbaric eastern plot.

"You don't believe this, do you?" he snarled at Elad. "You don't believe that Salia *isn't* a prisoner, do you? You don't believe that he's going to meet you *weaponless*, surely?"

Elad showed him a grave stare. "I know your daughter better than you do yourself, Imbur. And as a king, I am the equal of this potentate. I believe that more may have happened here than we can properly assume, without learning more. And I believe that it would do Agors absolutely no good, for whatever reason imaginable, to meet tomorrow with bared steel, or to provoke conflict over some folly of Salia's that—"

"Some—*folly!*" Ogodis rankled.

"I will indeed," Elad told him deliberately, "go to this man's palace at dawn. And I will indeed take sheathed steel with me—as well as my retainers and above all Lord General Thomo."

A nod, which Thomo acknowledged with a proud lifting of his chin.

Ogodis swore, "And *I* will certainly—"

"You certainly, will *not* attend this parley, Imbur! And if you insist upon—"

"He is holding *my daughter* in—"

"*And if you insist upon it,*" Elad repeated, voice rising in a strangely convulsive mixture of impatience and real wrath, "I will have you chained to the mainmast of this ship, I will have your mouth stuffed with *straw* until you agree to cease these *adolescent whinings!* Do you understand?"

Ogodis quavered in shock. Never in his entire life had anyone dared to speak so to him, ever—never in his entire—

Elad looked beyond him to meet the steely gaze of Major Thytagoras. "I trust, furthermore, that I am perfectly understood by any others who might look upon this incident as an excuse to further their own interests against the Salukads."

Thytagoras said nothing.

"I intend, then, to go below now and take my rest until dawn. Major Thomo—if you will see that I am not disturbed?"

"Certainly, Lord Elad."

"Good night, then, gentlemen. Have our messenger return to the *ghen* with my agreement.

"I seem to recall a conversation we had some months ago, brother," Nihim reminded Agors, "when your infatuation with this woman had not yet begun to wane. You boasted then, as if this were some game of *usto*, that you were 'raping the queen' of the Athadians. No?"

Agors growled underbreath and turned from him, stalked to a chair, slumped and glowered.

Nihim reproached him with words that bit like acid.

"And what did I tell you last winter, when you so proudly proclaimed your superiority over the ways of the west? 'Agors, if you think too much like your enemy, you become your enemy. Who then is left to make war upon?' This is why I play *usto* with the westerners—not to defeat or humiliate them, but to reach an accord with them, a balance. You have looked at your maps and you have polished your swords and dreamed your dreams of conquest but, o my brother, how can you truly conquer anyone, when you have not yet conquered yourself?"

"I did not order you here," the *ghen* growled at Nihim, "to allow you to upbraid me!"

"I am not upbraiding you; I merely remind you that when you were excited and wild as a free river, you failed to consider that there might be rocks or shoals somewhere in the future. Now you are rushing toward the rocks."

Agors stared at the floor, flexed his hands into fists.

"This action on the part of the Athadian king should not surprise you. Recall something more: recall when I told you that these men of the west, as they bend over the *usto* board, like children often form strategies in which they sacrifice everything to gain one goal. Would men like this offer their entire nation on the altar of war, over something as foolish as the whimsies and moods of a young woman? They would indeed! Would they not draw weapons upon us, were we to besmirch their pride in some unsavory way? You, too, would do the same, Agors. It is less a difference between east and west, I think, than it is the similarity of men everywhere to deem their pride and ambition worth more than their tolerance. Wrath and anger, intemperance and fury are always easy—see how quickly the skies can cause a storm. And it is left for the patient to clean the wreckage after the storm."

"You think I am a storm?"

"I think that you believe there is more integrity in the storm than there is in the patience of the victims of that storm. Our mighty father caused storms for a purpose: now his first son is full of woe because there are no more lands upon which he might descend like a storm. So will you create artificial lands? Will you storm upon this city because you lack lands in the west upon which to storm? And why? Because you have made a move on the *usto* table? Because your dreams and ambitions have reduced themselves to the antics of a foolish young woman? The *ghens* of Salukadia do not make war upon their enemies because a foolish woman has—"

"*Enough!*" Agors slapped his hands on his chair and stood up. "Enough! You tell me things I know already! Have I decided to go to war with this king of the west? I am no fool!" He began to pace the floor, head bent, eyes burning, arms swinging. "I know what I will do, Nihim. This king of the west, this Elad, comes to me on the dawn for the return of his wife. I have written to him already, consenting to his returning with her to his capital, at the other end of the world."

"Most wise." The sarcasm in Nihim's voice was not lost upon his brother.

But the *ghen* continued without acknowledging it. "I do not intend, however, to bring myself down to his place. He has come to me; shall I show respect to him in any way? To a barbarian?" He stopped where he stood, faced his brother sternly. "I know that *you*, Nihim, sincerely care to insure peace and maintain talk with these dogs."

"Do you know this?"

"Letters . . . and other proposals—"

"I see that, truly, nothing escapes you."

"I am the *ghen*. Shall I jeopardize myself, even for one moment? Even for sentiment?" Agors shook his head. "So . . . knowing how important it is for you to honor this 'balance' you so religiously devote yourself to, I intend to allow you to do better than simply address letters to this Elad of Athadia. I will let you speak with him personally."

"What do you mean?"

"Tomorrow at dawn, when King Elad comes here to this palace to retrieve his wife, you may greet him and act in official capacity to entertain him as you see fit, and apologize in any way that does not dishonor our father and our ancestors. Then you can send him back to his ships and order him away from us. Surely, arbiter, you find this accomodating?"

"*I* . . . to meet him," Nihim repeated slowly, "rather than—the true *ghen*. When he expects to be greeted, as an equal, by the king of this nation?"

"Precisely."

Nihim worried his head sadly. "Still, all this pride in you, this anger. . . . Face him as a man, Agors! Ah, but how much anger must fill you, that you have so much to spare strangers whom you regard as enemies." Nihim shrugged and crossed the room to the door, slippers whispering, robes flowing. "I will do as you suggest. And proudly will I do it. For I remind you of one thing more, Agors, which separates us when we should be bound by blood: more than our father, more than our ancestors, more than our empire, I pay homage to the ceaseless Way. And the day will come, my brother, when you will say to me, 'Save me from myself, for I have been a fool in my pride and false in my anger, and I too wish to place the Way before all else.'"

Agors chuckled cruelly. "And what will you do with me, Nihim, when I come crawling to you, begging for your sympathy and your forgiveness?"

"I will open my arms to you and allow you mercifully to place your burdens upon my heart. I will console you and comfort you and treat you with more graciousness than I would allow even myself."

"Nihim," Agors told him, "you are weak. Strive to rise above this need to depend on others."

"And I will treat you," his brother continued, ignoring the slander, "as you yourself should treat this king and his strangers from the west—not even as strangers, but as some lost part of you returned home at last, with marvelous tales to tell, and richness of experience beyond what we experience. But then—" Nihim sighed, and his voice turned grim with his reprimand "—what else should you do with these men, o *ghen*, seeing that you regard yourself as one of them?"

When he left Agors, Nihim hurried through the palace to the chamber of Queen Salia. She admitted him only after he had knocked repeatedly, but she was pleased (in her way) to see that it was him, for in the past weeks they had become confidantes of a sort—Nihim offering this strange young woman whatever comfort or conversation he could, and she responding to that comfort with speculations and hopefulness.

"So. . . ." Salia seated herself on a divan, curled up on one side of it. "My husband has come for me?"

126

"He has indeed." Nihim remained standing in the middle of the room, arms clasped before him, watching her.

"And—" the queen's voice shivered "he has come with war ships . . . and soldiers?"

"He has. But Agors tells me that he does not intend to answer your husband's challenge with arms."

"There will be no war, then?"

"No war, Queen Salia."

Almost silently, so quietly in a whisper that she could not be overheard, Salia muttered, "Good. . . ." and pressed one hand to her cheek. To Nihim, then: "Agors will not come to tell me this himself? No . . . no . . . of course he won't."

Nihim crossed to her. Salia's face tilted up, her eyes traveling the long length of his robe until she was staring into the young man's kind, tired expression.

"Your husband has come to take you home," he told her. "Is this not all that matters? Whatever else has occurred here . . . well, are we not all on this place to learn? Inevitably, to err—but to learn?"

"How can you always be so optimistic?" Salia asked him, voice heavy. "How can you always—"

"Not so optimistic," Nihim corrected her. "I am merely being realistic. Experience has taught me so."

Salia sighed lightly. "One a moral man, the other a passionate man," she murmured. "Have you ever, Nihim, been tired—tired unto death, almost? So tired and confused, not knowing who you truly are, so *frightened* that you could—you feel you could reach inside your head and try to force the pieces of yourself into something whole and complete?"

He was somewhat surprised at the lucidity of her observation. He assured Salia: "I have, indeed. It is a feeling familiar to many who have devoted themselves to *Wo Ahyat*."

That seemed to make her brighten. "Is it?"

"We refer to it as the Parceling of Selves; what you of the west might call it, I do not know. Remember when I told you about the three selves, the three parts? Yes. And . . . have you seen any light in your mirror?"

"There is no light in my mirror," Salia confessed glumly. "No light from me."

Nihim laughed at her, as though he were delighted by her failure. "It will come, it will come," he promised. He moved slightly; Salia jerked her head, saw that Nihim had reached out a hand.

To touch her? To touch her cheek, perhaps? Or her hair?

They looked into one another's eyes, and Nihim gradually withdrew his hand, clasped it in the other, turned softly and backed away, turned again and eyed Salia almost with tenderness or affection.

Something had happened within him, in that brief moment, and the queen suspected it. But her intuition was lost as Nihim said to her, changing the course of their conversation: "Agors . . . has determined that you must return to the west with your husband."

She started.

"Isn't it best that you do so? Is there any reason for you not to return to your husband, and to your throne?"

Salia looked away, began picking nervously at her robe. "No . . . I suppose not. Whatever reasons I had . . . I suppose I've forgotten them, now."

Nihim was disturbed; this was not— This woman was perilous, she was lost, she had changed. He had tried, he had worked— "Your king, then—" he breathed to calm himself "—arrives here on the dawn to accept you back to him, and to escort you again to your land. If you will be prepared to visit the hall downstairs in the morning—"

"I will be prepared," Salia answered him lowly, in *Hasni*.

"Excellent. Agors has asked me to preside over this . . . exchange."

"He will not be there?" She stopped picking at her robe.

Nihim shook his head.

The queen made no comment to this, and so Nihim, after a pause, decided to leave her. He was in need of sleep. But as he made his way out, Salia asked after him:

"Nihim? Is my father—is the Imbur of Gaegosh with my husband?"

"I am given to understand, Queen Salia, that the Imbur is with the armada, but that he will not be coming here tomorrow morning."

"I see. . . ."

128

"Good night, Queen Salia."

"Yes . . . of course. . . ."

Nihim went out. Salia continued picking at threads in her robe. She did this for a long time, until one of her pet birds began to make noise in its cage. This disturbed the queen; she sat up angrily and strode across the floor, twirled the cage on its hanger and yelled at her pet, "Quiet, be *quiet*! What's the matter with you? Stop it, be *quiet*!"

Her actions only served to further upset the bird; it chirruped and squawked very loudly. In desperation Salia tried to undo the latch of the cage door, but she fumbled with it and cracked one of her fingernails. Infuriated, the queen quickly lifted the cage from its hanger, carried it to an open window and hurled it out.

"Go away, fly away, *go away*!"

The cage dropped, vanishing into the dark, whistling as it fell.

"*Go away, fly—*"

It made a distorted, hollow noise as it struck the ground far below. The bird shrilled sharply. The brazen, circular noises of the smashed cage as it rolled still filled the darkness with a metallic echo—an upsetting sound, unfamiliar amidst the night's usual noises and whispers.

Salia, not wanting to hear it, slammed closed the shutters of her window, hurried across the room to her divan and buried her face in her pillow; she chewed on the pillow and stuffed the heavy cloth of it into her mouth, nearly suffocating herself in an attempt to prevent herself from crying. . . .

Why had she done that (she wanted to ask the light in her mirror) to her bird?

Why had she done that to the favorite of all her pets?

In the middle of the night, before the gray that harbingers the dawn, the first of them occurred, heralding that shadowed place on humanity's path where history began to move faster than time. A sailor sitting in a tavern down by Kurad Square slumped forward onto a table and did not move. His companions ignored him, thinking him drunk. But before another hour had passed they, too, began to feel nauseous; three of them dropped to the floor and began to writhe and vomit, while the fourth rose to his feet and, in a daze, managed to stagger to the door before falling to his knees in the road outside.

The young fellow behind the bar, whose father owned the shop, hurried around to examine these men, for he suspected that they were not victims of ordinary drunkenness but of something more. His fears were confirmed when he rolled over each of the sprawled three and saw that their faces had already gone white and were breaking open in red pustules. None were awake; yet they shivered terribly, arms and legs jumping spasmodically, and the sweat poured from them in widening puddles.

Terrified, the young man hastened into the street and ran until he came to the door of a leech. Frantic poundings roused the angered physician, but his temper abated when he heard what the taverner's son had to report.

And in other public houses along the square, other men and women fell victim to the same sudden exhaustion and vomiting, the same trembling and discoloration.

And in homes throughout the city, lamps were suddenly lit, footsteps quickened in the night as husbands and wives, children and parents awoke from sleep shivering uncontrollably, vomiting painfully, sweating as though caught in a downpour.

And in the temples, in the wineshops, in the guard stations and in the homes of food tenders and butchers, dye-makers and chandlers, tar manufacturers and oil pressers, in the houses of prostitution and in gardens where young lovers were hidden in secret trysts—

—the same shivering, the same vomiting, the same death.

And aboard the *Crown*, as it sat in the harbor of the Usub, General Thomo was roused from his slumber by an eager, frightened young officer. Thomo, grunting and swearing, followed him into the hold, where a number of soldiers were lying too still for sleep or were still in the violent throes of illness.

"What is it?" the general asked, coming fully awake. "Name of the gods, it—"

"Lord General, I am too afraid to say!"

"Name of the gods . . . not here, it can't be, not—"

"The king," whispered the young officer.

"Oh, *gods*!" Thomo threw a hand to his face. "Elad!" He turned and raced down the gallery, pounding on the wall as he went, ordering the young officer behind him to summon the *Crown*'s physician.

"Not here," he whispered, wiping sweat from his forehead—even as he feared that to be the beginning of it. "Not here . . . not now, not . . . Elad. . . ."

PART III

War

1.

Galvus was breakfasting alone, sitting on a rooftop patio, when Abgarthis interrupted him. The prince-regent was sifting through damage reports, tallying the destruction sustained by the brief earthquake on the fifteenth. He had reviewed them once already, cursorily, looking for some word of Omos: Galvus knew that it was too soon for his friend to write him, but he was concerned for his safety. When Abgarthis came up, Galvus regarded him expectantly—but realized then that his minister's visit had nothing to do with Omos.

"If you have a moment. . . ."

"Certainly." Galvus pushed aside his plate, leaned forward and took up his tea. He nodded for Abgarthis to take the chair across from him. "What is it?"

"I thought I should tell you about this now so that you can mull it over today, perhaps discuss it with some of your friends on the

Council. I've been receiving informal reports—gossip, really—about the problems we've been running into recruiting these people's representatives."

Galvus frowned. "What sort of 'gossip'?"

"Oh—these, as well," Abgarthis remembered, placing on the breakfast table a fat package. "The latest dispatches. From the Emarian front."

"I'll get to them. Tell me about these rumors, this gossip."

"I'm afraid," his minister declared, seating himself, "that leashing Rhin and the others may be only a beginning to your troubles. There are far too many out there who are sympathetic; they fear the abrupt change. Now, I don't think anyone intends to turn against you or challenge you, but you've got to bear in mind that Lord Rhin's influence is quite extensive, simply because of his vast business holdings, the many offices in which he sits, the highly-placed acquaintances he—"

"I'm aware of this, Abgarthis."

"I only mean to remind you, Galvus. For example, his suggestion of the *Khilu* was eagerly acted upon by many city administrators—"

"He set the waves in motion himself."

"Yes. Precisely. And meanwhile, these same administrators are uncertain about the contradictory edicts coming from the throne, giving them a great deal of *freedom* in choosing representatives to sit in government."

"They want to be told what to do."

"Sadly, yes, to a large degree. It's the method they're most familiar with. Things move too quickly for them."

Galvus sighed heavily. "I know that . . . but I supposed that with my declaration—" He let it go, lifted his tea cup to his lips.

"It's simply a matter of habit. We can't sweep away what's already there and begin fresh. There is far too much tension in the empire these days. With Elad gone, many of our businessmen and politicians are leery of making any kind of decisive move. They'll procrastinate, they'll vascillate— They don't disrespect you, Galvus—they are simply in the habit of dealing with things as they always have been. The people whom they see every day have much more effect on them than any document issued from the throne—especially from a prince-regent who, after all, commands what might easily be interpreted as a temporary or a provisional government. So much has happened. . . ."

"Yes, yes. . . ."

"I'm only saying that you must be realistic. Patient and realistic."

"What I need to do, then," Galvus decided, "is not alienate these merchandisers and plutocrats further, but come to terms with them."

Abgarthis nodded sagely. "Yes. Strike a bargain."

"Compromise."

"Exactly."

"And . . . undermine everything we were trying to accomplish in the first place."

"No, no, don't say that," his minister insisted.

"But that would be the effect of it, wouldn't it? If I were to go to Rhin and offer him something in exchange for something else, just so everyone would get the impression that the political winds are blowing in the same direction they always have been?"

There was a bitterness to Galvus's tone that warned Abgarthis not to pursue the topic further. He nodded briefly—"I mention it only because I know you want to be kept informed"—and rose to leave. But then: "There is one thing more. In addition to these." Once more he tapped the package of war dispatches.

"And what is it?"

"We've had reports, some from the city and some from outlying areas, of a sudden outbreak of disease."

Galvus went cold. "Disease? What do you mean? Explain yourself, please, Abgarthis."

"We don't have all the details yet. I'm waiting for a report from Sotos to determine exactly what—"

"Plague, Abgarthis?"

The old man stared at him, fear and sorrow apparent in his features.

And what had that prophet Asawas warned them of? *"The fifth sign will be a day and a night of plague. This is the sign that the end has begun. . . ."*

"Name—of the *gods* . . . Abgarthis. . . ."

"We don't know that it's the plague," was the cautious reply. "There's so much poverty . . . so little food . . . the summer has been so hot and dry—"

135

"Asawas." Galvus grinned sadly. "You remember, certainly."

"Yes. I remember." Quietly.

"He was wise, I know he spoke the truth as he believed it to be. . . ." Galvus slumped in his seat, nervously pulled at his lower lip. "I know he is probably a man of this one god . . . yet how can anyone allow himself to trust completely the *visions* of— some farmer, some—" He stopped, shook his head. "This isn't the old days, when people walked around producing miracles, talking to fires and spirits. But . . . it's quite frightening, isn't it? To suppose that he has the vision to have foreseen something terrible. . . ."

Abgarthis said nothing.

Galvus shook his head. "Now I know what Mother meant, and Elad. Sitting here—the gossip and the rumors and the news and the reports brought to me first of all. I can't rely upon anyone else, and it's hard to tell the difference between what might be a miracle and what be someone else's selfish lies. So it all seems, after all, as though it's falling apart. Wars and prophets and plagues and starving people. . . . No one person should pretend to be in command of it all. No *one* person can possibly—"

He paused again; he seemed very agitated. Abgarthis bent his head to one side.

"Yes, Galvus?"

"I suppose we had best take precautions. Issue orders immediately. The palace is to be sealed at once. No one enters, and no one who has entered today is to be allowed exit."

"Don't you think those are rather extraordinary—"

"Yes. Yes, I do. But . . . if this *is* the plague, then I want to take no chances, Abgarthis. I'm lord of the kitchen, after all, aren't I? Issue the command to take effect immediately. The Khamars are to bolt all doors. Issue the order for all government offices to be suspended for the day, as well."

"Very well."

To his minister's doubtful expression Galvus commented: "I don't think I'm being alarmist, Abgarthis. I am being realistic. Now—please. . . ."

The journey through the streets of Erusabad was a grim yet enlightening one. From his carriage, Elad peered through the curtains to catch glimpses here and there of the life of this strange city. He had never once supposed that he would ever visit the Holy City; and far from it, in Athad, the impressions he'd had of Erusabad had never truly given him a real idea of what the place must be. Long sheets of merchandise reports and legal statements had given him only a dry, statistical abstraction; lively details gained from businessmen, travelers and military officers had conjured pictures of wild color, peoples of many kinds raising a pandemonium of different languages—an imbalanced vision as unreal, in its way, as the unlively statistics. The reality was sobering.

Between the moving horses of his Salukadian escort, Elad saw whole crowds of people dressed in rags, living in huts they had built against great stone walls. He saw herds of goats and cattle and other animals being lashed through the streets as if the Holy City were little more than an outsized farming village. He saw beggars, and people roasting fresh pieces of dog meat over open fires. And corpses lying discarded or ignored, everywhere—in doorways, on the cobblestones, in alleys, bunched into tall piles. Corpses that were swollen and pale, bleeding and blistered.

Victims of the plague.

Thomo and the others had been insistent with him this morning about not entering the city. When the *ghen's* soldiers had arrived at the flagship with the warning that Erusabad had fallen victim to a sudden outbreak of disease, Elad's commanders of arms had resolutely decided that, after this long sea voyage, their king could delay meeting with his wife and the eastern monarch for another few days or another week or even another month. They were safe aboard their ships, away from any chance of being touched by the illness.

But Elad's reply to this caution had been a cold, "Let the plague take me, then. I intend to see my wife, whatever the gods will"— followed by his direct orders to lower the launch and prepare to follow the Salukadian escort into the harbor. All who did not wish to accompany him were free to decline; yet not one did so. Thomo, the first to speak out against entering the disease-ridden Holy City, was yet the first to swear allegiance to his king when Elad had made his decision. Majors Hadd and Ostorian, as well, had asked for the privilege of accompanying their lord into the foreign monarch's palace. And so it had been done.

The farther they moved from the districts near the harbor, the wider the streets became and the less densely populated. Elad noticed whole stretches of avenues and boulevards totally vacant, save for a loiterer or two. And to him came then, from a distance, the sad and nauseating stench of burning human flesh. . . .

When they reached the renovated palace of the Salukadian government, their escort was prompt in leading King Elad and his three retainers inside. Up the stairs and, to the sounds of a loud gong, down the central corridor to a hallway on the left. Elad and the others realized at once that this palace was not more than the elaborate home of some displaced Athadian aristocrat: the architecture and design, the tile marble and mosaics, all betrayed its western origin.

They were ushered through an open atrium toward great doors of cedar inlaid with ivory and gold—certainly *not* the craftsmanship of any western artisan. The doors were pulled open by soldiers dressed in fine fabric and steel, and Elad and his men were taken into the Audience Hall of the *ghen* of the east. It, too, was open to the sky; dull sunlight poured in and birds chirruped and flew among tall trees that reached through the ceiling. A great fountain at one end flowed and tinkled and splashed; great bronze lamps, smoking with incense, hung everywhere, creating a light aromatic fog. But Elad's attention, as he walked down the carpeting that led to the dais on the far end of the hall, was on none of this. He noticed peripherally many chairs stretching away on both sides from this dais and realized that some of the seats were empty. The smaller of the two thrones on the stepped dais was vacant, as well. But seated in the larger one was a very young man with shaved head, dressed in a plain white robe and rough sandals. Strange attire for the *ghen* of the Salukads. And standing erect beside him—

Elad had not seen his wife in over three and a half months. She had changed.

She was slimmer than she had been, even when he had married her. Her hair had grown longer, and it fell freely down past her shoulders. She wore almost no cosmetics, and yet she was dressed in an elaborate robe that fell in loose folds of colorful cartouches and interwoven symbols, all gold and silver, red and blue and yellow. Jewelry hung from her throat and her arms. Her sandals were gilt.

Elad stopped in his advance as the soldier before him paused, moved aside and bowed from the waist, lifting his palms briefly to his forehead.

"O *Ghen-usu*, I present to you Elad, King of Athadia and all the lands of the west."

Elad, aware that his gaze was fierce, tore his eyes from Salia, who had not yet looked at him. He stared at the man on the throne. In a crisp voice that revealed his bitterness and anger, he asked loudly: "You are Agors, then—the king of the Salukads?"

The young man on the throne leaned forward. "No, King Elad, I am not."

"You are *not*?"

"I am Nihim, the brother of the *ghen*. I sit here in my brother's place to greet you, and to tell you that my brother has been taken ill and is unable to meet you himself."

He felt anger swell within him with a real force; he heard his voice erupt before he was aware that he meant to speak. "What sort of treachery is this? Salia!" He faced her, and only Thomo's arresting hand on his shoulder warned Elad to remain standing where he was. "*Salia*! What sort of *treachery* is this? *Tell me!*"

His wife turned her eyes to him and looked upon him. Her head shivered slightly as enormous tears suddenly poured down her cheeks.

She staggered and fell back—

"*Salia!*"—as Elad lurched forward.

Nihim quickly rose from the throne, took hold of her, and forced Queen Salia to seat herself in the smaller throne.

Adred was just coming down one of the walkways in the garden when Orain called to him from the low wall of her balcony.

"Adred! Come here, get inside, quickly!"

The distress in her voice shocked him. He came around a tree and stood in the shade of it, looked up so that he could see her clearly, three stories above him. "Orain? What is it, what's—"

"What are you *doing* down there?" she yelled back. "Why did you get up so early?"

He breathed a faint laugh; what an incredible question. "I was going for a walk before breakfast! What do you mean, 'what am I doing down here'?"

139

"Please, just come here. Just come here!"

Very perplexed, Adred trotted down the walk, slipped under the arched entranceway and crossed the brick path so that he was nearly under her window. He went so far as to hoist himself onto the marble base of a small column. Hanging by his grip onto the carved robe of some deity, he threw back his head, "What's the matter with you, Orain?"

"They're closing up the palace! No one can get in or out!"

"*What*?"

"Galvus has ordered it!"

"What in the name of the gods *for*?"

"Plague! Adred, there's an outbreak of *plague* in the city! Now get inside before they lock you out!"

Thomo had reminded him, "Nihim is a good man. He is not his brother. They are night and day, white and black. He is a good man, King Elad."

And so, with the calming of his temper, Elad had accepted the *Ghen-usu's* invitation to meet privately with him in a chamber upstairs. There they sipped tea, and as Elad sat, frowning, working to maintain his irascible pose, Nihim had paced back and forth, robes whispering and slippers creaking, and had explained all that had come about since Queen Salia's arrival in Erusabad.

Elad, listening, discerned how Nihim carefully avoided placing blame for the situation on either Salia or Agors. In his talk he used metaphors that seemed to be drawn from mystical or religious teachings, and from his own wise observations of human behavior. The effect was to place this specific turn-of-events into a general context: to strip away the facades of royalty and power and present everyone concerned as human beings, complex and uncertain of themselves, and dealing with confusing situations in their habitual, if not entirely reasonable, ways.

Nihim complimented Elad on Salia, describing the queen as an intelligent woman who felt confined by the people around her. She was used to being dominated by powerful men, yet some part of her wished to assert herself; she was tired of being lauded for her physical beauty alone and wished to make people aware of her other attributes; she wished to escape, and yet she knew that

140

escape from life's difficulties is impossible; and she had been thwarted by all attempts to act reasonably or maturely.

As the *Ghen-usu* spoke, Elad felt the wrath in him drain away. He admitted to Nihim that he had come here to test the Salukadians: yet all he truly wished was to retrieve his wife. He had always hoped that, as distant from one another and as divergent as they were, the Athadian crown and the Salukadian throne might coexist on mutually respectful terms.

"That, too, is all I have ever wished," Nihim replied. "It seems to me that men everywhere fear what they do not understand, or launch their own fears onto what they do not understand. And conflict results, because men are not strong enough to learn the things they do not understand. There is wisdom in patience and in recognizing one's own ignorance: but men everywhere refuse to admit this. They see the world in their personal terms and the result is—" he smiled sadly "—confusion."

"Well, I don't mean to bring confusion to this city," Elad told Nihim, trying to speak more slowly than he usually did, so that the *ghen's* brother might not miss anything he said in his Athadian tongue. "And I would be happy to learn of your people. I wish now, however, only to regain my wife and return her to my empire."

Nihim nodded his assent. "Be patient with her—that is all I would suggest to you. We are never as patient with others as we expect them to be with ourselves."

Elad smiled. "Can you reduce all of life into these . . . these phrases of yours, Nihim *Ghen-usu*?"

"Yes. Do they seem to you simplistic? Think of these—phrases—Lord Elad, as the beginnings of concepts, not as rules or laws to be followed as though they are inviolate. You see, we deal with the world as though it were complex, it seems to me, but that is only because we are confused. I speak in the words of the Way, which is a path of balance. I fear, Elad King, that men will never be equal in their happiness and joy, but only in their loss and pain: for those are common to everyone, high and low, but only so many can be elevated at one time. Yet, still—if men can bring the conflicts and confusions of the world into a balance, they will astonish themselves, I think, and achieve those things they claim to desire so much."

Elad was moved by this. "I must say that I agree with you about that."

"Perhaps now it is time to meet again with your wife."

"I agree with you about that, as well."

Thomo, Hadd and Ostorian were waiting in an ante-chamber in the company of bin-Sutus and several Salukadian palace soldiers. All stood up immediately as the door of Nihim's office opened and the two leaders emerged. Thomo and bin-Sutus each exhaled sighs of relief at seeing the calm expressions on their faces.

"Queen Salia?" the *Ghen-usu* asked of bin-Sutus. "Is she in her rooms?"

The *aihman* shook his head. In a concerned voice he answered: "She has gone to see after Agors, on his sick-bed." To Elad: "To make her farewell before leaving with you, lord of the west."

Elad didn't care for that; he scowled at Nihim and grunted: "If you don't mind," and lifted an arm before him, indicating that the *Ghen-usu* might lead the way.

"My brother is quite ill," Nihim replied lowly. "Most probably he is dying. This—plague. . . ."

"I understand," Elad nodded. "Still—if you don't mind . . . ?" And he lifted his arm once more.

"As you wish." And Nihim led Elad, bin-Sutus and Elad's retainers from the chamber, down the outer corridor to the *ghen's* room.

He spent the day with Orain. Time went by slowly, slowly, and there was little to do. The most astonishing thing to Adred, initially, was the fact that, with all that had happened recently, with the enormity of events growing and stretching like great clouds of darkness over the country, he and Orain really had very little to talk about. They were very much in love with one another, and yet they spent the morning sitting on opposite sides of her room, glancing up occasionally from whatever each of them was occupied with, looking at one another, smiling their questions and answers, but otherwise saying very little. It was as though this enforced isolation did not free them or give them time to do things they might have been postponing or neglecting; rather, this enforced isolation trapped them, held them as though they were prisoners.

Adred was reading poetry. It was not encouraging poetry. It was verse by one of those romantic poets Abgarthis seemed to favor, and grim were the sentiments expressed.

Each leaf, each stone, each mysterious tree
Grins at me in foul mockery,
Men shall love the world in its dying night,
Pray to the images of ancient gods,
Recall Man's goodness and his temperance,
His soul shall fill with momentary love. . . .

"Did you hear that?" Orain asked him suddenly, looking up from her needlework.

"Hear what?"

"Listen."

It was deathly quiet. The whole palace was quiet. It seemed that—

"There," Orain said, voice quavering. "Oh, Adred. . . ." She set aside her sewing and jumped to her feet, hurried to her balcony and leaned over the rail. She could see nothing but the garden, pale and brown and silent as it was. But still there came to her—those sounds. . . .

Adred stepped beside her, lay a hand on her arm. "What?"

"Voices. . . ."

And now he heard them, as well. From far away, true, but many voices, a chorus of voices—moaning and sobbing and crying out in wild despair.

"Oh, Hea!" Orain exclaimed, staring at him, gripping Adred's shoulders. "It's *true*! *Adred*! People are *dying* out there!"

2.

It seemed so artificial and contrived. Not at all the way Elad had anticipated it, his first meeting with the powerful and feared, temperamental *ghen* of the Salukads. No angry posturings . . . no challenges and retorts . . . no testing of wills between strong men standing boot to boot, with their empires and millions of people hovering behind them like crowds of guarding souls from the netherworld. Only—this. . . .

The king of Athadia, dressed in his armor, standing in an

orange-glowing and incense-fogged, darkened room, witnessing the last moments on earth of the man against whom he had brought swords and ships and the standard of war. No prowling lion here; no roaring cat or swift-taloned vulture. Only a man.

Agors lay shivering, his face damp and running with sweat, his dark skin pale and broken with pustules and discolorations. His long hair and the hair of his beard were damp and matted, soggy with perspiration. While all around him, around his great wide bed of cushions and pillows, stood tier upon tier of tall burning candles; all around hung oil lamps and incense braziers.

From a far corner a group of old men, almost completely hidden in the shadows, were reciting oddly mellifluous, rhythmically coaxing sentences—some litany to the dead or dying, Elad supposed, from their barbaric religion.

Agors trembled beneath his blankets as though he was frozen in the middle of winter. His gasping mouth opened and closed stickily; his breath inhaled and exhaled audibly. His teeth chattered. Between his hands, which rested upon his chest, he held a strangely-shaped longsword—a *yagu*, Thomo had called it, of eastern manufacture.

And whatever the *ghen* was whispering or muttering or praying, Elad certainly could not decipher it; nor, he supposed, could anyone in that room. The words were unintelligible.

Becoming increasingly uncomfortable, not wishing to stay very long in this room, Elad looked meaningfully at Nihim, frowned and glanced at Salia. Nihim nodded quietly, moved his eyes from Elad to General Thomo, behind him.

Thomo understood. Leaning close to his king, he whispered into Elad's ear: "The *Ghen-usu* thinks it might be appropriate for you to pay respect to his dying brother. One leader to another."

Elad did not answer.

"A gesture, my king," Thomo reminded him. "The man you thought would make war upon you, whom you feared had stolen your queen—he is dying, King Elad. Suffering like any man. You need say nothing. You need only—"

Elad raised a gloved hand, indicating silence. He looked again to Nihim, studied his wife. Salia was kneeling on pillows on the floor, beside the *ghen's* bed. Her back was to Elad; she was unmoving, staring at Agors on his pillows.

Elad stepped ahead. Unconcerned with matters of protocol or

144

custom, he held a brief dialogue with himself and did what he considered best, under the circumstances. Close by the bed, only a short distance from his wife, he knelt onto one knee and joined his hands loosely together at the fingertips, lifted them to his lips, bowed his head.

He heard Salia's clothes rustling as she turned to look at him.

Elad closed his eyes, breathed deeply a few times. The aroma of incenses in that room and the darkness that he saw took him back in time, removed him to that ominous cave of the Oracle at Teplis. . . .

As words came to him, Elad spoke them.

"Gods of life and gods of light . . . in the name of Bithitu our Prophet . . . speak now with my voice to the gods of this land . . . tell them that I come here not in anger or in vengeance . . . tell them that I look upon a king and see only a man . . . as I—am a man . . . and you gods . . . of life and light . . . protect Agors *ko-Ghen* on his passage from the night of life into the bright day of your home . . . be generous with him . . . for I humble myself before you . . . for his sake . . . for his sake and mine. . . ."

He looked up, almost startled. Elad dropped his hands from his mouth. He didn't know what to say, or how to say it. He hadn't petitioned the gods since boyhood. He stared at the face of the dying Agors, and tears came to his eyes. It might have been himself on that bed. It might have been himself with that sword. It might have been—

He looked across the room, saw the shadow-hidden robes and the shadow-hidden faces of eastern men, their eyes on him, their expressions grave, their language incomprehensible and their thoughts, and the strangeness of the room, the colors and the tapestries, the incense, everything here so foreign and unusual—

Truth, here?

Elad choked, drew in a breath, looked again at Agors.

Whispering, in a nervous voice, as tears wet his eyes: "O you gods, you gods . . . look down upon us . . . we are *men*, he and I! We are . . . only *men*. . . ."

Salia sobbed in anguish. Elad jerked his head, stared at her. She fell forward. He threw out his arms and caught her. Held her. As she hugged him and pushed herself against him, clung to him, there in that room of the dying *ghen*, in the candlelight and the lamplight, in the smoke of incense.

"Oh, Elad . . . *Elad*!" And she sobbed terribly, wept and shivered as he held her.

Nihim looked away. He regarded Lord General Thomo, over there with the others, and saw in his eyes—

Yes, the same thought . . . the same thoughts. . . .

We are only men. . . .

As Queen Salia held her husband, while Elad gripped her as though to protect her—

As Agors's sword shivered in his hands, as he dreamed things he could not communicate, in his illness and his delirium. . . .

"I'm trying to imagine what it must have been like," Adred said from his side of the room, "to have lived through something like . . . well, the civil wars, maybe. Something as violent as that, something that chaotic. Caught in the middle of it, there would seem to be absolutely no order or sense to it. You'd be caught in a flood, you'd be pulled in all directions. . . . It must've seemed to them that the world was coming to an end, that people were simply—"

Orain, lifting her head, saw that he was watching her intently.

Adred set aside his book and stood up, crossed the room to her. He didn't sit down but leaned over the table nearby, to turn up the wick in her lamp. "You could use some more light. . . ."

Her sewing lay still in her lap while Orain stared vacantly, not at Adred but toward some memory or insight. "Hasn't it occurred to you," she asked hollowly, "that with all those people dying out there, becoming sick and—dying . . . hasn't it occurred to you that at any moment you or I, both of us, could just start shaking and sweating and . . . that it could happen to us?" Now she looked at him. "Hasn't it? Occurred to you?"

The room was so quiet. Adred touched her hair. "Yes," he admitted. "It's occurred to me. Of course it has."

If she meant to reply to that, Orain was interrupted by a light knocking on the outer door. Adred moved to answer it, but the door opened before he reached it and Lord Abgarthis stepped in.

"I believe," the minister smiled tiredly, "that I smell the aroma of brewing tea."

"You do, indeed," grinned Adred. "Care for some?"

Abgarthis nodded and signaled hello to Orain as he seated himself at the small table where Adred had been reading.

"You look exhausted," Orain noticed.

The old man rubbed stiff fingers against his forehead. "I have a headache," he informed her. "I've never seen a day like this, never in all my—" He coughed a bit—and caught Orain's stare. "No, no, I'm not ill!" he reassured her. "The palace seems to've been spared; Galvus was quite correct in acting as he did, and so efficiently. But . . . out there—" He turned in his seat, stared at the closed windows. "They are burning bodies in every street. Can you smell the stench, or have you gotten used to it? Maybe that incense helps. Mountains of . . . bodies. . . ." Abgarthis turned again to accept his tea from Adred. "Thank you."

Adred sat down. "But no one in the palace has been stricken?"

"No." A shake of the head. "And the worst of it seems past. It's absolutely incredible, absolutely incredible. Our population is decimated. It strains sanity. In one day—" But Orain's expression caused Abgarthis to withhold further comment. "Yet the worst of it seems to have passed."

"In one day," Adred echoed. "A day and a night of plague."

"That's what Galvus said, too."

"Asawas."

"Yes. . . ."

Silence, for a moment.

Followed by the sounds of Orain as she resumed her sewing.

Abgarthis cleared his throat, sipped. "This tea of yours, Adred, is really quite ex—"

"It's just the beginning, isn't it, Abgarthis?"

"No . . . why, no. As I said, Sotos informs me that the worst seems to have passed. I don't think we'll—"

"I don't mean that. I mean—it's hard for me to think this way— but I don't mean the plague."

Abgarthis watched him.

"I mean," Adred said, "it's . . . only the beginning of it, isn't it?"

Abgarthis only stared at him, said nothing.

* * *

It had not been Elad's intention to stay any longer than necessary in the Salukadian palace; however, when Nihim invited him, Queen Salia and his retinue to share a meal, the king found himself willing to delay his departure. To some degree this was because Elad felt very uncomfortable in having his wife with him again under these circumstances, and he did not anticipate with any pleasure the first hours they must spend together alone. Dining with the *Ghen-usu* would postpone that. Besides, with the tension they had all undergone, Thomo, Hadd and Ostorian deserved some sociableness at the expense of these easterners.

The dinner was not a lavish affair. They sat with Nihim and one of his court advisers, bin-Sutus, at a table in the main feasting hall. Ten musicians played on stringed instruments and pipes while efficient servants busily placed trays and goblets and removed used dishes and utensils. Elad and Nihim engaged one another in moderate conversation, but the atmosphere was conducive neither to informally polite dialogue nor more serious discourse. Salia spoke not at all; yet with her posture and her expression she proclaimed more than she might have with words. Elad noticed this, as did General Thomo and Nihim. Her sadness, and her nervousness. The chance clanging of a fork against a goblet would cause her to react with shock; the yapping of a dog from some distant hallway would nearly bring Salia to weeping.

By early evening, then, Elad indicated that he had best return to his ship. He told Nihim that they would lift anchor in the morning.

"I trust," the *Ghen-usu* told him in carefully phrased Athadian, "that we may meet again one day and under more tolerable circumstances."

"It would please me greatly," Elad asserted. "I believe our businessmen and lawyers have concluded new documents with your government in regards to trade? That is fine. I will see to it, Lord Nihim, that in the future relations between you and I, between our thrones, remain on a more . . . elevated plane."

Nihim nodded to him in thanks. Taking Queen Salia's hand: "Patience," he encourged her. "Patience, my lady. And when you regard yourself in your mirror—" he betrayed a slight smile "—patience, as in all things."

"*Imdo, Ghen-usu-su*," was her simple reply.

"Mirrors?" Elad asked her, then looked at Nihim. He was thinking of something else.

Nihim explained, "It is a thing which your wife and I have discussed. Perhaps she will speak of it to you."

"I see. . . . ."

They were escorted outside by Salukadian guards, and there in the unnatural quiet of the evening, as they exchanged formal farewells, Lord Thomo made a request.

"I am certain," he said, "that Lord Sirom has by this time heard of our arrival. I think it wise, King Elad, that I inform him of what has occurred, and perhaps invite him aboard the *Crown* for a conference before we set sail tomorrow."

Elad was agreeable to this; he had intended to invite Lord Sirom to accompany him to the Salukadian palace, but plague rife in the city had argued against that. "Let me know as soon as possible," he instructed Thomo, "how Lord Sirom and his ministers fare. In regards to—" He gestured.

It was understood. "With the *Ghen-usu's* permission, then," Thomo stated—and Nihim was quick to offer him a carriage and the privilege of an armed escort.

Salia remained quiet and elusive during the carriage journey back to the harbor. Although once or twice Elad made hesitant motions or suggestions to her, his wife was remote. Half-way across the city, Salia whispered to him: "Please, allow me a little time . . . my husband. . . ." He did not know if she grieved for Agors or feared his own wrath at being cuckolded or was perhaps terrified of seeing her father again; perhaps she was saddened at having been taken from the Holy City, or was merely upset with herself and all that she must be held responsible for. . . .

There were crowds collected on the quays of the harbor. Angry crowds. Dung and bricks were hurled at the Athadian coach as it came to rest, and at Elad, Salia and their retinue as they were escorted by the Salukadian soldiers to their launch. Cries of "Death to them!" and "They brought us plague!" lifted in loud choruses. Elad was astonished. The soldiers did what they could to protect those in their custody, but still a thrown stone struck Major Ostorian on the cheek, bringing blood. The Salukadians helped Elad and his people into their longboat and stood guard as they were oared to the flagship.

It was as they approached the *Crown* that Elad felt the first stirrings in him. A slight uncertainty or fluttering in his stomach; a dew of perspiration on his brow and cheeks. For a moment, the dull voices of those around him seemed to recede into the distance; then the swinging lamps of the flagship blurred and danced away from him. He felt something knock him on the head, and only when strong arms grabbed him and lifted him up did he realize that he'd fallen forward in an attack of dizziness.

Salia cried out to him, "Elad? Are you all right?"

Hadd whispered something in a distraught voice.

He tried to speak but could not; his skin suddenly erupted with perspiration as though he'd been washed with sea spray. He couldn't hear the people around him; he could barely feel Salia's arms clutching him.

"Elad? *Elad!*"

He supposed that she was shaking him, but he was shivering so greatly that he could not be certain. The violence in his stomach burned hotly up his throat, threatening to strangle him. Earnestly Elad threw himself against the gunwale of the boat and dropped his swollen head over the side; he clutched his stomach with both hands as the hotness blurted from him, choking him and freeing him, drying his mouth, staining him, bringing tears to his eyes and vicious waves of pain to his bowels. . . .

"*Elad!*"

Watching from where he sat, Major Hadd swallowed and felt his own throat for any symptoms of illness. "Name of the gods," he whispered tensely, "now it's got King Elad!"

Nihim watched from the roof of the palace as the small dark shadow on the waves blurred into the shining dots of small light that marked the Athadian flagship. In him, a million thoughts, a thousand feelings and doubts, urgencies and—

bin-Sutus's footsteps were like the silent pads of an animal.

"Yes?" Nihim did not turn. The hazy wind of the evening was yet cool, and he was intrigued by the hundreds of ships in his harbor with their thousands of burning lamps like eyes.

"*Ghen-usu*, I regretfully bring you word from our physicians that your brother has gone on from this life."

Nihim took in a shuddering breath. "*Sharu n'ghen.* . . . Thank you, bin-Sutus."

"The physicians are ready to speak with you, whenever you wish, *ko-Ghen-usu*."

Nihim turned and eyed bin-Sutus critically. "Do not call me that, my friend. Do not call me that. And rather than speak with physicians, it is better that we call into council our *aihman-sas* and ministers of the *Hulm*."

"Nihim, what do you mean?"

"I have no intention of taking the throne from my brother's ghost. I have no intention, bin-Sutus, of becoming *ghen* of my father's empire."

In the evening, in the darkness, in Herulia.

The sharecropper had given Asawas a ride in his wagon; together they sat as the young farmer guided his skeletal horse down the winding dusty road, back toward his homestead. He complained to Asawas that he had gone three days without food, save what he could scavenge; his corn had all dried up and blown away long ago, and the man who had sold him his land had died, too. He didn't know what he would tell his wife, who was waiting for him in their small hut—awaiting his return with the food he'd promised to find at the nearest village.

"I'd intended to sell my horse, even my cart, for whatever anyone would offer me. Not even money. Money doesn't mean anything when there's no food to buy; food is more important than money." He was fatigued, his head ached, and as he spoke he nearly broke into tears several times. "I don't care about myself," the sharecropper told Asawas. "It's my wife and my little daughter. My wife and I would gladly give our lives to the gods if it would keep our little girl alive."

When they reached his hut the young farmer was alarmed to see three ill-groomed horses tethered in his yard. Excited, he leaped from his wagon, failing even to unhitch his horse, and ran to his home, bursting in through the door. Asawas suspected his fears; but he took the time himself to free the mare and tether her at a tree, so that she might graze on the parched grass, before following his friend through the opened door.

When he entered, Asawas saw three bruised, tattered soldiers wearing Athadian armor sitting on the hearth of the fireplace. The sharecropper was crouched beside his wife, who was kneeling beside their daughter's crib. It was apparent to the prophet that the young husband's foremost fear had been unfounded: these soldiers had not molested his wife, nor had they ransacked his home, and they were now sitting content and sipping small bowls of soup. None spoke to him as he came in, but all stared uncertainly at this tall, gray-haired man dressed in his robe and worn sandals.

Asawas closed the door of the hut and crossed the room to the farmer and his wife; his staff knocked hollowly as a gigantic heartbeat on the floor. As his shadow fell across the crib, the young man looked up at him and pronounced:

"My daughter is very ill. She has a fever."

The prophet shook his head. "More than a fever . . . ." He urged the sharecropper to his feet, looked into the eyes of the wife, then knelt beside the crib himself and examined the small child, pressing his rough fingers upon forehead, cheeks, throat. Without announcing his intention Asawas lifted the little girl from her blankets and embraced her, held her close to him. To the mother's expression of shock: "Do not fear. She will be well."

She looked to her husband. He was resigned already to what must be and could offer her no comfort.

Asawas moved to a stool in a corner of the room, sat and held the child in his lap. So feverish was she, so silent and nearly gone, that she made no sound or effort, even as she was taken from her mother's presence by this intruder.

One of the soldiers sitting by the hearth asked Asawas: "What are you? Are you a priest?"

"Yes," he answered. "I am a priest."

"Priests don't seem to be doing much better than soldiers or farmers, these days."

"That's true, I'm afraid."

"Where are you going? Are you going south? You'd better go south, and get away from the fighting. There's a war on."

"I can't go south, my friend. I am traveling east."

"The only thing east of here is Emaria."

"That is so."

"We came from Emaria. Our whole unit was wiped out. We're the only ones that survived. There's a war on in Emaria, don't you know that?"

Asawas smiled faintly. "Yes . . . I understand that there's a war on."

152

"King Thameron's soldiers are murdering everyone. They're not even soldiers, they're butchers. You won't be able to—"

The young mother, filling a bowl with soup for her husband, suddenly sobbed in anguish, dropped the wooden bowl, threw out an arm to support herself against the fireplace. The farmer went to her and held her; she shook her head and after a moment gently pushed him away, retrieved the bowl and ducked it into the pot that simmered over the low fire. He took his bowl to the table in the center of the room while his wife, wiping her face, cautiously approached Asawas. She looked at him deeply, then knelt beside him on the floor, at his feet. She lifted one hand, placed a finger in a tuck of her baby's clothes and sat that way.

"Nothing but . . . war in Emaria. . . ." the speaking soldier said quietly.

"How far," Asawas asked him, "am I from Lasura?"

The soldiers stared at him, thinking him mad.

"Please—how far? I have a reason for asking."

"Three days on foot. Two and a half days."

The farmer's wife whispered to Asawas: "There is soup—"

"Do not fear; I won't hurt your child. And I am not so hungry. Share your food with these men. They're fatigued and need the nourishment."

"Will—" Her voice choked; she coughed slightly, licked her dry lips. "Will—will my baby live?"

The prophet stared into her eyes and read her entire soul in them. He nodded. "Your baby will live, yes."

The sharecropper, at the table, made a noise as he set his bowl down. He glanced at the prophet and ducked his head once, thanking him for so comforting a lie. *Our child will live on in the bosom of the gods, no, priest?*

Asawas reassured him, "Your daughter will live. Take your rest, my friend. Your daughter will be well in the morning."

The mother sobbed, one of the soldiers whispered to the other two, and the young farmer stood up to fill his bowl with another helping of soup.

3.

Mankind is a storm passing upon the face of the world.

Trapped on earth, trapped by our hopes and memories, where is our answer if not within ourselves? Where is our cause, if not within ourselves? O many-faced, all-voiced humanity, your enemy is astride your shoulder, it is fast-held in your mirror, it breathes with your breath, quickens with your life, dreams with your dreams.

O Time, your face is human.

O Death, your name is Man.

O Man, your names are legion. . . .

Everywhere, in all the lands and provinces and places, in all the cities and towns and villages of all the places: humanity, answering itself with itself—

Young men with their young girlfriends, as jealous of them as they would be of possessions, hovering close by them, seeking to impress them and yet wary of them, doubting that they will be understood, speaking with gross movements, awkward but hopeful—

In a tavern, a woman speaking to her husband, her voice caressing him cruelly with planned insults: "She's the one? Over there? That one? I really thought you had better taste than that!"—

Children and old people sitting on benches, sharing wonders with one another, telling truths, recalling memories as young as hope and as old as bone—

Two young men, companions, and when one burps because of the beer he has drunk the other tries to pass wind in a contest of noises, and they laugh and giggle at their foolishness—

A gravedigger falling asleep at his toil while the crowds around him weep and scream in the lamplight in the tossing darkness, because of all the death that has come, all the death that has made its home with them where they had assumed there were other kinds of promises—

Beautiful courtesans with shimmering oiled bodies, aromatic, their breasts rolling softly with their movements and their painted fingernails sparkling, with coiffed hairstyles and their legs wrapped in ribbons of gold and silver, laughing with men in the room full of draperies and incense and pillows, far from home and laughing at jokes or passing kisses around the table, sharing grapes they have plucked with their mouths—

In an alley, one man attempting to rob another—

In the streets, growing boys, tattooed and laughing, trying in earnest to accommodate the fashionable dangers of the day as they walk along, trading curses and taking dares—

In a barracks house, a group of soldiers playing cards, and one of them (drunk) intimidating another: "I told you not to touch that wine, didn't I? Didn't I tell you not to? Then why are you doing it? Why do you want your arms broken? Do you want your arms broken?"—

And in this place high in the attic where he sometimes comes to hide, and where although he doesn't know it is his older sister comes to make love with the youth she is infatuated with, a young boy by candlelight works patiently at his drawings, using a stick of charcoal on old pieces of parchment and worn paper, trying to become a great artist like those men and women he has seen in the square—

And a distraught young woman is weeping in the arms of a dark-eyed priest, terrified because the one she loved died during the plague: "He told me we'd be together forever and that we would be married and that he wanted . . . I have his *baby* in me! and now he's dead, he *lied* to me, I believed him and why did he do this to me? why? *why?*"—

While in a dark patch of forest in Emaria a soldier lies dying in the cool of the night, listening to the sounds of his blood, listening to the insects and watching the fading moon and the stars high above him, disgusted and terrified and angry, very angry, because the world had promised him much and it had lied to him, because his body so strong and pliant and quick had betrayed him—

And on a ship, one of hundreds in the harbor, the king of the world lies dying and shivering, sweating, groaning. He cannot hear the speech of the voices around him, he cannot hear the arguments of his commanders of troops or the hot words exchanged by his wife and her powerful, wrathful father. The voices he hears—

The voices he hears belong to other times and all are in his memory, all are out of the past, reminders of his guilt that confuse him, torment him, carry him away anguished: and they do not carry him away carefully and peacefully, as voices and memories should when men pass on from this burial ground of woe, this earth filled with crowds of corpses hidden from our view beneath our hurrying feet—

"Elad!"

"Oh, gods, is he dead, is he—"

"Elad! *Elad*!"

"Salia, come—"

"As each human being has three selves, so do you have three enemies. Your first is a mirror, your second a blade, your third a foreign countenance. Mirrors betray depth while having no depth. Blades have two sides, two edges and one point. Countenances are masks for the minds beneath."

"Gods, live! Dursoris, live! Oh, gods, I do not want this! I do not want this throne!"

"Your father used to compare the actions of a king to the stone that is dropped in a pool of water. Concentric waves speed out from all around the dropped stone—from the king—"

"Ab—Abgarthis. . . . ?"

"Quiet, he's speaking, he's—"

Sweating and groaning. . . .

"The gods test me, Abgarthis; and they test me to test the empire, they test our history, they test every great man and every shallow man who calls himself an Athadian. And I have failed the gods, haven't I?"

"We live in troubled times, and these prophets play upon the fears of the people. They argue that we are living at the end of time, and they say that people should prepare for the world's destruction."

"You will take the throne, and none other after you, and you will rule to see everything precious destroyed, every hope ruined, every man and woman wailing in torment."

"S—Salia . . . Salia, listen to—me. . . ."

"Don't go near him, can't you see—"

"Imbur, leave the room! Leave this cabin immediately! You're only—"

"Elad, I'm here! I'm here, I'm so sorry—"

"What holds all this together? If tomorrow we decided to end the pretense, we could. It's all held together by only a thread, as if

156

all of us concealed some great deep secret. One real doubt—one voice loud enough—and it's over."

"Elad. . . ."

"Do you know what we are? Do you know what Man is? Man is a fearful animal; he is an anxious animal, a doubtful animal. Man is an animal of fear. One doubt, one whisper . . . the awful truth returns."

"Salia . . . Salia . . . ?"

"I'm here, Elad! I'm here, my heart! I'm so sorry, I never meant to—"

"I'm going to live, Salia. I—I'm going to live. . . ."

"Yes, Elad, yes, you are, you are! You're going to live!"

"I'm feeling better . . . I can see you . . . my strength's returning, it's so—aston— I feel much stronger . . . tell Iso . . . the physician . . . I am going to live—"

"Yes, Elad, *yes!* Hold my hand, hold it . . . can you feel it? My heart, I'm so sorry I ever did this to you, I'm so sorry I ever— Hold my hand, Elad! Elad . . . *hold my hand, Elad! Hold my hand!* You're going to live, you're feeling better! Don't— Elad, don't die! *Don't die!* You're going to— My heart, *don't die!* Quickly, get the physician! Bring him in here, get the— Hurry! *Elad . . . !*"

What holds it all together? What?

Dawn, gray at the porthole window.

Tapers burned low, some extinguished.

Salia crouched above the bed, still applying the damp cloth to his brow.

Iso, alone with her in the stillness, watching.

Watching

Listening. . . .

Placing hand to forehead, neck, breast, mouth.

Iso, tired, pushed away Salia's hand. "No more, my queen. He is past all that."

Tapers burned low, some extinguished, smoking.

* * *

A little before dawn one of the sentries on lookout in the watch nest of the *Crown* called down that a small launch was sighted coming out to sea. It was close by and unlighted. The Imbur Ogodis, in command, ordered twenty archers to stand at the ready until the intention of the craft could be determined.

As the early gray of dawn lit the misty waters all around, Thomo perceived that the craft was listing, being pulled out to the ocean on no fixed course. As the small boat veered around off to starboard, Ogodis judged that it contained but one passenger, a man in weakened condition. Against the advice of Major Thytagoras, Ogodis ordered a launch sent out to recover the vessel.

The Imbur, Thytagoras, Elad's commanders of legions and other officers and soldiers watched patiently as the sailors from the flagship steered out to retrieve the Salukadian boat. They managed to help its passenger into their own craft and quickly rowed back to the *Crown*. As they came within clear sight, the Imbur called down: "Who is it?"

"General Thomo, my lord! And he is sorely wounded!"

Thytagoras struck a gloved fist on the railing. "Name of the gods! What has happened?"

Within moments Thomo was hauled aboard. His clothing was in tatters and bloody, his armor dented and in places undone; he was bruised and cut on his face, arms and legs; he had lost his sword. Ogodis eased him to the boards and ordered water brought; Thomo slurped it, coughing and gasping.

"What is it?" Ogodis demanded. "Tell us! What—"

"I must see . . . King Elad . . . immediately!"

The Imbur told him: "But the king cannot see you."

"Where is he? This is of . . . the utmost—"

"Elad is dead."

"*What*?"

"He died during the night, Thomo. After he returned here. The plague."

"Name of the—" General Thomo sank back, head and arms trembling; he slapped one gloved fist repeatedly on the wet boards of the deck. "No, *no! Damn* all the gods, they can't let this happen *now*!" He lay there for a long moment, stunned, gasping, staring, teeth clenched.

The Imbur cleared his throat. "General Thomo, I think it best—"

"Help me up." He raised his arms.

Ogodis and Major Ostorian bent forward, took hold of Thomo and lifted him to his feet. The general stood himself against the rail; he wiped a shivering hand across his mouth, which still seeped blood.

"Get a doctor," Ogodis ordered Ostorian—and then, more loudly, to one of the guards who'd collected there: "Get Iso, get the physician!"

"And . . . wine!" Thomo called after him. "Get me—"

"Lord General." Major Hamaro moved forward, proffering a flagon. "Silesian."

"Thank you. . . ." He unstoppered it and swallowed a long draft before handing it back.

"Now," the Imbur asked him, "can you tell us what happened?"

Thomo nodded quickly, sucked in another breath, tried to move around so that he might see the city. It was yet all dark, shadowed beneath the night's clouds, save for distantly flickering lights of lamps and torches, very small. "Sirom. . . . Lord Sirom is dead, as well. Beheaded." When the amazed, angry voices around him died down: "There are riots—there is blood in the streets—"

"These *easterners*?" Thytagoras barked, interrupting.

General Thomo replied with a stern stare and proceeded: "From what I can make of it, we're being blamed for bringing the plague to Erusabad, and for . . . the death of Agors. It's an excuse. It's an excuse . . . for bloodshed. Thousands of them, avenging the *ghen* and killing the westerners. Us. . . . It's broken loose at last. It's all broken down at last. It . . . it had to, finally. . . ."

"By the gods!" swore Thytagoras. "I won't stand for—"

"Be quiet!" Ogodis snapped at him. "Thomo! What about Nihim? What about him?"

The lord general shook his head. "I didn't see him. I'd have been killed, too—almost was. Except I was using one of Nihim's carriages—that's the only thing that saved me. I hid in it . . . hid. The drivers brought me back to the harbor. Couldn't get near the palace. Blood everywhere, people— Did what I could—stole that boat. Had to fight three of them. Killed them. . . ."

"You did the right thing!" Major Thytagoras assured him. "You did the proper thing, General!"

Thomo ignored him, faced the Imbur anxiously. "Elad is truly . . . dead?"

A solemn nod.

"And Salia? Queen Salia?"

"No," Ogodis told him. "She yet lives."

"Thank the gods."

"Iso the physician!" a voice called out, and some of the officers crowded near Thomo moved back so that the old leech, accompanied by three young guards bearing torches, could examine the lord general.

"If you'll make your way to your cabin, sir," Iso suggested, "I can treat you better. Be able to see."

"In a moment, in a moment. Get this cut in my mouth to stop bleeding."

Iso grunted and from a sack slung over one shoulder retrieved a small wooden box. He opened it and fingered the green paste inside, asked General Thomo to open his mouth. "Give me more light, here. . . ."

Thomo hissed through his nose as the bitter paste touched his cut mouth. Iso rubbed the gums and inside the right cheek, then wiped his fingers on his robe.

"This tastes like—"

"Leave it alone, don't lick it off! Let it stay there. It'll stop the bleeding."

Thomo sneered at him and asked Hamaro for another sip of wine.

Abruptly, Major Hadd exclaimed, "The city! Look at it!"

Thomo pivoted. Voices rose, cursing, while the skyline of Erusabad blossomed with a warm orange glow, flagrant and brilliant against the black night and stars.

"Damn them, I expected it!" the lord general swore. "That's from the east end!"

"Setting fire to their own city!" Hadd said, as though he didn't believe it.

"They're burning Athadians," Thomo told him. "They're setting fire to Athadian apartments and buildings."

Thytagoras chuckled cruelly; his tone was so obscene, it

threatened to burst into true laughter. "So it's come to war at last! *At last!*"

"No!" Thomo lifted an arm, pointed a finger at him. "No, it has *not* come to war at last, Major Thytagoras! It has *not* come—"

"They're killing *Athadian citizens*!" Thytagoras reminded him. "They're killing our—*your own people* in that city!"

"The fact of the matter is that no direct provocation has been made against—"

"Damn you!" roared Thytagoras. "Provocation? *Provocation?* Those *barbarians* are *slaughtering*—"

"Erusabad, Major!" Thomo nearly yelled. "Erusabad is *not* an Athadian city! Do you understand that? Do you understand what that *means*? Do you—"

"Do *you* understand what it *means*, Lord General? Those are *your people*! It doesn't matter whether—"

"Major Thytagoras!" the Imbur shouted. He stepped between the two of them, facing Thytagoras and daring him to speak further. Thytagoras reined his temper. Slowly Ogodis looked to General Thomo. "Surely," he said in a whisper, "you cannot mean what you say?"

Thomo, tongue working inside his mouth, replied adamantly: "There has been no direct provocation upon us, Imbur—not upon this fleet. And what happens in that city is no concern of ours; it's outside our jurisdiction. Erusabad is a Salukadian city, now."

Thytagoras, moving away to stand in the shadow of the forward bulkhead, grunted: "And that was only the *first* of Elad's mistakes!" He stared directly at the Imbur.

Ogodis recognized the slander but refused to make reply; keeping his eyes on Thomo: "Be that as it may, Lord General, I ask you again—surely you cannot mean what you say? Those are your people being murdered!"

Thomo stared at him frankly. Behind Ogodis he saw the hardened, impassioned expressions of his Athadian officers.

"No. . . ." he whispered, his voice troubled. "I do not mean what I say. And I will give the command to siege and occupy that city, if I find it necessary."

"You don't think it necessary *now*?" Major Dever asked him.

"Nihim," Thomo told him, "is a good man and an honest one. I want to give him time. We would ask for as much, ourselves, were we in his position. Too much has happened too quickly, far too quickly. If we begin an attack now, then we must see it through; and I refuse to begin it unless it is the only recourse left us. We must remain patient and . . . *objective*, until it is absolutely imperative that we draw our swords." He stared at every officer there, letting his gaze linger on the bellicose Thytagoras, who yet stood half in shadows. "For now . . . you officers had best take command of your vessels. You'll be signalled."

Now Thytagoras strode forward. "How much 'time,' Lord General?"

Thomo was exhausted, wounded, and at the end of his patience. "I am ordering my arrow sent up immediately, Major! And I'll await Nihim's reply! And if he doesn't reply by dawn, then I'll order up *another* arrow! And perhaps a *third*!"

Thytagoras sneered. "And if we're provo—"

Thomo growled at him, "Take your sword and swim into the harbor if you're so eager to kill them, Thytagoras! Now lower those longboats!" Loudly, to the hands on deck: "Lower those longboats! These officers are returning to their flagships!"

The flaming arrow was released into the dark pre-dawn sky; but Thomo had already gone below to rest for the few hours remaining before morning. He had intended to enter Elad's cabin and pay his respects to his king's memory, but Iso told him there would be time enough for that and ordered him into his own bunk, where the physician could examine the lord general's several wounds. Thomo had been cut in the right side and in the leg and had as well sustained numerous bruises and scrapes. None of his injuries were severe, but Iso nonetheless washed them thoroughly and applied poultices and bandages.

"I should give you something to make you sleep."

"Not right now, Iso; not just yet. I'll take my rest when this has passed."

Lying in his bunk, Thomo tried to rest but could not. From time to time he overheard Queen Salia's and the Imbur's voices, speaking loudly from her cabin. But he could not decipher their words.

At last, knowing he would never calm himself, Thomo ordered King Elad's maps and plans of strategy brought to him, and he

162

pored over these as the gray light of dawn gradually filled the porthole window above him.

4.

As dawn broke over Erusabad the *aihman-sas* and ministers of court and the tribal lords collected with Nihim *Ghen-usu* in the Audience Hall of the Salukadian palace. Nihim, like the others, sat in a chair on the lowest level of the floor; both thrones on the dais remained empty, for with the death of Agors there was no *ghen* to inherit the throne or claim eminence over the *Hulm*. To this collected body of eastern lords came officials of the city guard to relate the list of incidents that had happened so quickly during the night.

Groups of militant fanatics, Salukadians armed with torches, farm implements and weapons gained on the black market, had charged into several quarters of the Holy City and attacked Athadian homes, businesses and citizens. Included in this first wave of violence had been the Athadian government's Central Authority Building, and the official Athadian ambassador in residence, Lord Sirom, had been slain.

In response to this, groups of westerners had quickly organized and, led by outraged units of the resident Athadian armed forces, had clashed with them in the streets, predominantly on the westside around the Himu Square, on the east side in the vicinity of the Kinesh Square and Avarra Bridge and by the northside dock areas in the region of the Kurad Square. These locales had been evacuated as well as could be managed and were now blocked off.

In Lekusa Street and for an area comprising four city streets to either side, a gang identifying itself as the *Ghenluks*, or "Ghen avengers," had attacked the Temple of Bithitu and the offices where the cult known as the Doom-Soulers were prone to congregate, and they had taken a heavy toll of lives. A number of these *Ghenluks* had been arrested.

Presently, in four barricaded sections of the westside and the northside near the palace, groups of Athadian citizens were assembled under the protection of loyal city guards and *hetmuk-sas*, and these citizens wished to leave Erusabad as soon as possible.

Furthermore, the carriage opertor who had been ordered by Nihim to deliver the Athadian Lord General Thomo to the Central Authority Building had reported that he had been unable to do as instructed because of the violence and so had followed General Thomo's directions in returning him to the harbor. The fate of General Thomo since that time was not known. But the watch on the western walls had reported a signal arrow released by the Athadian government's flagship *Crown* shortly before dawn.

Nihim and the lords of the *Hulm* quickly discussed these matters. As apparent as it was that the distresses of the night had been directed toward the westerners in Erusabad, it was likewise apparent that King Elad had not yet seen fit to retaliate and declare open hostilities against Salukadia. Nihim felt, deep in his heart, that the signal flare had been ordered by Elad as a sign that the two of them should meet on a neutral territory and decide between them how to resolve this crisis before it should escalate further and lead to open warfare.

With this assessment of the situation his lords concurred, although a few held reservations regarding the wisdom of the *Ghen-usu* placing himself in jeopardy while tempers were yet prone to excess; and thus one elder seated there, Utto-sen-gar, advanced a proposal for military preparedness. sen-gar was the *hetmuk* of all Salukadian military forces and police troops in Erusabad, and he had been awarded that post by Huagrim *ko-Ghen* for having faithfully served both Huagrim and the late *Ghen's* father Huabrul in their wars of conquest. His counsel was mightily respected. And though it was accepted by the men of the *Hulm* that Nihim should be given deference in this hall (albeit Huagrim in his will had left the throne to Agors and Agors's progeny, and none other), still all agreed that Erusabad itself and all of Salukadia must be certain of their defenses—and Nihim, with his pacifistic and religious views, should not alone be entrusted with the weight of such matters. Nihim himself concurred with this, and allowed Utto-sen-gar sole discretion in alerting the army of Erusabad into preparation for possible conflict.

This resolved, Nihim ordered a torched arrow sent up from the western walls of the Holy City, so that Elad on his flagship might see it and know that the *Ghen-usu* wished to parley.

And as a man of the guard left the Audience Hall to accomplish

164

this, and while the lords and ministers of the *Hulm* slowly disbanded, conversing and sharing opinions, Nihim found himself recalling a somber passage from the *Wo Ahyat* of Toshin:

> *The sharp faces of sword and axe*
> *Become the faces of funeral crowds,*
> *Wan beneath the sky gray as steel.*
> *No warrior inherits the world as it was*
> *Before he unsheathed his weapon.*
> *The child is ripped dead from the womb*
> *Before it has life-shi to protest.*
> *Grim wheel: the dying murder the dead.*

Onboard Ogodis's flagship, the *Jewel*, Major Thytagoras sat with Udi, a Minesian conscripted into the Imbur's service and by profession a thrower of bones and a star reader. As the first full light of morning hazed the window of his cabin, Thytagoras leaned forward in his chair, his expression taut, as the cross-legged Udi, crouched on the floor, read the patterns of the colored bones he'd just cast and compared them to the horoscope he had drawn up on the night the Gaegoshan fleet had left Sugat.

Every night during this voyage Udi and Thytagoras had met thus, and the seer had thrown his bones and informed the officer of how the portents read and what the future suggested.

"Today," the Minesian nodded, looking from chart to bones and back again. "Today . . . yes. Here you are, commander—" He pressed a finger on the parchment.

"Sidru in the sign of the Wolf," Thytagoras grunted.

"Yes . . . you were born in the Wolf, and Sidru is the Wolf's planet. And all these planets have come around, finally, above this city."

"War." Major Thytagoras breathed the word as though personally infusing life into its syllable. "I, the man of war born in the sign of conflict, here in the city in the shadow of war."

Udi's own attitude was grave. "War, yes. A great destruction. . . . The Lion is in the sign of Water."

Thytagoras chuckled. "At last we'll put these savages to the sword! I suppose it was necessary for things to wait until—this moment. A purpose in it."

"A purpose." Udi, slim and bearded, stared at him. "You hate these people—almost too strongly. I must ask you a question."

"Ask what you please."

"Your mother was born in Erusabad, commander; I know this. But your father—"

"How do you know it?"

Udi ducked his head. "You told me."

"Did I?"

"When I asked you for the events of your birth. Your mother was Sabhite."

"Is it there? Is it in my chart?"

"Yes."

Thytagoras smiled grimly. "I'm avenging her," he allowed. "I'm avenging her spirit." He stood up, stretched, stared at the window. "So war will come today."

"The signs say a conflict will begin today. The Lion is in the sign of Water—the throne of Athad, in water."

"A naval battle?"

"I assume so. That—or we bury Elad their king today, in the water."

"Every night I ask you to interpret those bones and that chart, Minesian—every night for a month. And you can never tell me anything for certain. Don't the stars ever tell you what *will* happen?"

"Men decide what will happen, commander. The stars suggest; men accomplish, or they do not accomplish. The stars—they are the current of a river. The fish is pulled along by the current of the river, but it can swim against the current, too."

Thytagoras sneered. "Well, we'll see who swims against currents today." He walked to the window, stared out.

The Minesian collected his bones, dropped them into the pouch that hung from his belt, leaned to roll up his parchment. "But . . . *why* do you want to kill so many people, commander?" he asked.

"Must there be a reason, Udi?"

"Yes. Yes, there must be. Somewhere in you is the reason for this hatred of the Salukads."

Thytagoras turned to face him. "No," he said. "No reason. I can give you many excuses, yes, for hating these people—for wanting to destroy them, for wanting to cleanse the earth of the very idea, the very memory of them. Yes . . . excuses I can give you. But . . . 'reasons'? I'm not so sure, Udi. I don't think there are any reasons. I am simply here to hate the Salukads as passionately as other men hate other things."

Udi was much troubled by this. "Still," he pursued, "there must be a reason. For a man to feel so strongly about one thing that he degrades everything else in—"

"It's a game, Minesian. No one but me seems to realize that. We play the game passionately, but the game itself is dispassionate. Why did the gods give us life? Is there any good reason for it? Excuses, yes—many excuses that the priests and the philosophers love to rattle on about. But—reasons? It's a game. Perhaps there is no other purpose to a game than that it *is* a game."

Udi spoke softly. "All . . . those people. . . ."

"There will always be people," Thytagoras reminded him. "Kill as many as you can—there will always be more. Always." He lifted a hand, regarded it as he clenched it into a fist.

Near the wrist was a deep scar, half-circling his forearm, the result of a deep wound Thytagoras had once inflicted on himself. He had been young. He could give no one any reason for having attempted such a thing, while in the prime of his youth, and he had come to the realization that there was no reason for trying to take his own life. No reason to do so, no reason not to do so.

But that had been many years ago, when he had taken things very seriously—before he had learned that there were no reasons, and that everything was nothing more than—

A game.

Lord General Thomo answered the torched arrow from the Salukadians by ordering three longboats lowered and rowed halfway toward the outer harbor of the city. There, he waited as two flat-bottomed eastern skiffs put out to sea and moved toward him. In one, Nihim *Ghen-usu*; in the other, a coterie of armed warriors, their bows notched and ready.

As were the bows of the soldiers standing at attention in the longboats to either side of Lord Thomo.

When Nihim, alone in his boat save for two oarsmen, broke from the armed vessel and came into open water, Thomo ordered the rowers in his skiff to move ahead, as well. Shortly the two of them joined their crafts together and, in a somber mood, spoke.

"My king fell ill during the carriage ride to the harbor," Thomo told Nihim. "He died last night, aboard the ship."

"Believe me, Thomo-*su*, when I say I grieve for you and wish rest and peace upon Elad King's spirit."

"I do believe you, Lord Nihim."

And when he asked of the fires they had noticed last night, Thomo's fears were proved well founded: portions of the Holy City had erupted with violence just before dawn and much blood had been shed. Many Athadian citizens were dead.

"Yet I hope," Nihim said, "that you will not place the blame for these excesses upon me, or upon my government."

"I do not, Nihim-*su*. But my officers encourage me to answer such violence with arms. We must make certain that our citizens in Erusabad can live safely and at peace with your people. This was the first condition set down by my late king when he agreed to acknowledge your proprietorship of the city."

"This is true, and I respect your concern. What can I teach you about the human heart that you do not know? Be assured that these acts were performed by outlaws and untrustworthy soldiers, that the incidents were not planned or in any way done with my permission or the permission of my council, and that they shall not recur. I—and my men of the *Hulm*—would like to make a generous show of good faith in this regard."

"And what is that, Nihim *Ghen-usu*?"

"Many of your citizens in Erusabad wish to leave the city, for they fear for their lives. I feel that their fears are unfounded, despite the occurrences of last night. But I will allow these people to quit Erusabad, if you will offer them refuge and transport."

Thomo considered the offer. "I will agree to do this, but on one added condition."

"And this is?"

"I know my officers will demand some form of restitution for the atrocities committed last night. Before they pursue this matter further with me, may I offer them payment from your government, in a gesture of indemnity for these taken lives?"

Nihim answered without hesitation. "You may. Name your sum, and know that I will fill the belly of your flagship with

168

riches, if you so desire—although a ship's hold of wealth cannot compensate for one stolen moment of life."

"I thank you, *Ghen-usu*. I know this gesture of respect will help to ameliorate the dissension among my officers."

"The *Hulm* has also agreed that certain select members of your officers may witness the executions of the perpetrators of these crimes, if that too will help to satisfy any doubt among them."

Thomo smiled ruefully. "I am sure that, for many of them, that will be more satisfactory than the promise of money. I accept."

"This we plan to accomplish in a day or two. To let the passions wane, in the meanwhile."

"A wise decision."

"Your Queen Salia," Nihim asked, "—is she well? Or was she—"

"No. She is well, and survives her husband."

"That is good."

"And you will begin this morning delivering refugees to us, *Ghen-usu*?"

"Yes. The moment I return, I will relay your agreement to my hetmuk, Utto-sen-gar. You have met him."

"Yes, I've had the pleasure." Thomo eyed the great walls of Erusabad and saw the many soldiers lined there, weapons bright in the day's new sun. "I see," he observed quietly, "that you have regiments of troops along your fortifications. These are for defense?"

Nihim grinned. "I see," he replied, "that you have warships in our harbor and many men with weapons. These are for your defense?"

Thomo laughed openly and honestly, nodding his head in approval. "Yes, for defense! For we know that no one will attack us with such a display!"

Nihim glanced around toward the city. "Yes . . . for we know, too, that no one will attack us." He faced the lord general, lifted a hand to shield his eyes against the glare of the sun on the open water. "I say to you what I said to your king, Lord Thomo-*su*, too short a time ago: When this has passed, I hope we will meet again, and under more tolerable circumstances."

"I pray so, *Ghen-usu*. I look forward to the day."

They shook arms, then, and unhooked their crafts, and each ordered their oarsmen to return to the armed escort.

169

When Thomo reached the decks of the *Crown*, he informed his officers of what had transpired between Nihim and himself. Some of them—Dever, Hamaro, Ogodis—argued that the lord general had been much too lenient and generous in his bargaining with "the savage prince," and announced that they were offended by Thomo's accepting gross money and jewels, even as a token payment, in restitution for murdered Athadians. To which Thomo replied with a question: Did these officers prefer to repay these Athadian citizens' lives with many more Athadian soldiers' lives, and make of this a cause for war?

Tensions relaxed. King Elad's body, which had been prepared for purification during General Thomo's conference with Nihim, was now brought onto the middeck for a funeral service. This was performed by a priest from the Temple of Bithitu, one of the fourteen who had accompanied the armada. Queen Salia, who held close to her father, was unnaturally—and somewhat suspiciously—silent and still throughout the service, and remained so even when Elad's sarcophagus was lowered over the side and placed in an oil-soaked longboat.

And the queen continued to watch, silent, unmoving, as the boat was heaved out to sea and set upon its course in the ocean. Lord General Thomo himself, breathing his own private prayers to the gods, loosed the flaming arrow that set the longboat and coffin ablaze. As the flames grew tall and the oily black smoke poured up into the blue sky, the longboat seemed to steer its own course through the hundreds of galleys and biremes that stretched away in ranks to either side of it. And as it was carried out by the currents, great trumpetings and the beating of drums sounded from all those warships—the hailing of the king of Athadia into the throne hall of the gods and to a seat beside that of Bithitu, with his father and grandfathers.

Late in the morning Ogodis escorted his daughter back to their flagship, the *Jewel*. There, Queen Salia removed herself to her cabin, secured the door, and allowed no one entrance. Ogodis, aware of her grief, self-anger and exhaustion, was tolerant of this.

On the forward deck Major Thytagoras, when he heard from Ogodis of Thomo's agreement with the *Ghen-usu*, was unsparing in his denunciation of it. Bitterly reviling the lord general's fatuousness, Thytagoras openly declared that Thomo had been duped and that the cost would be counted in additional Athadian lives. Ogodis rebuked him harshly and sternly forbade his accompanying him when the Imbur returned to the *Crown* to witness the initial evacuations.

But, not to be thwarted, Thytagoras ordered a second skiff lowered as soon as Ogodis had gone and had himself rowed to the decks of the *Iviton*, a galley which, along with the Athadian flagship and fifteen others, was positioned in the first line facing the harbor of the Holy City.

The first of the refugees were brought out aboard a *surk* and were taken on by the crew of the trireme *Falcon*. The *surk* was a long, two-masted vessel built for rapid cruising along shorelines, and it had been adopted by the Salukadians (not a sea-going people) during their conquests of the coastal cities and towns. Lord General Thomo and his officers watched as the *Falcon* lifted anchor and began to make its way out to sea—and Port Abustad.

By mid-afternoon a second transport of Athadians was accepted aboard the *Pride*. And even as the *surk* that had relayed them returned to harbor, another took to the waves with a third group of Athadian evacuees.

But as these passengers were making their way onto the decks of the *Star*, a brown-sailed *surk* moved out from its mooring farther north, beyond the general activity of those ships passing in and out of the main harbor areas. This brown-sailed vessel came on quickly, under full speed, apparently making for a fourth Salukadian transport which, anticipating the third, was moving toward the Athadian armada.

General Thomo, at the forward rail of the *Crown*, watched attentively, uncertain what this stranger intended. To his surprise he saw the crew members of the brown-sailed vessel hail deckmen on the latest *surk*, and in response the *surk* veered toward the newcomer, slightly altering the direction.

The fleet vessel with brown-sails altered its direction as well—oddly aiming for the *surk* amidships. And before the fourth transport could react promptly enough to save itself, the brown-sailed ship's sharp prow had plunged into it.

"By all the gods! They've rammed it!"

Howls and screams carried across the sunlit waves as both ships, creaking and roaring, exploded in geysers of sea water, flying splinters of timber and hurled bodies—Salukadian seamen and Athadians alike.

Thomo and his officers, stunned, stared in amazement.

Caught, the *surk* nearly toppled as it slid on the waves, pushed by the force of the still-moving brown-sailed ship. Its great masts cracked and smashed into the water, the shrouds and lines and sails bursting free, throwing tangled bodies high into the air. Blood spread upon the sea like a dark oil and mighty spumes erupted as, shuddering, the *surk* at last broke apart and quickly began sinking underwater. Armed men from the brown-sailed ship, screaming, leapt aboard the dying transport. Swinging weapons, they killed any survivors they caught before being pulled under by the two ships' boiling whirlpool.

It had happened so swiftly that the third *surk*, its oars still fighting the waves, had not yet moved free of the *Star*.

"More of them, more *madmen*!" Major Hamaro roared at Thomo, who was staring in grief at the bloody, littered sea and twisting his gloved hands around and around the railing. "This is *war*! *They want war!*"

Major Dever groaned in anguish, "Name of the gods, how can they call themselves—"

"War," Thomo whispered.

Behind him, drums began to beat on every ship in the armada.

5.

Night.

Lord Thomo was sure the movements of the Athadian armada could be discerned in the darkness because of their lamps and torches. From the walls of Erusabad it must appear as though some absent-minded god had dropped a tray of glittering yellow gems upon the carpet of the ocean. Yet these gems coursed in patterns, aligned themselves in purposeful formations, and boasted to any observer that the greatest empire in the history of the world had been reduced to this: answering with arms stupid acts of vandalism and bloodshed. Thomo had seen enough conflict in his life to understand that warfare is just only when it is finally necessary to restore order to chaos: but too many wars had come and gone and had never restored any order permanently. It occurred to Lord General Thomo, as he stood there on the forward deck of the *Crown*, that if wars no longer served a nation's policy, if they no longer embodied ideals or were unable any more to restore order to chaos—then it must be chaos that reigned, and war must be only the most obvious sign of that chaos. Who had ever determined that order was an absolute and chaos only a temporary aberration?

He dwelt upon all that had happened in his life and sorrowfully decided that if there had been any order to things once, then his own passage of years upon this earth had witnessed the gradual erosion of stability and order, the progressive decline of the pretense that tolerance and wisdom and empathy could endure in an angry, petty, destructive humanity. . . .

The irony of it was that now he, wishing to resort to arms only to oppose anarchy and to reestablish order, was trapped by his training and habits and position, and must now resort to war not to oppose anarchy, but to salvage whatever he could of the anarchy which posed as order.

Madness. Humanity idealized madness by calling it reason. . . .

"Lord General?"

Thomo faced the man next to him, then looked quickly in the direction the soldier indicated. Another flame was rising from the walls of the Holy City.

"They must want to parley again, General."

Thomo grunted. "Yes. . . . I expected this. Have Majors Hadd and Ostorian returned to their flagships yet?"

"No, sir. They're still aboard, awaiting your command. You asked them to delay—"

"Yes, yes. Have them come up on deck, soldier."

The man saluted and went off.

Thomo continued to stare in silence at his stretched, rocking armada, and before its sails the high dark ancient walls of Erusabad. From behind him, then, came a voice—and Thomo was momentarily startled because he had not heard the intruder's approach.

"So . . . they still wish to talk peace," commented the Imbur slowly.

There was a note of irritation in Thomo's voice as he replied. "It will do them no good; my patience is at an end."

"Unfortunate . . . unfortunate," drawled the Imbur.

Thomo couldn't tell if he were sincere or not; curtly: "If I were

173

you, Ogodis, I'd send my daughter back to the capital as soon as possible. If this doesn't end as soon as it begins, every ship out here will be a target."

"I am ordering her returned to Athad tonight."

Thomo nodded brusquely.

His soldier returned, accompanied by the armored Majors Hadd and Ostorian. The two saluted their lord general.

"We've been signaled again."

Ostorian asked, "Do you intend to respond?"

"I do. I must. And I wish you men to escort me." To the soldier: "Have an archer brought to me. We're answering their flare."

They met aboard an armed *surk* which, brightly lighted and marking its advance with crashing cymbals and drums, dropped anchor half-way between the harbor and the Athadian armada's first line of defense. Thomo had come out in a longboat and he, Ostorian, Hadd and twenty swords were brought aboard Nihim's ship for the conference.

The *Ghen-usu* was the only man on deck not donned in armor. He was clothed as he had been when Thomo met with him earlier in the day: in his plain robe and plain sandals.

"It seems to me, *Ghen-usu*," the lord general told him, "that I have been played for a fool. Or both of us have. I know you'll assure me that the savagery of this afternoon took you as much by surprise as it did my officers and myself."

"It did, Thomo-*su*."

"Be that as it may, Nihim, my patience is at an end. I can no longer allow any of our citizens to live in such jeopardy. They've asked for evacuation from Erusabad, and you cannot guarantee their safety in doing that. I must request that you allow squadrons of Athadian soldiers to enter your walls to accomplish this."

Nihim did not answer. But from behind the *Ghen-usu*'s chair Utto-sen-gar, *hetmuk* of Erusabad, rose to his feet. Garbed as he was in boots and armor and helm, colored as he was by the swaying lamps and torches that illuminated the deck of the *surk*, he gave the appearance of being gigantic, like some angry spirit that had pulled itself from the earth and clothed itself in the flesh and armor of a Salukadian officer.

174

"We cannot," Utto-sen-gar pronounced, "allow your troops access to our city."

Thomo said to him coldly: "You close us off from our people—a direct breach of international policy. You will not allow us to communicate with those soldiers of ours inside your walls—another broken agreement. Yet you cannot guarantee the safety of our citizens, although they dwell in a city which you administer."

"We must protect ourselves, as well as your citizens, Thomo-*su*."

"I will ask you again, *hetmuk*: will you agree to let squadrons of Athadian troops enter your city, for the purpose of escorting Athadian citizens to safety?"

"And I answer you again, General Thomo—no, I will not do that."

Thomo clamped his teeth together and sighed heavily. He threw his arms behind his back, stared at Utto-sen-gar, stared at Nihim and the troops collected on the deck.

"You leave me no option, *Ghen-usu*. I do not wish to endanger these people's lives on the pretext of rescuing them, but I will do so if that is necessary. It is the custom of my country, in circumstances such as this—when offering an ultimatum—to explain the ramifications of its refusal to an—enemy . . . three times. You ask us to commit ourselves to a siege, and to warfare. I can only ask you once more: will you agree to let squadrons of Athadian troops enter Erusabad to—"

"No, General!" Utto-sen-gar shouted, angrily and impatiently. "No! And *no* again! If you cannot trust us to do as you request, we cannot answer you in any other way than this!"

"So be it." Thomo swallowed heavily. "So be it." He then saluted sen-gar, nodded to Nihim, and turned on his heel to leave the *surk*.

"Thomo-*su*!"

He turned once more, faced Nihim. "What is it, *Ghen-usu*?"

"It was never my intention to have . . . trivial events progress to a crisis of this sort. You understand that, do you not?"

"Neither was it my intention, *Ghen-usu*, and that is not why this fleet was brought here. And yet it comes to this inevitably."

"Forgive us, Thomo-*su*. I thought the true crisis had passed."

"As did I, *Ghen-usu* . . . as did I. But I must ask forgiveness of my own gods. You, I cannot forgive."

Nihim bowed his head and did not look up.

Thomo moved across the deck and took the ladder down to his longboat, and his officers and soldiers followed after him.

"Why do I think," Ostorian asked him, when he was in the skiff, "that there are no Athadians left alive in that city? That if any *were* still alive in Erusabad, the *Ghen-usu* would have agreed to let us escort them?"

Thomo confided to him, "The same thought occurred to me."

While above them, on the deck of the *surk,* as the last Athadian soldier moved down the ladder:

"We had no other choice, Nihim," Utto-sen-gar protested.

"I understand that, *hetmuk.*"

"If we had let them into Erusabad to protect the lives of . . . corpses—then half the war would already have been fought, and not one of their soldiers dead in bringing down our walls."

"I know this, *hetmuk.*"

"They will exhaust themselves, Nihim, in storming our walls. It can never be done."

"We should have been honest with them, *hetmuk.*"

But Utto-sen-gar disagreed. "No . . . no. It would have come to war anyway, Nihim. For one reason or another, the gods seem to wish our empires to clash. But do not be sad. If men did not die in war, they would die sooner or later by some other means. There is glory to war. There is glory and honor, duty and—"

"There is pain, *hetmuk.* There is pain and loss, grieving and wailing, disease and hate. That is what there is to war. And there are never any solutions gained, never any answers won. For if that were so, then the solutions would have been gained long ago, correct? The answers would have been learned long ago, correct? Yet they have not been. And so the old contempt of war turns around like a man in his sleep, and we will pretend that pain is suffered for glory, and death for honor, and that true strength prides itself in destruction. And when this war has ended, then we will praise life again as we praised this war, and we will praise peace as we praised conflict, and we will praise the peace makers as we now praise the hate mongers. And it will never end, *hetmuk.* It will never end, so long as the mothers of men continue to give birth to warriors, and the schools of men continue to teach mistrust.

"I should have been honest with him. To be honest with one's enemy—that, perhaps would begin to show us answers. . . ."

Utto-sen-gar sighed and told Nihim, "I respect you, *Ghen-usu*, but you are a sentimentalist."

"No, *hetmuk*, not a sentimentalist—only a realist. . . ."

Upon his return, Thomo discovered Major Thytagoras aboard the *Crown*, and the Imbur gone back to the *Jewel*. Hadd and Ostorian remained on deck only long enough to grip the lord general's arm, promising honor, before entering into combat.

"You know our plan of siege," Thomo reminded them quietly. "You've familiarized yourselves with the code. Keep a watch at all times for our semaphores, and follow your instructions." He took a breath. "And pray the gods that we can end this quickly."

They saluted him, then made their way to longboats. Thomo ordered the men on watch to alert him the instant any change became apparent on the walls or in the harbor of Erusabad; then he made his way quickly to his cabin.

Thytagoras followed him, dogging his steps. "War, Lord General?"

"I am certain, Major Thytagoras, that the Imbur wishes to have his chief-in-command onboard the *Jewel* at this hour."

"And I am leaving promptly. But not before I present you with an idea."

Thomo saluted the guards in the gallery as they opened the door into his cabin; as he seated himself behind the wide desk and turned up his lamps: "What 'plan,' Major?"

"This." From a pocket inside his vest Thytagoras produced a scrap of paper. On it he had drawn a section of the Holy City, marking a means of access. "A most cunning operation," he complimented himself, "and indispensible to us in a time of siege, don't you agree?"

Thomo regarded him coldly, spread open his large map of Erusabad and compared Thytagoras's sketch with the official version. "You have passages indicated here, Major, which are not included on our map."

"I did not spend years of military service here, General, without learning a great deal about these Salukadians *and* Erusabad."

"I can see that."

"I would request only a small force—a very small force—to gain entrance, Lord General. Attach this unit to a squadron deployed along the northwest section of the city. That's the ruse. Utto-sen-gar will think us simply making strong efforts at a straightforward siege, but the action will blanket what my men and I are actually accomplishing."

As he spoke, Thomo carefully studied his drawing. "I'm not going to throw away lives, Major, on a crude sketch done by a man whose hatred of these people—"

"My hatred, Lord General, is your weapon! And this plan is your only hope for seeing this operation concluded swiftly and successfully! Give me twenty men—*twenty men!*—and under cover of a false siege we can get you into the city. I've indicated— here—old mining tunnels which have been totally forgotten. The Salukadians will never suspect that we're aware of these tunnels— but a few hours of digging will drop us underground far enough to use them to get inside."

"And where do they lead? Here?"

"I learned of these channels when I ordered certain sectors of the northside fortified during the Salukadian occupation last year. They come into Erusabad right here—nothing but tenements and warehouses in that district. This is where the old city wall's foundations used to be."

Thomo mulled over this information carefully. "It seems . . . too much to hope for," he suggested.

"It is true, all of it. If Sirom yet lived, he'd confirm it."

Thomo was silent.

"Once inside," Thytagoras continued, "this postern gate is only a few streets over. Under shield of night we can reach it easily, and it takes only a few marksmen to subdue any guards and open that gate. Then you can march in with as many legions as you like. And the palace is here—a stone's throw away. We can send troops in through the Vilusian Gardens as well as through the streets, and have it surrounded before anyone knows we're inside."

Lord General Thomo tapped his fingers nervously on the table. "If you're telling the truth, Thytagoras—and I don't trust you, not completely—but if you're telling the truth—"

"I wouldn't lie about this, General."

"—then we'll save many lives. Many lives." He looked up. "I don't accuse you of lying; but I know your interest in seeing Erusabad taken by the Athadian government has more to do with politics than with military prudence."

"I hate these savages, sir, there's no secret about that. But I think the surest method of getting control of the city is the best method."

"And I agree with you." He continued to study the map. By concentrating his forces in the harbor and against the southern fortifications, Thomo would be doing just what the Salukadians must expect him to do—and he would thereby gain the element of surprise and speed from any surreptitious activities in the north. To the east, poor defenses and many fields, which could be torched, once the wind changed its direction. . . . "All right, Major. Return to the Imbur and tell your watch to keep their eyes open for our signals. I'm going to make use of your little discovery."

"Excellent. All I ask, Lord General, is the opportunity to lead that unit inside the walls."

"You shall have it, Thytagoras. You shall have it. . . ."

Aboard the *Wing*, one of his fleet's swiftest galleys, Ogodis bade his daughter a temporary farewell. "For you will see me in Athad again very soon," he promised Salia.

"I trust so, father."

"You are the queen of Athadia, Salia. The first woman of the empire."

She faced him, pale and exhausted, distraught, her eyes dark, her face thin and bloodless. "I am, father, at this moment, only a very tired and very disillusioned woman. I don't want to think anymore about being a queen . . . I don't want to think anymore about these . . . corpses I've left behind—"

"Salia!"

"I don't want to remind myself that I'm the cause for two governments going to war with one another—"

"But you're not!" Ogodis laughed at her. "You're not! And this will hardly be a war! Elad developed a masterful plan, and with it we—"

"And I don't want to hear anymore about Elad, father."

"Salia. . . ."

"I don't! Can't you understand?" Then, in the privacy of her cabin, with the noises of busy seamen above her, and as disoriented and weary as she was, Salia tried to speak honestly and plainly to her father, as she had been able to do only a few times in all her life. "I'm not—the person you think I am, father. I'm not even much of a woman . . . certainly not much of a queen. I know you don't understand me—I don't think it's possible for you to truly understand—"

Ogodis began to protest, but Salia interjected: "I'm some kind of symbol of death, father! My mother . . . Elad . . . Agors . . . even my animals! They . . . they are with me for a while and then they die. Plagues come— No, listen to me, let me speak! I know you don't understand! You've never thought this way! Can't you try to understand what's happened to me in these past two months? This past year? I . . . I feel like a ghost! I'm not a real person! I think I am but—I'm really some kind of trap for people! I'm supposed to be beautiful but inside me—*What's inside me*, father? What am I, *inside*? I try to look in the mirror but all I can see is—is *this*!" Salia lifted her hands to her face, dug her nails into the skin and pushed and pulled, drew lines of blood.

"Gods!" Ogodis cried in shock. "Stop it, Salia! What are you—"

Quickly she moved away from him, grabbed hold of a chair and whispered to him, as the blood dripped down her white face: "All this time . . . my whole life. . . . I supposed that if I'd listened to you, if I'd tried—" She laughed heartily, brutally. "Send me back to Athad, father. I'll be a queen! I don't want to be a queen! But you won't die, will you? It's come to war, now, and *you* won't die, you'll *never* die! Look at me! I can bleed! But all I want to do is run from the world like a shadow . . . I *am* a shadow . . . and I want to talk to Elad again—he couldn't hear me when I—"

Ogodis gasped.

Salia stared at him.

The Imbur was trembling terribly, appalled, frightened by his daughter. "What has *happened*?" he asked her, trembling and afraid. "Why are you doing this? What have you done to your *face*? Salia! What has happened?"

"What . . . has happened?" she replied, voice distant. "Only . . . life." And she began to laugh some more— "Remember how you told me to laugh, father?"—before falling backwards to the floor.

She curled up, wiped her bloody face with her blonde hair, and sobbed and laughed.

PART IV

The Storm

1.

The old farmer, whose name was Essor, had felt quite guilty at discovering Assia wounded by the side of the road. He now realized that that night he should have directed the young woman toward his farmhouse; and yet the uncertainty of the moment, the natural mistrust of strangers, had stayed his voice—and thus, his immense sorrow and regret, his guilt at feeling to some degree responsible for the crime done against her.

When Essor returned with Assia, his wife took care to comfort him when he told her the story. "On," she reminded him, "sees all things, and surely there was some larger purpose even for this crime, and for her coming to our hearth under these circumstances." Having faith, believing where most would have scorned, Essor had taken his wife Halis's words to heart, and did the best he could with the results of a situation he might have prevented.

Assia slept through her first day with them, ate the meal they gave her that evening, and sat quietly by their fire. The old couple did not inquire after her to any great extent and asked only her name and where she had come from; neither did Assia volunteer much more information than that. Harmed in her body and bruised in her spirit, her logical reaction to their solicitude was that which she had learned habitually to expect from apparently reasonable people: given time, they would reveal themselves, show themselves to be no better than most of the men and women whom Assia had ever met in her life.

During the second day, as she recuperated from her assault and began to feel better, Assia offered to help Halis with the work around the farmhouse. The old woman, knowing that this young girl had come from the cities and so knew almost nothing about farmwork, asked Assia to help clean soot from the hearth, wash dishes and clean clothes. And, in the manner of two women tentatively opening their hearts to one another, Halis began to inform Assia of her own background and her thoughts, and Assia confessed to Halis a little more of her own life and what she had suffered.

She was somewhat surprised that the farm woman did not judge her or condemn her for her life; indeed, Halis revealed to Assia: "I believe that everything that is, is for a reason. I don't know everything, so how can I pretend to decide what's good and what's bad? Only the god knows things such as that." Assia was intrigued by the solid simplicity of this, but she did not ask Halis to pursue her philosophy.

That evening, after the three of them had eaten a meal of soup and bread and eggs, they relaxed, each to some chores. Halis mended clothes and Essor repaired tools and Assia helpfully made tapers for the winter from beeswax. The conversation, after a time, led to the old couple mentioning how their lives had been transformed by a wandering priest they had seen in Mustala; they asked Assia if she had heard of this man, if perhaps he had made his way into Abustad or Elpet or some other port city.

"His name," said Essor, "was Asawas, and he was a real miracle worker and a very wise man. He swore that he was not the Prophet come back, but he was so comforting with his words, and he performed such remarkable things, and yet what he said was so frightening—well, I know many people think him a son of the gods, and perhaps indeed Bithitu come back."

Assia was as intrigued by this story as she had been by Halis's philosophy that afternoon. She asked what kinds of miracles this Asawas had performed, asked what he said that was so profound, and what he said that was so frightening.

"He said that there is only one god," Essor explained. "Not many gods, but only one god, and everyone on earth helps to create this god. Which, I suppose, is why things are as bad as they are and why we should try to do better. But he also said that there would be a famine, which has happened, and a plague, and many bad things. A terrible storm will come and many people must perish. But this will happen so that the earth can be cleansed, and then the world will be reborn."

Assia's interest waned. She was tolerant of what these people believed in gratitude for what they had done for her, so she didn't have the heart to remind them that a hundred new prophets and priests came every year to announce the fall of kings and the end of the world. She asked a few more questions but then fell silent. It would take a very great storm and a very great prophet indeed to cleanse the world of all the harm that had been done by politicians and businessmen; she herself was very familiar with that kind of treachery and corruption. And yet, that night, as she tried to fall asleep in her blankets by the hearth, in the darkness and the silence and the comfort of that farmhouse, Assia privately wished that such things as honest prophets and goodness in the world might come about. Everyone claimed that they desired such things, yet everyone acted in ways that insured such a world would never occur. It was unfortunate.

Over the course of the next few days, as Assia regained her spirit and her health, she began to talk about moving on from Essor and Halis's farmhouse, and she asked what towns or villages were closeby. The couple warned her that Mustala was the closest city but that with times so bad she might find it difficult to look after herself there. To this Assia secretly smiled, for the life she had led with her father she'd kept from them. They allowed as how she could remain with them through the winter; certainly the extra pair of hands Assia provided was useful, and so it was not charity that prompted them to ask Assia to stay. Also, Essor and

183

Halis had noticed that Assia's illness had not improved, and could she honestly expect it to in the city during the winter?

Assia did not force the issue, although as the days passed she began to feel that she was intruding upon the couple and should be going on. Yet she had never known real comfort or friendship or such calm peace as she did here, and so she lingered.

On the afternoon of her sixth day with Essor and Halis, Assia was outside feeding corn to the chickens when she noticed a figure coming towards the farmhouse from the north. When she finished with the corn she went inside and mentioned the fact to Halis, and the farm wife commented that there was enough soup in the pot to share with another body. Shortly the chickens began to squawk loudly, and there sounded a rapping on the door; Assia opened it. The stranger nodded his head and excused himself for intruding, but mentioned that he had been walking alone for some time and was tired, thirsty and hungry. He offered to pay for whatever food or drink could be spared him.

Halis urged him to sit at the table, while Assia dipped a bowl into the kettle at the hearth and served the newcomer. He was tall, a rather handsome man who, with gray in his beard and hair, nevertheless seemed a hale and hearty fifty or fifty-five years old. As Assia set a cup of barley beer on the table for him, the stranger made a compliment to Halis, remarking: "Your daughter is as kind to travelers as she is pretty."

Halis smiled and explained that Assia was not her daughter, and related how, alone on the road with only a horse and no place to stay, she had come to help with the farm for a few days.

The stranger introduced himself as a homeless refugee. "Forgive me," he apologized over his soup. "My name is Iramdos; I am from Emaria and am fleeing the war there. I was in Mustala for a time, but I think it might be better to stay south, along the ocean, for the winter."

Halis did not have much to say in regards to this, although she mentioned that her husband Essor would no doubt be interested in hearing about conditions in Emaria. Assia, for her part, was instantly attentive, as she wondered if this Iramdos had, by the faintest chance, heard of Thameron or could perhaps tell her how he was, or what he was doing. Yet she refrained from mentioning her friend, for the moment: his was a common name—even the king of Emaria was now called Thameron—and it seemed too much to hope for, at this late date.

But tomorrow sometime, or even this evening, she would mention the matter and speak with Iramdos before he went his way.

Smoke and ashy fumes from a nearby burning barn blew across the road as Asawas, leaning on his staff, came up the hill. Though he was the only man in sight who was not dressed in armor, the straggling lines of wounded soldiers that passed by him did not call out for Asawas to identify himself or demand that he halt or ask why he was there. So the prophet continued on his way, staring sadly at the spectacle of the war's wake.

On both sides of the road, stretching up the hillside and into the fields all around, lay the bloodied and the dying, dressed in stained blankets. Moans and sobs carried in the air. Here, as Asawas looked, a blind man with his head wrapped in a dirtied, blood-wet rag, crawled along the road on all fours, crying out and babbling, as flies and gnats swarmed about him. Over there a man with the bottom of one leg wrapped in an old coat was hobbling between two companions; his head was slung low and the sweat dripped from his face like rain as he muttered, "I can't feel it . . . I can't feel anything . . . I can't feel it. . . ." Farther on, by a fire that was little more than a soft bed of glowing coals, three soldiers were holding down a screaming, writhing man while another, his chest and face all bloody, held a notched sword over the coals, then moved to apply it to one of the screaming soldier's mangled arms. "Let me die! Don't do it, *don't do it*! Let me die, I'd rather *die*! Don't cut off my *arms, no-oho-ooo*!"

There were horses ahead, kicking up clouds of dust as they moved back and forth across the road. Asawas approached and one soldier, wearing the double gold stripes of a sergeant hailed him.

"What're you doing out here? Get back to your farm!"

"I am journeying to Lasura."

"*Lasura*? Damn it, get back to your farm!"

Asawas noticed the torn pennant that flapped atop one of the tents. "You are the Twenty-ninth Athadian Legion?"

"I said, *Get back to your farm*! We're pulling back and we're leaving our dead behind!"

Someone yelled from across the road, "Sergeant! Please!"

Growling an oath and warning Asawas again to begone, the officer reined his horse around and crossed the road.

Asawas continued up the hill. When he reached the height of it he stepped off into the field, all dead and wasted as it was, all parched brown grass and broken trees. The road had been blocked with wagons and logs; tents and horses and several long tables and fire pits formed a camp off to one side, where a large company of men were congregated. It was from this group of soldiers that an ear-splitting horn call sounded.

In answer to it, hundreds of men all across the landscape mounted horses and waved swords and began moving toward the encampment. Many of those who passed Asawas called to him or made remarks, but the prophet ignored them. He walked through a copse of burned trees and started down the other side of the hill.

Now he could see a wide panorama of devastation. Huge fields had been put to the torch, and in places the blackened earth still sent waves of gray smoke into the sky. There were piles of corpses everywhere—men and animals—and everywhere, too, lines of slow-moving, bedraggled men pushing up the hillside, toward the Twenty-ninth Legion's campsite. Farther away, almost hidden by the haze of the scorched land, was a bulwarks of stone and logs that seemed to stretch a third of a league long. An Emarian rampart, Asawas guessed. He would not be able to pass through it; it would be necessary to go around.

Moving down the hillside, heading northeast, he noted those areas where the battle had been fiercest. The dead were heaped in hills, with many of the corpses stripped of their armor, weapons and boots. Everywhere . . . war's feast. Insects swarmed in black clouds, and from nearby trees huge buzzards and other scavengers fluttered down, croaking, to pick and feed. Here skin was mottled on grimacing heads that hung lopsided, suspended on torn bits of ligament and flesh. Asawas saw a naked foot lying alone in the brown grass—only a foot. Over there, half an arm, the hand of it a battered stump. Asawas spied a wild dog savagely growling as it tried to pull a bloodied arm from beneath a mound of legs and bent torsos. Two crows, flapping their wings, fought over a prize of meat that made sounds like tearing parchment as it was ripped from a staring skull.

The prophet walked on.

He could feel in his heart, feel in his mind, the agony and terror and the fury of this place. He could sense still the fear and the hatred, although a day at least must have passed since the end of this battle, perhaps a day and a half.

The land continued to swell and dip, but Asawas realized that it was gradually rising, as it must the closer he approached Lasura. By late morning he was past the last of the remnants of the battle on the hillside and climbing another stretch of steepness. And when he reached the height of this rise he saw before him, beyond more wide fields and further scenes of devastation and the blackened frames of more huts and barns, the walls of Lasura.

Only a few leagues distant, then.

His long journey—and the accomplishment of it—only a few leagues distant.

As he scraped up dust clouds, moving down the slope, the prophet listened for a moment, for he suspected that he heard the sky rumbling above him. He looked up.

Gray clouds . . . the hint of sun just behind.

For months those clouds had moved across the reaching sky, giving no rain, while beneath the parched earth had continued to rumble as though respirating, as though stretching to awaken like some great beast caught too long in an artificial posture.

No . . . he had not been mistaken.

The sky was growling.

From very far away—thunder. . . .

When Adred entered Galvus's office, he noticed that the prince-regent was in a better mood than he'd expected—and in a better mood than was Adred himself. The reason was a letter that had arrived just that morning.

"From Omos!" Galvus smiled, waving the pages. "He arrived in Sulos four days ago. He says he's staying with Rhia and someone named Mirhu and her husband Endric."

Adred was taken aback. "*Rhia's* husband?"

"No, no, *no*! This woman Mirhu's husband. No, nothing about

187

a husband for Rhia. However—" he cocked an eyebrow "—Omos says that she's pregnant."

"Rhia, you mean?"

"Oh, yes. Doesn't mention who the father is." Galvus noticed that his friend, already in a glum mood, was made uneasy by this, and so he continued: "He says that earthquake four days ago didn't reach Sulos, but they saw some damage done in Bessara during their layover there. He says things are still rather quiet in Sulos, but there's tension. Vardorian, gods thank him, opened one of the chambers in the City Administration Hall for public discussions. Debates there every night. Omos says that these 'Khilu' police aren't doing much . . . Vardorian seems to be keeping a leash on them. Maybe because I have their boss locked up in the attic, and they don't know what to do without him." Galvus looked up, frowning, and set down the letter. "What's the matter with you, Adred?"

He was staring out a window, nodding absently to everything Galvus said; now he turned around, moved to a chair and slumped into it. "It's not worth it, Galvus. None of it is."

"What's bothering you?"

"I don't know, I can't— All—that." The window. "Bodies of people filling up hundreds of buildings—the police can't dig holes fast enough to bury them, the priests can't pray fast enough, people can't— Hell." He turned his face away.

Galvus sat back, showing his deep concern.

Adred sighed, tapped his fingers nervously. "Your mother's off someplace talking to some leaf reader or something. That's what Abgarthis told me."

"She's a sensitive woman," Galvus remarked in a still voice. "This is all very difficult for her. Everything that's happened in the past year. . . . She's strong, but she just needs to have her strength—well, strengthened, occasionally. I'm not sure *I'm* willing to wake up every morning, anymore; there's more gone on in one year than my grandfather could expect to have happen in *ten* years when he was on the throne."

"It's all gone lunatic," Adred grunted, staring at the floor.

"You're exhausted."

He shook his head. "For the first time I'm seeing what humanity's really like, what it really is, and it's senseless, Galvus, it's senseless."

188

"You're very depressed, aren't you?"

"Yes, I am . . . I am. And everyone should be as depressed as I am right now. Can't they open up their eyes and *see*? It's just been— Gods! there are crowds in the street fighting about the *corpses*! The damned *corpses*! There are people out there who want to make sure that all the followers of Bithitu are buried in the same hole! Are there any dead foreigners mixed in with them? Some people don't want their relatives buried, they want them *cremated*! And some of them don't want them cremated, they want them *buried*! Some of them—it goes on and on and *on*! They're so damned—" he stared at the window angrily "—*stupid*! Four days ago they were cringing under their covers praying *not* to die! And now that they're still *alive*, well, they take it for granted like they always did! They turn as petty and as squabbling as— I don't know; it's disgusting. Can't they *see*?" He slapped a fist on the arm of the chair, but that only served to make him wince and rub the hand with his other one. When he looked at Galvus, he saw that his friend wasn't amused.

"I know exactly what you mean," Galvus told him darkly. "I understand exactly what you're saying."

"Oh, I know you do. . . ."

"It'd be so much easier if we could just be businessmen, wouldn't it? Or if we could spend our whole lives with books, or running a tavern, or cooking food, or just—anything. Whatever it might be. Anything we might become obsessed with. That's what it is, Adred. Maybe all we needed was to've been born with a few less brains, or with less sympathetic temperaments. Or maybe all we need to do is put on blinders, like everyone else in the world seems to do. Believe in one thing—just one thing—and judge everything else by that *one thing*. But we can't do it. You and I . . . we can't do it."

Adred didn't say anything.

"And on top of all that, we're in the government. It's almost comical. We're fighting for the good of people who don't even seem to know what *is* good for them . . . who won't appreciate it until *we* deliver it to them, even though they can't imagine it before that, imagine it and try to help make it happen. We're fighting for the intellectual freedom of people who don't even seem to *have* intellects. I know what you're saying, Adred."

"You can't—" The mildly arrogant decisiveness of those words rankled Adred a bit; they ran counter to everything he and Galvus had discussed. Was Galvus changing? Or had he phrased it that way to get a reaction from Adred? To challenge him, and so break him out of his mood? "You can't refer to people as if they're brainless cattle, Galvus," Adred reminded him.

His friend smiled.

"You can't say that because they're not *us* they'll never—"

"Oh, no, no, *no*, I'm not saying that!" the prince-regent corrected himself. "You know me better than that! Adred! But you and I are in a position to see possibilities . . . potential. But we have full stomachs and get a good night's rest every night, don't we? We'd be less worried about society's potential if we had to go to bed hungry every night; we'd be a lot more worried about out next meal, than we would about high-minded ideals."

"I'm afraid you're right."

"I almost wish I weren't."

Adred looked at Galvus, then, and he was touched by what his friend had just accomplished: simply, easily, in a moment of conversation. He smiled.

"You said it yourself one time, far better than I can now," Galvus continued. "That long talk you had last winter with Uncle Elad? Don't look so surprised! He told me about that; he told me some of the things you said about . . . well, what he remembered."

"What did I tell him?"

"That . . . if we don't do the best we can to show people that there *are* better ways to do things and think about things, than what we have right now . . . then we can't blame them if they act poorly or think poorly. I'm paraphrasing, but that's the gist of it. That, and fear. People will turn to anything, Adred—*anything*—to save themselves, in their fear. And people are apt to be afraid of anything and everything. And that's why so many of them out there act the way they do. They're afraid, and we haven't really shown them a better way to deal with that—a good way that benefits everyone—and so they're going to stay with what they *do* know." He glanced at the marked candle on his desk, moved a little to see past the glare the flame made on its glass cover. "Which is the perfect reminder for me, I suppose, that I'm supposed to interview Lord Rhin about now."

"Oh, yes." Adred shook his head as he stood up. "That's why I came up here. Abgarthis told me to tell you that the Khamars have arrived and were taking Rhin into the Audience Hall.''

"Good, good. Were Osudu and Ellu down there?"

"I believe so."

"Good. If you want to come along, Adred, you can. I'm going to see what I can do about stoking some of the coals that're warming under Rhin's chair. He's had about half a month to himself; it's time to see what he's been up to. And if I have to come to some sort of compromise with him—well. . . ." He gestured.

Adred made some sour comment.

Galvus grinned. "You have to keep in mind what we're dealing with. It'd be wonderful if I could just wave my hand from the throne and make the kind of world we think we want simply appear. But if we're going to start carving things up in a new way, we're going to have to do it one step at a time. And we've got to be practical. We've got to make it clear that—"

He stopped suddenly, as a shuddering rippled through the room.

"Gods!" Adred exclaimed. "It's happening *again*!"

Yet in a moment the tremor had passed, and both men breathed in relief and traded shaky, meaningful glances.

Galvus cleared his throat. "Maybe whatever it is down there that just rolled over in its sleep," he remarked, "just had a stomach ache, this time."

"Maybe. . . ."

"I think it's time we went down to the Audience Hall—while we still *have* an Audience Hall!"

2.

Despite his protracted isolation under house arrest, Lord Rhin appeared in the Audience Hall as relentlessly arrogant, as defiantly self-certain as he had ever been. He gave Galvus the impression of being a proud beast caged or held at bay, yet still able to lash out with real strength and fury: without doubt the precise posture Rhin wished to convey.

The great stone walls and marble pillars of the hall rang with echoes as Galvus opened the session by stating frankly his purpose in having the aristocrat escorted there. He openly suggested that

191

Rhin and the Athadian throne, rather than being antagonists, were actually partners intent on maintaining the strongest economy possible in the empire. And if their views or methods differed, then perhaps that was simply a matter of degree that could be reconciled. Indeed, Galvus emphasized, their differences *must* be reconciled. And soon.

"It seems to me," the prince-regent spoke, watching from his throne where Rhin, seated alone behind a stone table, eyed him contemptuously, "that the system we have *allowed* to come into being—sometimes by actively pursuing policies, sometimes by looking the other way when businessmen such as yourself influence the throne for your own benefit—is not the best we can hope to obtain for the benefit of the totality of the Athadian people. And if we're going to insist on referring to ourselves as civilized, then we must address the welfare of our people at some level above mere survival. But I assume that your interest, Lord Rhin, is *not* necessarily in promoting so beneficent an economy, is it?"

Rhin smiled snidely. "The economy we have now, Prince-Regent, suits me very well."

"Then I must induce you by some means either to aid me, or at least not interfere with me, as I go about promoting a more equitable economy."

"Prince-Regent, may I say something?"

"Certainly."

"When you begin talking about the economy, all you're talking about is one of many different kinds of human enterprise. And when you talk about human enterprises, all you're talking about is simple human nature. And when you're talking about simple human nature, all you have to keep in mind is one fundamental principle: people are going to look out for themselves. All I'm doing, as a businessman, is looking out for myself. That doesn't interfere with you at all, and it doesn't interfere with someone else looking out for himself. If it ever does, then he has to use a little ingenuity—and there's nothing wrong with that. You want an economy that works for all the people all the time? All of those people, Prince-Regent, are going to be looking out for themselves anyway, whether you try to look out for them or not. If you start interfering with that, then you're just creating more problems. If you don't give the people what they think they want, they'll work

192

around you to get what they *do* want—to look out for themselves. The throne's already interfered enough by creating all these work quotas and personnel requirements and laws about safety on the docks and safety in the mines and on the farms and fair prices and on and on. Prince-Regent, leave people alone! Leave businessmen alone! A man is going to do what he does, whatever it is, because it's in his own self-interest, because he's going to look out for himself. It's as simple as that. It's just as simple and direct as that."

Galvus stared at him for a long moment. He pressed his hands together, lifted them to his mouth, studied Rhin for a very long while before replying. "No," he said, shaking his head. "No. You reduce society with your argument, Lord Rhin, to your personal level: and society must be the aggregate of all personal beliefs raised to the highest level practicable. By your argument, someone would sooner or later gain everything that there is to be had: because you and I know that human nature dictates that emotions come before reason, unless reasonableness has been proven more effective. More effective habitually, and on a social level, not a personal one. If we're going to come together to form a society, Lord Rhin, then that society takes precedence over the individual; if you want to be an individual, then you may leave the society and be an individual as you like, where you like. There is a social contract here, an unspoken agreement which men like you flaunt too often, whenever you please, for short-term benefit. You work for your own self-interest, but inevitably that will run, sooner or later, counter to society's interests. You want to take what you like and need, when you want it, and that means that you will take more than you need as insurance, or for redistribution at a profit, on your terms. You're interfering with what other people want and need, you're hoarding money, you're hoarding property, and that puts you at an advantage and society at a dis—"

"Prince-Regent, just send me back to my villa! Do it now! Send me back to my prison, please! I have nothing to say to you, you can't convince me that these tactics of yours are somehow going to improve society, and I'm sick of arguing with you! I'm a businessman and I'm not going to defend that! Not to you, not to anyone! I don't have to!"

Galvus glanced toward Lord Osudu, who was seated at a table

with Lord Ellu, just below the throne dais. Osudu leaned forward and said to Lord Rhin:

"It was the prince-regent's intention to approach you on an elevated plane and so speak to you, Lord Rhin, as one cultured and educated noble to another. Obviously, the prince-regent misjudged you, so we'll dispense with such formalities or the more—rarefied or philosophical aspects of all this. Would you prefer that?"

"I would."

"I see how highly you regard the philosophical in men."

"Don't be snide, Lord Osudu. Business is one thing, philosophy something else altogether."

Osudu grinned. "Perhaps that attitude explains why we're in the predicament we're in. But—let's talk business, then. The first thing I want to say to you is that everything the prince-regent has done so far is entirely legal. I mean, in terms of your house arrest, your property and so forth. You'll be given copies of these papers—" he displayed those he had withdrawn from a portfolio "—and you may review them at your leisure. The second thing I'd like to point out to you is that human nature is a bit more complex than you care to interpret it, Lord Rhin; and that's why we have laws in this empire, to keep in check some of the more questionable or debatable tendencies in our human nature. And since we have laws to do that, and since you hold human nature in such high regard, I should inform you now that *these* papers—" Osudu held up another batch "—implicate you on a variety of charges, and over a very long period of time—"

"What are those?" Rhin growled. "Let me see them!"

"—*period of time*, Lord Rhin, in which you pushed your precious human nature very much beyond the limits the social law has allowed for! I will read you—"

"*Let me see those papers!*"

"*In time*, Lord Rhin!"

"Lord Rhin!" Galvus yelled at him. "Lord Rhin!" He motioned to the Khamars behind the aristocrat.

Adred, seated at a separate table beside Osudu and Ellu, groaned in disgust as Rhin, ranting and pounding, screamed profanities, while the two Khamars came forward and coaxed him into his seat once more.

"Lord Rhin!" Galvus called. "This is *not* a legal procedure!

There are *no* scribes or secretaries present! You are not being formally charged with any criminal—"

Above him, the ceiling groaned.

"—activities which could—"

"Galvus!" Adred cried, rising suddenly to his feet.

The ceiling groaned. The great chandeliers, suspended on their heavy chains, began to rock as bits of mortar and chips of stone block rained down in a heavy dust.

Galvus stared up.

The chandeliers swung back and forth like pendulums. The very walls of the Audience Hall trembled, shuddered, fell quiet—then shuddered some more.

"It's happening again!" Rhin shouted. "*It's happening again!*"

From outside, even through the enormously thick walls of the palace, everyone there heard abrupt crashing sounds, the tremendous noises of explosions or eruptions.

"Name of the gods!" Galvus breathed. "It's coming, it's happening!"

Adred ran up the stairs of the dais and crouched beside him. "We've got to get out of here! *Now*, Galvus!"

"To where?" he whispered. "To *where*?"

Loud choruses of screams and shouts sounded hollowly and distantly, through the walls.

The great marble pillars began to creak, threatening to buckle.

Rhin tried to run for the doors. "Get *away* from here!" he howled.

"Hold him!" Galvus yelled to the Khamars, although they had already moved to restrain the aristocrat. "Hold him! Wait . . . *wait*!"

More screams—crowds of screams—

Osudu and Ellu, on their feet, were leaning on the table before them, listening, watching Galvus, waiting—

The great doors of the Audience Hall swung open.

"Prince-Regent!" A Khamar ran in. "Prince-Regent! It's another earthquake! It's already—"

Galvus stared across the chamber. The outer wall was moving; he heard it moan, saw the huge blocks of it push and pull against one another as though they were alive.

"Oh *gods* . . ."

He grabbed hold of Adred, gripped one of his arms—

The wall began to break. Great stone blocks suddenly shivered and slipped, and three marble pillars quickly twisted and snapped apart, crashed down—

"It's happening again!" Rhin screamed, above the blowing dust and the roar of collapsing stone. "*It's happening again!*"

Orain's carriage was passing through the Odasian Square as the first of the tremors erupted.

She was glancing through a small book she'd purchased for Adred when her carriage suddenly veered wildly, throwing Orain from one side to the other. Crying out, her first thought was to look out the window to see what had happened; and then the carriage began to tilt—Orain heard the snapping of its axles—she heard the frightened whinnying of the horses, and the howling of her driver—

She was thrown against the window as the screeching, teetering coach slammed onto its side and skidded noisily over the bricks. Breathless and dazed, Orain tried to right herself as it shuddered still. The door opposite her—above her, now—flew open, and with a grunt that yanked one leg into a painful position she managed to reach an arm through the opening, then her head and shoulders.

What she saw stole her breath.

Before her, the driver was staggering, hands to his bloody face, in a weaving path; and above him—across from him—on the other side of the square—

Orain found her breath, and screamed.

The massive monument atop the *Firtel Kos* was falling. A huge statue—a man with arms outstretched, flowing robes, a dove in one hand, a lamp in the other—and the legs suddenly snapped, one arm dropped free, and in gigantic blocks of rubble the monument collapsed. Eight stories below packed throngs of shopping in the square stared up in horror, were thrown back and forth defenselessly as wave after wave of shocks ripped through the ground. Unable to move, they howled in anguish as the stone debris fell upon them. The wall of a building next to the *Kos* suddenly pushed outward, as though some giant fist had shoved it deliberately. The very bricks in the street rippled and burst free, flying into the air. People were thrown in all directions.

And Orain screamed her anguish as the great arm and lamp and

196

dove, the broken legs and the massive stone torso of the monument showered down in a mist of dust, smashing into the screaming faces, the waving arms and legs. Children . . . women . . . running boots, hoarse yells, startled animals—

The billowing dust blew up in massive clouds as great lakes of blood began to pour down the twisted bricks of the square.

Orain couldn't move. She was too terrified. She looked around, tried to find her driver. The horses, still yoked to the carriage, had fallen atop one another and were kicking their legs and shrieking, hurting themselves, jarring the coach. Orain struggled to pull herself up through the open door. Before her the dust began to clear from the collapsed monument and now she saw blocks of stone the size of ships shuddering still, with the crushed, pulped remains of hundreds of bodies beneath them.

She tried to look away, began to vomit, tried to look away—

The very wall of the *Kos* seemed to twist on an axis; then it burst apart, showering the screaming, dazed, red-splashed victims below with a second collapsing mountain of stone and brick and glass.

"Oh . . . *Hea*. . . !"

Screams, very close to her. Orain looked, stared, tried to see. Dust cleared. Faceless people—their smashed heads pouring with blood—were crawling on the ground, waving their arms in the air, falling upon one another. There came the sounds of hoofs as horses galloped through the square, trying to keep their footing on the jumping earth. Khamars. Orain saw them. They called to her.

Four Khamars on horseback surrounded her imperial coach; one leaned from his saddle, wrapped an arm around Orain's waist, roughly lifted her up and pushed her behind him.

"Anyone else?" he asked, glancing into the coach.

A Khamar on the other side yelled, "No, no one!"

"No," Orain whispered, hugging the guard as his horse danced frantically. "The—palace—?"

"As soon as we can make it, Lady Orain! Gods, *look out!*"

He reined quickly as thunder burst beneath his horse; he fought with the animal to keep it under control. Orain was nearly pitched to the ground.

On the other side of the coach, behind it, the square was open; only a tall pillar dressed in flags stood in a grassy park between two old buildings. Orain saw the pillar begin to topple, saw the carved facades of the buildings tear loose and slide down the sides, smash thunderously onto the street.

"Hurry, *hurry!*" breathed one of the Khamars.

Orain's rider reined about, warned her to hold onto him tightly, and slapped his mount forward.

Behind, the screams, and more eruptions of noise—

Bodies, everywhere—smashed and bloody, staggering, wailing in torment—

They passed through the west entrance of the square, hurdling piles of rubble and the endless disarray of fallen bodies. The gates protecting the wide palace gardens were twisted all out of shape. Orain wanted to see what she could, although one cheek was pressed so tightly to the Khamar's back that she kept one eye closed, and her vision out of the other danced and bobbed and jumped with the reckless galloping of the horse.

"The palace . . ." she whispered. "Galvus . . . Adred. . . . !"

The horse's hoofs were clomping on a cobbled pathway; the Khamar had slowed his gait. The noise behind had quieted. Orain straightened herself, looked back.

The Odasian Square no longer existed. Everything was hidden beneath huge piles of dust clouds and fallen rubble, collapsed buildings and walls. Farther away, through the glimpses she caught beyond the square's east entranceway, it was the same— fallen buildings and landmarks disappeared, great clouds of black and gray smoke like hell fumes risen from the pits, hints of fires—

She looked before her, coughing and choking, fighting back the urgent need to vomit, and saw a wall of the palace tumbled in pieces.

"*Galvus!*"

"Careful, my lady, be *careful!*"

One of the other Khamars trotted beside her. His face was covered with grime, sheeny with sweat running in dirty rivulets.

"My *son!*" Orain sobbed. "Where's *Galvus?*"

"We don't know yet, my lady!"

"Oh . . . Hea. . . ."

"It's calmed down," Orain's rider declared. "I don't feel it anymore."

"It's only started," the other one said. He pointed. "Look."

Three immense domes had collapsed, including the huge cupola of the Imperial Library, so that the southeast of the capital could now be seen. There, very far away, the tall decorated pillars of the *Kirgo Amax* were shivering and cracking, tumbling down and down, just as though they had been built of mud and were now being whisked away by an angry child. Hundreds of them. And as they fell, some quickly, some very slowly, columns of black smoke and dust rose up to obscure the view, lifting to hide the sun itself.

"The games were on," the Khamar said. "Two hundred thousand *people*—" His voice choked.

"Galvus," Orain moaned, numb and dazed and terrified, as she hugged her rider and swayed with the moving horse. "Oh . . . Hea. . . ."

"Galvus?" Adred could barely see him for all the dust and smoke, but he felt him, felt his arm beneath his hand.

"I'm—" The prince-regent coughed. "I'm . . . all right. . . ."

They were staring into the Audience Hall. Sunlight pouring through the fallen outside wall glowed through the mist, obscuring everything.

"My lord!" called a voice. "*Lord Galvus!*" A Khamar.

"Here, man! I'm safe! Count Adred and I are safe!"

The guard stumbled toward them. As billowing fumes of dust curled away, Galvus and Adred saw that where the throne had been there was now a pile of debris and broken rock that had spilled into the center of the hall.

"Gods!" Galvus whispered. "Can you see Ellu? Osudu?"

"Dead!" gasped the Khamar, as he crawled along the wall toward them.

They saw blood streaming down his front from a great wound in his left shoulder.

"Your arm?" Galvus asked him.

He swallowed thickly, nodded, flexed his hand. "Ellu and . . . Osudu. . . ." He shivered his head grimly.

Adred groaned and threw back his head; it knocked against the stone of the wall.

Galvus asked him, "What made you think . . . that we'd be safe . . . here?"

They were beneath an archway, one of the side entrances to the hall. Before them, the chamber with its collapsed ceiling and tumbled outside wall, scattered pillars; behind them, rubble in the passageways inside.

"I . . . *didn't* know. . . ." Adred coughed, and tried to smile. "I wanted to get—through!"

Galvus looked up. That bench arch of stone had held, while the entire ceiling of the Audience Hall had given way. He asked the Khamar: "Lord Rhin?"

"Unless he ran out when we—when we didn't see him, Lord Galvus. It came down so fast . . . *so fast*. . . !"

Adred staggered ahead, moving toward the piles of stone and block, into the sunlit smoke. Beneath a great smashed stone he saw a pair of boots; on the other side, under a pile of broken brick and fine dust, was Lord Rhin. His face was blackened, blood was pouring brightly from his mouth and nose. As Adred approached him, Rhin opened his eyes.

He didn't speak, but his stare beseeched Adred.

Adred looked at him.

Rhin blinked slowly, stared.

Galvus called, "Adred! What is it?"

"Here. Rhin! He didn't get . . . any farther than this!"

The aristocrat tried to move; or perhaps it was only the whispering dust, the trickling blood that moved.

"Gods," Adred muttered. "Gods, oh gods. . . ." He tried to crouch forward but, weak, fell to his knees. Lord Rhin's hand was stretched toward him. The rest of his arm was covered by bits of rubble and a great piece of metal that had broken loose from a chandelier.

Adred coughed, touched Rhin's hand, clasped it. The fingers didn't move in recognition, but the flesh was warm and damp. Adred looked at the staring aristocrat. "Rhin . . . damn you. . . ." Gripping the hand firmly, Adred pulled back to free it from the covering rubble.

Rhin stared at him, did not move, did not wince.

Adred pulled again on the hand.

The entire arm came free.

"Oh . . . *godssss*!"

The entire arm. Rhin continued to stare at him. Adred held the hand and the end of Rhin's arm gushered blood, trailed stringy

200

muscles and tendons that were coated with dust and bits of stone. Blood poured from beneath the rubble, where Adred had pulled out the arm.

"*Galvus!*"

"What is it? Adred? What—"

"Galvus, *Galvus, Gal*—"

"Adred!"

He tried to stand up, fell back. Shrieking, Adred attempted to throw the arm away. It was dead, lifeless and warm and dead, and it wouldn't let go of him—" ·

"*Gal*—!"

He began to vomit as he threw the arm to the floor.

Galvus's footsteps and, "Adred, *what*—?"

Rhin, blood pouring from his mouth and nose, continued to stare at him.

3.

Assia discovered when she stepped outside—"For a walk," she'd told Essor and Halis—that the evening had become very cool. This surprised her. She had become so used, throughout the drought-plagued summer, to the hot, dry conditions that a naturally cool, late season evening seemed peculiar. She wasn't prepared for it: she was dressed only in her skirt and shirt. Nevertheless, she didn't return to the house, where Iramdos was making his thanks and farewells to his hosts. Assia didn't care to interfere with that and, besides, she truly did want to be by herself for a while.

Crickets were chirping noisily all around. The chickens scruffled a bit as Assia walked by their pen, moving away from the lamp-lit farm hut into the dim shadows of maple and elm trees on the other side of the dirt road. There, in the calm seclusion of those trees, she crossed her arms over her breasts, leaned against a thick elm and stared at the night and the fields. High above was a full moon, eerily lighting the clouds that swarmed before it. She noticed a few stars. The night seemed somehow luminous, more brilliant than it should have been with only the moonlight and the starlight. Assia wondered if this had something to do with her:

perhaps she was catching a fever or becoming more ill. She hadn't suffered any real coughing attacks in quite some time.

Quiet. So . . . quiet. Assia felt incredibly alone, but this awareness didn't depress her now as it had in the past. She seemed to be complete and whole for the first time in her life, here in the shadows of these trees, in the soft night with the faraway moon and stars and the warmly-lit farm house behind her. She almost wished that she could stop time at this very moment—stop it, keep things as they were just now. She felt so complete and whole in her aloneness. It seemed somehow that all that happened to her must have been for some reason. It wasn't a rational deduction; it couldn't be analyzed; it was simply a feeling, a mood. It felt very right.

Far to the west, as Assia languidly watched the night, she saw brightness swell on the horizon. It was almost a glow. An immense glow, as though yellow starlight, a haze of it, were being pushed from the earth up to the sky. It was most peculiar; Assia had never seen anything like it.

She moved to change her posture, because her legs were beginning to ache and her arms were becoming tired. As she shifted her weight she heard a noise behind her—soft footfalls on the dry grass. Assia turned.

Iramdos was standing in the darkness beside her. At the sound of the young woman's gasp, he asked carefully, "I'm sorry. Did I startle you?"

"Yes . . . yes. . . ." Assia waved her hand at him, caught her breath, whispered: "I've been daydreaming out here . . . I didn't hear you. Are you—leaving now, Iramdos? Going south?"

"Yes. I want to thank you for your hospitality today. You've been very kind to a stranger."

Assia sniffled. "Not me, so much; thank Essor and Halis. I'm as much their guest as you are."

"Still. . . ." He watched her for a moment, then glanced toward the west. "Odd," Iramdos muttered.

"What? Oh, those lights? Yes, I noticed that, too. Can't imagine what they—"

"Those are volcanoes," he said.

"Volcanoes?"

"Volcanoes, and earthquakes . . . the tides will rise . . . the earth is attacking itself. . . ."

"What are you talking about?" Assia asked him. His strange tone, his words, frightened her. He was so somber.

"What am I talking about? Why, the end of the world, Assia. The end of—" he looked around "—all of this. A conclusion to what we have begun."

She stared at him, didn't say anything.

"Do you think I'm lying. Do you think I'm out of my mind?" He made a sound in his throat, then moved from beneath the elm tree, went into the field and bent his head back, stared up at the night sky.

Assia watched him, wondering if she should run back into the farm house to get away from him.

After a moment, Iramdos pointed. "There. The clouds have moved. You can see it now. Imgor had moved into the sign of Sath, the Dragon." He glanced at Assia.

She stepped away from the tree, approached him, stared at the stars. "The dragon that swallows its own tail."

Iramdos chuckled. "So, you know astrology?"

"Not really. But . . . someone I once knew, he talked about it. Imgor in the sign of the Dragon, and something else that had to happen. I don't know."

"You can't see it now," Iramdos remarked, "because the clouds hide it. But Meb and Sidru are in conjunction."

"What does that mean?"

"It means that they're as close together in the sky as you and I are right now, and in the sign of the Wolf, Grem. And they are opposite Elru—that planet, there—in the sign of Oloros, Water. These aspects have never before occurred in the history of the world."

Assia didn't say anything. She glanced at the stars again, then moved back to the elm tree. Shortly, Iramdos followed her.

"I don't mean to upset you," he began, "but I thought you might be interested—"

"You say you came from Emaria," Assia curtly interrupted him.

"Yes. From Emaria."

"I want to ask you a question."

"Ask."

"Do you know a man named Thameron?"

She saw, despite the night and the shadows, Iramdos's reaction to this. "*Thameron*?" He let out a shuddering breath. "The lord—the king of Emaria? The man who usurped the throne from King Nutatharis . . . *his* name is Thameron."

"I know that. It can't be the same man. But . . . I was deeply in love at one time, Iramdos, with a man named Thameron. He was—well, he had been a priest." Assia looked away, stared out at the fields. "But something happened to him. He left, he said he'd become some kind of mystic. He became very—not the same man. I still loved him, but he didn't want me anymore. He left . . . we were in Abustad, and he left, he said he was going into Emaria. I haven't seen him since. And I—think about him, I worry about him. . . ."

Iramdos asked her, in a very low voice: "What kind of mystic did he become? Did he tell you? Did he join an order, or did he mention any name, any scholars or towns, any—anything?"

"No. No. . . ." She faced him once more and recalled: "He had some kind of marks on his hands. On the palms of his hands. One was a star, the other was very strange—it almost looked like—"

"Two crescent moons, intertwined."

Startled, she said to him, "Yes. Yes! Those were the marks! You know where Thameron is then, don't you, Iramdos?"

He could barely speak. He was numb, he felt frozen, he could barely utter what he had to say.

"Iramdos? You *know* where Thameron is, don't you?"

"Thameron . . . that priest you loved? Assia—he is the king of Emaria."

Her stare. . . .

"Did you hear me?"

"It can't be." She laughed a little, shook her head. "It can't be the same—You're mistaken. Can he? Can he be?"

"He slew Nutatharis. He has stolen the hearts and minds of an entire nation with his infernal—*sorcery*! His *evil*! He is *evil*, Assia! He is—"

"No!"

"—*ro kil-su*, the enlightened *evil*! Your *Thameron* is the *evil king* of the world—"

"No, Iramdos, *no!* I don't—"

"—the Bringer of Hell!"

204

"*No!*" Assia shrieked at him. "No, no, *no!* Don't tell me that, don't tell me that Thameron is—not *Thameron*—"

"Oh, *gods!*" Iramdos moaned. "Oh, gods, *gods!*"

He threw himself forward. Assia screamed. But the stranger wound his arms about her in a strong embrace, held her tightly as he shuddered and groaned, as he began to sob. Assia struggled to get out of his hold; but she managed only to fall back against the tree, where she suffered his body's tremblings.

"He is evil, he is *the evil one!* He was *chosen* to do this! I tried to slay him!" Iramdos sobbed, "but *nothing* can kill him! He is evil! Don't you—" He pulled himself away, held Assia by her shoulders, breathed into her face as he groaned. "Don't you *understand?* Don't you understand what is *occurring?* The world is *dying,* Assia! We're falling into the *abyss!* Humanity has failed! *Humanity has failed!* The gods are destroying us! The world has *ended,* it is over, mankind *itself* has called these spirits into being, and they have *come! They have come!* They—"

"You're . . . no, you're wrong . . . you're out of your mind," she whispered tensely. "How can you even imagine—that. . . ."

Iramdos swallowed audibly, gasped, wiped his mouth. "Assia. . . ." Fumbling, then, he slapped his hands quickly over his clothes, asked her: "Do you have a weapon on you? A knife? A dagger? *Do you?*"

"No, I don't—I don't carry—"

"*Do you?*"

"Yes!" Assia cried, becoming angry and very frightened. "Yes!" She lifted her right leg, shoved a hand into her boot and withdrew a small dagger.

Iramdos fell back one step, ripped open his shirt to bare his chest. Silver moonlight glistened on the perspiration running between his nipples, coated the hair of his chest with frost. "Here," he murmured. "Here."

"*Stab* you?"

"Here."

"I—I can't—*stab* you, Iramdos!"

"Here! Strike me now!" he ordered her, tapping his left breast. "Listen to me! Your beloved *Thameron* is the Master of Hell! It is *he* who brings this ruination and disease upon the earth! He has slaughtered thousands! Tens of thousands! Hundreds of thousands! He feeds them grain, then he rips mothers open, he forces them to feast upon the children from their wombs, he tortures—''

"Stop it, *stop it*! Liar! *I won't stab you*, I don't care what you say!"

"*Here!*" Iramdos howled. And when Assia did not move, he swiftly lunged forward, gripped the hand that held the dagger and forced it toward him.

Assia gasped and tried to deflect the stroke, but Iramdos was far stronger than she and he forced half the blade into his chest, just at the heart.

"*Why are you doing this*?" Assia bawled fearfully, pulling back, still holding the dagger. "Why are you—" But now she saw.

No blood.

No wound.

Her eyes went wide, her lips dropped open. "You . . . can't be— You *made me stab you in the heart*!" she yelled "It *went in*, I *felt* it, I *saw* it!"

Iramdos told her, "I cannot die."

"*I pushed the knife into your heart*!"

"I cannot die, Assia. Stab me a thousand times, you will never draw blood, you will never make a wound, and I will never show a trace of one. I cannot die. I have never died. I am cursed by the gods. Look—look at me! *I cannot die*! *Thameron* could not kill me! *Cyrodian of Athadia* could not kill me! A hundred thousand men throughout *time* have tried, and *none* could slay me! I cannot die! The *world* is dying, and *I* cannot— I will not die!"

Shivering . . . weakly . . . she dropped the knife . . . stared at him. . . . *No—no he must be this isn't possi*. Her knees buckled, her skirt ripped as Assia dropped to the ground, curled up and tossed her head back and forth. Back and forth. "Not Thameron!" she screamed, lost. "Not *Thameron*! *Thameronnnn.* . . !"

Weeping, Eromedeus knelt beside her, and after a while wrapped his arms about her and held her.

"I have heard mountains groan," said Eromedeus, his voice somber, full of aches and dread at what he revealed, poignant, his words terribly true, as true as the mystery of life itself. "I have heard mountains groan; they sound like men caught in troubled sleep, although one must pause and listen for ten thousand years to hear the breathing of that slumber. I have seen seas dry. I have witnessed the deaths and births of stars in heaven, as age upon age has passed beneath my tread. I have even seen complete forms of life become stunted and pass on, and other forms of life subtly change as the seasons and the world and its currents have changed. That gives me hope—hope that man will be surpassed, in some dream life far in the future. For I have seen no transformations in men. But there is a change in things, a slowly progressing mood to life itself.

"And I have listened so many times, so many times, to the rise and fall of cycles of existence—birds and animals and all the creatures mating and being born, growing to mate with others, perpetuating the mystery that has no end. Tribes and nations and civilizations . . . everything born, living to complete itself or to enhance the world, or confound the world, then passing on and dying. Yet I have never died. Yet am I flesh, like all mortal things—deathless flesh. I am a monster. I am bone and muscle and nerve, though I cannot die and am a monster. I cannot rend this unhappy flesh. I cannot plunge from a height and be dashed. I cannot be dismembered, but that the parts crawl back and rejoin themselves—to my never-ending shame. I cannot fall ill; no disease will touch me. I reach a limit of years where other men begin to turn from the world, reflect and wonder of their rewards, and then I slumber and awaken again to breathe, unchanged—the fleshy clay still wrapped upon these bones. And I cannot die. I have no spirit."

Assia, silent, watched him as he spoke: haunted voice like a distant wailing wind, ancient eyes drawn with sadness—eyes that had seen so much, so much more than they wished.

"Don't you think I have prayed to the gods for my death, petitioned them and tried to make bargains with them? I am no adventurer; I am no poet, nor even a philosopher. Men of numbered years build beauty from life's limits: I have seen verse fossilize, and I am familiar with the rot that comes to all dreams. The gods are cold and they will not listen: the gods are not human, they are not warm and they have no humor in them, no touch of change, no sense of time's patterns. Better that the gods die. Yet have I prayed to them, these cold gods—prayed to be forgotten, as forgotten as those with whom I first lived, so long ago that no road leads any longer to where we lived, no stone remains from those houses that we built. I have beseeched the gods to strike me with the most painful and debilitating of diseases, and to have that disease linger and hold and continue for a thousand years within me, for ten thousand years. I could endure it, did I but know that there would come an end to it. Those cold gods . . . they hear, and they refuse me. I am forgotten, but in life and not in death.

"And I have called myself by so many names that there are no words left that I might use. And I have desecrated temples, I have caused wars, I have made butcheries happen and I have sought out every means I could to enrage the gods and all men everywhere. But I might as well have been a storm, for all the vengeance that I kindled in men's slow-knowing hearts. There are no abominations I have not committed, no dishonors grand or small which I have not performed. Life without loss is—meaningless."

He fell silent.

Assia thought he would speak again and so she said nothing; but as the moments passed, as her heart beat and still Eromedeus, in his pride or profound agony, did not say more, she at last asked him:

"Love?"

"What of it?"

"Have you never, in your unending life, loved? Or committed abominations in the name of honest love? Or offered your soul to the end of time itself, out of love?"

He smiled at her. "Love is as much a thing of men as is food and drink and clothing. There is no love that outlasts the lover."

"Or hate?" she inquired. "Then there is no hate that outlasts the one who hates passionately, as passionately as he might love?"

"Hate is not love. Hate remains, love dissipates. When love is gone there remains only—nothing. Nothing. Love might be smoke, and hate a rock."

"I . . . love," Assia confessed. "And I want to die, feeling that love."

Eromedeus frowned.

"I love Thameron," she told him.

"You don't realize what you're saying."

"But I do. You told me that—that Thameron—the king of Emaria—that he is evil, that he has become an evil spirit. That may be so, Eromedeus, but the evil man on the throne of your

208

country is not the Thameron that I love. The Thameron I love—he and I—we are back in Erusabad, we are still there, and in love."

"You don't understand love at all."

"I do, Eromedeus. I do. Thameron has not ceased to love me; he has merely become confused, and so he has turned away. Perhaps he supposes that our love is no longer relevant, has no currency in his heart. But the love is still there. And my love for him . . . still there. And, Eromedeus, I want to die in love, feeling that."

"You don't know what you're talking about," he insisted again.

"Yes, I do. You don't understand, but you don't need to. My love for Thameron—it has never gone away. It still is. I made it happen—we made it happen—and it will never go away. We created it . . . I still feel it . . . and I still feel *his* love. I don't know if he and I will ever come back to this kind of life, or if we'll go to the gods—your cold gods—or we'll go to a pit. People make those things up, I think. But—*love*, Eromedeus! I don't mean passion . . . I don't mean—lust or fear or jealousy or— Just . . . love."

Love, o king, he had told Nutatharis, is a storm; it is not a quiet dawn, it is not placid, it is not warm flesh coupling to sate lusts. Were you ever to confront true love, it would demolish you with its power.

How pretentious he had been. How he stared at this young woman. His mouth went dry; he began to tremble. "What . . . are you saying?" Eromedeus asked her.

Assia told him: "I have never felt so complete as I do now. Everything that you've told me . . . at first, it frightened me. But now—I seem to feel something, I feel—*bright*. Isn't that strange? Maybe—maybe it's not true, but it *feels* true. I'm not tired anymore; I'm not ill; I'm not afraid. I want—"

She looked at him.

Eromedeus whispered: "Assia. . . ?"

"You told me that the reason you can't die is . . . because no one was ever willing to give up their life for you, Eromedeus? I will."

"Assia—"

"I will do it, Eromedeus."

He was trembling uncontrollably; the ground itself seemed to tilt; the stars above him began to spin; the shadows of the dark began to fill with light. "You don't—*understand*!" he moaned, lifting his hands.

Assia smiled at him. Tears dripped down her cheeks, shined on her lips, hung on her chin. "But I do understand," she answered. "Oh, I *do* understand, Eromedeus!" She crouched forward, smiling at him, her face damp and slippery; she lifted a hand to his cheek.

"*No!*"

But in that moment Assia's fingers touched him; and in that moment she sighed, still smiling, and slumped forward.

"*No! No-oho-no*!" Eromedeus screamed it, threw his head back and screamed it to the night.

Assia fell against him; Eromedeus drew her to him, forced her to sit up.

"Listen to me, Assia. *Listen to me!*"

But she had gone limp. Still smiling. Eyes closed. Unmoving.

"Assia! No!"

He roared at the night; the stars revolved in a great wheel, and they seemed to revolve around him, as though he were the center of a universe of whirling lights. A breeze sighed low in the darkness; leaves fluttered in trees everywhere. Assia was still warm in his arms.

"Oh . . . *gods!*" he screamed. "Oh, gods, *godsss!*"

A numbness seized him, and nausea gripped him. He felt cramps buckle and coil within him; he felt himself being pulled through a warm tunnel of moist darkness. Though his eyes were open, Eromedeus could see nothing—nothing. The stars had gone, the trees and fields had gone. All was utter darkness, completely black, and he heard nothing save for the violently pounding secret thunder of his own heart, the rampaging cascade of his own mind. He felt nothing, he was floating, he was powerless, a victim, or a moment about to be exposed to time—

And suddenly the universe erupted all about him. The stars returned, brilliant and profound, blatant, to explode with blossoms of blinding light that washed down so heavily upon him that Eromedeus could feel the pressure of the brightness. Noises became sounds and he could feel the weight and pressure of the noises of the world. Huge sounds, marching and throbbing, stretching and rolling with screams and many violent echoes, the tumultuous groaning of oceans as they moved upon the surface of the world, and the tiny evanescent colors of mere grains of sand blowing upon a stone in whispers, and the sounds of animals coupling, the sounds of roots growing and pulsing and the shining sounds of mountains bursting upward, rocks singing with their inorganic strength, perfect waves of wind and air rushing in cold patterns and in hot streams upon the seas and over the deserts and through the forests, high into the mountains. Rainfall. Laughter. Insects. Fingers parting moistly in the new hand of a newborn child. The sounds of eyes opening. The tumbling noise of death stretching and pushing against the insides of dying bodies and the merest trace of a hum, a single shared note, as the spirits slipped or fled from those bodies, happy and joyous in their reunion with the soul of all that had gone before and all that would follow after—

"No-oho-oooo—!"

His body was very heavy. Eromedeus slumped, fell sideways, dropped onto his back. He stared up at the revolving stars as they slowed . . . slowed . . . fell still again upon the endless surface of the black eternal night.

His body hurt, his lungs labored, he suffered, his fingers felt stiff, his legs and his eyes—

His body hurt.

Eromedeus lay there panting, gasping, reborn, and his chest hurt where someone had wounded him—

Where he had forced Assia to stab him.

He shrieked with fear and understanding. He began to sob and wail in torment, like a newborn child pulled from its complete universe and dragged into a cold world of noise and light and heavy flesh, aching bones, failing senses.

He shrieked.

"I want—to—*live!*" he screamed to the stars, to the night, to the cold gods. "*I want to live!*"

Above him the stars growled, thunder echoed. Beneath him, the earth groaned.

He felt Assia's body still slumped upon his, sprawled and unmoving, unalive.

He felt drops of rain sprinkle upon his hot face, and the cool promise of the late night breeze.

4.

Through the heavy shadows and in the darkness of the night, Major Thytagoras with twenty men moved furtively among the trees and over the low hills toward the northside of the city. Erusabad's walls lifted tall and gaunt and solid above them, the fallen shadows protecting their progress. High above, the stars were hidden by mighty clouds, and those clouds growled and heat lightning flashed as droplets of rain swept down, carried on long trailing breezes.

Thytagoras slowed, motioning his men to pause in their advance. He studied the walls, he observed the landscape all around. He glanced behind and saw where the huge armada with its thousands of lights had deployed into formation, the flagships leading their vessels into positions before the harbor, upon the northern beachhead and—farther away, where Thytagoras could not see—against the southern beachhead.

Continuing his cautious advance, Thytagoras waited again when he heard a hiss sound behind him, a whisper. He glanced back, followed the pointing hand, and saw. Beyond the tall shadowing walls the darkness of the sky gave way to glowing orange and crimson and white. Then Thytagoras and his men heard screams—a few pitched howls that shined brightly through the general clamor of rising shrieks.

"Major!"

Thytagoras saw it. "Fire ships!" he grunted. "The damned bastards are sending out fire ships! *Damn them!*"

Ten of them. Long *surks* piled high with wood and refuse and doused with oil, set afire by crews that dived from them (sparkling in the black waters of the harbor as they escaped) while the fire ships swept out haphazardly, moving with their tall flames and crumbling masts to scatter the formations of the Athadian fleet.

Then in the sky came flaring comets. Great bundles of flame loosed by catapults on the walls of Erusabad, flying out in streaking orange arcs, smashing into the ocean and exploding in geysers of steam, some of them finding their targets and crashing into Athadian galleys and biremes with wild eruptions of fire. Sails caught aflame; decks suddenly roared into life with great howling whirlwinds, as bursting comets spread their oil and splashed their sparks and greedily began consuming the war ships.

From where they observed, Thytagoras and his men saw small moving bits of whipping flame jump from the ships and sink into the shadows of the ocean. The screams followed, crossing the distance as the flames vanished, swallowed by the blackness.

"Damn them, *damn them*!"

But this panorama of destruction, these episodes in the opening of a war, could not deter Major Thytagoras. Already he had concluded that they had reached the area he'd indicated to General Thomo: this copse of trees, the fall of the land, the distance from the walls assured him of that.

"Break out your shovels," he ordered, "and begin digging over there!" He stood up himself and moved away from the trees, staggered down an incline in the darkness, pulled free his sword and jammed it into the ground. "Here!" He pushed the sword around, making a crater, then yanked it up and wiped it on his pants.

Twenty men, making as little noise as possible, moving toward him—ten with shovels to begin digging, ten with steel bared to keep a watch.

Hardly had the unearthing begun when great comets ripped through the sky above them, arcing high and dropping bits of raining fire, smashing into the woods and hills beyond and setting fire to the earth. Two of them—three of them—six—ten in all, arcing and reaching through the darkness and dipping and exploding, their remnants growing into a hurrying wall of fire.

"They know we're here!" gasped one of the men.

"No!" Thytagoras barked. "They're trying to see if Thomo has forces on this side of the city! Stay down! Low, low!"

Loudly through the darkness came the noises of trotting horses, the hollow clanking of armor and weapons.

"They know we're here!" grunted the same man again, throwing down his shovel, pulling free his sword and falling into a crouch.

Thytagoras yelled for them all to do the same, and as the last man dropped to his knees flashes of silver and gray and bronze and the moving whiteness of horses climbed into view before him. Thytagoras tried to discern the numbers of the patrol: more than twenty, in any event. And as they rode past, disappearing in the direction of the beach, further thunder followed them—a true force of riders.

Major Thytagoras swore under his breath. He and his men were caught wholly in the open, were completely unprotected. Not even a copse of trees could—

Stay down, stay down. . . .

Behind him, then.

Whinnying horses, calling voices, heavy pounding on the earth. One of his men called out.

The snapping of bowstrings in the darkness brought out loud grunts and screams as some of the shafts found their marks.

"Major! *Major!*"

One of them took off, fleeing for cover.

Two loud horses overtook him, steel flashed, the helmeted head flew away on a brilliant spiral of wet shimmering blood—

"Damn you!" Thytagoras howled, rising to his feet, holding his sword with both hands in a basic posture of defense. "Come here and face me! Come here and face me! *Damn you all to hell-lllll!*"

And the riders came at him, flying hoofs and bouncing armor, swinging swords and heavy axes—and the thunder and noise and the howls and screams sundered the night in all directions—

"*Damn you all to—*"

Gasping. Howling. The swift plunge of weapons into him, at him, upon him.

The night went red and suddenly silent. . . .

The *Wing.* Its first night out from the armada as it made its way north toward the Isle of Odossos, food and water, and then the long way to Abustad and the sea road back to Athad.

Not one man among all the crew had seen or heard from Queen Salia since she had locked herself in her cabin last night. Her food trays had been left in the gallery; when a cook's hand brought her supper and found that breakfast and lunch had not yet been taken inside, he knocked on the cabin door and called the queen's name.

No answer., Properly alarmed at last, the hand alerted the master of the *Wing*, who made his way down into the gallery and, too, hammered upon the wood and called out for the queen.

She answered Captain Lathen's temper, told him that she wished to be by herself and assured him that she was not hungry. His cook could remove the food trays.

And that was all, until the watch sang out the fourth hour after nightfall. The first mate was making his way from his bunk to the stern deck when he heard something smashing in Salia's cabin. The sound of glass breaking, or a mirror shattering.

Captain Lathen was notified but he was too occupied to investigate; at five bells after sunset, however, he decided that the queen had best come to terms with her childish pique and eat something. So he took a tray down to her himself, held it in one hand while he rapped on her cabin door with the other. No answer. Becoming irritated with this temperamental game, Captain Lathen called out sternly to Queen Salia and, as a matter of habit, pressed his free hand to the latch to jostle it.

The latch gave way and the door swung open, surprising Lathen so much that he nearly dropped the tray.

But Queen Salia was not inside.

Lathen set her tray on a table, called out again—then cocked an ear as a voice above him sang out: "Man overboard! *Overboard*!"

His belly dropped.

Stepping around the strewn particles of glass that had been a mirror on the back of the cabin door, Lathen moved into the gallery and raced down the corridor and up to the poopdeck. A crowd of hands at the leeward rail hailed him and he hastened to them.

"Salia? Is it Queen Salia?"

The men jabbered. One of them grunted and pointed. Out behind them, trailing in the wash of the ship's wake, was a brilliant white object. Lathen ordered his boats down, but already the tackle was clattering, lines were hissing, skiffs splashing loudly.

As men at the rail moved to join those jumping into the boats, Captain Lathen noticed something on the deck boards. Groaning, he knelt to inspect it and found not one but three rose petals fallen there.

"Eh?" muttered a man beside him, taking one. "Flowers?"

"Yellow . . . rose petals," the master frowned, not understanding.

The white shape was retrieved quickly. Captain Lathen called from the poop rail, asking if the queen were safe. But as the boats

215

continued to circle in the water, the rescuer oared back to the *Wing* and one of its mates cried out:

"No sign of Queen Salia, sir! We only found her clothes!"

The *Wing* listed at anchor all through the night. The boats circled, torches bloomed in the breezes and lines were thrown out at shadows and moving currents.

But Queen Salia's body was never found.

Lasura.

The city of austere elegance had been betrayed. Even at night, lighted by torches and lamps, the clean wide streets were noticeably littered and rubble-strewn, the alleys filled with trash and with hobbled crowds of frightened people. The great fountains which once had sparkled with columns of water and nets of spray now showed the burnt remains of bonfires—and in the ashes of charred wood and soft peat coals, bones.

The bones of animals, perhaps.

From the roof of every building flew the new state flag: the star of the Emarian League. The black symbol hung from windows, was draped over balconys and doors and decorated the promenades and courtways of all public buildings. Stern emotionless soldiers, dressed in black and scarlet and silver, marched through the boulevards and rode through the squares, proudly displaying armbands patched with the sign of the star. The soldiers moved in long unswerving columns; passersby veered out of their way, and children crouched into huddles, shopkeepers behind their windows did not glance up.

In every street, in every mall, on the steps of every important building, men garbed in scarlet and black and silver, lit by huge cisterns of leaping flames, hammered at lecterns as they addressed crowds of people who cheered in unison, laughed as one, raised fists in the air when mention was made of the enemies of the state. Imperial armies at the Emarian border . . . children who refused to acknowledge the failed ideals of their parents . . . insurrectionists who plotted against throne and family, who plotted against the spiritual and moral values of the star—enemies all.

Occasionally, in the night, in Lasura, a scream would sound—distant, muffled, hidden somewhere underground but escaping through a broken window or finding its way into the open through a drainage tunnel. Another enemy, meeting his or her just punishment. Someone protecting a guilty friend or sibling? Someone from a derelict army unit, planning revolution? Bent, all of them, and resisting the unified flow of the will of the people, the heart and mind of the people, fighting the truth the people wished to hear, declaiming the truth the new prophet of the star had come to proclaim. Enemies were everywhere. . . .

As he was brought down the broad avenue leading to the state palace, Asawas saw the hollow remains of a great stone building—charred blocks, fallen timbers, and some brown-eaten skulls mounted on posts in the center of the blasted foundations. He asked the leader of his escort what that building had been. The reply was terse.

"The legislature."

The yard before the main entrance of the palace had been barricaded: fresh walls, obviously only months old, were patrolled by sentries. Asawas, accompanied by his escort of ten soldiers, was led through the tall iron gates and brought before an officer seated in a booth. This man asked many questions in Emarian, which the prophet did not understand; the leader of the escort made replies but did not interpret for him. Finally Asawas, accompanied now only by the leader, was taken across the yard toward the palace steps leading to the entrance portico. All around the square stood gleaming soldiers, proud and at attention, weapons glowing orange in the torchlight, the leather and bronze and silver of their armor shimmering. From the low darkness of hidden corners and other enclaves came the growls and snarls of dogs—hundreds of them, leashed but dragging their chains, showing their yellow eyes, white teeth.

Asawas took the steps to the entranceway slowly. He felt numb and exhausted, but not only because of his long journey. The earth beneath him extruded waves of tension; the drizzling sky above him rolled and breathed with the promise of storm; and this palace, these steps, this entire city clamped upon the prophet like a gloved hand upon the throat. It was the feel of evil; it was the dark, alive sensation of soullessness, the weightiness of corruption and untruth and inversion—the very feeling of evil which slowed the prophet's steps, brought a burning to his lungs and an ache to his heart.

The evil.

Everywhere. . . .

And the pathetic signs of evil—the lost hearts and minds of the people, the urgent and perilous sameness of the soldiers who had sold their lives for a common bond of flagrant repression, mistrust, hate. The oppressive shadow of *fear* was everywhere. The numbing certainty that all was weak asserted itself as strength; that individuals had given up their voices in return for one voice. The betrayal: the false and insulating security of steel and commands, human authority, force, intolerance. . . .

Great doors were opened; Asawas was led down a long nave festooned with black flags, the polished marble glistening wetly in the endless torchlight. He was directed into a small room, little more than a cell without a door; he was told to stand there and wait while Lord Thameron was notified of his arrival. And there he stood, a tall gray-haired, gray-bearded man dressed in a worn robe, worn sandals, with only his staff to lean on, in full view of the armored men who observed him from the entrance hallway.

The empty hollow distant echo of retreating boots. . . .

Outside, dogs barked. Men laughed.

Thunder bristled, high above.

The prophet felt very weak, very tired. Privately, he murmured a prayer.

The hollow echoing sound of boots returned to him, and the officer who had escorted him here announced to him blandly:

"Lord Thameron refuses to see you."

Asawas was momentarily startled. "He . . . refuses?"

A blank stare.

He remembered something. "Does he . . . he doesn't know —who I am?"

"Why should he know who you are?"

"Give him this." He handed his staff to the officer.

"Lord Thameron is much too occupied to give attention to—"

"Show him the staff."

The stare.

"Take . . . this . . . staff . . . to . . . Lord Thameron."

He held it outstretched in his veiny, boned hand, where it quivered.

The officer squinted. Took it. Retreated.

Hollow, echoing bootsteps. . . .

Asawas studied the soldiers across the hall as they carefully watched him.

The bootsteps returned, clicked abruptly as they stopped, farther down the polished marble hallway. Asawas could not see the officer, but his voice was loud.

"Bring this man into Lord Thameron's presence at once!"

Orain remembered.

"I love you, daughter not born of my flesh. Orain, how can I face the goddess, when to face her is to look into my own mirror? These crimes have come, so awesome, because we have refused our deep secret, and we cannot share or understand what we refuse. Orain—the gods are within us. We are the gods. We are their masters, and we are very poor masters, poor masters indeed, of the gods and ourselves. . . ."

Yta. . . .

In the garden, in the whipping torchlight, as the rainy drizzle fell and collected in shining black pools in the cracked walkways, one of the Khamars looked to where footsteps were coming and announced grimly: "Count Adred! Lord Galvus, are you ready?"

He nodded silently, rose to his feet from the damp stone bench. He glanced at his mother.

Orain turned to face Adred as he entered the garden, carrying over one shoulder his satchel. Letters, his father's letters, notes, books—those things important to him. Ideas.

"I've brought a few clothes," he said quietly. "But I'm hoping this won't last too long."

Eyes in the darkness watched him mutely. Adred's glance moved from Galvus to Abgarthis to the ring of Khamars. Orain slipped her hand into his.

"We're ready, then?"

Orain asked Galvus, "Are you sure—you don't want to take anything?"

He nodded his head.

"All right, then," said one of the Khamars. He motioned to the others and they gently urged the prince-regent and his group ahead, down the path of the garden. "We're going to take Othad Avenue to the Undorian Boulevard," he told Galvus. "From

219

there, the northwest docks. We can't make it through the city to get to the royal quay."

"That much damage?"

"I'm afraid so. Half the city's gone, Lord Galvus."

Orain made a sound; Adred squeezed her hand tightly.

As they made their way toward the fallen western wall of the garden, more dull rumbling quaked beneath their feet. The Khamars helped Abgarthis and Galvus over the piles of debris and twisted metal, while Adred guided Orain. The coach and some extra horses were sitting beneath a bent tree, hidden in shadows.

Abgarthis, Orain and Adred stepped into the carriage. As Galvus pulled himself up, he asked the Khamar: "Do you really expect much trouble?"

"Othad Avenue took some heavy damage, my lord. There may not be much left of the Undorian, either. But . . . the people— maybe we can't expect them to act any differently, under conditions like this. But we want to get you to safety as quickly as possible. And a ship at sea is the safest place possible, now." He added, anticipating a natural concern: "Never fear; Captain Mandoum will see to the palace until order is restored."

Galvus muttered something and moved inside, sat beside Abgarthis.

Leather creaked, metal clanged and bounced as Khamars mounted their horses and the driver the seat of the carriage. The whip cracked loudly; the coach bounced forward, rolled and rattled down the street, away from the ruined gardens and broken palace.

Silence.

Adred held tightly onto Orain's hand, glanced at the others.

But no one was looking at anyone else. They were all staring off into dark corners, shadows, staring at what their imaginations made of all this—not looking at anyone else.

5.

Thameron awaited him in a large chamber on the second floor of the palace.

Only the dimensions of the room lent it any atmosphere or auspiciousness, for otherwise it was somewhat barren and in no way ostentatious or overdone with presumptious trappings of authority. Drapes and arras hung against the walls; tripod braziers burned with coals of incense; long rugs lay used upon the stone floor. Oil lamps hung suspended from the tall ceiling, and there were several beautifully-wrought tables.

Curiously, Asawas did not notice a single black flag or star design anywhere in that chamber, other than on the armbands of the twenty soldiers who stood at rigid attention alongside the door and alongside Thameron's chair. For the sorcerer sat in a great stone chair behind the largest table in the room. Upon this table were a decanter of wine, a goblet, some books, parchment and pens, as well as Asawas's staff. Thameron himself was dressed plainly in a scarlet robe and he wore upon his head a blue *sulm*; he appeared in every aspect a youthful, energetic man, betraying not at all the forbidding or sinister appearance of a master of evil which an unsophisticated mentality might conceive.

As Asawas was ushered in, Thameron rose from his chair and leaned forward, pressing his hands upon the table. He displayed no emotion as the prophet was led before him.

As Asawas stepped still, the guard beside him growled: "Bow before the king of Emaria!"

Asawas did not move.

"*Bow before the king of Emaria!*"

Still Asawas did not make any indication that he intended to do so; the guard lifted a hand and roughly collared him, to force him to his knees.

But Thameron shook his head and muttered, "No. That will not be necessary with this man." His gaze never strayed from Asawas's burning stare.

The soldier lent his king an uncertain eye, but he released the prophet and stepped away a pace, resting his right hand on his sword pommel.

"So . . ." Thameron smiled, "as promised, you have come."

"Surely you did not forget me."

"No. Oh, no. I did not forget you. But I doubted that it was truly you so suddenly as this."

"So suddenly, *ro kil-su?* Time hurries."

"Indeed it does."

"Humanity hurries, toward its new beginning."

"Toward its long-sought conclusion, Asawas—through me."

221

"To its sundering and reunion, Thameron, through the will of On, and All and the All Forever."

Again Thameron's bland expression was touched by a hint of smile. He leaned back, dropped into his chair, made himself comfortable. "I assume you have come a long way, on my account. May I offer you food? Drink?"

"No."

"Any service whatsoever?"

"The only service you may render me, Thameron, would be to dispense with these pretensions."

"Pretensions? I see no pretensions."

"All of . . . this. These mortal trappings; this vain assumption to power that cloaks your actual purpose; this lying pose as the liberator of humanity."

Thameron chuckled. He noticed the soldier beside Asawas, and the others in the chamber, becoming anxious at what they overheard. The king said to the guard: "This man, like myself, is learned in the profound arts. He has come here to beg my leniency in the name of his god."

"I have come here," Asawas said plainly, keeping his sight on Thameron, "to condemn you, and to force you to reveal yourself as the thing you truly are, to wrestle away your grip, which you hold clamped upon the throat of humankind."

Thameron's eyes narrowed; his voice gained an edge. "To reveal myself, farmer?" To condemn me? Proud words!"

"You are *ro kil-su*, the sower of discord, the prince of liars, the hiding shadow, the evil one, master of hell—the arbiter of human fears. You are the black womb, Thameron, from which issues nothing but terror and fear; you are fear incarnate."

"You," Thameron retorted, watching, sensing, "condemn yourself when you condemn me, priest."

"Unmask yourself now," Asawas challenged him, "before me. Face me, Spirit. Do not prolong mankind's agony, for even now the storm builds."

"And I hear the storm building, Asawas. Reveal *yourself*."

The prophet pressed his hands together, a delicate, controlled gesture. "What shall I do," he asked in a whisper, "that might force the evil spirit from you, boy? Shall I battle you? Shall I prostrate myself before you? Shall I offer myself as a sacrifice

222

to—" he glanced at the soldier beside him "—the lowest of your order, these whom you have duped and provoked?"

Thameron saw that his man was eager to punish the prophet for these slanderous words; but he withheld giving any order. Instead: "Go, Ioris."

"Lord Thameron!"

"*Go!* This will be resolved on my own terms! Go, now—all of you, go!"

Disgruntled, not understanding, the man frowned to the twenty, who saluted, raised their arms and moved from the chamber. Ioris himself was last to go, and he regarded his king keenly as he backed out and shut the chamber doors.

As the sounds faded: "Men are beasts," Thameron remarked. "They are low, they are fallen, and they yearn to be caged."

Asawas replied: "Men are animals seeking the expression of wisdom deep inside them. They are spirits, Thameron, searching for freedom. Sometimes their search leads them into cages, and such as you confound them with your shadows. They worship you and adore you because they believe you embody a power they do not have. Yet you are a vampire, sucking the life from them, returning to them only husks and shells. They forge their own chains from their own weaknesses. To them, sorcerer, you seem to be life itself, all in one vessel, coherent and actual and whole; and what they do not comprehend, you rationalize for them. You are the necessary lie."

"They are eager children," grinned Thameron. "And who are you to reprove me for solacing that wild herd? If they did not turn to me for authority, they would turn to another. I willingly sacrifice myself to them! I am their will, their life, their answer! I guide them with the wisdom they give me! For they are so weak. . . ."

"No. They are very strong—only they have not yet found a direction for their strengths. Every young thing is that way, yet it is why humanity seems ill and wicked, weak and incoherent and its own enemy."

Thameron seemed to ponder this; he moved from his chair, stood up and walked around his table in long, slow strides. Hands behind his back, he seemed to contemplate the prophet's words with curled brow, frowning mouth. He stopped at the end of the table, faced Asawas. Watched him. Seemed to wait, as if to hear more.

"We both know the truth, Thameron; we both have been touched by the All. But you allowed yourself to become invaded by the least of things, while I was touched by the glory of the highest. You and I are only men, after all. Shall I tell you my secret, Thameron? The power that visited me as I lay near death, was no other power than that of myself—myself, raised to the height that humanity can reach. Shall I tell you the secret of yourself?"

Thameron frowned.

"The spirit that entered you, that uses you as a vessel, is only yourself in another guise—a fragment of yourself, a fragment of the All which you use as your mask, here in this place."

Thameron sneered at him. "Words . . . words. There is no power in words."

"In words resides the only power, for when men name a thing they may either destroy it by possessing it, or they may become it, and so transcend it."

The sorcerer maintained his frown and began to walk slowly in a circle around Asawas. "You are wise, you are learned," he admitted. "Yet you come to me, asserting your simple strength, piously, self-righteously, and you invite my very dangerous anger, shaman—and for what reason? Did you come here to discuss humanity? Surely there are better places for that! Did you come here to judge me? Surely you are not so foolish! Did you come here with a power to defeat me, to destroy me? A noble desire, but you know that such cannot be. My strength is vast."

"Vast though it is, sorcerer, it will be a simple thing to defeat you, for I know your secret."

"Do you?"

"To look upon the crowds that worship you, is to know your secret. You yourself saw me deny the crowds that sought to worship me—such is my secret, and my strength. I have come here only to cast out from you this creature that holds you, this shadow in your heart, this emotional demon, this fear that has become Fear itself. I have come to do away with the wall you have forged, and to build a bridge. For there is nothing that separates us, although you feel there must be."

Now Thameron laughed aloud at him.

Outside, thunder growled.

The sorcerer remarked on it. "Do you hear? Do you? That is

224

humanity's storm, shaman! That is *humanity*, eager to destroy itself! *Humanity*, preparing for its own annihilation! And why? *Why*? Because humanity fears *life* more than it fears *death*! And you? *You* come among men and ask them to stand *naked* in their fears? They come to worship you, and you bring them only ugliness and discomfort, you bring them the *truth*! Men do not want the *truth*! They want their fears exorcised! They want enemies punished! They want their guilt and fear and unreason fed! They want to slake their guilty thirst at being alive in pools of blood! They want to devour the meat of their guilt and their shame with the carcasses of their fellow men! *I* offer them nobility! *I* offer them pride! *I* sustain them! But *you*? You ask them to open up to their fears as they might split open old wounds! Those wounds are as old as humanity! Men already *know* the pain of those wounds! They no longer wish to feel that pain! They wish to *escape*! And *I* offer them escape! And there is no reason why they should *not* escape!"

"No reason," Asawas replied, shaking his head slowly, "other than that one day they shall awaken to their own fears, as I have warned them—and then they will wish no more escape. They will accept. Humanity will accept itself. Then you will be seen as the shadow you truly are, and not the light."

Thameron laughed again as he continued his slow pacing around the prophet. "When I at last understood this creature, man—when I at last cast away all that was young and confused in me, priest—it was then that I saw humanity for what it is, and understood my own purpose for being here, now, at this glorious moment, this culmination of mankind's rampant, angry fear. Humanity has finally attained what it has sought for so long. Through countless generations it has petitioned Nature to place itself upon the altar of sacrifice, and at last this strange breed of animal is accomplishing its will: its mighty fears are to be expiated at last. For I discovered . . . sensed . . . that humanity is a most strange combination of creatures. It realizes that it is peculiar, but it does not know what it should do about itself. And what does this strange thing do, when it feels peculiar and awkward and uncertain about itself? It has the ability to ask questions, but lacks the means by which to answer them. It stares at its reflection and is faced, not with an image, but with a million ideas. Its guilt at even existing and not comprehending its own existence is enormous. It realizes, but it does not understand! How can a thing which understands so much not understand itself? Mankind is in love with its imagination of itself; it is in love with its illusions, and these are the illusions, priest, that have moved around in countless cycles, like a great wheel of flagrant agony. Illusions themselves seem to be illusions; Life becomes its own enemy, and that is senseless. Men grapple for excuses, reasons, ideals, more illusions—and on and on it goes. Tribes and villages and cities, warriors and soldiers, money and business empires— on and on it goes, the ceaseless search. And so the contradictions appear, as bright and glowing as flames. Fear awakens love; and love cannot resolve itself without fear! Fear is more necessary than love! Fear gives *meaning*, but love gives meaning only in the context of fear—when it gives limits, when it chains and binds, when it issues commands. You will tell me that love is freedom, and that men wish to be free: I will tell you that men do not know what freedom is, because freedom means knowledge, and true knowledge—self-awareness—is the thing men fear most of all. Do men truly wish to *know* themselves? To stand naked before the truth you bring them? They do now! And so the sublime horror reasserts itself, and I come to men, I make illusions real and make reality an illusion. I tell them they are not animals, but gods; I give them answers to questions before they can ask me to rationalize their fears; I turn them against one another, and they rend one another in the name of love. The words are meaningless; they are not powerful—they are meaningless. No, priest, no. . . . If men truly *aspired* to the truth, they would have no need of me; but men *need* me, they desperately need me, because they *conspire* in their lies, they do not aspire to *truth*! Men beg to be trapped by their freedom, so that their guilt may be assuaged in rituals of blood and pain, fear, animal life—death. That is the truth they know."

Having said all this, Thameron held pause where he stood and stared proudly, almost malevolently at the prophet.

Asawas pressed his fingers together and shivered his head. "I am not afraid of you, Thameron, because there is no fear in me. I am not afraid of being alive; I am not afraid of death. And because I do not fear those things, I have become love, and the spirit. I tell you that what you try to push away will build a bridge into your heart. What you try to isolate will come to you in a communion of spirit. I tell you, Thameron, that humanity will transcend itself, and that it aspires to that. Thameron—don't you think that *I* know what it is that you feel?"

The sorcerer glared at him.

"Man will never be free, evil one, until he understands that he can never be as free as his dreams, his imagination: but man can dream of that, as well, and understand it. And man will never know God until he can look into his mirror and see that his ideas are simply the faces of other men, and know those faces as the one face of the one god. And man has mirrors, and will see into them. And man will never become human until he can banish the fear of his own knowledge of death, and thus his fear of life. But by banishing that fear of death man opens the doors of love that lead to the gates of the spirit, and man will do that. Deny himself, to become himself. Be, in order to become. You cannot refuse this, old shadow, for you yourself once felt the power of God, the All, in you, and God itself *is* man. For there can be no God *without* man."

Thameron did not reply with words but, staring into Asawas's eyes, he unleashed a low growl, the voice of the shadow within him.

"This is not you," Asawas told him "—that boy who was lonely and afraid and seeking, but only the thing you have allowed to happen. For those things we allow to happen . . . those are our spirits."

"I have drawn around you a circle!" Thameron warned him. "I am a mighty power! You are caught within this circle! You have foolishly trapped yourself, priest!"

Asawas smiled sadly. "This?" he asked in a whisper. "Another illusion? I am not entrapped, here, Thameron. I have banished all such things from myself. Now yours, too, are banished. We are humanity, Thameron, you and I; we are God. I do not deny you, and I shall not allow you to deny me." He lifted a hand, stretched out an arm toward the sorcerer.

If indeed there was any power in the ring which Thameron had outlined, it gave no evidence of itself as the prophet reached beyond its perimeter.

Thameron felt a profound weakness sieze him.

"Flee, spirit," Asawas spoke. "Leave this boy . . . join the storm that rages, fighting for itself, and be defeated. Thameron

227

. . . touch my hand. Touch me. Let it be done. Touch me, touch what I have become, and you will join me."

Thameron, as he stared at Asawas, began to tremble. He felt himself dizzying and weakening, he felt a light begin to envelop him, he felt himself shrinking.

"Free yourself," Asawas whispered to him, holding out his hand.

"Free yourself from this evil!" Guburus had shouted to him.

Sweat poured down him; he felt as though he were falling, collapsing. He tried to think of words to say . . . he tried to remember rituals . . . he knew no words. . . .

You are chosen, the vessel, the being, the embodiment of the days. . . .

"Free yourself," Asawas whispered to him.

He lifted his hands; they seemed to float before him. He stared at the marks on his palms.

They were glowing. Burning. Smoking. Yet he felt no pain. Vanishing. . . .

It's guilt at even existing and not comprehending its own existence. . . . Men already know the pain of those wounds! They no longer wish to feel that pain! . . . Do men truly wish to know themselves? To stand naked before the truth you bring them?"

"Touch me. . . ."

"Deny himself, to become himself. Be, in order to become. You cannot refuse this, old shadow. . . . We are humanity . . . we are the god. I do not deny you . . . I shall not allow you to deny me. . . ."

"Touch—"

It is a door . . . a door . . . a door. . . .

"Touch—"

"I need you, Assia. I love you. . . ."

. . . we are the god. . . .

"Touch me—"

Ioris heard it first.

Sir Jors, only now alerted to the fact that an outlander priest had been admitted into King Thameron's presence, was hastening

228

down the corridor as Ioris, glancing in alarm at the other guards, bent his head to the door of his lord's chamber and listened.

The sound of whistling wind.

Frightened, he pounded upon the wood and loudly called out Thameron's name.

"What is it?" Jors demanded angrily. "*What is it?*"

No answer.

As the sound of the whistling trapped wind died out.

"Get this door opened!" Jors yelled.

Ioris threw back the latch, put his shoulder to the door and shoved. He was a strong man, but there was a resistance to his effort, a suctioning or a pressure from just inside. Jors growled to some of the other men there and they leaned against the door beside Ioris.

The door gave in, nearly spilling those guards as they stumbled inside.

"Lord Thameron!" Ioris howled.

And Jors: "*My lord!*"

But as they and their crowd of soldiers raced into the main hall, they stared in amazement at the flagged floor. Lord Thameron was not present, nor the strange priest. Yet upon the stones lay their clothes—only their clothes—and these seemed to glow as though lit by some unseen candlelight.

"Lord Thameron?" Jors shouted. "*Lord Thameron!* Ioris— check those rooms! You men—behind there!"

Yet as the guards moved off to make their inspections, Sir Jors already suspected what had happened. What must have happened, although he could not visualize it, imagine it as real. . . .

"No . . ." Ioris gasped, returning to Jors. "No . . . sign of them—either of them, my lord!"

Jors knelt, fingered the clothes. . . .

The shutters of one window creaked open slowly. Ioris stared, Jors looked, but outside was only a strong breeze, a drizzling rain dancing on the stone casement, and the distant sound of thunder in the air.

PART V

Harvest of the Storm

1.

The lyrical thunder of war, the beauty of the movement of flames and shadows in conflict: blacks and grays and no false, limiting colors . . . rawness and fury and honesty, no deceptive wonder or remorse.

Place civilization on an altar and set fire to the altar, smash it, sunder it. Demolish it, so that we may rebuild the broken pieces with that same mortar we used to construct it.

The excitement surges like a hot liquid, surges like a swelling arousal, a fever, at the promise of destruction and waste. Smelling the poisonous, acrid fumes of destruction, we are reduced to the terror and aliveness of death at any moment. No rose ever smelled so sweet as those acrid fumes; no woman in her love throes ever tossed like the stretched and writhing bodies thrown by the whirling tumult; no sounds were ever raised in joy or exultation like those of mobs of humanity escaping from the clutch of terror into the arms of fear. What proud and momentous meaning there is in contributing to the annihilation of all things it has taken generations to form! Humanity is at home in its own feces, its own blood, its own rot, at home in its graveyards, in the smoking pits and necropolises it has made for itself.

For when did the voice of humanity ever sound more true, than when it has been raised by a small child, crying alone in the ruins of the aftermath of a war?

Dawn, raining and thundering, lifted obscurely upon the harbor of Erusabad, where smoking ships listed in the gray waters as they sank. Fires still threatened two Athadian galleys, and already Lord General Thomo's armada had lost twenty-seven ships. The Salukadians, in their fiery attacks, had lost forty *surks*. There were bodies, some in western armor and some in eastern, bobbing amidst the charred timber and floating wreckage.

And in the hollow haze of the rising dawn there came to General Thomo, aboard the *Crown*, the far off sounds of rocks smashing upon rocks, and very faintly the thin metallic noise of metal striking metal. Yet through the morning mists he could not see any sign of how his siege of the southern walls was developing. The latest report, hours before dawn, had not promised much.

Thomo ordered semaphores run up his main mast; shortly after, he heard answering trumpets from Ostorian's flagship, and very soon the *Valor* was leading its ships with their deckfuls of ready troops into formation before the choppy waters of the harbor. Thomo signalled Ostorian to a hasty council.

"I have a dangerous plan in mind," he confided to his second-in-command, as he watched Ostorian's longboat splash into the water. "We will lose many lives—but it may end this warfare quickly. . . ."

In the palace, where Nihim could not take the throne of state, the *Hulm* sat in deliberation. Outside, the people moved through the streets in fear, and defenses were mounted upon the high, heavy walls of the Holy City. Reports of successes had come to these men of council: the siege against the southern wall repelled twice during the night, and a furtive attempt to tunnel beneath the northern walls discovered and eliminated. But there were failures, as well—setbacks: part of the tall wall near the Sujha Gate had collapsed under repeated volleys from the Athadian catapults and men on the walls had been slain, brick and stone had destroyed several homes and buildings. Hundreds of lives lost. Fires ignited by high-thrown burning refuse had caused much devastation in the southern quarter of Erusabad. The best method of quickly and efficiently decimating, if not entirely eradicating, these warmongers, seemed to be with fiery ships launched at them, as had been done last night.

As Nihim listened and allowed his glance to wander—from the empty throne to the stern visage of his *hetmuk* Utto-sen-gar to the many expressions revealed by the many *aihmans*, *aihman-sas* and landed lords of the *Hulm*—he realized that he himself felt as empty as a breeze, and as chill as one. He seemed a stranger to this very room, and the men here (whom he had known all his life) seemed strangers, as well.

With the dangerousness of the hour, with the urgency of the moment impressed upon every heart, much pretense was done away with, and while Nihim sat in his calm dispassion, Abru-o-binar, an angry and volatile man, rose to his feet and addressed his peers with much vigor and gave to them a challenge.

"We have no *ghen*!" he yelled—to the men of *Hulm*, to the heights of that Audience Hall. "Who stands fearless and as mighty as a god before these invaders? Who embodies the wisdom and the courage, the vision and *do-shi* of the chosen of the gods? Listen to me, for I have had a vision of greatness! I had a vision of power and glory last night, as I stood upon the battlements of this our city and heard the crashes and the screams of warfare! We are a people of blood! We are a people of old strength and might! Where has the spirit of Huagrim the great *ghen* fled, now in this grim hour when we need his sight and the meaning of his conquering heart? Who has felt his presence? Listen to me! For I tell you that as the walls thundered last night my heart thundered, and as the city trembled I trembled, and as the skies shook I also shook! *Wah nebbe ka yi Ghen! Ummu! Wah nebbe ummu!*"

Heads ducked, hands fluttered, voices lifted and fell in a surf of noise.

Utto-sen-gar stole a glance at Nihim and understood that the

dispossessed son of Huagrim seemed more intrigued than cha-
grined by this transparency.

"*Sah wah nebbe ummu ka yi Ghen!*" exclaimed Abru-o-binar,
falling to his knees, lifting his trembling hands toward the
curtained ceiling of the hall. "I heard the voice of the *ghen* speak
to me! I saw his flaming sword! I heard his smoking voice! I felt
his vision! And he entrusted to me his plan!"

Such was the anguish and dread of those *aihman-sas*, and the
fiery nostalgia of the old horse-chiefs, that this claim of spiritual
visitation did not seem to them a political gesture. They assumed
that the pride known to dwell in the brooding heart of o-binar had
attracted the pride of Huagrim's restless ghost; the anger of o-binar
suggested the anger of Huagrim's shade; the vision of a great war,
Huagrim's great vision. So eager were these men for victory, so
tempted were they by memories of past glories, that this blatant
attempt to wrest power from the many so that one might secure
dictatorship appeared to the *Hulm* as divinely inspired and not
maliciously contrived. So be it. *Wah hono yi ko-Ghen!* The voice
of the *ghen* had spoken! Such things had happened before in
troublous times: so the legends spoke. The sword falls into the
strongest hand.

Nihim could not protest. He had no legal recourse, neither had
he any desire to confront or expose the ambitious Abru-o-binar.
Perhaps, after all, active fire must do what it should, for a time,
where passive water had failed. Surely there was a cause. When
heads turned toward him, expressing anticipation at his reaction to
this claim of o-binar's, Nihim shot a look at his *hetmuk* (who was
very grave and much disturbed by this) and rose to his feet to
announce:

"It is possible that my father's spirit did indeed return to guide
his children in this, our sad hour. Should we not cast spears to
decide the merit of Abru-o-binar's claim? Surely if his vision was
correct, my father's ghost is with us even now, and will guide
those spears into Abru-o-binar's favor."

This suggestion met with approval. The casting of spears had
not been done in three generations, not since Nihim's great-
grandfather Guragu had proclaimed himself *ghen* of the Salukads
and begun his war march against all the lands that were the lands,
unto the sea where the sun dies. The sun's dying place. Erusabad.

Servants took down the spears from where they hung, ceremonial and unused, upon the walls of the hall. Each man of the *Hulm* received his father's, his grandfather's or his great-grandfather's ornamental weapon. Huagrim's family shield was taken down and placed upon one of the stone pillars in the center of the chamber.

Twenty-one strides, for the twenty-one great tribes and families that had joined Guragu and his progeny in their march to empire. For though some of the men who might have cast spears there had been taken by the plague to their ancestors, still the twenty-one long steps were walked out by Utto-sen-gar. His pacing led the *hetmuk* nearly to the area before the *Hulm*'s gathered seats. sen-gar regarded these men carefully; could so many middle-aged and old men cast such heavy weapons accurately?

One by one they stepped up to Utto-sen-gar's boot mark, hefted their spears, called out prayers and cast.

Some shot wide of the shield; others glanced off; but a majority struck and did the shield damage. When Abru-o-binar himself, the last man there, hurled his own spear to test his claim and challenge the favor of the all-seeing gods of the *Endowui*, it split the shield of the *ghens* in two.

Applause and calls and prayers boomed in praise to him.

While Abru-o-binar was led by his friends to the throne, Utto-sen-gar walked to Nihim and grunted: "You should not have allowed that. You should not have!"

"If I had refused, *hetmuk*, it would have been done anyway. Some were against it—" he glanced at bin-Sutus, who stood alone, apart from the others, watching Nihim "—but it would have been done, anyway. Besides, the spears were already cast before Abru posed his challenge, don't you think?"

Utto-sen-gar growled something but did not contradict him.

"It is as it was predicted, *hetmuk*. This war of titans, this whirlwind between the empires of the earth. It is . . . as it was predicted. He will die in terror, just as my brother did."

Utto-sen-gar's brow wrinkled. "What do you mean, Nihim?"

He was recalling events prophesied in the days of Guragu *ko-Ghen*—that the *ghens* of Salukadia would die three generations in peace and three in terror. Huabrul and Huagrim had died easily, taken by the gods as a reward and not a punishment. Agors had been stolen away by nightmares while deep in his fever.

Now, Abru-o-binar.

It puzzled Nihim somewhat, because he suspected that Erusa-

235

bad certainly, and Salukadia perhaps, would not survive to witness the succession of another *ghen* of the empire. He could not quite decipher the prophecy.

But there were many things he had been unable to decipher in his life. . . .

"Can it be done?" Thomo asked Ostorian.

The officer nodded, looking up from the lord general's map of the Holy City. "Yes . . . if you'll order a decoy to attack on the south, so that it seems as though we're reinforcing our legions on that wall. And have someone coming up behind."

"Major Dever."

"Dever, then. His ships behind me. Have them move norther-ly—that's deceptive enough—and as my ships head in—"

"—they'll swing around behind. Exactly. Exactly."

"It will cost us an enormous number of lives," Ostorian remarked.

"Anything we do, Major, will cost us an enormous number of lives. Our choice now is either to prolong this siege, or finish it in the shortest amount of time possible, don't you agree?"

"Yes, yes. . . ."

Quickly, then, they left Thomo's cabin and made their way up on deck. It was apparent that during their brief time below the skies had become more ominous, the waves of the sea choppier and showing whitecaps, and the winds blowing eastward, into the city.

"Destiny," Thomo commented, "seems to be with us."

"Destiny. . . . Alert Dever to meet me aboard the *Valor*."

The lord general nodded. "Tor will be south of you. Like so many cavalry, marching for center. Striking—hard."

Ostorian pulled on his gloves and ordered a man to prepare a boat. "For the throne, then."

The vow sounded hollow. "For the throne, my friend. And if we do not see one another again—"

The two warriors faced each other, and Ostorian grinned slightly. "If not in this life, then—*seh nu nebbe ke arka-shi*, eh, Lord General? Is that how they say it? With the next turn of the Wheel?"

"With the next turn of the Wheel, Ostorian."

Thomo walked him to his longboat and for some peculiar reason wished to prolong this moment: some odd sensation or quiver of inspiration. As though instants could alter the course of years. But he did not delay his officer's departure.

Ostorian stepped into the longboat, held onto a line. He tilted his head, eyed the sky. "Gods," he muttered, "but this is a foul day to die."

When it was perceived that a fleet of seventy-six ships was moving to augment the land forces besieging the southern walls, Abru-o-binar ordered Utto-sen-gar to increase the number of defenders on those walls, as well as the number of fiery ships to be launched at the first available moment. The *hetmuk* of Erusabad was against this plan: to increase the troops already mounted on the battered southern walls he must borrow forces from other locations in the city.

"We have repulsed their attacks so far!" was his outburst. "We will do as they expect if we move our troops back and forth whenever they send a few ships forward! Don't you understand that this could be a ruse? They'll attack on the north again, o-binar! Mark me! They'll attack full on our north!"

Abru-o-binar was not swayed by this argument, and the swelling of approval among the ranks of men eager for leadership—eager, even, for divine guidance in the form of any man daring to call himself *ghen*—forced Utto-sen-gar to take men from the north and west and place them on the southern walls.

And there they stood, as the morning lengthened, as the sun lifted through the rain, while the Athadians far below did not appreciably increase their catapulting of the Holy City or intensify their excavating at the wall's foundations.

Utto-sen-gar did not join his troops; suspicious of this obvious Athadian multiplication of entrenched forces, he mounted the western wall overlooking the harbor, and so was present to observe the true Athadian plan as it took shape.

A fleet of ships, two abreast, was moving under full sail straight into the harbor. The *hetmuk* watched, astonished at the audacity of the tactic; he could not at first trust his eyes. But when a second fleet, sailing north (as he had anticipated) altered course to fall in behind the first lines of war ships, the awesome truth spoke to him at once. It was a device as old as the plains wars that had raised Salukadia to its greatness.

One hundred and fifty ships, rail to rail and prow to stern, bearing down at all speed upon the harbor, intent upon charging directly up the Usub River, splitting the city in half.

Utto-sen-gar almost laughed out loud, so admirable did he find the brashness of the scheme, the sheer enormity of it.

He ordered horns blown, calling his reserves to the western walls.

On the south, Abru-o-binar ordered further horns sounded, as the Athadians began to assault the walls in earnest. Catapults swung and jounced in the fields; mighty towers of timber and hide and steel were rolled against the tall defenses; arrows were loosed in swarms; flaming piles of refuse and wood were flung high, to hurdle the walls and smash into the inner streets and buildings.

From the ships that sat at anchor came great rafts piled with logs, which were transported by horses and men up the southern beach and into the fields, to be raised and hammered and lashed together into more siege towers and armored burrowing equipment. To protect these operations, huge jars filled with oil and poisonous insects and serpents were catapulted onto the fortifications, and Salukadians shrieked and screamed as showers of burning flame and explosions of insects and snakes crashed into them. Huge battering rams, protected by frameworks of steel and hide, were driven continuously against the base of the wall, so that the stone blocks shuddered and the buildings within were shaken into rubble. The anguished people of Erusabad began to collect in swarms on both sides of the river. Some, in fear, moved down into the sewers, supposing that they would be as safe as possible underground.

Abru-o-binar pleaded with the ghost of Huagrim for a sign that might lead to the repulsion of these invaders. He traveled the southern wall, hurrying along the parapets, urging his men to the fight, bestowing upon them praises and blessings, promising them divinely-inspired victory and torment for their enemies. He fell beneath a clutch of arrows. Men nearby witnessed the newly-enthroned *ghen* stagger and scream as many arrows caught him, some in the head and throat, others in the breast and side. Toppling, Abru *ko-Ghen*'s body crumpled and rolled sloppily down a wide ramp of steps that led into a courtyard. While many wailed and moaned, more desperate and determined soldiers unceremoniously clambered over the dripping corpse to aid the defense of the southern wall.

The *Valor* rolled and swayed in the wash of the hurrying ships; Ostorian gripped his rail and watched intently as the long line of war galleys and merchanters sped toward the harbor of the Holy City. With the powerful wind of the building storm pushing them on, and the soldiers on every deck yelling chants and beating drums and clashing cymbals, the lead ships—two triremes with high decks and strong prows—crashed into the Usub.

There were *surks* moored to the quays, and men aboard them; and there were crowds of hurrying Salukadians jumping on and off the ships, running up and down the docks with weapons and torches. Mobs of people from the city, intent on lending aid, only interfered with a hastily contrived resistance. A number of *surks* were boldly oared into the paths of the oncoming triremes in a vain effort to halt or stall their advance. Those *surks* were smashed and scattered like kindling, while the screaming men aboard them were thrown high into the air or sent limp and crushed into the waves of the harbor. And as the Athadian triremes forced their raw path up the river, archers in their masts and at their rails rained volley after volley into the stunned crowds on both sides. Howls and shrieks erupted; horses flailed and bolted; men and women jumped into burning *surks* or fell from the quays to splash in the water and be torn asunder by oncoming Athadian keels.

The fortifications shouldering the docks were neither as tall nor as strongly built as the city's outer walls, nor were the wide entrance gates leading into Erusabad well defended. Warehouses loomed above open boulevards; merchants' stalls and taverns sat beside towering trading offices and government buildings. The river front was a jumble of unplanned, chaotic urban congestion. Where the southern wall offered a strong, unified defense against the Athadians in the field, here the clogged wharves and docks were protected only by intermittent guard towers rising from urban slums. By its very nature, the dock area of the Holy City was indefensible.

Behind the successful triremes came the war galleys and biremes, their shrouds and masts filled with men launching plagues of arrows upon the inner city. And the soldiers at their rails moved in leaping waves onto the docks and quays, pushing forward in an onslaught that took the limited squadrons of defenders both by surprise and by sheer weight of numbers. Stones and arrows, spears and corpses were dropped from the surrounding heights by desperate Salukadian soldiers. Additional troops, responding from all directions, moved through the city and sought to block paths leading to the major boulevards; they overturned carts, spilled burning oil, toppled monuments across avenues and back alleys, summoned cavalry and war chariots to guard the streets leading from the quays.

And still the swift-moving Athadian warships pushed and crushed and forced their way up the Usub, until their momentum at last wore down. The mainmasts of the lead triremes smashed into the low Bisht Bridge. Breaking from their sockets, the timbers groaned, tilted and smashed heavily into the low walls on either side of the bridge. Frenzied Athadian soldiers scaled the fallen masts to bring the battle to the Salukadian defenders on their own walls and rooftops. Swords clattered, men screamed and pushed and shoved, bodies dropped waving and spinning into the streets and the clogged river.

Outside the harbor, Major Tor's fleet veered again to the north, for it was apparent that his ships would have no access into the harbor area. A handful of blazing *surks* were launched against his galleys from the north dock area, but they died smoking on the waves before doing any damage.

And Utto-sen-gar, still on the western wall, stared in astonishment at the confusion of the battle: forests of ships' masts, blowing lines and fragmented sails, leaping flames that devoured the wreckage in the Usub and threatened to burn warehouses and office buildings. The screams, the waves of moving men, the mobs of Athadians all red and silver battling with sword and axe, pole and knife in every street leading into the city, on both sides of the river. Flaming clouds reached to the skies, curling and coiling and spewing black smoke that obscured the overhanging storm clouds which added their own thunder to the carnage. A tremendous rain, all hail and wind, swept down upon the city. Howling mobs of men and animals lurched through the congested avenues as burning buildings fell, monuments toppled, and whole crowds pushed back and forth on bridges and quays.

When Utto-sen-gar saw the Bisht Bridge begin to sway
dangerously, he thought it the result of the battle, the consequence
of a hundred Athadian war galleys smashed and nearly up-ended
along Erusabad's docks. It wasn't until he felt the tremors himself
that he understood what was occurring. The crowds of men
fighting atop the bridge were hurled back and forth by its sudden
lurching. The rumbling tremors caught hold of smaller buildings
facing the river, and began to affect the churning river itself.

And Utto-sen-gar understood—understood, when the very wall
upon which he stood with hundreds of others began to creak and
rock and threaten to collapse.

Understood, when the Bisht Bridge, which had for centuries
spanned the Usub, abruptly cracked and split and fell in a
thousand fragments of stone and mortar into the river and took five
hundred howling, plunging men with it. Understood, even as the
stone embrasure upon which he leaned disappeared from beneath
his hand, the suddenness of it almost pulling him over the side.

The Athadian ships in the harbor began to lift on swollen tides.
The heavy wind, and the groaning earth, began to twist those
ships as though they were wood chips in a child's puddle.

Utto-sen-gar understood.

Earthquake. . . .

2.

Midday—but with the ferocity of the storm, it might well have
been midnight. Captain Lathen, in the middeck of the *Wing*, could
barely see the forward rails of his ship. Above the howling din of
wind rose the yells of seamen trying to communicate with one
another, while timbers groaned and stretched, threatening to
topple, and ratlines and shreds of canvas sail snapped and blew in
the driving hail.

Through the chaos, Irded, Lathen's first mate, crawled on hands
and knees down into the middeck.

The captain was hugging the jambs of the doorwell leading
down into the hold; the door panels had ripped away and blown
across the deck.

"Captain Lathen!"

"What is it?"

241

"We've lost three more men, sir!"

Above the shrieking tempest, through the noise of rain and storm thundering on the *Wing*, Lathen heard the mounting screams of his crew. He saw the prow sink beneath a gigantic wave that curled and nearly reached the middeck; Lathen was tugged forward. He lost his precarious hold on the doorway. Falling to his knees, he skidded on the running deck until he crashed into the foot of the stairs—where Irded had slid, thrown too by the massive swell.

"She's smashing up, sir!"

"Gods, I know it!"

"She's breaking apart! She can't hold—"

"I know it, *I know it*!"

Above them the great mainmast twisted, groaned—and ripped from its socket, toppled toward them.

Irded screamed.

Instinctively, Lathen threw himself away from the falling mast. A tide of wind caught the great pole and spun it around; lines snapped, voices shrieked. Through the haze of a brief dip in the wind, Lathen saw five men struggling in a fallen shroud. They were no more than insects caught in a web, caught by the flying lines—and in a moment the crashing mast took them with it as it toppled into the sea.

Water began to boil up in a geyser in the middeck, where the mast had uprooted.

"We're sinking!" Irded shrieked. "We're sinking!"

Lathen pulled himself up the slippery, washing stairs. He crawled to the larboard rail and hugged it, looked out to catch a glimpse of whatever land there might be. He couldn't know what direction he faced; there was no way to judge how far out to sea they were, or whether or not they might be just within reach of shore.

"Captain!"

Another respite—the howling wind stopped, the driving rain lessened for a moment so that the film of the tempest hung in the air like gauze. Lathen stared.

Saw—

"*Captai—*"

He glanced over his shoulder at the screaming Irded. The air

242

filled again with mist and rain. The *Wing* reached skyward once more and Lathen's stomach pulled toward his mouth.

Irded was hanging onto the portside rail, on the other side of the glistening deck. He was caught in the railing, his arms twisted around, one leg wrapped awkwardly, the other jerking nervously. Lathen stared as Irded screamed at him. What could he do? He could scarcely breathe in the storm; to cross the deck would take half the day—unless a wave grabbed him. Irded's terrified eyes . . . the black cavity of his silently shrieking mouth. . . .

Lathen began to crawl toward him.

The railing gave way.

It was gone in the space of a gasp. One moment Irded was hugging onto it for safety, and in the next—

The wave had risen and quickly washed the decks, as if to erase any memory of that railing or that screaming man who'd clung to it.

Gone.

Lathen wiped his dripping head, turned back to the larboard rail, stared toward—where? What? What direction?

Land?

The *Wing* heaved, the sky opened a bit, and Lathen saw it again—that glimpse of what he'd caught before—

Land.

A city.

"Oh . . . gods. . . ."

A white city on a stretch of brown rock. Towers . . . wharves . . . walls. . . . Very far away, yet—

The city disappeared.

Lathen tried to climb to his feet.

The air filled again with rain, sleet, gray wind, mist.

The city had disappeared.

Quickly, Captain Lathen wiped his right hand over his face to clear away the sea water and the sweat. It had to have been an illusion. He was dying, he was going to die, there was no city—

More screams, behind him.

Lathen turned, stared.

Half the *Wing*, from stern to middeck, was under water. There were only a few men still alive—three or four that he could see—and they, too, were hugging railings or pieces of shattered decking. But those would not save them. None of them would live. None of them would escape alive.

The wind died a little. The swirling mists, the crashing waves held back for a moment.

Lathen knew the gods had done this to the storm, to the ocean, just so he could be certain before he died that there had been a city, that he had died in sight of land.

He stared through the railing, whispering.

The city had gone.

No— There.

"Name of the gods. . . ."

Two towers—only two towers still standing. And around them—what? Gray water? Gray fire? The towers toppled. Lathen saw them topple; it wasn't his imagination. The entire city of Elpet was being destroyed as quickly and decisively as the *Wing* was being destroyed.

The world was dying.

It was the end of the world.

Lathen tried to pull himself upright. He stared in complete shock at the falling towers, at the rising tides of water swirling with huge remnants of debris.

"*The whole . . . city!*" Lathen screamed.

The *Wing* lifted again and spun around. Lathen was jerked back; he held on desperately with his left hand as he was torn from the rail, and he heard his left arm breaking in its socket before he felt it. He never felt the pain. He never felt his fingers slipping from the rail. He slid across the rocking deck on long sheets of water, stared up into a massive black shadow. Lathen tried to scream, but before he was prepared for it, the descending shadow took his breath away.

Despite the heaving and swaying of the ship, Galvus was pacing the floor of his cabin, unable to ward off the grim unease that filled his mind and soul. One moment he felt, in the wake of the enormities that had occurred, only numbness and artificiality, perplexity; but the next moment he seemed to hear thousands of voices, see thousands of faces screaming like a plague of riotous cacodemons. There was no sense to it, there was no pattern—and he was trying to comprehend all of this by using past experience as a measuring line. Yet no one had ever experienced anything like this.

When the knocking sounded on his door, Galvus's hand was on the latch in an instant; he tugged the door open against the weight of the rolling ship and stared into the ashy face of a Khamar.

"What is it?"

"My lord . . . your mother—Lady Orain . . . requests your presence on deck—"

"She's ondeck *now*? In *this*?"

"The . . . capital, my lord."

"What *about*— Gods . . . no."

He moved past the Khamar and hurried down the gallery; when he reached the stairwell Galvus was nearly thrown backwards by a sudden movement, but he held onto the railing as the Khamar behind him held out a supportive arm. When he pushed open the door that led onto the middeck, he was met by a gray wall of rain and stormy wind.

"*Mother!*"

His answer was a man's voice—"Over here!"—and Galvus saw Adred, dressed in a long dripping robe, wave to him. Orain was beside him, dressed too in a long robe as protection against the tempest.

Beyond the rising and falling waves that moved like angry gray mountains, Galvus saw the boiling, roaring sky swarming toward them; abruptly, it veered off, then turned again with lightning and clouds in their direction. But it wasn't the sky that moved so violently; it was the ship. The ship was rocking directionlessly on the sea, wholly at the mercy of whatever waves or winds might batter it. As he made his way across the deck, Galvus saw other sails and other masts come into view beyond the rising and falling rail. Some of them were barely afloat; others were turning and twisting like wood shavings in the pounding sea. And beyond these ships, beyond the cavernous waves, gigantic and climbing, glistening with foam, larger than the sky—beyond lay the harbor, and the capital.

Athad.

Or, rather, what remained of Athad.

For half the capital had completely disappeared.

"The . . . earthquake!" Orain gasped to her son, as she held onto Adred.

245

Adred showed Galvus a white face dripping with spray, staring and emotionless.

"Gods on high. . . ." the prince-regent whispered. He gripped the railing and stared in disbelief. Athad was so distant, it appeared small and unreal. The buildings that still stood might have been thin blocks of wood, or carved from bone or charcoal for a child's decorations. They seemed that insignificant—and they crumbled apart as easily as wood or charcoal might have.

Galvus felt himself beginning to shudder and tremble uncontrollably, as with a rage. "The *lives*!" he roared. "The *people* in that city!"

Orain, not facing him, sobbed, while Adred gave him a blank stare.

There were a thousand ships spread in all directions, disappearing into the mist and the waves to the north and south. And bodies—everywhere, bodies and wreckage, parts of ships jumping and dipping in the sea. The capital was covered by a gray haze that glowed with furnacelike fires and parted occasionally to show where now one building had disappeared, now three or four others. Great columns of smoke poured up from the earth. And waves as tall as mountains roared across the surface of the crashing ocean, smashed into themselves in tremendous explosions of steam and erupting water, rolled back to engulf twenty ships at a time, or thirty.

The earthquakes. Galvus understood. The earth was ripping itself apart; chasms were opening far beneath them, tunnels were opening or parts of the world for some reason were colliding. Perhaps the earth itself was breaking apart. So the seas must smash, cities must crumble, lives, bodies must be thrown in heaps or discarded in pieces, hurled into the air or pulled underground like so much useless flotsam and jetsam.

"Gods . . ." the prince-regent sobbed, looking upon it. "The humanity . . . the people. . . ." He thought of Asawas, thought of what the prophet had said; yet it meant nothing. The end of the world? A war between the elements of humanity? A death to the world, so that it might be reborn?

Words. Nothing would be reborn. Everything would be—destroyed.

And Galvus was alive to see it. Not that he would live much longer: he realized that and he accepted it, accepted it in the abstract—for what else could he do? But even to have survived this much of it—to have actually witnessed a holocaust, a series of holocausts on a scale so vast that it didn't even register emotionally. . . .

A Khamar approached to warn Galvus and Orain and Adred, "Might be best to get below. It seems to be storming stronger than before."

"*Stronger*?" Galvus was astounded.

"The worst, my lord, has been to the south of us, so far. But this—" He shook his head.

"We'll get below," Orain whispered, watching her son.

He looked at her, looked beyond her.

The sky curled and leaped, rushed toward them and pulled back. Galvus leaned into the railing, gradually was pushed away by the rolling tides and the wind.

Far away—he saw it through the haze and the mist and the raging wind—far away, another building in the capital crumbled apart and fell into the reaching jaws of the waves as if it were a piece of charcoal, a friable old piece of bone—just crumbled apart.

"Galvus?" Orain whispered.

He seemed to be laughing, laughing at it all; his face twisted into a sneering grin that seemed almost malevolent. "What does it . . . *mean*?" Galvus looked at his mother, looked at Adred, at the Khamar. "What does it *mean*? How can it—*mean* . . . anything. . . ?"

"He's sailing off!" the sailor called to General Thomo.

"Are you sure? Can you see him?" Then: "Gods, *gods*!" as the *Crown*, creaking and twisting, nearly tore apart beneath a wave that struck portside and slid the galley around.

"Can't— Lost him!" cried the hand.

Thomo was furious. Running ahead, slipping, he grabbed the railing and tried to see what he could of Ogodis' *Jewel*. "Damn you, Imbur!" he howled. "*Damn you*, Ogodis! *Ogodis*!"

He was slapped in the face by a cold wall of wind. Thomo sank to his knees but held on. All around him—the whistling, roaring winds, the gray air, the driving rain, the rising screams and the

247

crashes of hundreds of ships as they were pulled and pushed, shattered and pummeled—

"Eller!" Thomo screamed.

His sailor let go of a line, ran toward him.

"*Eller!*"

The lord general had no time to cry out further. Before him, lifting through the rolling wall of storm, came the hull of a trireme. Thomo was lifted into the air. Shining wood tilted toward him—smashed oars—small bodies dropped over the side, were devoured by leaping waves—

Nihim, last of the lineage of the great *ghens* of Salukadia, sat in the throne of the empire and waited for death to come.

Outside, the crashings and the groanings, the noise of the sea rising to engulf the collapsing Holy City, the screams and the shrieks and the howls of mobs, and of the winds.

Inside, a strange silence, punctuated by shiverings and rumblings, the creaking of great stone columns, and the drip of water as the first of the rising tides and falling rains began to flood the palace.

Nihim stared at this Audience Hall. The wide floor was a lake, and small whirlpools and explosions took place in that lake as the pouring rain blew in through the open, smashed roof. Part of a wall had caved in and its great blocks now shuddered and twisted, dislodging themselves further. There were a few corpses—Wensa-go-Illu, Ansu-o-Kem—but most of the *aihmans* and the servants and the palace personnel had rushed out into the city with everyone else.

Nihim closed his eyes, tilted back his head, grinned. His private thoughts—of dooms, of the way of the world, of spirit and matter, soul and flesh and light and shadow—brought a thin smile to his lips. His throne trembled, a spray of leaking storm washed upon him, but Nihim did not move.

He heard splashing sounds, then, and heard bin-Sutus call out to him. The sounds passed, stopped. Nihim roused himself, looked at the *aihman*.

bin-Sutus stood before the dripping steps of the dais; he stared pale faced and shadow eyed at Nihim, appearing betrayed.

"What is it, my friend?"

"The city—" bin-Sutus began, voice choking. "Half our city is—gone, fallen—or inundated by floods—the ocean, and the rain. And . . . still it does not end."

Nihim was silent.

"The deaths . . . there are too many to count, Nihim!" He staggered forward, splashing water, and reached out a hand to steady himself on the dais. The old man sat down on the damp, running stone. "Utto-sen-gar . . . he was on the western wall. . . . The western wall has fallen into the harbor. Abru—dead. His son proclaimed himself *ghen*, and the moment he did so a building fell upon him. Our ships—all destroyed. . . ."

"The Athadians, bin-Sutus?"

The old *aihman* looked up at him. "Washed away. Their ships—perhaps twenty, thirty remain. Wreckage. . . ."

Nihim whispered, "*Nebbe tani arka-shi.* The turn of the Wheel. So be it. *Seh wah nebbe ummu endowui.* The voice of the gods speaks, my friend. Listen."

The rumbling . . . the screams . . . the crashes of falling stone, rising waters.

"We must leave—" bin-Sutus suggested.

"This all comes for a reason, I think," Nihim said softly. "But I cannot decide what that reason might be. Can you, bin-Sutus? One reason? Many reasons?"

The old man watched him with teary eyes and trembling lips. Had Nihim lost his senses? "We must evacuate . . . leave the city. Get aboard a ship, sail away—"

"If we are meant to live, *aihman*, we will live. Shall we challenge destiny, and invite death to overtake us more quickly?"

bin-Sutus shivered his head. "It came so suddenly," he grieved. "No one suspected. We were in the middle of our lives—there was order, there was purpose— And this came so suddenly, interrupting the . . . the flow of meaning, the—*becoming* that men were involved in. No signs . . . it gave no signs. . . ."

"There were simple signs, bin-Sutus. Hundreds of signs. Only we did not heed them; we misread them, we—men in ignorance, caught up in our purposes. . . ."

bin-Sutus, at a sound, lifted his head quickly and groaned. The ceiling was shifting; more water poured in, more blocks gave way in the wall on the other side of the chamber. "Are you not afraid?" he asked. "Are you not frightened by this?"

Nihim shrugged. *Nebbe tani arka-shi.* "I feel . . . nothing, my friend. I feel, I suppose, as the gods must feel about this. It is occurring; I am part of it, but my *shi* is outside of this. It occurs, but it does not matter whether I am aware of its occurring or not."

The blocks of the wall opposite them gave way and with a thunderous explosion of noise great waves of water rushed in, sending up leaping fountains of brackish water, and the shattered and tumbling stones. Many bodies were swept in with the pouring flood.

Nihim regarded them dispassionately.

bin-Sutus stood up and moved to the top of the dais, knelt beside the throne. Resigned to the inevitable, still he wished to protect himself for as long as possible in this small island amidst the devastation. He stared at the waves of water flooding the Audience Hall.

Nihim sat silent and still.

Two corpses floated toward them—two of many. One was a man; half his chest was ripped open and his features showed a startled, wide-eyed stare, immobile, frozen onto his sheeny face, his gray skin. The other corpse was that of a baby, perhaps four or five weeks old. The baby was gray-skinned and bloated, as though it had been pumped full of briny water. It floated face down, and when it was swept by the swirling waters against the bottom step of the dais, one pudgy arm and its head knocked softly against the carved stone.

3.

Down below, in the rolling hill lands and the open fields—

The city should have been there.

"That's . . . *it*, Commander—isn't it?"

Captain Uvars was so astonished that he could only stare, mute and befuddled.

"Commander?" his lieutenant asked again.

Uvars regarded the sky, glanced in one direction, in another, looked all around. Behind him his five hundred men crouched in their saddles, waiting for his signal—five hundred men barely alive, hungry and exhausted, their clothes in shreds, their armor

250

stolen from corpses on battlefields, their weapons and food stolen from—corpses. . . .

Uvars could only stare, mute and befuddled, at where he knew—*knew*—Lasura to be. There, directly before him, in that valley.

But was it all now beneath that lake? Was it all a lake, now? Had it become an inland sea? *Overnight*?

Captain Uvars had not taken seriously the few reports of widespread, large-scale destruction that had come his way. Most he had dismissed as hearsay, done to undermine morale. He and his men had witnessed, of course, signs of great fires from a distance; they had felt the rumbling earth and so they had realized that this area was gripped by earthquakes of some intensity. But it had not interfered with their dogged advance, and in the six days Uvars and his men had spent fighting through the northern defenses of the dwindling Emarian army they had seen little sign that the rumors they'd heard were to be taken seriously. Lies, all of it, composed by connivers to unnerve the conquering Athadians.

But now—now, as Uvars looked down upon what should have been Lasura. . . .

He shook his head to clear away the anxiety that filled him, the dread. "No horns!" he commanded the retainers behind him. "But dismount! Dismount!" He signaled with his hand. "We bivouac here until nightfall!"

Nightfall. . . .

In the blowing, raining darkness of the early night the ruins of the capital, still as far away as ever, glowed with a soft phosphorescence. Rather, Galvus imagined, the way the soul must glow upon the death of the body that had housed it. Everything collapsed and ruined, gone, and the glow and brightness of—what? Fires . . . fires lighting mists, lighting walls of smoke that fumed to the skies. . . .

The storm had somewhat abated; it was still raining heavily, there was no sign of stars behind the tar black clouds, and occasional muffled sounds—as of breakers or thunder—came intermittently from far away. More earthquakes. Or volcanoes. Or the destruction of another city.

It had all been so sudden and complete, so awesome and

random and . . . complete, that Galvus now could only react to it with a sense of utter calm and absurdity. The gross injustices he had fought against in Sulos and in Athad—those had been enormities that could be felt and measured because they were so precise, so calculated; they could be measured in human terms, they had taken place within a human scale. But—this? The end of the world? One hundred and fifty families losing their farms because of some businessman's greed—that was manageable, that was a calamity everyone could understand and deal with. But ten million people destroyed in the course of a day and night because the earth had suddenly opened to let the sea pour in, because the earth had decided to rip itself apart? That could not be understood; it could not be measured. It was too enormous, and it could only be endured and endured in only the smallest and most private of ways. A smashed finger was a good reason for anger: the loss of ten million people was outside the range of human focus.

Galvus smiled sadly and glanced at his right arm. His forearm had been twisted, sometime during all of this, and now he saw that it had begun to swell and was affecting the dexterity of his hand. It would pass.

But he flexed his hand, wincing, and wondered about the blind selfishness of human nature. . . .

The sound of boots on the deck intruded as a Khamar came to Galvus and saluted.

"Yes?"

"Captain Sallus wishes to know if you'll take survivors aboard."

"Survivors?" Galvus stared at him. "What survivors?"

"A skiff, sir. Appears to be fourteen, maybe a few more survivors to her."

Galvus swallowed thickly; hope bloomed within him—others besides himself and his mother, Adred and Abgarthis and the handful on this ship had survived. Yet the hope withered swiftly as he pictured it, realized—

"Shall we haul them aboard, Lord Galvus?"

"Yes. . . . Yes! Immediately!"

And he followed in the Khamar's footsteps as, together, they crossed the deck.

* * *

252

Dusk came quickly, and with it the irritating rains that had followed Uvars and his company for days began to fall more heavily. A number of his retainers brought word to the captain that thirty, perhaps forty of his soldiers would not be mounting saddle in the morning to take up the trek: the retainers would see to it that the bodies were buried during the night.

These wasted lives sombered Uvars's already grim mood. Yet the quickening rainstorm and the falling night brought not only additional deaths to the Athadian company: they brought the suggestion that the war against Emaria had not come to an end in this swamp, but was still a very real thing.

"Campfires!" reported one of the scouts, when he returned from an early evening mission to the south. "At least three of them! Difficult to see in this weather, but they were campfires, Captain! Twenty or more Emarians down there!"

Uvars sneered with undisguised pleasure. "Twenty will lead us to twenty hundred," he decided. "Are you fit enough to take us back down there?"

"Yes, Captain. But—"

"In this weather?" Uvars interrupted. "Tonight? Is that what you were going to say?" He fixed his rider with a hard stare.

The man did not reply; he wiped his running face.

"Who would expect an Athadian party to raid them on this night, under these conditions? Hey?" Uvars grunted, and chuckled as he gloated. He turned to Lieutenant Hendru. "Fifty men. Our fittest. We ride immediately."

Hendru didn't care for this decision at all; worn, feverish, and more aware of the temperament of the men than was Uvars, the lieutenant was of a mind to refuse the order and face whatever charges for insolence Captain Uvars might care to bring against him.

But then he reconsidered. They had come this far to find Lasura destroyed—another city utterly demolished by this frightening chain of natural (or gods-willed) events that gripped the heart of every strong man in the company with dread. Soon enough, Hendru knew, the men themselves would refuse Uvars—refuse to mount their horses, refuse to continue this mad campaign. Soon enough, this absurd progression of illness, death and human waste would come to an end.

It occurred to Lieutenant Hendru, as he nodded to Captain

Uvars, saluted him and went off into the mud to rouse fifty victims, that the Emarian troops and commanders he had mocked months ago were actually no different than he himself was, now. The same ill, haunted, malnourished and driven living corpses that now dozed in this sullen encampment. To defeat your enemy, Hendru reminded himself, become your enemy.

Yet . . . become your enemy, and what becomes of the war those enemies had fought?

Lieutenant Hendru took so long to choose even the first ten of Uvars's requested fifty, that the captain himself (in a hot-tempered burst of impatience) strode through the camp and randomly decided on the last forty for his squad.

"Where are we headed?" asked one of the drenched, fatigued dogs as he pushed back his hair and got to his feet. "What's the old man so bent about? Where are we headed, Lieutenant?"

"To hell," Hendru told him, adjusting his helmet. "You can die here, or you can die out there, in hell. It no longer makes any difference, does it?"

There had been seventeen survivors in the skiff, and they had escaped the destruction of the capital (explained one of them) only because the merchanter they'd been aboard had been delayed in its departure from Bessara. It was making for dock at Athad when the first of the earthquakes and subsequent tidal waves had occurred. Though her master had done his best, eventually the merchanter had sustained enough damage that it had been necessary for all aboard to abandon her, and this was done once the captain had ordered it as far out to sea as possible. He'd ordered twenty to a longboat, although the persons aboard this particular skiff had forced twenty-two into her, and five had been lost in the turbulent seas.

Only three of them, in any event, were in a condition even approximating good health, for the smashing seas, driving winds and rain and gas and blowing smoke had taken their toll. Galvus ordered the survivors bunked in every available cabin and spare room, and this led, quite naturally, to a discussion with Captain Sallus regarding the stores and supplies on board.

"Enough for the few of us," the ship's master reported— meaning Galvus and Lady Orain, Count Adred and Lord Abgarthis, the six Khamars, and his crew of twenty as well as Sallus himself. "With seventeen more bodies to keep fed and warm, Lord Galvus. . . ."

"What are you suggesting, Captain?"

"Only—for the time being, I suppose—that each of us do with as little as we can. At least until we see how far we've been blown from shore, and see what other boats are out here—see what our situation is."

"We can't possibly be the only survivors."

"I agree, Lord Galvus. But these rains aren't letting up, and the sea and sky's so dark I can't judge. There's lights out there, but what does that mean? One ship? Twenty? A hundred and twenty? You see where I'm pointing to. There haven't been many who've made it through this. And what of the city? Can you see it from here? I can't. It's like some hand just pushed us half-way across the world, my lord. For all I know, we'll slip off the edge during the night."

"I think the world's a good deal larger than that, Captain Sallus," Galvus smiled.

"Oh, I know that. But still—you say what you like, my lord; we still might be sliding over the edge right now, slipping straight down into hell."

"Even if that were so, Captain Sallus," Galvus cautioned him, "I'd keep that sort of speculation to a minimum onboard this ship—don't you agree?"

"Yes . . . Lord Galvus."

"And I have another suggestion for you."

"What's that, Lord Galvus?"

"Stop calling me 'lord.' I'm not lord of anything anymore. I'm not sitting on the throne of anything left to sit on, and if anyone deserves any titles, then it's my uncle. And it's liable to be some time before we see King Elad's ship hailing us to. Quite . . . some time, I fear."

"Aye. Aye. . . ."

"So from now on, Captain Sallus, I'm simply Galvus. You understand. All of us . . . nobility—we're just our names. We're just people."

"Very well, Lor— Galvus."

"You'll get used to it."

"I expect I will," smiled Sallus.

255

With that, the captain left the forward deck and moved down toward the middeck and the way to the hold. Galvus cleared his throat and crossed to the railing; he leaned on the iron-braced wood, watched the dark sky and the night and the endless waves, but saw no sign anywhere of land or the capital. A few yellow lights flickered far away, to—well, to north and south, he supposed. The falling rain and blowing chill wind obscured them, covered them with mist, as though the yellow eyes of the lights were grown over with wens. Galvus threw his head back, looked up; no stars were visible, and he could barely make out the signs of dark clouds traveling swiftly high above him.

This ship might have been at the bottom of a well. At the bottom of some enormous well.

And Galvus himself felt so strangely alive at this moment that he also felt guilty or self-conscious about it. Perhaps it was similar to what he'd heard the men and athletes of the arenas had experienced or soldiers in the middle of combat: the apprehension of death, or the nearness of one's own death in volatile, dangerous circumstances made life itself seem more vital. It gave one the sense—a thrill, an excitement—of the mere appreciation of being alive. Alive, in a world so full of immediate death and large destruction, and so many perils.

Galvus turned at the sound of someone else approaching him from behind.

He had anticipated that it must be Sallus returning for some reason or perhaps Adred coming up ondeck. But it was a young man, perhaps his own age, no taller than Galvus but dark haired, dark bearded. He was dressed in simple garments, and the only extraordinary thing about him was that he carried a well-polished dulcimer in one hand. No, Galvus saw, as the youth moved from the shadows of the stairs onto the deck, the dulcimer was slung upon his shoulder by a strap and he merely rested one hand upon it.

Galvus nodded to him and the young man stepped up to the railing. He blinked at the rainy drizzle and immediately slipped his dulcimer from his shoulder and covered it over, sliding it beneath the short cape he wore. Then he relaxed and watched the waves in the darkness.

"Thank you," he said.

Galvus grunted. "Couldn't let you just float out there, could I?"

"Two other ships did."

"Perhaps they had their reasons."

"Perhaps. . . ." The young man sighed. "You're the prince-regent."

"Yes, that's right. Your name?"

"Sossian."

"Are you from Athad, Sossian?"

"No. Bessara. I was living in Bessara and returning to Athad to visit some friends."

"No family?"

"No. No family." He laughed roughly, as though at some rude jest, then took in a deep breath, leaned back on the rail and stared at the ship. "The end of the world," Sossian muttered.

Galvus didn't say anything, directly; but after a moment: "You play that instrument, do you?"

"Oh, yes."

"Since it appears we're liable to be aboard this ship for a longer time than any of us anticipated, may I count upon you to entertain us?"

Sossian nodded.

"Is that your trade?" Galvus asked him.

"Yes, my lord. I play the dulcimer. I compose songs. I compose rhymes, and verse. Tales and stories and poems."

"Yours is a literary talent, then?"

Sossian shrugged agreeably. "Meager as it is," he confessed, "I tell the truth that I know in the best way that I can."

Galvus commented, "If everyone had, perhaps none of this would have come to be."

"Do you sincerely believe that?"

"I do."

Sossian kept his eyes on him. "Perhaps, then, I ought to tell your story, Lord Galvus—in a poem."

"*My* story?" Galvus chuckled. "No, not mine, Sossian. But—" He crossed his arms upon his chest. "If you want a story to tell, poet, then tell the story of my family—the story of the throne, and the story of the empire. There's the tale for you to tell. Sharpen your pen on—everything that we were."

"The tale of the empire—ah!" Sossian laughed. "Of what it did, and how it died."

"What it did . . . how it died. . . ." Galvus whispered.

257

"There was much that was wise, there, poet. Much that was wise and simple, and much that was true. And much that was weak and too proud. . . ." He turned on the rail, stared at the sea and night, and felt suddenly very uncomfortable and self-pitying. "Tell that, yes," Galvus said in a very low voice.

"My lord?" Sossian leaned close; he hadn't heard him.

"Tell it!" Galvus shot back, slipping quickly into a bad mood. "We might have been gods! We had the truth and the hope in our hands—here! In our hands! And in our hearts! And we failed! Tell it, Sossian! Tell it! What we did . . . how we died. . . ! Gods! *Tell it*!"

4.

Within the sounds of the washing rain the noises of the sloshing boots were lost. Against the darkness of the hillside and the shadowed forests, the movements of the fifty soldiers were obscured. Not until Uvars bellowed an order was there any actual indication of what was occurring in the dripping fields just outside the haze of the fires; and not until fifty swords emerged like the teeth of a dragon's jaws, shining and shimmering from the darkness, was it evident that the Athadians far outnumbered the few startled Emarians.

"Keep your hands *away* from your *weapons*!" Captain Uvars yelled. In the night, his seemed a disembodied voice. "Remain sitting as you are! My soldiers will remove your weapons for you! Stay as you are!"

Silence . . . for several long moments. . . . Then, the soldiers came forward and began as the voice had promised: they removed the weapons from the trembling hands and from the belts and boots of the Emarians.

Meanwhile, a bold Captain Uvars stepped into the area of shared campfire light and faced the one man there who appeared to be a leader, perhaps the chief-in-command.

"You understand Athadian?"

"Yes, I understand Athadian—" a glance at Uvars's badges, dim in the wet night "—Captain."

Uvars sneered at him; the Emarian was an obese man—or, rather, he must at one time have been obese. Now his gray skin,

258

oranged by the firelight, sagged from cheeks and chin, and he had the haggard, dark-eyed appearance of a once-proud individual reduced by circumstance and sudden change to a shadow of what he had been. "I am, sir, Captain Uvars of the Imperial Athadian Cavalry, Second Legion. Your name?"

The obese man swallowed, cleared his throat and offered: "Jors. Lord . . . Sir Jors, Captain. Once Acting-Major of the Emarian Army under our late King Nutatharis." He nodded slightly to the giant seated beside him at the fire: a huge man, dressed in armor, all burning eyes, drooping moustache and long beard. "This man is Thamu, my retainer."

"Have him turn his weapons over to my men immediately, Lord Jors. Have him remove his weapons now and drop them to the ground."

"Are we your prisoners, Captain?"

"You are indeed."

"You are," Jors informed him, "the first Athadians to manage this far alive into Emaria. Was it your intention to capture Lasura, Captain, with—" he made a swift count, a guess "—forty men?" Jors smiled blandly.

Uvars was not to be mocked—or made to reveal more than he himself intended. "Tell Thamu to remove his weapons, Lord Jors."

"Certainly. Thamu?"

The giant looked at Jors, and Jors nodded quietly.

"What does it matter now, Thamu? Everything you were led to believe . . . everything I had hoped to believe in. . . . We're not going to get out of this alive, in any event."

"Oh, I don't intend to kill you," Uvars promised him. "No, no. I won't oblige you in that way. I fully intend that you should live, Lord Jors, because I have a number of questions I'd like answered."

"Captain Uvars . . . it strikes me that you have not seen what's become of our capital city."

"Lasura?"

"It was destroyed in the space of one afternoon. Inundated. It was hurled to the bottom of the valley and flooded over. How many men do you see before you, Captain Uvars? Fifteen? We're the only ones who escaped alive. And I nearly wish I hadn't."

Uvars did not reply to this.

Around him, the clacking and scraping and clatter of soldiers collecting Emarian weapons fell silent.

"I don't know how you and your men managed to find your way up here," Jors continued, "but these highlands are all that remain of our entire nation. Are you aware of that? Are you, Captain?"

"What do you mean?"

"The rivers flooded. The far seas have swept over our northlands like—like water over a lakeshore. Don't you realize that earthquakes have destroyed half the world?"

Uvars chuckled grimly. "Lying Emarins told us—"

He was cut short by Sir Jors's howling laughter. "'Lying' Emarians, Captain Uvars? 'Lying?' You truly don't understand, do you? We may be the only people still alive on the entire earth! Don't you see?"

Uvars wasn't sure what to say. Anger and anxiousness began to ache in his bowels, fill his lungs, burn his heart. He glanced at some of his men near him.

"We're sitting on the last bit of dry land in the world, Captain Uvars. Or the northern half of the world, at least. Where my men and I were two days ago—it's all underwater, now. Athadian! The world has been tipped upside down! Are you blind? How did you manage to climb this far, when everyone else has been drowned or sucked down into the hells?" Lord Jors's voice began to rise in panic as he described what had happened—and relived it all afresh, himself. "The world is *dying*, Captain Uvars! The world is already *dead*! We're all corpses! Even the gods are dead! You're still fighting a war that dead men started!" And he began to laugh uncontrollably—sadly, and uncontrollably. "Dead men, Captain! A *dead men's war!*"

The night had grown late, and so Galvus was unable to ask after any of the survivors he'd ordered retrieved. One of the Khamars told him that the refugees had fallen asleep in whatever bunk or corner or spare space of floor had been allotted to them.

But Galvus needed to talk. He found Adred still awake and sitting in the galley. He was alone at the single table in the kitchen, sitting in the gloom broken only by a swinging oil lamp above him and a stubby, almost-gone candle fuming in a tray beside him. He

260

was sipping a cup of tea and he looked up, momentarily surprised, to notice Galvus in the doorway.

"Ah," Adred nodded. "I'm making too much noise. Keeping everyone awake. I was afraid of that. Running around at all hours of the night."

Galvus smiled and walked in; he sat down on the other side of the table, folded his hands together, rested his chin on them. "I suppose we should all be grateful we're alive."

"I suppose you're right."

"Does anyone have any idea where we are?"

Adred shook his head. "None. Far too cloudy and stormy to get a reading by the stars. And I heard Sallus complaining that the magnetic needle he uses to help judge his course isn't working, either."

"That's certainly very strange."

"Certainly is. The gods thought of everything when they planned this."

"The gods." Galvus made a face. "Does any of this seem . . . *real* to you, yet?"

"No." Adred examined his tea cup with his fingers. "No. . . . I still intend to wake up—wake up, open a window, listen to Abgarthis complain about Elad—" He stopped, not caring to pursue any further that particular train of thought.

"How *is* Abgarthis?" Galvus asked him. "I haven't seen him since this morning. Seems more like years."

Adred shrugged. "Alive. Very quiet. Maybe he's dying." He waited. "I'm afraid he's becoming ill." He sipped his tea; it had gone cold, but he finished it anyway. "I'm afraid a lot of us are going to get sick, the longer we have to stay on this ship. It's not healthy."

"I always thought you liked ships. Sailing."

"I do. But this isn't a healthy mentality, having to *live* on ships without anyplace to *go*. With all the places there *were* to go to— The hell with it."

Galvus regarded his friend uncertainly. "Without anyplace to go? Adred, we're not trapped, you know! You give it another day or two and we'll make certain where we are, we'll navigate to the nearest port—"

"The 'nearest port's' at the bottom of the waves, Galvus."

"Oh, Adred! That's not possible and we both know it!" the prince-regent replied gruffly.

His friend only watched him, his reply in his eyes.

"What are you saying? Have you given up? Are you telling me that there's *nothing* left?"

"Galvus . . . you know as well as I do what we've gone through—"

"Are you telling me there are *no cities* left? *Are you?* Because it's physically impossible, Adred! It's impossible!"

Adred looked away. He complained quietly, "What we've just lived through was a physical impossibility."

Galvus was truly vexed. "How can you sit there— Adred! Is that what you're saying to me? Who told you that? Who's up there talking about no cities being left?"

"No one has to *talk* about it. No one has to come right out and say it!"

"Well, it's not true. Damn it. . . ." Galvus stood up, crossed the galley, impatiently punched one fist into a wall. "It's not true."

Adred, too, rose to his feet; he moved across the floor for the door.

"Where're you going?"

"I want to look in on Orain."

Galvus stared at him for several long heartbeats, strong moments; his expression made Adred feel uncomfortable. The tension on this ship was becoming almost tangible: random individuals left alive, saved from the overwhelming destruction almost as afterthoughts, and uncertain how to cope with that, how to answer the startling question of their meager aliveness.

"What is it?" Adred asked, becoming testy.

"I just. . . . Gods! Why did you have to *say* that?" Galvus asked.

"Say what?"

"I have to have—*we* have to have . . . *hope*! Don't you realize that?"

Adred licked his lips, stared at Galvus; his eyes were strained and sore, so he rubbed one of them, then the other. "I'm tired, Galvus. You're tired. We're all—"

"We have to have something to believe in, you know. We have to have *hope*."

262

"Whatever was there, Galvus—it's gone. The world's broken into a million pieces. We're lucky—maybe we're lucky—that we've survived, but that doesn't mean there's any *hope*, it doesn't mean there's any *meaning*, it's just—"

"You don't believe that. Why're you saying it? You're frightened, that's all. I don't blame you."

"Everything's over, Galvus. It's ended."

"There are still *cities* out there, damn it!" *People* out there! We just picked up a boatful of them! Why are you insisting that— Hell! We might as well all just jump overboard! Give up! Tell me why it's so important for you to believe that we're *dead* already, Adred!"

"It's not important to me," his friend corrected him. "It's just— I'm being honest. Galvus, if you don't realize what's happened, if you think we're going to be able to just sail back to wherever it was we came from, then you're a—" He caught himself. "I'm tired. I'm very tired."

"I'm a what?"

Adred shook his head. "I'm very tired," he apologized lamely. "And I've been staying awake because I'm afraid that if I go to sleep, I'll never wake up again. Some storm'll come along and—" He sneered, motioned with one hand in a curt, crude gesture of death.

His admission softened Galvus's temper. "I know. I know . . . exactly what you mean."

"Either I wake up dead, I don't wake up, or . . . I wake up tomorrow to this. No land. No cities. Just a shipful of sick people not sure what to do with themselves, when to do it, waiting for whatever isn't there to come back for them. It's like some tremendous mistake was made. This wasn't supposed to happen. Not this, not now. I'm sitting here, I'm sipping tea, and I *know* this wasn't supposed to happen! And there's no reason for it. I know there's no reason for it, but I'm a human being, I've been taught there are reasons for everything, so I'm sitting here trying to figure out the reason for there being no reason. . . ." He snorted a cruel laugh, wiped his hands over his face. "Good night, Galvus."

"Adred? Yes . . . good night." After a moment: "You *will* wake up tomorrow, you know." Galvus showed him a slight, hesitant smile. "We have to start making plans. What to do, how to do it—just what you said. We're *alive*. Maybe there's no good reason for it other than—just that . . . that we *are* alive. But whatever we can do with that, we'll have to do it."

Adred was in no mood for such determined inspiration. He waved weakly, turned and glided through the door.

Galvus frowned as he listened to his friend's vanishing footsteps.

"You're just tired," Galvus whispered to himself. "You're just tired, and afraid. We're not dead, Adred." He sighed heavily, there in the dimness with the rocking lights of the oil lamp and the wavering light of the stubby candle. "We're *not* dead. We're people. We're humanity and we're men and women . . . damn you. And this *did* happen for a reason. . . ."

The stubby candle burned out at last, going away with a drowning hiss on a spiraling trail of smoke, taking half the room with it.

Galvus, still in the mood to talk, was alone in the silent shadows.

Dawn.

It betrayed itself at Ogodis's porthole window with bars of gray light that swam with dust. Yet there was no warmth to the dawnlight, and by the sounds of the sea beyond the bulkhead and the noise of the blowing rain all around, Ogodis knew that there was no warmth in the world this morning, as well.

He had not slept at all. He had been on the middeck until halfway through the night—not particularly due to bravery, nor because he was helpful in times of peril, but only because Ogodis had been afraid and curious in his fear. From the middeck he had seen great towers in the Holy City fall; he had seen tremendous mountains of fire and smoke boil and rise against the storm; he had seen whole lines of ships in the Athadian armada whirl and crash and burst apart in the powerful winds and the lashing seas. Many of his own ships, too, the Imbur had seen splinter and sunder and die under the waves.

He had witnessed all this, becoming more and more agitated as the night progressed; at last (for his own safety, he was told) he had been urged down below into his cabin by Captain Thars, the master of the *Jewel*. Ogodis had complied, more out of fear for his own life than in response to Thars's commands. And he had gone complaining and fussing, asking if the men there thought he was a coward—because he could fight with the best of them, and was a trained soldier. . . .

And here he had stayed for the remainder of the night—rolling back and forth in his bunk as the ship rolled, waiting with gurgling stomach and trembling hands and feet for the ocean to burst through his walls and capture him and pull him down to the depths.

It had been a strange night. After a time of fear and tension that had nearly exhausted him, combined with being isolated in his cabin while all around him men screamed and died and worked for their lives, Ogodis had a sensation of animal-like vitality. He had almost come to feel that a protective nimbus surrounded him; and this odd sensation had increased when, at a calm hour in the ferocity, he had dared to move from his bed and retrieve from his things one of the bottles of wine which he kept with him. Drinking the wine as he sat huddled in the warmth of his covers, there in that lightless cabin, had affected Ogodis profoundly. He had even come to a moment when he felt compelled to pray to the gods, and he had done so. The starkness and the humiliation and terrifying doubt of that moment, in the night, during the storm, while so many died and so few lived, made the Imbur aware that he was actually, in a curious and private way, making a sacrifice to the gods—the sacrifice of his pride, the sacrifice of his own dignified place among men.

He remembered it now, this morning, as he lay awake in the dawn. In some strange way his fear had placated the gods so that, however many others had died last night, Ogodis and the men of the *Jewel* had not died, and that was due to the Imbur himself.

Grunting, Ogodis managed to sit up and hold himself by his arms at the edge of his bed. He dropped his feet to the floor, coughed to clear the dry itching in his throat, then stood. He weaved across the floor to his porthole window; he did not open the thick glass, but even without doing so he learned what he had suspected already: that the seas were still restless, that there was no true sunlight to the day, that the *Jewel* floated in the sepulchral calm of the afterstorm. He washed himself quickly, changed his clothes, pulled on his boots. He was still somewhat drunk, but nevertheless Ogodis managed to make his way (leaning continually with one hand on the wainscoting edge or the railing) down the gallery and up the way to the middeck.

There he was met by strong winds and blowing rain. He spotted Captain Thars on the forward deck and started across the waist. As he did, Ogodis noticed a number of the hands there regard him doubtfully, then quickly look away.

As he came up the steps, Ogodis wished Thars a good morning; the master of the *Jewel* returned the greeting with a grunt. The Imbur stepped beside him and scanned the cold gray seas; he saw no other ships nearby, only hints of broken wreckage in all directions.

"Where," he inquired, "is the reminder of our fleet?"

Thars eyed him askance, then nodded and pointed.

Ogodis perceived, far out on the horizon, perhaps three or four dull sails.

"The rest of them," Thars reported, "are gone. Either blown far from here or gone to the bottom."

Ogodis indicated the far sails. "Those were blown so far to the west?"

"South." To the Imbur's stare: "South, my lord. Those ships are south of us."

Ogodis reacted by quickly staring in a number of directions; startled, he wiped rain from his face. "But . . . if they are south of us . . . then we must be sailing—away from—"

"*We're* west, my lord."

Ogodis was very confused. Everything seemed to tumble together in his mind, with his sense of direction wholly confounded.

"My needle's off," Captain Thars told him. "I got a reading off her last night and she told us we were blowing west; now all she does is point south. Whatever that means, Imbur, we're to the west of the Holy City, and that—" he pointed "—is now north."

Through the mist and chill winds Ogodis noticed now a pile of rubble far to the north—to the south—where the other ships were. "That city?" he asked.

Thars shrugged. "Hard to say; they've all been smashed to pieces and sunk to Hodul's belly. Elpet, perhaps. More likely Ovoros. There's no telling now."

Ogodis realized that the storm had done a great deal more

damage last night than he'd realized; earthquakes, tidal waves, storms—

"The *Wing*?" he asked. "My daughter's ship?"

The master only looked at him.

Ogodis drew in a long breath; when he exhaled, he noticed that the air clouded. "It's—very cold," he commented. "It's the middle of summer . . . and it's so cold. . . ."

"I believe the cook's got some breakfast ready in the galley, my lord."

Ogodis accepted the suggestion and began to make his way down from the foredeck.

Thars turned, leaned on the railing and watched him go, shaking his head in disgusted wonder.

PART VI

Sunless

1.

A sense of order and purpose established itself aboard Captain Sallus's *Doron* in the days following the great destruction. The fear of imminent death, the anticipation of further harm, were forestalled by an anxious but simple dedication to industry. There were sails and lines to be repaired, and siding and block and steering tackle. Partitions and bunking, cots and mats needed to be constructed in the hold and in the few cabins below the forecastle. For the forty-eight refugees on the ship the limited amount of stores meant strict rationing. The most precious of their commodities, however—water—was amply provided for by the same gods that had plunged the people into this abyss of uncertainty: rain fell endlessly. There were wounded and ill to be tended to, five children to be protected, all sorts of comforts and necessities to be managed. It was in accomplishing these things that the survivors of the deluge were able to resist concentrating too

269

greatly on the storm they had passed through: attention to immediate things kept nostalgic recollections and terrible apprehensions at a distance.

There was no one person who deliberately took command; rather, a shared attitude of common selflessness governed the people of the *Doron* far better than any active voice of authority might have. There were numerous talents available, and the many tasks that needed to be filled fell to the most experienced or willing hands. Galvus and Adred, while helping out wherever and whenever they could, nevertheless shared knowing smiles from time to time—for here, on the *Doron*, during these days of gray skies and endless rains and memories, was being practiced the sort of society both of them had dreamed of creating in those old days on the other side of the horizon. But they were, after all, rather pathetic smiles that the two men shared.

Captain Sallus and his men knew their ship and knew what was needed to repair her, manage her, keep her afloat. The six Khamari had been schooled in matters of military survival, in weapons and in self-discipline, and so from flotsam and wreckage and whatever was on hand they fashioned tools—especially for help in repairing the *Doron*, and then for the purpose of finding food. Quickly they made spears and lances, bows and arrows, fishing poles and iron hooks; there were seven young men who'd been on that drifting longboat, and these the Khamars instructed in the best methods of spearing and casting for fish; Sallus's seahands—and the women, as well—lent aid by fashioning netting and weights, and those served much better in gathering up loads of fish. Orain and Irysa, one of the women who'd been rescued from the skiff, took charge of the kitchens alongside Sallus's cook, Casio; and the three of them kept the stew pots and soup kettles warming continuously.

The first days thus passed with activity and labor. The ship was repaired, the wounded were healed, the ill rallied—and those who did not were given sea burials by Sallus. The people took turns climbing the mainmast and sitting in the lookout nest to scout the wide-ranging seas through the endless drizzle, for any sign whatsoever of other surviving vessels. Songs were sung, and occasionally prayers were lifted—and curses. At night—every night—they huddled in small makeshift families or in pairs in their cots and bunks, under their blankets, and whispered promises or badmouthed the foul luck that had befallen them. But blaspheme though some of them might, they did not protest too greatly their hardship: for whatever the circumstances of life aboard the *Doron*—life it was.

For six days Sallus kept his eyes on his magnetic needle, and in those six days the needle did not waver. It continued to point due south.

The world, indeed, had changed drastically.

Sallus couldn't explain it, but there was really no need for him to be able to explain it. It was enough that this alteration in the behavior of his needle remained constant. West (he explained one evening to Galvus and Sudon, one of the Khamars) was still west, and east east; but the north had changed places with the south, at least as far as the directional needle was concerned.

Still, taking that into account, Sallus could rely upon those things that hadn't changed for whatever information he needed. And now that the *Doron* had been repaired and could respond to an honest sea captain's demands, he assured Galvus that they would learn soon enough where they were and what had become of the rest of the world.

Sallus, of course, already had his suspicions. Every evening for the past several nights he'd pored over his maps of the western seas, and he'd tried to make educated guesses about their general vicinity, taking into account the duration, strength and direction of the storm winds, tides and waves.

"My best guess, I suppose," he volunteered, "is that we're here." He placed a finger on a map.

Sudon whistled. "We're in the middle of nowhere, then?"

Sallus smiled grimly. "Which is why I want to bear east as true as I can—and we should be able to, now that this needle's making some kind of backwards sense. If we were blown asea this far, so were other ships. I haven't seen sign of a flag or pennant or signal for six days and nights, but there have to be others out there."

Galvus agreed.

"So . . . we'll sail east. Make for—well, for what used to be Athad, I suppose."

Galvus sighed. "Athad. . . ."

Sallus glanced at him and at the Khamar. "Or whatever they're calling it these days," he amended.

* * *

Adred, as the days passed aboard the *Doron*, found himself
falling victim to a vain but very strong feeling of depression, and
an uneasiness bordering on melancholy. At first he had worked as
diligently as the others to ensure the safety of the ship and the
survival of everyone on it; but now, as the people seemed to
habituate themselves to this new environment, seemed actually to
accept its closed world as they might have accepted an apartment
building or life in an old warehouse, Adred felt frustrated and
resentful.

The tolerance of these people to this new condition, their
reaction following so closely upon their near-annihilation, filled
him with revulsion. Who did these people think they were, to
accept so calmly and as a matter of course this precious
opportunity, while around them the sea was filled with bloated
corpses? How many brothers and sisters, mothers and fathers had
these people lost? How much fear had they suffered intensely and
actually, and how dare they forget that fear, blandly barter it for a
cup of soup or a piece of fish? What would they do when the food
ran out? Or if fresh water ran out? It seemed to Adred that this
steadfast denial of reality on their part, this acceptance among
themselves of a community of equals, was a pretense. Were they
all blind? Or was it simply that they no longer cared to anticipate
the future? Had that been frightened out of them? Were they living
for the moment only?

This mood that gripped him and held him was a strange one.
Adred knew that it wasn't shared by Galvus, who'd been spending
much time with Sallus and with the Khamars and the sailors; and
he knew that he could not explain how he felt to Orain, who was
also keeping occupied, working with the other women and with
the children. The destruction, and her survival of it, had changed
Orain, just as it had changed Adred himself, and Galvus—
everyone. Abgarthis, who yet lay abed in the hold, weak but
recovering from the illness that had nearly claimed him—
Abgarthis might understand this unease of Adred's, but Adred was
certainly not going to waste that man's time with grim speculations and aimless intellectual tunnelings.

He had tried, nevertheless, to begin explaining it last night to
Orain, as they lay together in their cot pretending to drift off to

sleep. From beyond their thin partition the silence of the hold had been punctuated by the coughs and mutterings and whispers of other refugees. And the rocking and swaying of the ship, the endless dance and beat of the ceaseless rain against the *Doron*'s sideboards, had seemed to the preoccupied Adred reminders of their entrapment—as though all of them had been captured and were being held prisoners.

He had tried to explain this to Orain, but she hadn't understood.

"Maybe," Adred had whispered to her, "I wish things were the way they used to be."

"You don't," Orain had reminded him in a careful voice. "You know you don't."

"But people aren't going to let go. These people . . . they aren't letting go."

"What do you mean?"

He'd held her close in the darkness, the only warmth the warmth they shared, and he knew what he wanted to say but was unable to speak the words. Not now; not yet. It would have hurt too much.

"We have to believe in something, you know. We have to have hope."

"What, Adred?" Orain had coaxed him.

He'd only held her and not answered.

How could he have told her? She wouldn't have understood. Neither would Galvus have understood. Maybe Adred was wrong, after all. Maybe it was simply nostalgia. Something was holding him back; it was his own fault. All of them had died somehow, in some way, because of what had happened; perhaps he was less honest about that than the others were.

But how could he have told Orain about what he felt when he read his father's letters and diaries? How he felt when he read the letter he'd received so long ago from Rhia? When he read some of the things he'd written himself? They might as well have been communications from ghosts inhabiting another land—ghosts that Adred still recognized, dimly recalled . . . and ghosts that he still believed in. The way a child believes a flickering candle flame is a living thing.

The memories. Sunsets on crowded brick streets. Food cooking in kitchens and in restaurants. His mad joy at finding Galvus again in that snowy street in Sulos, and in finding out again something he'd already known for a long time—that he was in love with Orain. His utter terror that night when Cyrodian had held him by the throat in the palace prison. The boulevards and the docks and the bath houses and the taverns, the gambling houses and the incensed rooms and the public squares of Athad and Bessara, Sulos and Pylar. . . . And Elad yelling at him, and Adred yelling back, demanding that Elad change the course of the world, change the laws of the world, for the sake of justice and tolerance, for the sake of life. . . .

Men shall love the world in its dying night. . . .

Yes, Adred considered—in the way men love so dearly those things they've taken for granted all their lives, once they realize that they'll soon be lost.

He felt tears well in his eyes, warm tears. Self-pity. Orain had chided him about that last night, and had told him, "You'll work through it, my love. You're too strong a person not to."

Perhaps.

He knew there was no reason for all of this, all that had happened, but that still didn't satisfy Adred. Perhaps there was something very simple that ached in him, and he—his intellect—his pride—his vanity—had to make it seem more complicated than it was. It had helped him through crises before, this reliance on his own perspective.

Perhaps it was simply the uneasy realization that if everything he'd fought against was gone, then everything he'd fought *for* had probably vanished, as well. Life would continue—some kind of life, some kind of living, at least for these people aboard the *Doron*. But perhaps Adred was finding it more difficult than he'd assumed, adjusting to this.

Perhaps he was, or had been, more committed to things the way they used to be than he'd realized, up to now.

Then again . . . perhaps it was simply the result of a sunset upon the endless seas. Perhaps his nostalgia and his self-pity were simply his way of giving meaning to things which were, after all, quite meaningless.

With thoughts such as those, small wonder that he felt so isolated from everyone else. . . .

* * *

Adred and Galvus, along with two Khamars and Amella, a large beefy woman, were sitting at the table in the galley the next morning when Sossian came in, dulcimer on his back. Galvus asked him how he was progressing with his poem.

"Poem?" Adred asked.

Everyone was intrigued.

"It only seems fitting," Sossian explained, "that someone should . . . eulogize . . . the empire. I don't want people to forget. And I want all of us to remember, too." He glanced at Galvus, who seemed to smile wanly.

Adred offered, "There are lessons to be learned, I think. Anything you wish to know, Sossian, I'll tell you. I'm sure all of us will."

Everyone at the table assented.

"Thank you," Sossian acknowledged them. "But I've only just begun it. My first canto deals with the creation of the world. I set it, you see, as a . . . parable for the empire."

"Play it for us," suggested Galvus.

"Yes!" exclaimed one of the Khamars. "Play it for us! We'd like to hear what you've composed so far!"

Sossian seemed hesitant—secretive in the way many artists are before they feel prepared or confident enough about their work to reveal it to an audience. But those in the galley were so insistent that he finally assented.

"I'll play the first canto for you. It's too bad I'm no Hordos or Indimion—I haven't the voice of a great poet. But I've tried to fashion the words properly." And so he began it for them:

"Es atu teh odos. . . .
Of the lost earth, and the days that were
Before the rise and fall of Time
Brought the storm and flood to claim
The fullness of a glorious place,
Completion of a proud beginning:
The end of thrones and sturdy laughter,
The surge of tears, forever after.
Hearken, Vision, to my poem,
And come with answers for the sorrow,
Teach the skies and teach the rivers
Of humanity's stern tomorrow.

275

The mystery of humankind
Renews itself in turning Time.
  When earth was first sundered from heaven,
  When God first rejoiced in the skies,
  When evil announced its intention
  With death to imprison all life:
  Then man was born from the clouds and rain,
  Man was born for limitless pain,
  Man was born for tears and lies,
  And made to wonder all his days,
  And made to wonder all the days. . . ."

When Sossian was done the room was filled with silence—silence and awe, and a number of tears.

For the poet had given back to these refugees what they had held private and hurting in their hearts—private and hurting, their wounds and memories. Even Adred—melancholy, depressed, eager to resurrect ghosts and find meaning where there was no meaning—even Adred was affected, and his tremblings showed it.

For Sossian had done for all of them what all poets do, what good priests and successful physicians and all healers do: he had taken the many parts and weaved them into a whole, to make from the fragments a truth. Life made valid through the tongue of art.

Abgarthis was sitting up in bed when Adred came in. The old man had been given one of the few true beds on the *Doron*, the one in Sallus's first mate's cabin. And he was very nearly alone in the room, for the others who stayed there had improved and were helping with the ship's work.

Abgarthis himself was eager to quit his bed and join the rest of the people; but Sallus and Galvus, Orain and the Khamars had all insisted that he prolong his rest.

Now he was sipping broth from a wooden bowl; a small plate of steamed fish, brought to him by Orain, was on a table beside his bed.

"You're looking well," Adred complimented him, sitting in a chair alongside the table.

"And feeling much better," Abgarthis assured him. "Except for this . . . back and forth rolling. I'm afraid I'm a land animal, Adred; you can keep your ships and your sailing. It's not my calling."

Adred smiled.

"Set this over there, will you, please? Thank you. Yes, hand me the plate. Orain insists that plenty of fish is good for me." He winced.

"That's because," Adred told him, "fish is the only thing we *have*." He passed Abgarthis the plate; the old man speared a piece, lifted it to his mouth, sighed and chewed on it thoughtfully. "I suppose we're fortunate to have it," Adred continued. "There's plenty to catch; the schools are acting oddly. One of Sallus's seahands told me that, anyway."

Abgarthis nodded as he chewed and swallowed. "I . . . have had strange dreams, my friend."

"Have you?" Adred was alert.

"I thought I was delirious. Because of my fever—the storm. But—the dreams were real."

"What kind of dreams?"

Sharp, piercing eyes; shadowed face; gaunt cheeks. "They've all been taken by the gods, Adred. You know that, don't you?"

He didn't reply.

"It was a dream, but . . . no dream." Abgarthis eyed the younger man meaningfully. "Are you bearing up?"

"Yes. I've been depressed, though."

"Memories."

"Memories and . . . other things." To Abgarthis's insightful stare: "They're all so eager to prove to themselves that they're still alive, Abgarthis. They're making plans, they work hard. I'm not ready for that, yet."

"You will be, sooner or later."

"I suppose so."

"You really won't have any choice."

"I—" Adred shrugged, smiled weakly "—suppose so."

Abgarthis chuckled at him, grunted as he moved to set aside the fish. "I'll be growing gills, pretty soon. Gods! Well . . . do they have any idea where we are? We were lifted on strong winds, weren't we?"

"Very strong winds. Waves as big as Mount Teplis. Bigger."

Abgarthis nodded. "Yes. . . . That prophet of yours certainly knew what he was talking about, didn't he?"

Adred was cautious. "I suppose he did. I don't know. . . . How he could feel it coming—I'll never understand. And to interpret it as he did. . . ." He watched Abgarthis, saw that the old man's head was beginning to sink into his pillow. "I'll be getting on deck, now. But I wanted to look in on you."

"Thank you, Adred. I appreciate it."

"Not at all." He rose up.

"Adred."

"Yes, Abgarthis?"

A smile, in the dimness of the cabin. "When you people decide to do away with the . . . existing order—you certainly don't do it in half-measures, do you?"

Adred laughed out loud—the first honest laugh he'd unleashed in a long, sad time. "Gods!" he exclaimed, "but I'm glad you've made it through this, Abgarthis!"

"Umh." The old man grunted. "I believe I prefer to . . . withhold judgment . . . for a few days more. . . ."

2.

That afternoon Adred spent time with Amella and one of Sallus's ship hands, making candles in the waist of the *Doron*. They were heating tallow (gotten from the ship's stores) at a kettle; Adred would ladle the melted tallow into molds held by Amella, while the sailor inserted the wicks made of gut threaded with oil. It was a smelly chore and Adred did not much care for it, so as he mechanically ladled out the melted fat he let his thoughts roam as they would.

He was watching the two-year-old boy, Irysa's son, entertain himself on the other side of the deck. The little boy was giggling foolishly as he closed his eyes and spun around, then stopped short, went into a posture and opened his eyes. His happy shrieks carried across the ship as he surprised himself over and over again, discovering where he'd wandered to.

"Little ones," Amella said.

Adred couldn't be certain, from her remark, whether she meant it in amused exasperation or if Amella perhaps truly didn't care for children. He glanced again at Irysa's two-year-old and saw the boy

278

wandering around now with his arms thrown out and his tongue wagging. After a moment, Adred realized what he was doing.

It was snowing, and the boy was trying to catch snowflakes on his tongue.

Snowflakes.

Adred smiled in astonishment. "Do either of you," he asked, "have any idea what the date must be today?"

The sailor didn't know, and he didn't seem to care very greatly about it. But Amella guessed: "Elru, something, isn't it? Are we still in Elru?" Then, answering her own question, "Gods, who knows what month this is! Who knows!"

Adred decided that they were still in Elru, and mentally he calculated the number of days he'd been on the *Doron*. Tracing back, he added the days to the last date he recalled in Athad and decided that today must be the thirty-first of Elru, or perhaps the first of Hutt. Late summer.

"Late summer," he remarked. "And it's snowing."

The sailor looked up, glanced around, gave an eye to Irysa's boy. "You're right," he agreed. "The whole world's really gone to hell, hasn't it? Now it's snowing in the middle of the damned summer." He shook his head once but never interrupted his labor with the candle wicks.

Adred, slightly annoyed, decided to keep any further insights of a profound or remarkable nature to himself.

Late in the afternoon, as the snow was replaced by driving rains, a wind came up from the northwest and began to challenge the helmsman's guidance of the ship. Captain Sallus ordered everyone below, save for those hands who routinely were scheduled to be on deck at this time of day. Adred was among this number, for he was standing by as a second for Kedrom, the Khamar acting as helmsman; as well, Galvus remained above, for it was his turn to serve in the lookout nest atop the mainmast.

It was Galvus's excited voice, then, that rose above the howling wind shortly after the decks had been cleared, to alert all hands: "To portside! Flags flying to portside!"

Sallus hastened to the poopdeck and ordered Kedrom to tack leeward. "Ships?" the master of the *Doron* wondered aloud, grabbing a line to steady himself, trying to see through the increasing gale.

Adred stepped up beside him. "Land, perhaps?"

Sallus couldn't say.

The storm rapidly became fiercer. Galvus, alone high above, refused suggestions that he climb down and remained in the nest, which was whipped back and forth more and more strongly. Sallus, rather than take any unnecessary chances, ordered his forward sails reefed. Orain and a few others, hearing of flags sighted, came up on deck and moved to portside in an attempt to catch a glimpse of whatever might be there.

Late afternoon became as dark as dusk. The sea began to swirl with whitetops, the air was a rushing void of drizzle and splashing mist. Several times Galvus cried down that the flags had been lost to sight, yet they always reappeared, faint shadows in the murky gray distance. Sallus commanded Galvus to at last come down from the nest and not tempt the spirits further. "We have them in sight now, lad! We're sending out boats! Get down here!"

Yet Galvus did not.

The waves continued to roll and swell, and the rains swept in tall curtains across the *Doron*. Sallus at last gave permission to eight of his hands, Sudon and another Khamar, as well as Adred, to man three skiffs and move out to see who was left alive on those ruined craft, for they were close enough now to judge that the signal flags were flying from poles or masts mounted on dangerously damaged small launches.

Just as Adred and one of the hands were grabbing lines and beginning to heave the first boat over the gunwale, Galvus called down in alarm: "Hold! Hold up! We've lost them! Both of them are gone!"

Adred whipped his head back and forth, slapped rain from his hair and shielded his eyes with his hands to look up at Galvus, who was swaying wildly in the nest in the driving wind.

"They're gone!" Galvus cried again. But he didn't move for the rigging to climb down.

Adred looked across the ship to where Orain was standing in the waist, a long coat half-pulled over her head.

"We've lost them!" Galvus yelled.

Adred looked out to sea; no sign of them at all. . . .

"We've lost them, Sallus! *They're gone!*"

280

"Come down, Galvus! Now!" And to Adred and the others: "Lock those lines again! Helmsman! Kedrom! Steer back to our charted course, helmsman!"

"Damn it!" Galvus yelled—and Adred recognized the sob in his cracking voice. "We lost them, and they went under!"

Orain and the others, their appearance that of damp ghosts in the gray drizzle, moved back across the waist and disappeared through the door leading into the hold.

The storm reduced itself to a strong rain and the winds, while violent, never grew fierce enough to actually threaten the safety of the *Doron*, nor its passengers. Dusk fell, colorless and slow.

Adred was not in the mood to eat supper that evening. Everyone aboard was by this time showing symptoms of malnourishment and fatigue, the cold and the damp. Adred wondered how long it would be before the first of them died from fever or severe congestion.

He was on his cot, reading by an oil lamp, when a regular wooden tapping sound warned him of someone approaching. Adred looked up when he saw an old ivory walking stick move around the corner of his partition.

"Abgarthis!"

"Up and . . . walking about," the old man smiled. "Not walking too steadily, however. As I said—I'm a land animal."

"Sit." Adred quickly stood so that Abgarthis might relax on his cot.

The old man moved slowly to do just that. "Thank . . . *you*!" he grunted, as he fell back on the blankets. "Yes, yes . . . much better. How these frail bones got the best of a . . . the biggest damned storm the gods ever—" He let it go, expelling a deep breath.

"What can I get you?" Adred asked him. "Tea? Soup?"

"Oh, stay where you are," was the reply, with a hint of impatience. "I'm not an invalid, I'm just an old man. What are you reading?" Abgarthis reached for the papers Adred had strewn on the bed. "Do you mind?"

Adred was tempted to apologize and take the papers from him; yet when he saw the expression on Abgarthis's face as the old man

281

scanned what was there, he relented. "No . . . no . . . I don't mind."

Abgarthis studied the lines critically, shuffled three or four of the papers. "Count Diran," he nodded. "Your father."

"Yes."

"A good man," Abgarthis remarked. "A good, good man. We treated him . . . shabbily." He lay the papers aside. "'Diran' . . . 'Doron.' You've remarked the similarity, I suppose."

"Oh, yes."

"Destiny, I think, tends to play . . . pranks like that." Abgarthis sighed again, readjusted himself and his walking stick, then leaned forward on it. "I would have thought," he began, "that you and . . . Orain would have asked this Captain Sallus to marry you, by this time."

This took Adred wholly by surprise. "Abgarthis, I—"

"Well, I've been meaning to say something to you *and* her about it . . . and there doesn't seem to be any better method than to just . . . blurt out what I—"

Abruptly, Galvus's voice carried to them, and Abgarthis stopped what he was saying. The quick sounds of hurrying footsteps grew as loud as thunderous heartbeats. Both men stared as Galvus hurled himself around the partition in a frenzy. They feared a new calamity—

But Galvus was smiling. His face was wet and dripping, his hair curled and falling down to his shoulders from the storm.

"Land!" he breathed to them, gasping.

"*What*?"

"It's *land*! Adred! Abgarthis! We've sighted *land*!"

It was late in the evening when the people of the *Doron* heard the sounds of breakers—waves crashing into something other than the hull of the ship itself. Land. Tedium gave way to that excitement which accompanies important mysteries. Yet so little could be discerned in the darkness that what seemed to be land, what promised to be land, might have been to the eye no more than a deeper mist of shadows in the night.

Sallus, Galvus and the Khamars discussed the possibility of sending up a volley of fire arrows. But this idea was rejected. "If

282

we can see all there is to see with a few arrows," growled Kedrom, "then we might as well sail on past it!"

An alternate suggestion to send forth a longboat and half a dozen men with torches was similarly put down. "I'd feel more comfortable," Sallus declared, "doing something like that, if we had a better idea what we were heading into. Give me one good reason for doing that now, rather than waiting till morning—other than impatience."

And so everyone on the ship settled down reluctantly to see what the rising dawn would reveal.

Few aboard slept; some of the older men and women napped, of course, and the younger children dozed off. But otherwise, people gradually drifted up from below to sit in the waist or quarterdeck and gossip. As the drizzling skies moved on and torches and lamps were brought out, an urgent excitement filled the ship. Clothes and shoes and weapons were mended in the midst of the talk; Casio the cook's precious deck of cards (the only set on board) was brought out, and he and two other sailors and Amella crowded together cross-legged on the forecastle and began playing *Triple Death* and *Cuts* for imaginary bets. Other deckhands cajoled a few of the women and some of the younger men into sets of pins, and all night long echoed the hollow sound of wooden balls rolling down the boards, clattering into the makeshift wooden pins. Sallus stayed on the beakhead deck, chewing absently on a splinter of wood, tapping his feet impatiently in awkward time to the flapping pennants high above him on the forward mast. Galvus stood nearby, amused by the captain's anxiousness.

Adred, meanwhile, had discovered the intellectual companionship of Irysa's older son, the eight-year-old Davar. While Sossian sat on the other side of the quarterdeck (leaning against the bulkhead, stringing his dulcimer and singing old love ballads) and Orain sat on the last step of the stairwell leading to the forecastle, Adred and Davar engaged in deeply ruminative and complex matters of thoughtful inquiry.

Where did the sea come from? Davar wanted to know. Did it come from the rain? If it came from the rain, then where did the rain come from? And why did the rain seem like clear water when you caught it in your hands but change colors everyplace else? And did rain and snow come from the same place? Just from the air? And if they did, then how did the air make rain and snow? And if they didn't, then where *did* the rain come from and the snow? And why were some people girls and some people boys? And was it true that little girls grew up to be mothers and little boys grew up to be fathers? And if that were the case, then why were there more mothers than fathers?

"More mothers than fathers?" Adred chuckled. "Whoever told you there are more mothers than fathers?"

"Nobody had to tell me. I just know it."

"You just know it?"

"There are lots of boys and girls and so there must be lots of mothers. More mothers than fathers."

Adred glanced at Orain, who was listening to this and politely keeping one hand over her mouth. "Did it ever occur to you," he asked Davar, "that a mother can have more than one little boy or little girl?"

Davar tilted his head to one side and squinted. –

"It's true, you know."

"Are you *sure*?"—slightly exasperated.

"Well, look, now . . . you have a little brother, don't you?" Davar nodded.

"Well, don't your little brother and you have the same mother?"

He had to admit that that was so.

"Well, then, there must be other little boys out there who have brothers, and they have the same mother, don't they?"

"Not *my* mother!"

"No, no, it doesn't have to be *your* mother, they could have their own mother; but that mother could have more than one little boy, right? Isn't that possible?"

"Yes," Davar admitted carefully, "I guess that's possible. . . ."

And where did stories come from? And if people just made them up, then were the people lying or were they telling the truth? Because you're always supposed to tell the truth. And if everybody lived on boats now, what'd happened to the people who still lived in houses? And. . . .

* * *

Dawn.

Initially they perceived only shades of gray, some darker than others. As the purple on the horizon gave way to deep blues and reds, then whites, then grays parted and through the drizzling haze there appeared mountains.

Everyone at the crowded rails of the *Doron* was ecstatic. Mountains. Land.

Land.

But shortly the massive grays were revealed to be, not mountains, but great slabs of stone. Domes . . . columns and walls . . . portions of a ruined city fallen into one vast, sea-washed heap.

Orain groaned.

Galvus suggested that a longboat be sent out and an investigation made, to see if the identity of the ruins could be ascertained: it might possibly give them a clue to their position. Sallus agreed; a boat was lowered and Galvus and Adred, as well as Kedrom, Amella and four sailors pushed off.

While all on board the *Doron* watched through vision obscuring mist, the craft slid into the fog and raised eccentric, hidden sounds. The lifting sun lit the swirling haze with sparkles and beams, while waves lapped against the boards of the ship then slid away. And before morning was fully light the eight had returned with reports of rotting corpses, nests of writhing serpents and other reptiles, mere fragments of debris—and an ocean that was no more than a swamp, a sea of mud, for as far as the eye could see toward the east.

"This is all we brought back," Amella said, holding up a piece of pottery.

A glance told everything. It was obviously the base of a jug or some other moderately-sized vessel, and it had been stamped with the seal of the port city of Pylar.

Pylar, then.

The third largest metropolis in the empire, and here was all that remained of it: a pile of rubble, corpses, vermin and mud.

Sallus ordered the *Doron*'s anchor lifted and called for his helmsman to tack northerly. Maybe they'd find some clue as to what was left of the capital, or some other city. Maybe they'd find more survivors, or come upon an actual beach or shoreline.

The people of the ship returned to their routine tasks with somber hearts and lowered spirits.

Until midmorning.

That was when the great bell on the forecastle rang out for the second time in a day, indicating that land had once more been sighted.

3.

Two boats went ashore. Adred and Galvus were in the first of them, along with Kedrom and Sudon and three seahands. The other two Khamars came in the second skiff, as well as Sossian, Sallus's first mate Lodan and, at her own insistence, Amella.

They shoved the boats onto a beach that was no more than a heap of mud and rock. The earth was so drenched and soggy that the twelve made their way very slowly and stepped carefully; otherwise, they feared sinking in, as they would in swampland. They separated into a long line, staying within sight of one another.

For as far as the eye could see there was nothing but muddy land, upturned boulders, water running in rivulets and collecting in wide, brackish streams and ponds. No birds, no animals—no signs of life of any kind. Neither was there evidence of rubble or ruins from any building: if there had been any structures here they had obviously been buried or sucked under by the riotous earth. And everywhere, in every direction, the endless rainy drizzle made the very air seem gray and damp. Fog and mist hid any sense of horizon.

Slowly and carefully they moved to the height of a dripping ridge, each of them occasionally sinking knee-deep in the muck. Sudon was the first to gain the top, and when he did he paused, panted and looked back at the others.

"Something's here."

Kedrom pulled himself up just behind Sudon. "What's that?" But already he saw for himself.

Galvus joined Kedrom, and Sossian made his way to the top of the ridge, followed by Adred and the others. And as each finished the long climb—

"A house," Sossian suggested.

286

"No, not a house," countered Kedrom. "Too damned hard to see, with this rain!"

It was decided that some of them stay within visibility of the boats (the sailors agreed to do so, as did Amella) while the remainder moved ahead to explore.

It was another long, slow trek through grasping sucking mud, past fuming bogs and around giant boulders; but as they continued it became clear to them that what Sudon had spotted was not a house, but an overturned boat. A launch or a skiff. And as they at last came closer, all of them noticed a number of crude grave markers aligned just beyond the launch.

The men of the *Doron* came still, standing in a loose semicircle, feeling as though they were intruders come too late to act as rescuers.

The bow of the skiff had been punched in below the water line; obviously it had run aground or struck something in the water. Its oars held the boat propped up at an angle, so that it provided a protective lean-to.

Galvus wiped his face and looked around; he counted five grave markers. Then, still some distance from the skiff, he knelt down to glance underneath.

"A body," he announced.

A throaty growl, a whining sound, lifted from beneath the boat, and Galvus—astonished—backed away.

The others joined him.

"There's some kind of animal in there," he warned Adred and Kedrom. "Maybe a dog."

Adred and Kedrom crouched down to take a look. Adred saw a man's skeletal corpse lying in the mud, half-buried, wrapped in a wet gray blanket. The stench was not pleasant. Also underneath the boat but on the opposite side, away from the body, was a small dog. Some Kendian breed, light-haired and scrawny, with its ribs showing, all wet. It showed its teeth to the strangers and gurgled deeply.

"Oh, come on now, boy," Adred called to the dog, waving one hand at it.

Kedrom gave him a look; the dog might be mad, and poisonous.

Galvus walked partway around the skiff, his boots making deep sucking sounds in the shifting mud. "He wrote something here. Or one of them did."

"What?" Sudon called.

"Carved it into the boat. A prayer. And a date. Thirty Elru." Adred shook his head. "Only a few days ago. Damn."

Sossian let out a long sigh, wiped his forehead. Staring around, he said: "Nothing else here. Wherever we are. . . . No wildlife."

Kedrom grunted, "At least you'd think there'd be some horses running wild. Something."

"Some *meat*," Sudon seconded.

But there was nothing more to be learned, so they started back toward the ridge and the others. Half-way there, Adred glanced behind and saw the scrawny Kendian dog following them, picking its way through the slosh and muck. He knelt down and snapped his fingers.

"Come on, come on!"

The dog stopped and stared at him.

Adred gave up and continued toward the hill. When he looked behind once more, the dog was still following. And it followed all twelve of them down the hill to the beach and the longboats.

Adred was one of the last to climb in. The dog watched him from the shoreline.

"If you're coming," he called to it, "you'd better hurry up!"

But the dog waited until both boats were in the water before jumping in and paddling toward them. When it came alongside his gunwale, Adred pulled it in.

The dog, wagging its tail and jumping, shook the water from itself in a spray that dampened everyone in the skiff. The sailors and the Khamars cursed volubly and threatened that Adred had better train that pup speedily.

On the return to the *Doron*, Kedrom and the others reported what they'd found ashore and noted that there had been no survivors in the camp—save for the pup.

And Davar, when he saw the lean dog, yanked himself from Irysa's hand and ran across the quarterdeck, faster than a gusting wind. "Look what you found! Look what you found! Adred! Is he for me? Look at him! He likes me!"

* * *

Sallus decided to keep in sight of the shoreline. They would continue north—or south, as his needle now indicated—at least until the weather or circumstances argued otherwise; and they must keep in sight of land on the assumption that it would provide them with their best opportunity for discovering further survivors.

The captain's reasoning proved correct. Late that afternoon the *Doron* steered around a shallow cove and the people were surprised to discover, anchored there in the deep shadows of tumbled rock, a small single-masted galley flying a tattered pennant of the city of Mirukad. Sallus and his men hailed the craft, waving from the starboard rails of the *Doron*; the initial impulse was to lower a boat and send six or eight men across to communicate.

But the only figure on the single-masted to answer their calls was a shabbily dressed man who tottered on the forward deck and yelled back to Sallus and his crew:

"Stay away! *Stay away!* We're a *dead ship!* We're plague, on this ship, do you hear me?"

"Plague?" Sallus cried back. "*Plague*, do you say?"

"Sail on, Captain! We're a dead ship! We're a death ship!"

Night came down with no further sign of survivors. Talk began concerning the length of their stay aboard the *Doron*, for some of its passengers (especially those who'd been taken on from that longboat in the open sea) were of a mind to quit the ship and begin making do on what land there was.

Sallus—and Galvus and Adred agreed with him—thought it wisest to open this attitude up to a debate. And so beneath the fire of torches and in the wafting odor of burning oil lamps, that night the people congregated in the waist to discuss the idea.

At first, the matter seemed unarguable. Though the rains had continued unabated, the great perilous storms and the earthquakes seemed to have passed. The stores onboard the *Doron*, of course, were limited, and that death ship they'd cruised past today held a lesson for all of them: if they remained together for too long, without proper rest and care and nourishment, surely disease would settle in one or several of them, and if that disease were contagious—why, within a mere day or two the whole ship might become a slow grave, itself.

Sallus admitted that this was a dire possibility; but he maintained that thus far everyone had managed their health, and with the ingenuity and work all had so far contributed, it seemed that the threat of disease was not immediate, nor lack of nourishment. The captain claimed that he did not wish to interfere with the decision anyone onboard might make, but as he was an experienced sailing man and a practical fellow, it might be wisest to keep a few concerns in mind.

First of all, they had not yet discovered any settlement or encampment on shore, and this seemed to argue against the reliability of planning such a thing, at least so far. Granted, they had only been within sight of shore for a brief time: but if there had been any hardy survivors in this region, then wouldn't they have shown sign of themselves, even if only by a trail of smoke spotted from a distance? The land which the twelve who'd gone ashore earlier had trod was marshy, muddy, inhospitable earth, and it did not promise to yield much in the way of security for people who merely wished to trade a rolling deck for solid ground. That ground wasn't very solid at all.

Secondly, Sallus emphasized, he had discussed this matter briefly with his first mate, Lodan, and with Galvus, Adred and the Khamar Kedrom, and it seemed necessary to them all that, should anyone ever decide to quit the safety of the *Doron* for a sojourn on land, with the intent of staying ashore, it must be agreed to by all concerned that there could then be no returning ondeck the *Doron* at a later time. Sallus clarified the matter by saying that a scouting party or an investigating boat sent ashore was a different matter from any one or any group set aground with the intention of staying there. When that might happen, the *Doron* must leave those persons on land forever, and they could not take further accounting of them henceforward. Should it happen that the *Doron* might turn sail and ride past that settlement the very day after its people were put ashore, and even should terrible calamity befall those settlers in that short a time, still—the *Doron*, its crew and passengers could not take those people back. Sallus claimed that this was not meant as a punishment nor was any vengeance or ill will intended. It was simply a precautionary matter done to insure the safety and good health of everyone of them. People must commit themselves to one thing or the other, to staying aboard the *Doron* or taking their chances on land.

When the issue was presented in this light to all those assembled in the waist, it could be seen that Captain Sallus's reasoning made laudable sense. The people of the *Doron* were living in a precarious balance, and to jeopardize that balance might make the difference between life and death, survival or extinction, even in ways that could not now be imagined or forseen. A vote was taken; each adult seated or standing in the waist or on the forecastle was called upon to raise his or her hand in response to this agreement.

Overwhelmingly, it was accepted that all aboard should stay aboard, save for temporary expeditions to investigate the shoreline; and should anyone or any persons consider leaving the *Doron* permanently at any time, that decision was to be respected and those parting from the *Doron* would agree to quit the ship and its company forever.

Adred began to feel tired early that evening. As soon as the meeting adjourned he decided to retire. Sossian, on the forecastle, offered to entertain with his dulcimer and poetry any who cared to remain and several lingered, including Galvus and Orain. Adred whispered in Orain's ear, gave her a hug and kissed her good night, then left the forecastle to make his way below deck, to his cot.

He had just closed the door leading into the gallery when he heard a small shriek. A second followed immediately, in the same voice. Adred instantly recognized it.

"Davar?" he called. "*Davar!*"

"Don't you—*No-oooo!*" carried the boy's voice.

Heart racing, Adred hurried down the gallery, following the direction of the screams. They had not come from far away. When he reached the first of the small, cramped hallways that crossed the main corridor of the gallery, Adred threw himself down the hallway to his left—and immediately, he nearly stumbled over people crouched on the floor.

Davar was half-kneeling, half-fallen on the floor, backed up against the ribbed wall on one side of the hallway. He had the puppy in his arms, and when he saw Adred, Davar's eyes went wide. Towering over the boy, his back to Adred, was Lodan, Sallus's first mate.

"He wants to steal my dog!" Davar screamed. "He wants to kill my dog and *eat* it!"

Lodan, back bent and still turned away from Adred, who was panting behind him, began to turn; with a mild chuckle he explained, "No one wants to hurt your damned—"

"Adred!" Davar screamed. "Watch out!"

Lodan moved suddenly, lurching in the cramped nearness of the hallway; he pivoted on one boot and brought up his right arm, making a swiping motion at Adred. In his hand was a knife.

"Look out!" Davar screamed again, in a shrill whine.

Adred cursed. Still breathless and panting, leaning on a wall for support, he glimpsed Lodan's mean eyes and saw the blurred arm and knife jump at him. Instinctively, Adred kicked up with his right leg while at the same time throwing himself against the opposite wall.

Lodan grunted, and Adred felt him huff a gasp.

There was a clattering sound on the floor behind Adred, and to his surprise, in those crawling instants of fleet motion, he saw no hint of blood anywhere.

When he slammed into the opposite wall, Adred tried to rebound as quickly as he could; he brought up his arms, doubled-up his fists and, wholly unprepared, struck out at the wiry Lodan, jabbing quickly.

Lodan cried out in a gruff voice and whipped his head back and forth. Adred felt the first mate's nose buckle and smash beneath his right fist and blood erupted in a spray.

"Stop!" Davar screamed—while the puppy in his arms whined to escape.

Lodan, coughing and trying to speak, backed away from Adred and bumped into the wall. He waved one red-stained hand while holding his bleeding nose with the other. He didn't manage any words, but Adred understood.

He stepped back, glanced down, spotted Lodan's knife. Adred crouched and retrieved it, held it up in one hand, tempted to use it.

"He wanted to eat my dog!" Davar was sobbing.

"By . . . the *gods*. . . !" Adred gasped, breathing deeply after his exertion.

"I—I wasn't going—to. . . . *Gods*! let me . . . get to a pan!"

Thunderous footsteps charged down the stairs behind Adred

and filled the hallway and gallery. Adred turned about, knife in hand, to see Captain Sallus and Kedrom and many others shoving their way into the cramped space to discover the cause of the commotion.

"What the hell is going on down here? What in the name of hell is—"

"Lodan! What were you doing?"

"He tried to eat my dog! He tried to eat—"

"Adred! Is that boy all right? Are you—"

"Explain yourself, Lodan! Now! Damn you!"

"Bleed to death, you son of a—"

"So Adred did that to you, did he? Isn't that a—"

Once the pandemonium and gossip had calmed down, Adred was at last able to go to his cot and lie down for a night's rest. Davar kept a close watch on his dog, and both of them were put to bed by an upset and short-tempered Irysa. A few moments after Adred closed his eyes Orain slid into the cot beside him.

But now he couldn't sleep. He lay there, hands behind his head, staring at the darkness, as the mumblings and mutterings around him quieted and were replaced by snores and dull moving sounds. He listened to Orain's regular breathing, knew that she too was asleep, and tried to lull himself to slumber by imitating her monotonous inhaling and exhaling.

Finally, Adred decided to get up and go into the galley, perhaps have a cup of tea.

As quietly as he could he slipped from the cot and made his way around the partition. While he was doing this, Adred thought he heard splashing sounds, loud in the night, and several voices. But he didn't worry much about it; he pulled on his breeches and a shirt and his boots, quietly made his way across the cabin to the door and the gallery outside.

In the kitchen Casio made him a cup of tea. "It's fresh," the cook told him. He'd made it just now because it was time for the first watch to come off duty.

And just as Adred began to sip his tea, Kedrom entered the galley with Sossian. Both had served the first watch, one on the forward deck, the other in the lookout nest. But their topic of conversation had to do with those splashing sounds Adred had heard.

"Who was that, did you say?" he asked, as Sossian and Kedrom sat down at the other end of the table.

"Lodan!" Sossian winked at him. "Lodan and Sudon!"

"What about them?"

"Didn't that boat going over the side wake you up?" Kedrom asked him. "They didn't seem to care! It woke up just about everyone else."

"No, no . . . I heard it, but it didn't—it didn't wake me up."

"Well, that was the two of them," the Khamar reiterated. "One of my brothers of the badge, if you can believe it. And that first mate—though I never believed he was one to be trusted."

"They've abandoned ship, then?" Adred asked.

Kedrom assured him it was so.

"Why?" Adred asked. When Kedrom didn't seem to pay him any attention, he glanced at Sossian.

"Why?" the poet replied. "Who knows why? They just took a boat and headed for land, Adred. Maybe they got tired of eating fish all day long."

Adred shook his head back and forth, shrugged, grinned oddly. "Maybe," he agreed, "that's all it really was. That and— boredom. . . ."

4.

Another day passed as the *Doron* continued north—south, now. Snow began to fall again, heavy snow that came down so quickly it clung to the crossarms of the masts, drifted on the foredeck, swirled in the waist. Faced with the inclement weather and tired of constant disappointment in his search for other survivors, Sallus ordered his ship about.

Continuing to keep the coastline of the mudlands in view, the *Doron* returned by the route it had come, traveling in the direction that everyone persisted in calling south. The snowstorm followed them those first few days back down the coast; when it let up it was replaced by the ceaseless rainfall.

Many of the people onboard the *Doron* claimed to have

forgotten what the sun looked like, and the society that had grown upon the ship began to fracture.

Casio sent Orain into the hold for more oil; he'd run out of whatever he had in the kitchen, and fish oil had become such a necessity in his cooking that he needed it at hand continually. Not anxious to leave the steaming warmth of the kettles for the cold, damp passageway of the gallery, she promised to return shortly with enough fish oil to last for three days.

She didn't pass anyone on her way, but this was not surprising: a grim mood had settled over the *Doron*. The expectancy or excitement which the people had lived with had passed away, especially now when they were sailing in waters which they already knew harbored no chance for meeting other survivors. The unending dreariness, too, and the mist and cold and the damp, were taking their toll. People were beginning to sneeze, cough, shiver more frequently than they had previously; everyone was pallid and beginning to show signs of haggardness. Orain worried about the possibility of someone finally weakening and giving in to serious illness; as Adred and Sallus and Abgarthis had mentioned several times, if that were to happen, the remaining passengers onboard would be so many matchsticks crowded around one particular match caught afire.

The illness would certainly spread as quickly and savagely as that fire would among matchsticks.

Orain opened the doors to the hold just wide enough to allow herself entrance between them: that way, she cut down on the draftiness. The one oil lamp that hung from the center of the long, low ceiling was hardly enough to light the entire expanse of the hold, but Orain was familiar enough with the supplies by this time to know in which aisle the fish oil was stored. Taking a candle from the half-filled box on the floor by the doors, she carried it to the middle of the storeroom and clutched it to her while she used the pole that had bits of straw tied to it to light the candle. Matches were too precious to waste everytime someone needed to light his way in the storeroom, and so Sallus had devised this method: long straws tied to the end of a pole that would reach the oil lamp. The straws could be relit again and again, and the method saved the wooden matches for emergencies.

With her burning candle Orain made her way over two aisles to where the small ceramic jars and casks of fish oil were packed. The carton on top of one stack was half full; Orain was tempted to lug the entire half-carton out of the hold and down the gallery to the kitchen. But she knew she'd never manage that, and so she settled for two of the smaller jugs. She tied them together by their handles with a piece of rope she'd learned to carry in a pocket of her vest, draped them over her shoulder and began moving back up the aisle.

That was when she heard footsteps echoing hollowly somewhere in the storeroom.

Orain paused, listened. The footsteps seemed to pause, as well. When she started up the aisle once more, she heard the footsteps again.

Worried, she hurried and came to the end of the aisle, saw the doors of the hold just ahead of her, farther down the bulkhead wall. As she approached them she heard the odd footsteps more loudly—and nearer. A shadow flitted across her path and Orain gasped.

She stared up.

A tall man stood before her.

And Orain relaxed a bit, let out a long breath of relief. It was only Nolor, the middle-aged fellow Orain had sometimes seen talking with Amella.

"You . . . you almost scared me to—to *death*!" she whispered.

Nolor, tall and gaunt, his face shadowed with beard and mustache, smiled thinly and shook his head. "Sorry. I apologize." He kept his eyes on her. "Orain."

"Would you . . . help me with these?" She nodded behind her, meaning the jugs of oil; she was still a bit breathless.

"Yes, of course." Nolor came forward, stopped in front of her, helped Orain with the jars. Still, he seemed to be staring at her, watching her carefully.

She asked him, "Did you follow me in here? I didn't hear you come in."

"I had to—I just came here to—"

"You *had* to?"

"What?"

"Is that what you said, Nolor? You *had* to come in here?"

He was looking at her as he held the jugs of fish oil. "I . . . yes. I wanted to talk."

"All right. But could we talk out there? In the kitchen? It's cold in here."

"Yes . . . yes." But he didn't move.

Orain wondered what was going on and began to feel somewhat apprehensive.

"I feel like . . . I'd like to have some wine," Nolor confessed, smiling oddly. "There's no wine anymore . . . I miss that. I've been thinking about my wife."

Orain swallowed slowly; she knew that his wife had been killed during the great destruction. Nolor hadn't said very much about that, had talked not at all about his wife. That in itself seemed a bit peculiar.

"We could . . . talk in the kitchen," Orain suggested again.

"Yes, yes," he agreed. He turned his head to one side a little, cocked it on his shoulder. "You're a princess, aren't you? I mean—you *were* . . . a princess."

Orain felt nervousness flutter in her belly. "That was a long time ago."

"But . . . you were wealthy. You lived in a palace, didn't you? You had everything. I never— My wife and I, we never—" His eyes shifted; he looked past Orain, seemed to regard something behind her. Nolor scratched his stomach, smiled a bit, shook his head.

Orain noticed that he was breathing more rapidly and that his breath appeared in gusty little clouds.

"Nolor, I think it'd be better if we—"

"Think about it," he commented. "You're a princess. And do you know what?" He held up the jars of fish oil he held in one hand. "I imagine that if I dropped these and lit a match—" he let go of them; the ceramic jugs shattered and oil sprayed up, although Nolor did not blink a bit "—if I spread oil all over here, in the hold, I could set fire to this ship—"

"*Nolor!*"

"I could just light a candle . . . it would be easy. . . ."

"Nolor!" Orain backed up a step but she refused to cower; she told him boldly: "I can't imagine what you think you're trying to do, but you're only one person—"

"Be quiet, Orain."

"—one person onboard this ship, and you—"

"*Be quiet, Orain!*"

The threat was in his angry voice, although his head was still cocked to one side and he hadn't moved. Orain waited.

Nolor told her, "I've thought about this for a long time. I've had to give this a great deal of thought."

"What are you talking about?"

He reached down into his left boot, withdrew a knife. He straightened and said to her, "Take your clothes off."

Her heart jumped; instantly Orain tensed, and her hands curled into fists.

"Just take your clothes off," Nolor repeated. "Do it now."

She sneered at him and said, with nervousness in her voice, "It's really a little too cold for this sort of thing, Nolor—don't you think?"

"I'll set fire to this ship," he vowed, "and I'll hurt you, unless you keep quiet and do what I tell you to do." He began to move ahead.

Orain stepped back, bumped into a wall of wooden crates. "Nolor—"

"And don't try to talk to me!" he growled at her. "Just do it!"

"All right!" she yelled back. She came forward, lifting her hands as if she meant to undo her vest; suddenly Orain's eyes went wide and she stared at something behind him.

Nolor grunted disgustedly, "I told you to hurry! I don't believe there's any—"

A sound, behind him.

Shocked, Nolor glanced around.

Orain, screaming loudly, kicked out with one leg (trying to hurt him in the crotch), missed Nolor and nearly slipped in the pooling fish oil.

Casio came running into the storeroom, called, "Orain! What is it?"

"No, *no!*" Nolor yelled. He faced Casio, threw down his knife and cried out, "I didn't mean to, I didn't do it!"

Orain had begun to run away; but while she caught her balance, Casio reached Nolor, stared at him in surprise, and at Orain, and asked, "Orain? What's happened?"

Nolor sobbed, "I didn't mean to!"

"He tried to—" But Orain managed no more.

Casio understood. "You piece of vomit!" he yelled at Nolor, and struck out.

Nolor howled as Casio's hand caught him on the side of the head; slipping in the spilled oil, he dropped suddenly, crashing on one leg and a hip. He fell back against the wall of crates and sobbed, "I didn't even want to . . . I didn't even want to . . . my wife forced me to do it!"

Casio stared at Orain, moved toward her and offered her his hand to help her around the oil and around the whimpering Nolor. Orain was shuddering violently.

"How did he know you were in here?"

"Just— Please, Casio, get me out of here! Call Captain Sallus, do something— Just *get me out of here!*"

Kedrom and another Khamar kept a watch on Nolor in the galley, while Orain and Casio reported the incident to Captain Sallus. Sallus seemed more peeved than outraged and his first suggestion was to string Nolor up by his ankles from the mainmast—that, or keelhaul him.

Orain didn't care to discuss such things. When Galvus and Adred, quickly alerted, arrived to comfort her, she insisted that she did not wish Nolor any harm and personally had no appetite for revenge.

The afternoon deepened quickly into dusk; Sallus had to go above deck to be with his hands and was content for the moment to leave this situation unresolved. But Adred suggested that the matter be discussed as had been the issue of settlements: "Let's get Orain and Nolor both in the waist," he said, "and have Nolor face her with everyone else there and explain why he did what he did."

"He probably doesn't even know, himself," Sallus remarked.

"It may threaten him," Galvus commented "—but on the other hand, if he's sure he won't be punished—if he has to live with his guilt—let him be his own punisher. We have to maintain some kind of society here, on this ship."

Sallus impatiently waved a hand. "Garrot him," he opined, "and be done with it."

In the kitchen, Nolor asked to see the captain, to have a word with him.

"He's busy," Kedrom refused him, and followed it with an abusive aside.

"Then take me up on deck to speak with him," Nolor said. "What am I going to try to do? Attack you? Attack him?" He held up his hands, which had been lashed together at the wrists by a length of leather.

Kedrom looked at his partner, and the guard shrugged.

And so Kedrom got to his feet, unsheathed his sword and poked the point of it at his prisoner. "Get up, then," he grunted. "Topside you go."

Word of what had happened had spread to every ear, and as Nolor was led up and out into the waist, voices hushed, heads turned, quiet fell over the *Doron* as heavy as the darkness the ship swam through. Sallus, on the poopdeck, held still in his charting, shoved his wooden splinter from one side of his mouth to the other, and watched with narrowed eyes as Kedrom pushed the hand-bound Nolor up the way to the poopdeck.

"Kedrom!" Sallus cried. "What's your purpose in—"

Abruptly, all became confusion as Nolor lurched to one side— out of range of Kedrom's long blade—and ran across the poopdeck to the starboard rail.

"Stop him!"

"Damn it, he has no—"

"He can't—"

Grabbing hold with his caught hands, Nolor heaved himself up from the deck—swung his legs over the railing—

"*Nolor!*"

—dropped down the side of the *Doron.*

"He's overboard! He's jumped overboard!"

"Lower those lines! Lower those lines and get him!"

"Damn it!" roared Kedrom. "Lying son of a serpent! *Liar! Coward!*"

The lines were loosened and cast out, as were two boats; but in the darkness nothing could be seen, and in the dull gray light of the night only water and froth showed in the wake of the *Doron*'s passage.

When Orain was told of what Nolor had done, her sole comment was: "Perhaps, then . . . he has found his peace. . . ." And thereafter she did not speak again of the incident in the hold or of the pathetic Nolor's suicide, and bade Adred never to mention it to her again, as well.

Dawn broke gray and with the promise of a light drizzle rather than windy squalls—as well as the promise of something more.

Sails.

First one appeared on the northern horizon, then a second. Followed by another.

Three ships, tacking towards the *Doron*, signaling them with semaphore flags and, as they drew closer, trumpet calls.

Three ships.

By the time morning was as bright as it would be, the rails and lines and lookouts of the *Doron* were crowded with waving arms and smiling faces. And by early in the afternoon sails were reefed, oars lifted, anchors lowered.

Longboats were dropped splashing into the water from the *Doron* and the lead ship of the three, with Sallus himself at the bow of the launch that carried Adred, Galvus, Kedrom and four seahands across the rolling waves to a reunion with other—

Athadian citizens?

Could they still consider themselves, think of themselves as . . . Athadians?

The lead ship, the *Strong*, was a merchanter, large, three-masted, and filled with nearly one hundred refugees from the city of Sulos. The second, from Sulos as well, was a galley holding thirty-two survivors. The third, also a galley, had escaped from Bessara with fifty-two people.

Leron, the master of the *Strong*, was a soldier who had served in the Sulos metropolitan guards; by sheer good fortune he'd happened to be aboard the merchanter when the destruction began. The original captain of the *Strong* had been killed, along with several others, during the storms that had come with the earthquakes and fires; those who'd remained had held an assembly and had cast votes, and elected to have Leron command their vessel, with three veteran seahands as advisers.

Leron invited Sallus and his seven aboard, and this was done in full view of the cheering, clapping crowds that lined the rails of the *Doron*. As Sallus and Adred, Galvus and the others climbed aboard, they stared into long lines of faces, three and four rows deep, collected in the waist and on the forecastle. There were tentative smiles and many staring, hopeful expressions.

Adred and Galvus felt the same thing these people did: perhaps, by the will of the gods or the fate of the world or by the intervention of the Prophet, *perhaps* someone they knew might be aboard, and alive. . . .

Leron presented Sallus to his crew and then to the survivors of the *Strong*. There was little food, but soup, water and meat (from butchered horses that had been captured on an island two days to the west) were ordered set out in the dining room, there to celebrate the reunion.

Sendarian, the captain of the Sulosan galley *Usalla*, and Tasla, master of the Bessaran *Rover*, came aboard the *Strong* with a few of their crew. They brought with them rolled parchments containing the names and home cities of everyone living on their ships; Leron added the roll call of the *Strong* to theirs and invited Sallus to take these with him onto the *Doron*, keep the lists overnight and review them with his own people. There was always the chance that family or friends might be reunited. It had happened eleven times already, among these three ships.

The meal table in the dining room was filled with robust talk, hearty laughter, sad recollections that breathed new life into the men and women. Sallus learned that Leron, Sendarian and Tasla had entered into a compact: that their ships should remain together for as long as fortune allowed, in hopes of searching out a good stretch of beach, there to dock and begin building a settlement.

"The people of the *Doron* are of the same mind," Galvus confided to them all.

"We've been sailing north," Sallus explained, "intending to find any other survivors, or perhaps a sign of some settlement—anywhere."

"North of here," Sendarian told him "—or south, now, I suppose—is your needle acting as all of ours do? North of here is nothing but wasteland, Captain Sallus. My *Usala* was blown farthest north of any ship I've met and I promise you there is only frozen death there. Every port I used to visit is either demolished or disappeared. The whole coast is changed . . . gone. The first sign of life I saw was when I spotted Tasla and his *Rover*."

"I see."

"So we're sailing south," Leron nodded, "as we've decided

that, even if the damage of the storms and the quakes is as extensive there, maybe the climate is more tolerable. Either for us to unload and start making our way on land again or even for the possibility of others having survived."

"It's always . . . possible," Adred agreed.

When the meal was finished Sallus and his people thanked their hosts, then decided to return to the *Doron* and report all they had heard to their crew and passengers. "I'm sure the decision will be," he told Leron, "to continue sailing with you—with all three of you."

"Excellent. There is strength in numbers."

"Precisely."

Adred, however, feeling impatient and curious, borrowed one of the lists of names from Galvus; half-listening to the sea masters as they talked, he scanned the columns, looking for any familiar name. He did not expect actually to find anyone he—

His heart stopped.

Near the bottom of the page, in the second column—

"Who?" Galvus asked him.

"Rhia," Adred breathed, staring at him. "Rhia's here—on this ship! And Omos!"

"*What*?"

"Yes, yes—true!"

Excited, Adred rolled up the parchment and handed it, with the others, to Kedrom; he explained to the startled Sallus:

"Go on over to the *Doron*—I want to stay here. Someone I know is aboard!" He glanced at Leron. "Captain?"

"By all means!" Leron smiled at him. "Stay!"

"And my friend Omos's name is on that list, too," Galvus told Sallus and Leron.

"Omos?" asked one of the *Strong*'s hands at the table. "He bunks two cots down from me. I'll take you to Omos."

"Gods. . . ." Adred whispered under his breath, overwhelmed by it. "Gods! It seems . . . impossible!"

They were led, excited, anticipating memories that would return to life, down the gallery by Leron's first mate and into the several large cabins which (like those on the *Doron*) had been converted into barracks or dormitories.

"Omos!" called the first mate. "Hie, Omos! There's someone here for you!"

There were others in the cabin, sitting on the floor or on their cots, hanging in hammocks: and they witnessed a scene too few of them had taken part in, and then not often enough.

All the loss and the fear and the confusion . . . hopes waiting on a scrap of a letter saved from the end of the world . . . memories of warmth that had become mockeries. . . . They stared at one another, at first, as though not certain whether they regarded whom they truly hoped they saw, or if they were being confronted by an imposter.

Then, suddenly, Galvus and Omos rushed forward and hugged one another, embraced so strongly and for so long that it seemed they'd died in one another's arms.

And under the first mate's direction Adred found Rhia in one of the women's cabins. She was in bed; she hadn't even been able to come up on deck when the *Doron* was first sighted.

"Is she ill, then?" Adred whispered to the woman beside Rhia's cot. "I—"

"Mirhu."

He seemed to remember her. "Mirhu . . . is Rhia ill? Is she—"

"No, no! She's not *ill*!"

Adred knelt beside the cot. Rhia, murmuring and rolling over, awoke confused and groggy.

"Rhia? Wake up, Rhia!"

"Who . . . is it? Bors? I'm . . . awake now. . . ."

"No, not Bors!" Adred needed a moment to remember who Bors had been.

"Not—" Her eyes fluttered open, she shook her head. "Not—*Adred*?"

"That's right! Right!"

"By—all the— *Adred*?"

He laughed at her; she laughed back and opened her arms to him, hugged him and held him. As they searched deeply in one another's eyes: "How are you?" Rhia asked him. "Are you well? Are you?"

"Hungry," he smiled. "Hungry, all the time. Other than that . . . alive."

"Yes. Alive. . . ."

Her damp red hair . . . pale skin. . . . Rhia had become so

thin, she looked so tired, with the sheets and blankets piled over her. "And—you, Rhia?"

"Alive!" she whispered, falling back onto her pillow, staring up at him and continuing to grin. "And I'm pregnant. Can't you tell?"

"Pregnant?" He was astounded; she couldn't be very pregnant, or else—Well, she was so thin. And then he recalled that letter Galvus had received—weeks ago, months ago— Before the end of the world.

"What's it . . . like out there?" Rhia asked him. "Is it still all—just rain and storms?"

"No. No more storms. It's raining; all it does is rain or snow, I'm afraid."

"Well," Rhia promised him, "I'm not going outside until the sun comes out again. I'm staying right here until the sun comes out. And it'd better be soon."

Adred grinned.

She continued to look at him and asked him, then, carefully: "What happened to Orain, Adred?"

"She's alive. And Galvus is alive. He just found Omos here. We escaped from the capital on the *Doron*. Pure chance. Athad fell apart like it was . . . well—you know all about that."

"Yes," Rhia grinned, "I know." She closed her eyes, relaxed, kept her one hand in Adred's and squeezed it. "Rare breed of . . . tough people . . ." she whispered "—these aristocrats. . . ."

Adred gripped her hand strongly, watched her affectionately, and remembered.

PART VII

Resurrection

1.

The *Jewel* dropped anchor off a rocky stretch of coast, at an inlet whose waters washed calmly upon a pebble-strewn beach of green. Captain Thars, the Imbur Ogodis and the men of the crew were surprised to see so verdant and peaceful a strand: for days upon days they had pushed the *Jewel* westward, in rain and mist and occasional snow, and had spied only lifeless land, fallen cities, overturned earth.

As the galley rocked quietly in the gray waves, the man in the lookout swore that he saw movement inland, beyond a fringe of black forest. "Horses!" he called. "Or cattle!"

Food.

Thars gave orders to lower three longboats; he himself would lead one of them aground. Weapons were distributed and the Imbur himself decided to go ashore, as well. By late in the morning the three skiffs were lowered to the waves, and the ten

307

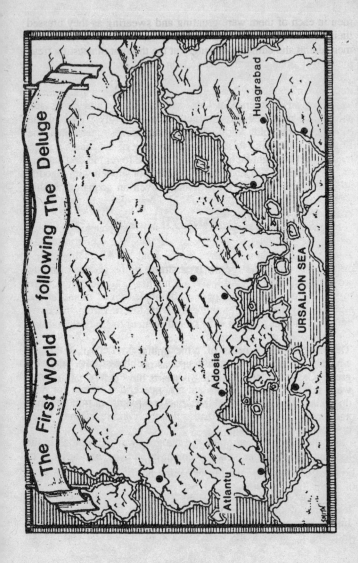

The First World — following The Deluge

Huagrabad

URSALION SEA

Adosla

Atlantu

men in each of them were grunting and swearing as they pressed their oars through the strong incoming waves. Shortly, thirty-four men, damp and chilled and hungry at the thought of roasting fresh meat over open campfires, stood on the green earth.

Among them was Udi, the Minesian. Ogodis felt uncomfortable in this man's presence, for the Imbur had been told confidentially by one of his soldiers that Udi, with his charts and bones and coins, had predicted the destruction of the Holy City and the passing of the old world. Ogodis had never questioned the Minesian concerning this, but once learning of the man's powers he had kept his sight on him and had noticed (over the past several days) oddities in Udi's behavior. This did not sit well with Ogodis; however, while he had yet to manage even an acquaintanceship with the seer, he decided that he held a begrudging respect for so knowledgable and insightful a reader.

Now, on this shore, Ogodis noticed that Udi seemed agitated, yet for no apparant reason. The small Minesian quickly hurried away from the others, as soon as the boat he was riding struck ground. He ran to a large flat rock sitting in the green brush, sat cross-legged upon it and tilted back his head, as though he were sniffing some odor in the air. He squinted, looked inland at the high waving hills that turned gray with the drizzling distance, rubbed his hands together briskly and seemed to study the tattoos that had been cut into his arms.

"What the hell is he up to?" the Imbur asked Captain Thars.

Thars's opinion of the foreigner was on a level with Ogodis's own. "Maybe his powders and his charts have driven him moon-gone at last," was his remark. "There's—"

He stopped short at the sound of local thunder, rumbling on the ground.

"Horses?" Ogodis blurted.

Hemmed in as the cove was on three sides by steep hills of grass and high rock, they could as yet see nothing, although the thunder boomed closer—the sound of galloping hoofs, the steady rumble of many feet hurrying—

Abruptly, Udi shrieked.

Heads turned in time to see him fly from his rock, stumble awkwardly and drop twitching onto the grass. An arrow protruded from his back.

Thars bellowed: "Into the water! Now, now!" as he pulled his sword from its scabbard.

Every soldier there did the same, as did Ogodis, and all began backing into the skiffs.

But in that moment the wild thunder revealed itself. Horses. Tens of them.

Horses with riders.

"Captain!" someone yelled. His voice ended in a gurgle as he, too, dropped with an arrow through his leather jerkin.

Armed riders. They came from three directions, from both sides of the beach and down the tall hills directly before Thars and his men. If there was a leader among them he was difficult to acknowledge, for all seemed dressed similarly: in tattered and patched clothes augmented with haphazard bits of animal skins, leather, bronze and steel armor. Some wore helmets, others did not. Some wore two or even three swords; others were armed only with knives and hatchets, axes, longpoles, spears. Shields clattered against saddles; and some of the riders did not even have saddles under their legs. And some, very obviously, were women.

Swift as a sudden thunderstorm the mounted warriors surrounded Thars and his group, warning them in a coastal dialect of Athadian to throw down their weapons and not resist.

"Your lives will be spared," yelled one of the mounted men, a tall warrior wearing a steel helmet and dressed in armor, waving a sword, "if you cooperate with us! We do not want to take your lives! We want only your ship! Now—which of you is the captain of that vessel?"

Silence—save for breathing, clanking metal, the wash of the water on the shoreline. Thars's soldiers watched the mounted warriors with glaring eyes but unmoving hands, stilled weapons.

"I will ask you again!" roared the speaker. "Which of you is the captain of that vessel?"

Still—the silence. . . .

The leader cantered forward, weaving in and out of the staggered groups of men from the *Jewel*. And from the ship anchored just beyond, a number of men yelled something. The leader of the warriors looked at them, could not quite catch what they said, but laughed garishly at the utterances.

He brought his horse to a standstill beside Ogodis.

"You! You appear to be a man of breeding! You are the captain of that ship?"

Ogodis, white-faced, shivering with barely subdued wrath, stared up at the helmet atop the horse and growled contemptuously: "Take your pack of dogs and ride back to the hell that vomited you, animal!"

The leader's response was swift: with a grunt he lifted his sword and brought it down in a sweeping, fluid movement. Even before Ogodis had time to flare his nostrils in anticipation, or begin to scream, the shining steel had sliced through his throat. The Imbur's head twisted slightly, emitting a suctioning sound, then jumped into the air and fell heavily onto the ground with the noise of a dropped melon. A torrent of blood gushered out of the naked neck, throbbing and pulsing in a spray that quickly painted his corpulent body a shimmering scarlet. The arms and hands shivered, the legs began to buckle at the knees and give way. In another moment Ogodis's corpse swayed to one side, like a sack of potatoes or grain shoved brutally, and slumped to the ground. The blood continued to pour from his severed neck like some loosened water pipe; the blood made splashing and trickling sounds, like a fountain.

Thars's men groaned and called out in shock.

The leader yanked on his horse's reins immediately upon making the cut, and pulled away, so that the spewing blood would not stain him. As the Imbur's corpse slumped to the beach, his eyes darted upon all the faces before him—and settled on Thars.

"*Dog!*" the captain swore. "That man was the *Imbur of Gaegosh!* You've slain—"

"Silence!" He urged his horse ahead, urged it still before the trembling Thars.

Two strong men, one an honored officer with many proud years to his badge, the other little more than a mask, stared at one another.

There was a great quiet on that shore, save for the horse's breathing and it's rider's, and the repressed sound of Thars's monumental fury, and the dying trickles of Ogodis's leaking blood.

"There are," came the mounted warrior's metallic, ringing voice, "no longer any Imburs. There are no longer any kings, and there is no longer any Gaegosh, or Ithulia, or any place. You understand that now, don't you?"

Thars's hot stare. . . .

"And you, I take it, *are* the captain of that ship?"

He could no longer deny it. "I am."

"You are Gaegoshan?"

A nod.

"That is a war galley, Captain. You were involved in that war to the east?"

Another nod.

"That is well," proclaimed the rider. "That is well. Your name, Captain?"

"I am . . . Thars. . . ." He gave it as though it were forced from him, twisted from his flesh itself. "Captain of the *Jewel* . . . out of Sugat."

"Very good. Very good," the rider thanked him, apparently pleased. "You will remove all your weapons now, Captain Thars, and you will order your men to come ashore in the boats remaining aboard your galley. And I will insist that everyone here lay down their arms, as well, and begin tying one another securely with their belts. As I say, we have no intention of harming you, unless you persist in refusing us what we demand. Warn those men on the ship not to resist us or make any plans against us; the force you see here is only a fourth of my army, and the remainder are watching us from beyond those hills. Be certain of it. They will attack this beach at the first sign of provocation."

Thars stared at him. There was no way to verify that claim, but at this moment—why should he dare refute it? What was to be gained? He looked askance at the Imbur's tumbled corpse.

"Am I understood, Captain Thars?"

A stiff nod and a formal, bitter: "Yes. . . ."

"Very well. Now turn around and call your orders to those men on deck. . . ."

It appeared from the distance to be a fort. As he came nearer, the wanderer saw that it was indeed a kind of fort, only a very small one. Tall walls of logs set in the ground and, around it, a trench. It was built upon a hill, the base of which was lost in a wide lake—the result of the deluge and the overturning of the world. A marshy stretch of earth passing through the brackish lake provided the only real access road to the fortress.

As he came across on this twisting, marshy stretch of land, the stranger heard someone hail him from the wall of the fort. He looked up to see a young man dressed in armor. Athadian armor, it looked to be.

"Who are you?"

"A traveler. Isn't that apparent?" He advanced until he came to the wide trench; it was partially filled with water from the constant drizzling weather.

"Where did you come from?" asked the man on the wall, as a second soldier appeared beside him.

The stranger's face broke into a grin as he called back, "Name of the gods, man! I come from what *remains* of the *world*! Who are *you* and how did *you* get here?"

The second soldier told the first, exasperatedly, "Get down there and open the gate, damn it! He doesn't look ill and he's walked a long way!"

The stranger let out a cloudy breath, carefully made his way half-way down the side of the trench wall, leaped across and clambered up the muddy opposite side. When he reached the top he saw that the doors of the fort had been pulled open. He entered on weak, shaking legs.

"Food. . . ." he requested of the soldier he'd first talked to, who was now standing by the tall open doors. "Food . . . rest . . . I assure you I have no weapons and—I have no intention of assailing—your fort. . . ."

The soldier made a face and pushed closed the doors, drove through the beam bolts. He then led the traveler across the wide yard, toward the single building that stood within the compound: a long, low, flat-roofed lodge outside of which were tethered horses. Otherwise, the other quarters of the place were composed of tents, lean-tos or shacks obviously constructed of timber and fragments and scraps of cloth and brush.

The odor of cooking food brought an actual pain to his vitals, as he was led inside the lodge by the soldier. The main room was a combined kitchen and dining area, although partitioning walls at either end suggested sleeping quarters. There were only a few people here—perhaps sixteen or seventeen men dressed in armor, another four or five clothed in woollen and cotton breeches and shirts (as well as leather and animal skins), and three women.

The women were seated together at the farthest table, which was set against a wall. There were two other tables; all had oil lamps and candles sitting on them. Cut logs served for benches and chairs.

Everyone in the lodge looked up as the stranger came in; the women particularly stared with interest. Over by the fireplace three soldiers at the hearth turned and stared for a long moment, while an obese man dressed only in pants and boots sweated above the roaring fire as he stirred the eight buckets that were being used for cooking.

"Another one," spoke the soldier, as he nodded for the stranger to sit anywhere he wished.

He moved slowly for the first table and fairly collapsed when he reached it, dropping onto a flat-topped log that wobbled unsteadily beneath him. He leaned onto the table, propping himself up with his elbows, and did not look at the curious faces around him, only stared at the grooved wood.

The obese cook wrapped his right hand in a rag and lifted one of the buckets from the fire, carried it to the newcomer and set it before him. From his belt he produced a greasy, stained spoon and dropped it beside the bucket.

"Soup," he grunted. "Don't ask what's in it. But it'll fill y'up. Eat. You want water to drink?"

"Yes. Please. . . ."

"Water's cheap. Rain."

"I'm very . . . grateful."

The cook snorted, turned on his heel and waddled away.

Now the stranger, invigorated by the aroma of honest food, looked up, glanced around, picked up his spoon and dipped it into the hot bucket. When he brought out the steaming spoon he found it filled with a greenish liquid. He sipped carefully, ignoring its sour taste, happy to have whatever it might be.

From their table, the women began to cackle smartly.

The door of the lodge opened again, but the stranger did not pivot to see who might be entering. As the footsteps crunched past him, he heard the soldier who'd escorted him call:

"Another one, Captain."

"So I see. Who is he?"

No answer.

"Traveler," called the captain. His voice was not unkind.

He looked up, eyed his speaker, looked at the man beside him. The man beside him. . . .

Name of the gods!

"I—know you . . ." the man standing alongside the captain said. He was tall, must once have been overweight but now appeared only bedraggled and tired, sagging. The eyes . . . the hair and beard . . . the timbre of the voice— "*I know you!*" he nearly yelled.

The captain's face wrinkled in astonishment. "What the hell are you—"

"Uvars! Uvars, you don't know him but—" He faced the stranger eagerly. "Stand up! I want to look at you! Ero—medeus!"

He lifted himself carefully to his feet, nodding slightly. "Jors. . . ."

"I should have guessed it! Should have realized! That even if the world died, *you* never would, of all men!"

The phrasing of that puzzled Uvars and the others in the room: it did not sound as though it were praise, nor was it spoken with pride.

Sauntering, Jors crossed the floor to the stranger; yet as he did, his expression changed, and when he came close he regarded this Eromedeus carefully. The pallid, gaunt face . . . the tattered clothing. . . .

"Your arm," Jors said quietly, as he noticed the bandage wound about Eromedeus's right forearm. "You're hurt; you're wounded. You're bleeding!" He looked deeply into the man's eyes.

Eromedeus was trembling.

"How could this have happened?" Jors asked him, voice tense. "How could this have happened to you?"

The traveler winced, an attempt at forming a smile. He glanced at the others in the lodge, but none came forward. Uncertainly, he sat down again.

Jors leaned on the table, hovering above him. "How?" he breathed in astonishment.

"How?" came the croaking voice. "Because . . . of all this. Because my soul, Sir Jors, was humanity's soul."

"But you—" Jors smiled faintly, beginning to comprehend. "You're only a man, now."

"Yes. Only a man."

Jors chuckled lightly, but not with cruelty.

Eromedeus eyed him, agony plainly evident in his eyes. "I must ask you," he whispered, "to let me stay with you. I fear I am ill . . . weak . . . very tired— How can I travel any farther?"

"Yes, yes," Jors replied. "You can stay with us. We have little, to be sure, but all of us, together— Well. You must stay with us, Eromedeus." He smiled again, shook his head in wonder. He decided to sit down opposite the wanderer.

Eromedeus looked at him, looked away. He dipped his spoon into his bucket of soup, but did not eat more.

"You were a brave man," Jors complimented him in a quiet voice. "I feared you at first. You were such a mystery. You seemed . . . evil. But when you tried to kill Thameron—"

"What happened to him?" Eromedeus asked.

"A priest came . . . they met with one another behind a closed door—and the world ended."

Eromedeus swallowed thickly. "The Man of Light . . . as was meant to be."

"The man of— Yes. Yes. The man of light."

"I have been transformed, Jors. Reborn—brutally. As has this world. . . ."

"Eat," Jors told him, reaching across the table to touch one of the time wanderer's veiny, pale hands. "Eat. You'll stay with us. And no one shall know, unless you wish them to." He stood up, wiped his beard, turned to leave. But then a thought crossed his mind and he said: "Transformed . . . reborn. What do you think of all this, Eromedeus?"

"What do I—think of it?"

"Yes. All of this. What's happened to the world. How it all happened. And what we're doing now. It's— How do you feel about it? What do you think? I want to know."

The wanderer looked up at him, glanced around the room, saw the faces, noticed a small, dirty window, felt the people. He told Jors, "All of this. . . . It's the way the world was, when I was a boy."

2.

By the middle of Hutt, the month of the Horse, the four ships were passing through what had been, before the Great Destruction and the Deluge, the Straits of Ithser. But that channel, once vast, once bordered on one horizon by the coast of Gaegosh and on the other by the distant Isle of Hea, was now so narrow that the refugees' vessels sailed in the shadows of towering cliffs of naked rock.

"Gaegosh?" Adred asked, standing at the portside rail of the *Doron* and staring at the tall, glistening coastline.

"More likely," Galvus replied, "what used to be underwater, and thirty leagues out from the Gaegosh we remember."

"Look at it," breathed Omos, standing close by Galvus. "It hasn't seen the sun since the beginning of Time. . . ."

And on the starboard side the people stared at gray beaches and green verdure newly risen from the depths.

"Those can't be the southern lands," Sallus commented, smiling his wonder.

"If they weren't before," was Kedrom's remark, "I guess that they are now. The southern lands—or the northern ones, I presume."

Sallus shook his head and shifted the splinter of wood between his lips from one side to the other.

The western coastline of the continent had collapsed into a sea of mud, but these new shores which greeted the survivors as they sailed into the new Ursalion Sea suggested precisely what Adred, Galvus and Omos had suspected: they had been thrust up from the bottom of the waves. It was as though the land had actually tilted, like a piece of cork in a puddle. The west had collapsed and fallen under, the south had risen. Sallus tried to map the new shoreline as well as he could but at last gave up in disgust and put away his old maps.

Where there had been the deltas of rivers before there were now sheer cliffs or rocky expanses; where there had been green coastal beaches there were now huge inland seas dotted with hundreds and thousands of small islets, some no larger than the deck of a

317

galley. Suda had apparently been heaved underwater or thrust much farther inland; the same must be true of Orbad. If any brick or foundation stone remained of Port Arsol, then the only place it might be was on one of those islands dotting the horizon off to portside. Hundreds of cities, towns, small beaches and docks—vanished.

The days and nights wore on, seemingly endless. Fishing the alien seas provided ample supplies of food, but occasional sorties onto the strange new beaches for food, information or fragments of what had been resulted in nothing useful or knowledgeable. Once, a boatload of investigators from the *Usalla* reported columns of smoke rising far inland, during an afternoon landing; twice men exploring from the *Strong* noticed herds of cattle roaming far in the distance. And from time to time claims were made that individuals and groups of people had been spied on the shorelines. But no contact was ever made with them, for even if those who reported seeing other survivors had been accurate, the people they'd spotted apparently chose to have nothing to do with the newcomers.

Better success was had from the infrequent meetings with other shiploads of moving refugees. Nearly a month had passed since the Great Destruction, and in that time the crews of the four ships could claim to have communicated with only seven other boats. Two had been those sighted by the *Doron* and lost in a storm; one had been the ship of plague victims which Sallus had hailed off the western coast, and there had been a sinking galley of screaming men and women which the *Rover* had tried to rescue only days after the Deluge.

But since entering what they still referred to as the Ursalion Sea, the four ships had made contact with only three others, two of them sailing west, one east. The eastbound merchanter, which had appeared heavily damaged, subsequently either tacked southward during the night or listed away from the route the *Doron* and the others had charted; in any event, it was never seen again. Nor were the two which had been determined to sail west. Both had claimed to be refugee vessels of Athadian citizens—soldiers who'd escaped the siege of Erusabad. But they had not stopped, had not furled sail or dropped anchor when the offer to communicate came from the *Doron* and the *Strong*. And only two days after the galleys had vanished to the west a brief but fierce squall blew in from that direction, forcing the four refugee ships to take drastic measures to save themselves. The *Usalla*, in fact, made for a small cove and waited out the storm, rather than be overturned and sunk in the maelstrom.

But save for occasional instances such as these, the survivors learned of few others fortunate as themselves. If many had lived through the Destruction, east or west, then it was apparent that their numbers were scattered and their opportunities random for meeting with the people of the *Doron, Strong* and other ships.

By late Hutt colder weather settled upon the sea and the waves, and the ships found themselves sailing eastward into a long stretch of coastline that interrupted the horizon for as far southward as any eye could see. Conferences among the four masters of the ships brought forth the decision to tack southerly, to gauge if what they had reached was either the coastline of the old Salukadian empire (it seemed impossible—but then, the world *had* been turned upside down), or if it were perhaps but a huge island, or perhaps an arm extending from what had been the province of Ithulia or Omeria.

Several days passed; it became evident that the land they'd run into was an arm or an archipelago extending southward from the continental coast. Rather than pursue their course farther, then, the four ships dropped anchor and the masters of the vessels met upon an islet to discuss their future. For by this time the separate captains, the various members of the crews and passengers were of minds to follow alternate paths, some wishing to explore one direction, others another. The masters, however, were unable to come to any clear conclusions, and so returned to their ships.

A full month had passed since the end of the world. The survivors were weary, frightened, exhausted. Some wished to give up in despair; a few wished to continue seafaring and exploring; and many were of a mind to go ashore and take their chances on the land.

There were many and varied opportunities by which to invite peril.

And still, through sailings and conferences, through despair and excitement—the gray, the endless lightless gray. Air and sky, water and land, fog and mist—endless gray. Gray cloudy skies, cold and stretching. Gray and black seas, the waves rolling

319

forever. The rain, the drizzling rain, that was relentlessly stealing the health of every person.

No one spoke with true voices any longer: the gray and the mist and the rain had taken their voices and now all of them mumbled, croaked, coughed. None felt truly strong any longer: the gray had stolen that from them, as well.

North was south, land was water, and what land remained was strange and dead.

Sossian, aboard the *Doron*, continued to compose his lyrics about the vanished empire, but his words and music now seemed hollow, reminders of some place that must have existed once, but perhaps only in the deluded imaginations of these ghosts who wandered the decks of death ships, caught upon the moving waves of endless, unending sea. . . .

When Adred awoke to the feeling of warmth on his face, he feared at first that it must be dripping blood. He sat up quickly in his cot, gasping, slapping his face.

He stared at his hand, saw that it was dry and unstained. The same pale skin, gray—

No. Not pale.

Bright.

Adred whispered, "Orain—"

But she wasn't in their cot.

Startled, Adred stared in awe at the brightness that filled the blankets where she had been. He turned around, looked up—looked up at the porthole window.

The brightness!

And, still half-asleep, he realized that what he'd taken to be the sounds of swelling waves, of breakers, were actually the noises of running feet and yelling voices. People yelling. *Happy*.

Adred continued to stare at the window as the tears began flowing down his face. He lifted his right hand to the brightness; it felt almost stinging, foreign and hurtful. He rubbed his right hand with his left, and his left began to glow and sting. It was wonderful.

Noisy footsteps, and Orain's voice. "Adred! *Adred*!"

He turned as she came around the partition, stopped, her face a great smile.

"Do you *see* it, Adred? Do you *feel* it?"

She fell on the bed beside him, hugged him, held him.

Her blonde hair glowed again, as it had always done before, before the death of everything. Her blonde hair glowed again.

In the sunlight.

Like creatures reawakened from a long winter's cold slumber, the people of the ships moved up onto the decks and stared, yelling and laughing and crying, at a sunlit world.

Adred, holding onto Orain, standing beside Galvus and Omos on the *Doron*, listened to the dripping sounds of trickling rain and stared at the high distant clouds. The sun hid behind them, came forth again. Heavy clouds, breaking up at last and hurrying over the horizon, to let the good sun pour through.

The ocean was so brilliantly dazzling that it hurt the eyes.

Colors were so vivid, they seemed alive.

Far away—very far away—Adred noticed flocks of birds wheeling and circling in the sky. For one painful moment he was taken back . . . taken back—

"Look at it," Orain breathed, hugging him, renewed.

The world.

Off to the west, someone noticed, was a large rainbow, spreading down out of the clouds and vanishing beyond the still dark horizon. Many on the ships applauded it, as they might a visiting god.

That afternoon the sun vanished again, more storm clouds rolled in and the ships were lashed with another tempest.

But by early evening the thunder and the rain had passed on and the sun could be seen in the west, an enormous orange ball swimming in an atmosphere of purple and red, sinking beyond the edge of the world. It was as gorgeous and plentiful as any freshly born child, as any resuscitated promise or lingering vow; and many of the sentimental and devout were so overwhelmed by the beauty of it—the sun and its twilight, the continuance—that they wept and even fell to their knees and made prayers.

On all four of the ships that evening and well into the night celebrations were held. The people of the new world danced and sang songs, played cards, laughed together. On the *Doron*, Sossian hastily composed a short series of lyrics which he called

"The Return of the Day," and response to it was so favorable that he was compelled to sing it over and again, at least twenty times that night, as the people memorized the lyrics and sang the song with him.

Many were yet awake the following morning when dawn rose with the new sun. Though the sky was still cloudy it was not overcast, and for the first time in many long days the survivors savored this opportunity of looking upon a sunrise, its colors and its promise of warmth.

As breakfasts were being cooked and served in the galley of the *Doron*, Sendarian of the *Usalla* came aboard with three of his crew and met with Sallus, to explain that he and his people had decided to make settlement on this shore and not sail on farther with the other three ships.

"This place means something," the captain said. "We saw the sun here, again—for the first time, really. And we consider it an omen."

Sallus could appreciate that, but he remarked, "I think you're being hasty."

"Perhaps, my friend. But, nevertheless—we have our ship's stores and there are fish in the sea. We want to live on *land*, now. And before the weather becomes too threatening, we want to build our huts, some dwellings, and live like human beings once more. If this coming winter is severe, Sallus, you'll have no better chance of surviving it than will we, in our settlement."

"That's true. But I don't intend to sail much longer. We're all . . . restless."

"Yes. And *we will survive*, my friend. Come back to see us in the spring. We'll welcome you with cooking meat and . . . flowers—all the comforts that can't be had aboard a trading galley!" Sendarian lifted his cup of tea in a salute, a toast. "To life!" he smiled.

Sallus grinned at him, sincere, hopeful where he had not been in a very long while. "Aye," he whispered. "Aye. To life."

By the calendar he kept in his cabin, Sallus conjectured that they were moving into the month of Gara the Bear. Winter, soon.

Well, they would not try to sail the seas in winter—he and Leron and Tasla had agreed on that. The sun, and the lifting of the stormclouds and the passing of the endless rain and drizzle, only encouraged them to keep that vow.

The three ships continued to sail north—southward—bypassing great islands and small inlets, exploring the great inland sea that seemed to go on forever. What lay beneath these waves? The great temples of Suda? The warehouses of Arsol? Hundreds upon thousands of corpses of merchants and sailors, farmers and priests, women and children?

Several times they spied upon distant shores the ruins of other attempted settlements, but no signs of any ships or ships' wreckage about. That argued one of two distinct possibilities: either the people had evacuated a ship, because it was damaged or sinking, or because they wished the master to set them aland—or the settlements had been founded by people who'd come from farther inland, and for logical reasons had supposed it most sensible to start new homes or villages by the sea.

That was the way history had begun the first time around—or so historians had always supposed.

Towards the middle of the month of Gara—and when at last the three ships sighted land ahead of them, it appeared as a verdant green shoreline. No suggestion of upearthed mountains or devastated cities. Only league upon league of oak and maple trees, elms and birches. So green a coast Sallus had never seen along the Ursalion in all his sailing years: trees this crowded, so tall and unspoiled, had only been left unmolested in the territories deep within the empire.

But such did not much concern the people of the *Doron* or the *Strong* or the *Rover*. Eager to be done with sailing and their lives aboard the decks, their decision was unanimous, as anchors were dropped into the calmly washing waves just offshore: their new life must begin.

Here they would build their settlement. Huts at first, mere cottages. Later, truly strong buildings of stone block and hand-made brick. Streets. A monument, dedicated to the memory of what had been before. A village, that would grow in their children's time to become a town and a port, and in their grandchildren's time into a city.

A new beginning. A new beginning in a new world, creating a

bridge between the present and a glorious, remote but splendid past.

The middle of Gara—and one evening as she watched the shoreline from the waist of the *Doron*, Orain was reminded of something. She turned to Omos, who was with her.

"One year ago," Orain whispered, "I was in Sulos, in Kendia. Celebrating the Feast of the Ascension."

"That's right, isn't it?" Omos recalled. "This is the holiday season."

"It's so . . . poetic!" Orain laughed. "The rebirth of humanity through the Prophet, and now—the very real rebirth of humanity here, on this shore. It seems so . . . right."

Omos nodded, making a sound in his throat. Then he sniffled.

Orain thought the youth was perhaps weeping, but when she glanced at him again in the moonlight, she saw that he was not.

"What is it?" she asked.

Omos told her, "I was thinking about . . . the *other* prophet."

"The other—?" Then she recalled him. "You mean, Asawas."

"Yes. Yes. . . . Asawas."

"Do you know what this means?" Galvus asked, as they sat alone at the kitchen table in the galley.

Adred didn't say anything; he noticed that one of the candles on the table was nearly burnt out, so he wet his thumb and first finger with his tongue and snuffed out the burning wick.

Galvus didn't seem to notice his friend's mood. "At first it seemed terrifying, didn't it?" he said. "Seeing the buildings fall . . . hearing the screams. That can't be changed, now. But—the libraries, the courts, the temples, the palace—all of them gone. All the records and the files and the laws," he mused "—the *history* of Athadia, the *history* of the empire, of what we were in our souls! Gone! All of it . . . gone forever." Galvus sighed heavily. "Do you realize what it means?"

Adred looked at him but still did not reply.

"All that was lost . . . everything that was washed away . . . we've been cleansed, Adred! Do you see? Much was taken from us, but in return we've been given everything. Everything! The chance to be *new*, to begin again! No more history! No more traps, no more mazes! No more having to deal with a past that hangs like lead around our necks. We've been given . . . *everything* again!" Excited, Galvus slapped a fist on the table top. "Remember what you and I used to talk about and dream about, what we used to plan? Look at what we have now, Adred! We're *free*! Guilt . . . money . . . history . . . all those traps, dead!"

Adred stared at him, slowly shook his head.

"Do you see?" Galvus laughed enthusiastically. "We can do it, now!"

Adred slowly shook his head.

"What's the matter with you, Adred?"

He let out a breath, sat back, leaned away from the table in his chair. "I'm sorry, Galvus. Maybe I don't feel well. I think I'm tired." With no more apology than that, Adred stood up, creaking the chair, and started walking toward the door of the galley.

"Adred!" Galvus called to him. He sounded hurt. "What's the matter with—"

"Oh, *you* don't see!" his friend told him crossly, half-turning from the door. "*You* don't see, Galvus! Guilt? Money? History? Heroes? All that—nonsense? Yes, we have a chance to begin again—yes, we do. And one of the first things we'll do in this 'new world,' Galvus, is start creating new guilts, start finding new heroes, start minting more money—" He stopped, seeing the look on Galvus's face. Adred shrugged and told him: "Nothing's changed, Galvus, except the new coastline. . . ."

3.

Adosia.

Before they had even dug the first trench or felled the first tree, the people of the ships had decided to name their settlement *Adosia*—"the new place," "the new city."

They set to work in days of cool sunlight and brisk breeze, using the tools they had forged on their ships. The organizing of the project fell by common accord to those men who had developed into leaders on the ships—Leron of the *Strong*, Tasla of

The *Rover*, Sallus and Galvus and Kedrom of the *Doron*. They drew up plans and sketches, made their lists. A few men from the *Rover* had been builders and so their advice was solicited.

The work was shared. Every morning the men (and those women who preferred labor to working indoors) drew colored pieces of cloth from closed boxes as they left their ships. The majority of the pieces of cloth were colored brown, which indicated work to be done on the settlement. Blue pieces of cloth meant the individual was to fish that day for food. Green pieces of cloth meant that the worker was to take weapons that day and scout the surroundings for any possibility of food—fruit from trees, vegetables in the ground, animals of the fields or birds in the forest. Any horses spotted that could be captured were to be taken alive. If their meat was needed during the progression of the winter, then so be it: but until that time came, horses would be invaluable for labor and transportation.

Before the sun had cleared the distant forests each morning, the loud carrying sounds of axes felling trees could be heard across the green fields and down to the beach. The longboats set out and cast their nets. The hunters returned almost daily with fresh food—fruit at first, later carrots and tomatoes and potatoes, and often pheasant and other wild bird. Horses were seen far away, but none captured.

But the leaders of the settlement wanted those horses. As soon as the main lodge building was finished, they promised themselves, traps could be set for the animals. Precious salt and sugar from the ships' stores were set out in the fields and in the sparse woods, in hopes of attracting horses, as well as deer and any other animals that might chance by. Sossian, as it turned out, was adept at making traps—a skill he claimed to have learned from his mother's father. And so he was kept busy thereafter, day after day, until he had so many traps constructed that he needed the help of another man and Irysa's boy Davar to set them and check up on them. Fairly soon, the poet's traps began to yield a good quantity of squirrel, rabbit and groundhog. Meat.

At the end of six days the lodge house was completed to the extent that as many people who wished to leave the ships and begin living there could do so. Nearly every woman decided to move into the lodge, and barracks had been built for them at the west end of the long log hut. The men's barracks were at the east end, and there was room to accomodate only fifty of them—fifty out of one hundred and thirty-two men. The fifteen children were placed in lofts above the dining tables.

Many of the men, however, preferred to stay aboard the ships; this was particularly true of the sailors and soldiers who'd come on the *Strong*. So there was ample living space in the lodge for the others, for those who tended to be craftsmen and artisans, toolwrights and farmers and erstwhile members of the gentry. (It had been proved advisable on the ships, as well, for erstwhile members of gentry and men who had made their lives with their hands and backs to tread opposite sides of the decks; yet despite this, tempers had flared on more than one occasion.) Initially this caused no real dissension, for the paths leading from the beach to the lodgehouse had become so worn that they were almost true roads. But once the lodge was finished and work was begun on other buildings, those men who stayed on the ships were less prone to come ashore and less willing to accept the authority of the leaders situated in the settlement.

The democratic argument that everyone must work together for the benefit of all began to show signs of strain.

Adred, who witnessed the development of this (and had predicted it), imagined what would happen when the spring came—when some of them here decided to carve out territory and plots of land for themselves, or decided that they were now in a position to own property that could be rented or borrowed but not used communally. And what would happen when, as it inevitably would, the animals they hunted and the fish they caught and the crops they grew became abundant? What would become of the surplus? What would happen when "ours" became "mine"?— not just clothing and toys, tools and utensils, a few books or a few baubles—but food. Property. The wood that was needed for fuel and heat and cooking. What would happen when claims to certain sections of the beach or rights to farm a particular area of land, became "mine" rather than "ours"? And what would happen when some ex-businessman or some nostalgic plutocrat, who'd barely survived the destruction of the old world, contrived some substitute for money here in the new? And who would rekindle the idea of compound interest? Sooner or later, one of them must. What would happen when it developed that someone owned a certain plow or a certain loom (both yet to be built) or someone else owned a certain tract of land and decided that the use of these things was no longer a communal necessity but a personal privilege—that the use of these things could no longer be had for barter or trade, but had to be rented for money.

It wouldn't take long, Adred knew. It wouldn't take long at all for one man to decide he was more deserving than the others, and for some to agree with him out of their own need to deny themselves, and so call him a leader, a visionary, a hero—while others, of course, would disagree and leave to start their own "Adosia."

New place. New city.

There was nothing new about it.

It was the same old place under the same sun, inhabited by the same human fears and ambitions, the same greed and selfishness.

Adred felt almost betrayed.

Betrayed by that one glorious moment he'd felt, with the warm sunlight on his cheek.

Adred was returning from the stream beyond the west hills, in the company of Irysa and Casio and Lelmi, a pretty young woman from the *Rover*. They were carrying water jugs to the settlement, and just as they came within view of the log walls being erected around the lodgehouse, they heard the loud slow clanging of the bell on the forecastle of the *Doron*. A warning. Groups of people were running down to the beach, kicking up cool clouds of gray dust. Davar, with his constant companion Hungry (the dog) was scampering down over the hills on the east side of the camp.

"What is it?" Lelmi asked, quickening her pace and looking out to sea.

Adred saw it now, beyond the finger of forested beach that guarded the cove where their ships sat at anchor. There, beyond the wind-tossed oaks and pines, came a hint of sail and a mast.

"It—can't be!" he breathed.

"Adred!" It was Galvus's voice, very small and thin because of the distance. He was on the beach, waving his arms. "Adred! Do you see—who it is?"

He saw.

"What does he mean?" Irysa asked.

"The marks on the sail," he told her. "It's a Gaegoshan ship. It was the flagship of the Imbur of Gaegosh!"

"What?"

"Ogodis's . . . ship. . . ." Adred was stunned. "I've got to— Excuse me!" he apologized, and began running down the slope toward the beach. The water jug jumped up and down painfully on his shoulder.

The *Jewel* steered into the cove, reefing her sails, dipping her oars into the thrashing, sparkling waters. The crowds on the shore cheered and waved. The *Jewel*'s foredeck filled up with faces and bodies; as he hurried, Adred saw them more distinctly.

But he didn't recognize any of the insignia on their armor. In fact, their armor didn't appear to be armor at all. And there were *horses* snorting and shaking their heads in the middeck of the *Jewel*. *Horses!*

Adred slowed down, came almost to a standstill, dropped his water jug onto the grass. Lifting one arm to his perspiring forehead, he watched the *Jewel* as it came in . . . watched as the crowds on the beach lost their initial excitement. . . .

On the *Rover* and the *Strong*, sailors and soldiers leaned on the rails and climbed the rigging, began to point and yell.

Adred stared. His heart began to beat faster. "That's not . . . the Imbur. . . ."

A flame flew into the air from the foredeck of the *Jewel*. It was swiftly followed by another.

Flaming arrows.

Adred, forgetting his water, began hurrying back down the hill again, as the people on the shore screamed and moved back toward the settlement.

The first fire arrow dropped smoking into the water; the second landed on the sterndeck of the *Doron*, where it caught some rigging afire. There were only a few hands on the ship, but immediately they were lowering buckets into the bay for water to douse the flames, and ringing their bell in an alert, and howling savagely at the *Jewel*.

The Gaegoshan ship did not slow down, but she began to tack away. Her lines were yanked and her sails dropped quickly, bellied out booming in the gusty wind. Her oars were hauled up and pulled in. It was apparent that she'd intended to enter the bay and attack the settlement, but at the final moment had concluded to do otherwise. Perhaps those men aboard her feared that they were outnumbered.

A few more fire arrows arced high and fell crookedly into the waves, and with that the *Jewel* was on her way out to sea again, rounding the western arm of the bay.

But even before the last sign of the *Jewel*'s sails had vanished beyond the treetops, Tasla of the *Rover* and his crew had come to a decision.

He wanted those horses. He could use an extra ship, true—but he wanted those horses. And so he quickly struck up an agreement with Sallus and Leron: Give me the weapons you have made, lend me men who wish to sail with me, and I'll run down that fat-bellied tub, kill her crew and take what she has. And when I return with her, a fifth of what she holds in her is the settlement's.

"A fourth of what she holds," Sallus argued.

Tasla slammed his fists, shook his head—"A fifth! *A fifth!*"—but time was short, he had to outrig his two-master as best he could, and so he agreed at last to a fourth of the horses and a fourth of the booty.

The people who had hurried so excitedly down to the beach were still panting, breathless, when Tasla and his fifty men hastened aboard the *Rover*, hauled anchor and dropped sail and steered out in pursuit of the *Jewel*.

It all happened so quickly that Galvus and Omos, Orain and Abgarthis stared in fascination at the disappearing *Rover*.

But Adred, when he joined them, chuckled cruelly. "Piracy," he said. "How noble."

"It's not piracy," Galvus corrected him. "They meant to kill us; and certainly if we don't do something, they'll return. It's not piracy; it's business. We need horses."

"Piracy," Adred insisted, and watched as Tasla's galley sailed out.

It returned three days later, the *Rover* with the *Jewel* in tow; and the story Tasla told was the one he had heard from the giant who'd commandeered the Imbur's ship. The pirates had taken charge of it when the sailors originally aboard had landed on some shore far to the east. Everyone on it had been put to the sword—Imburs and captains, soldiers and sailors—or so the pirate chief had claimed. And it had been a fierce battle, likewise, for Tasla and his men: seven of those who'd gone with him did not return. But they'd surprised the *Jewel* and its dogs, dealt swiftly with half of them by bow and arrow before outmaneuvering her and boarding with axe and sword.

Tasla was justifiably proud of his accomplishment.

There had been forty-four horses aboard her. One-quarter to the settlement meant eleven, but Tasla painted a portrait of such woe and suffering that Sallus, Leron and Galvus relented into accepting an even ten horses in exchange for the weapons and men they'd loaned him, as well as armor, clothing, coins and other tokens taken from the *Jewel*

And even though he had lost seven lives during this exercise in vengeance and pillaging, Tasla was not surprised to learn that every man who'd gone with him was prepared to sail out with him on his next expedition.

"Your *next* expedition?" Galvus exclaimed, as the two sat with others in the lodgehouse that evening.

"Tomorrow morning!" the captain answered boisterously. "Or the morning after! Yes! Keep your settlement! Keep your farming! That life is too dull for me! I need a more exciting business!"

"Business. . . ." Sallus remarked.

"I'm a sailor," Tasla told him, smiling with cunning. "And I know how to survive. I traveled nearly all the world before, when it was the *old* world. Now it's a *new* world, and I believe I'll spend the last half of my life exploring *it*! Whenever was a man born so fortunate, to have one foot in one empire and his other in a second?"

"Business," Galvus shook his head and smiled uneasily. He glanced across the room at Adred, who was sitting beside the hearth with Orain.

Adred saw him, heard what Galvus had said, and refuted him by forming a word slowly and deliberately with his mouth: *Pi-ra-cee*. . . .

4.

Winter came.

Snow began to fall towards the end of Gara, but it did not last. Intermittently the snow gave way to rain, and by the first days of the month of Saru the Eagle it was apparent to the inhabitants of Adosia that they might reliably anticipate a mild winter.

They continued to prosper with the food gained from their nets and traps, and work was begun on a number of additional buildings, smaller huts and cottages that would suffice for families.

For stability and habit and the promise of a future had given hope to the companionships and the romances that had begun to evolve. Old Abgarthis, who humorously referred to himself as a relic from the past, looked with affection upon the renascence of that most durable of emotions—love—and smiled with pleasure to see blossoms grow from the ash heaps. Sossian, as everyone noticed, was spending a good deal of time with Irysa and her sons. Amella regularly engaged in lengthy arguments with Kedrom, who was used to giving orders and was impatient with anyone who questioned his authority—which Amella did daily, chiding him with jokes, mocking his posturing and generally plucking hairs from his beard. But at the same time she would go out of her way to repair his clothes, and Kedrom, while reminding Amella endlessly that she didn't know everything there was to know, would gruffly thank the woman for her troubles by going with her to unload traps or chop wood. Sometimes they would be gone half a day.

Casio, to no one's surprise, asked Hemia, a friend of Irysa's, to join him as his assistant in the lodge's kitchen, and it developed very soon that their partnership promised to yield more than stews and plates of cooked fish. Omos and Galvus' loving friendship was regarded by some in the community as an aberration, but by others more tolerantly as an indication that warmth and affection, no matter its source, was more to be prized than scorned. Mirhu and Endric, Rhia's friends from their days as revolutionaries in Sulos, shared a relationship that—despite their politics—many found admirable: their love had weathered the crimes of the old

332

days and the violence of the Destruction and was now transplanted, full of vigor and humor and caring, onto this new soil. A long evening of feasting was held when the announcement was made that Mirhu was with child.

Rhia, meanwhile, progressed in her own pregnancy and discovered that Latus, one of the soldiers from the *Strong*, was very solicitous to her and preferred to spend his spare time sitting with her, talking about things, or running errands for her. Rhia was at first upset by this, because it seemed to compromise her beliefs—she, before the Destruction a fighter for the rights of the people, now inviting the attentions of a soldier who before the Destruction would have been among the first to have her arrested on criminal charges. Many days passed before she confessed her dilemma to Latus, and he was offended by the truth; he turned to Adred for support and insight: "I know that you and Rhia were close friends in the old days. I'm in love with her; maybe I wouldn't have been before, but now—things have changed so much. . . ."

Adred went to Rhia and talked with her, reminded her of many things—the letter she had written to him, their days in Bessara, the rainy afternoon they'd spent on the porch in the Diruvian Valley—and their reminiscing led to tears and much frank talk, and later to Rhia speaking frankly with Latus. Thereafter, the two seemed more companionable; very often they could be found sitting quietly in a corner, after the community meal, holding hands and trading private jokes and smiles. "She has beautiful legs," Latus would occasionally grin at Adred. "It was all his father's fault," Rhia would occasionally explain to Adred; "Latus's father filled his head with a lot of nonsense and gave him goals no one could ever achieve." And Adred would shake his head, smiling. "A happy Rhia. Happy at last. Wonders never cease, I suppose."

But Rhia, knowing him even better in some ways than Orain, would chide him with: "Yes, I'm happy now, and I don't care what anybody else says. But what about you, Adred? There's no excuse for all of us not to feel happy about something, right now. So . . . what about you?"

For he was not happy. Adred was torn, and in a way that would have seemed ludicrous, almost incomprehensible, to the others in Adosia. He looked at all that had happened, sought to interpret it, relied upon what he knew and what he'd read and what he felt—and Adred was frightened. Not for himself, but for humanity.

He and Abgarthis, one chill winter night, discussed it.

"Galvus doesn't understand," Adred told the old man. "He's still full of hope. He truly sees this settlement as a new beginning. He's content! He thinks people have actually changed or been improved by what has happened."

"And he's wrong, of course," prodded Abgarthis.

"Of course he's wrong."

"But, Adred, you must understand—Galvus knows as well as you what happens in people's hearts. He knows no one has really changed; but he sees this as an *opportunity* for a renewed beginning, not actually as something so radically different from the past."

"Then he'll be disappointed, Abgarthis."

The old man shook his head. "Somehow, my friend, I believe you're less concerned about Galvus being disappointed, than you are of your own disappointment. Is that what you're afraid of?"

"I don't know . . . I don't know. . . . I don't like to think that I'm that great a coward."

"That's not what I was suggesting."

"Oh, I know that, Abgarthis. It's just—" Adred thought for a moment. "It seemed like, before—when we were fighting *against* something, fighting for change—it seemed then for some reason that it was almost here, very nearly in our grasp. It was *possible*, Abgarthis. It was a philosophy that had been coming for a long time and no one could deny it, even if they were angered by it. But now—now that we're starting over from the mud and the bricks. . . . In another few generations everything we remember will be completely forgotten. People really will start all over again, but they'll do exactly what they did before. And there's no reason for it!" He was actually becoming angry—angered in the way a sensitive, honest person is when confronted with the blatant truths of a society, the blatant hypocritical truths. "Look." Adred nodded toward Irysa and Sossian, who were sitting by the hearth on the other side of the room, keeping an eye on the boys playing on the floor beside them. "I'm not being sentimental, Abgarthis. It seems to me that the love between a mother and her child is done more harm than good by the continued existence of humanity."

Abgarthis faced him sternly. "You'll find no one here sympathetic to that. Adred! I've never seen you so bitter. What's brought this on?"

"We . . ." he shrugged. "—we make up stories about ourselves, Abgarthis. We believe what we want to believe, and if the facts don't fit, then to hell with the facts. *We* do that—we . . . human beings. And in the short run it seems a comfort, and in the long run it produces only misery and despair and hate. Tell me I'm wrong! Tell me this 'new city' of ours doesn't fill you with dread! In a thousand years, Abgarthis . . . it will be Athad again, with everything in it that we fought in the old Athad."

Abgarthis watched him carefully.

"I'm being honest with you," Adred said, keeping his voice low deliberately. "I can't lie to you and I can't lie to myself." He glanced once more toward Irysa and Sossian and the boys. "I know it's very tempting to think that trust, that love between a parent and its child is somehow a promise, a second chance—or the millionth chance, maybe—for the human race. But it isn't. It never has been and it never will be. It only perpetuates part of what we are—the loving part—the sharing and the good part; but that's a very *small* part, Abgarthis, and it can be washed away in blood and flame very quickly. You know it, yourself, from your days at court."

"Perhaps I do; but I've been surprised often enough not to be as cynical about the human family as you are. Allow yourself some years, Adred."

He motioned absently with his hands. "I don't see it as cynicism. I see it as—as parts of ourselves warring against one another, no part ever besting the others. Never improving . . . never sacrificing greed for fairness, pride for tolerance, belief for truth—"

"And this is why you've been moping around here!" Abgarthis told him impatiently. "Adred! You're fortunate to be alive! Flex your muscles; take a good breath! *That's* what it means to be human! I'm an old man but, damn it, that means I've learned how to sift the wheat from the chaff! Adred. . . ." His voice softened. "You're right to be critical, to want the best—but you've become lopsided. Humanity must struggle on it's own!" Abgarthis smiled. "It won't always have you to help it along, you know!"

335

Adred sighed and grinned a little, appreciating the humor. He glanced across the room, saw Orain looking at him with worried, sad eyes. "Damn it, Abgarthis," he said, "—as soon as people become docile again—as soon as they start looking for answers—then they'll start listening to people who promise them the stars in return for a little slavery. And everyone sooner or later will sell a finger in return for some comforting slavery. You saw what happened when Tasla plundered that pirate ship."

Abgarthis replied, "You still want what Galvus wants, Adred—only you're talking yourself out of it! He still wants to *try*; you've given up. Life is a matter of survival. The survival of bodies . . . people . . . places—ideas."

"Abgarthis, once life becomes *more* than a matter of mere survival, it becomes a matter of philosophy. As soon as someone looks at the stars . . . as soon as someone has a full belly . . . as soon as there's a little extra grain or an intelligent idea—it becomes a matter of philosophy. And our philosophy is based on fear and mistrust and hate, and it's gone on for so long that people assume it has to be that way because it's always been that way. Give this settlement time; it'll happen again, because there's no end to it."

Abgarthis found himself becoming amazed. Here in the lodgehouse was warmth, food, drink, friendship, entertainment, and yet— "Why are you doing this to yourself?" he asked Adred.

Adred stared at him and, almost with tears in his eyes, answered slowly, in a quiet voice: "Because I've learned the truth; and the truth of it is that truth is nothing but chains. These people don't want the truth; society never wants the truth. Watch them and see. Hand them the truth, proclaim it, announce it—and if they don't reject it, they'll change it. They'll change it just enough that common sense seems like nonsense; they'll change it so that a few bloated toads can steal and rape and claim they're doing it for the good of everyone; they'll change it so that all you need to get into the afterworld is a checklist of saying the right things to the right people. The rich man can buy his way to the gods; the poor man starts tunneling his way the day he's born." Adred stared at Abgarthis. "We need a philosophy, but I'm sure we'll content ourselves with a few politicians and some compound interest."

Sighing, Abgarthis admitted that Adred was correct, as far as he went; but he admitted also that he himself would remain a bit more tolerant—and optimistic—of humanity, at least for the time being.

But within only a few months Adred's grim, cynical observation of his fellow men was begun to be proved correct.

Winter ended with a series of thunderstorms, and as the rains ended spring came with brilliant sunshine, golden fields, green forests and sparkling waters in the blue Adosian Bay. The people of the New City proclaimed their true rebirth and identified themselves as the survivors of an empire that had been blessed by the gods from the beginning of Time.

They set to work immediately, in the warm clear spring, building an altar in the center of their settlement, to praise the gods of the old order for their deliverance.

But it was Omos who, though young, hesitant and not used to public speaking, nevertheless stepped up before the committee of Adosia (a table at which Adred did not sit) and claimed that no altar should be raised to honor the old gods of a sunken empire:

"I mean those times no disrespect; but we have witnessed the ending of those days and the passing of the gods of those days. Those gods are no more, my friends. But before the Great Destruction visited us I spoke with a prophet who told me of a new god, the One God who *is* all of us. This is the God we should praise—the God of the people; for *we* are the people of this god! Let us build an altar to On and thank the One God for delivering us from the destruction of what was, to the bounty of what we have come to!"

Omos, young and emotional. Many applauded him, although many others had reservations concerning what he had said. Galvus, however, and Abgarthis, Orain and Adred were called upon to testify in regard to the matter, and they all honestly iterated that what Omos had declared was what occurred, insofar as they had witnessed it.

An altar to On was built in the center of Adosia, and upon it were placed the first of the gleanings of the earth of the new year: fruits and vegetables, animals from their traps, fish from the sea.

While Adred, shaking his head, whispered to Abgarthis: "This isn't what Asawas talked about. This is precisely what he said he didn't want to see happen!"

337

To which Abgarthis was forced to respond: "Yes, my friend, I know this. But men have always worshipped this way, haven't they? With icons and altars? That will never change."

Adred looked the old man in the eyes—and smiled.

Oloros, the month of the River, came with the first good weather of the new spring. For the first time since the Destruction the air began to feel dry and sunlit. Crops were planted with the aid of the ten horses and the plows that had been built during the winter. More buildings were begun, and most of these were huts and homes. Adosia already boasted, besides its lodgehouse (which had become a public meeting hall), two community baths, a stables and three barns, along with four storage buildings for extra tools and other items from the ships; as well, three residences had been built. Sallus and a woman he had become fond of—Beria from the *Strong*—as well as Sossian and Irysa, and Casio and Hemia, had been the first three couples to request the help of the community in building small, one-room cabins in which to settle as spouses to raise families and call their homes.

Very soon the practice developed that, when the request was made to the Adosian Committee for help in building a cabin, it was taken publicly to mean a declaration of marriage. Yet because it took at least several days for everyone available to help with a house—and much longer in the spring, when planting had to be done—a waiting list was drawn up. It became apparent after some time that many couples would be forced to wait half a year or longer for their own private dwellings.

Adred and Orain, however, had at long last done what had been expected of them for so long and signed up as third on the new list for help with building their home. Abgarthis declared that now he could go to his grave a contented man: waiting to hear this pronouncement from Adred's own lips had been one of the things keeping him alive, all during the floods and storms and the end of the world.

The winter had seen the passing of some of them: a few older people, one young girl, three men who'd been hurt while hunting during the snowy season. But spring brought with it the first of the new citizens of the new world: Rhia's son.

Orain and Amella helped with the delivery, while Latus assisted them. The child was born a month early (so far as Amella could guess) but he was a healthy boy. And when he was placed at Rhia's breast she answered Orain's, "What do you intend to name him?" with a whispered, weak: "I'm going to name him after his father. Bors. He'll be a farmer like his father was, a strong man." She saw that Latus was hurt by this comment; Rhia smiled at him and reached out for his hand, held him and told him: "But *our* next son will be a hunter, Latus. Not . . . a soldier. I'll have no soldiers in my family!" She grinned. "But I would like our son to be . . . a hunter."

"A hunter," Latus commented, "of proud, beautiful women—like his father."

The spring saw the arrival, too, of something else that occurred for the first time in the history of Adosia—the visit of a trading ship from the east. It was a *surk*, one that had survived the detruction of Erusabad, and its crew was composed of Salukadian citizens and soldiers, a few Athadians, other renegades rescued from various shores. Regarded at first with mistrust, the people of this *surk* were very quickly welcomed into Adosia's public house and feted with meat and fish, beer and wine (both concocted by Kedrum and Amella, who claimed that no place on earth was deserving of the name "civilization" if it lacked liquid spirits), music and dancing.

The sailors of the *surk* brought word of all that had happened in the east during the time of the arrival of the western armada and the storms of the earth. They told of Salia, and of King Elad's death from the plague, and the loss of the *ghen* from the plague; they told of the war that had begun, and of the utter end that had come to Athadian war ships and armies, to proud Erusabad and the eastern empire. They told of their fortunate survival and of other settlements they had discovered during their exploratory journey west. They had been welcomed in many places, including the village of Usalad, which had been founded by a man named Sendarian. There were at least ten settlements, the easterners reported, between Adosia and their home village, which they had built upon the ruins of Ilbukar and had named in honor of the last great leader of their people—Huagrabad.

339

Among the visitors on the *surk* was a middle-aged man named Sem. It was discovered by Abgarthus, in conversation with this man, that Sem was an Omerian and that his father—Omul, a farmer—had become a wandering priest following a long and difficult illness. He had renamed himself Asawas and had left Omeria to fulfill his calling to the one god. Abgarthis was astounded by this revelation; and when he made it known to Galvus and Omos, Adred and Orain, the five of them spent an entire night in animated discussion. Omos especially was entranced to speak with a son—the only living descendant—of the new prophet. Several times during the night Omos spoke privately with Sem, and Sem seemed pleased and heartened to hear what the young man had to say.

Aboard their *surk* the easterners had wine and animal skins, much fish and fish oil, gold rings and jewelries and other ornaments, which they agreed to trade with the Adosians in return for the fresh bread, good cloth or whatever else was available.

The Adosians had not yet grown enough grain to have made any bread; nor had they yet managed to fence any sheep for wool and cloth: they had been making do with what cloth they had and with the tanned skins of hunted animals. They did, however, have that which the easterners dearly desired—horses.

The Adosian committee came to a decision: they would trade one stallion for whatever the easterners could spare now, and if the *surk* would return at any time with sheep or cattle, the Adosians would bargain with them for additional horses. This was agreed to, and after several days' visiting the *surk* set off again, returning eastward and promising to return in the mid-summer, if not sooner, when they had additional goods to trade.

And so the world began again, as it begins again always throughout Time: with survivors of disaster and war and plague and famine rebuilding, replanting, creating and believing, manufacturing and struggling, making purposes and promises and toiling to deliver something of tomorrow into the hands of those beside them.

On an evening in the early spring Adred sat on a hill overlooking the settlement. It was a lovely twilight: the sky was blue and purple, the sun sank in the west behind green hills that

340

were filled with tall golden grasses. Water trickled in clear streams; laughter could be heard drifting up from Adosia, and the sounds of hammers on wood, and saws cutting. A few people were walking one of the paths leading from the beach to the low entrance gate, and beyond them Adred could see Sossian, Casio and Kedrum teaching some of the older boys and young men how to mount and ride a horse. The bell, which had been removed from the *Doron* and placed on the roof of the public house, clanged hollowly—six hours after sun-high, and only a little before sundown. Columns of smoke curled into the air from behind the tall walls of Adosia—smoke from cooking fires, hearths, furnaces. Homes.

He whittled at the length of wood in his hand, sighed and glanced up occasionally to see how far Orain had come. She was walking up the hillside toward Adred. And at last she reached him, panting and shivering, to run a hand through his hair, kiss him on the cheek and sit down (with a happy gasp) in the grass beside him, under the maple tree.

After a few moments, Orain said, "It'll be dark, soon."

Adred nodded.

"What're you carving?" She leaned close to examine it; it was a small wagon, and Adred was being very careful about doing the wheels, so that they would spin on their axle and move the wagon. "Very nice," she smiled. "Very good. You're becoming quite the artist, aren't you?"

"I suppose so."

"For Davar?"

Adred shrugged. "For one of them." He chuckled. "As long as people keep having children down there, I guess I'll be in the wagon business."

Orain lay her head back on his leg and closed her eyes; it was getting cool but despite that, insects were busy spoiling the pleasant evening. She blindly swatted a few mosquitoes, sighed, reluctantly opened her eyes and sat up again. She glanced at Adred—and made a little sound.

"Heart . . ." Orain breathed, "you're crying, aren't you?"

Adred shook his head firmly, carefully wiped his eyes with his knife hand.

"It's all right," Orain told him.

He tried to show her a grin. "I was just thinking. Remember-

341

ing. I've been up here . . . watching the town . . . thinking."
His voice was thick. "One moment I want to rejoice, because it's
all so exciting; but the next—"

Orain lay a hand on his leg, watched him. "Thinking about
what, Adred?"

He started to whittle again with shivering hands. "About
. . . people, and dreams. About what we had a year ago. A year
ago, Orain."

"I remember."

"A year ago . . . on the other ¹e of the world."

"Don't—" she began.

"And I'm thinking about all those people down there with their
hopes and their ideas and their faith, their lucky rings and their
precious monument in the middle of the town. And Galvus . . . all of it. The prophet's son. Trying to . . . interpret it
all, I suppose. I'll never stop doing that. Some people never
bother to stop and look around and ask questions; I suppose I'll
never stop *looking* around and *asking* questions."

Orain didn't say anything.

Adred set aside what he'd been carving. "But . . . it's faith
that fails us," he said to her. "It's belief that destroys
us . . . and hope that makes us miserable. But we can't really be
people without those things, can we? Can we? We're less than a
dream, Orain—and look down there: the dream's come true, for
those people. But they continue to exist, hoping . . . continuing. And it will never end. There'll never be any end to
the . . . rationalizations, to the lies, the storms and the hypoc-
risies and the arguments, to the . . . endless cycles by which
humanity *is* humanity. Do you see? There are no answers. There's
no order, except whatever we decide to decide on. No trust, except
what a few people can grab hold of in the name of love or
friendship. There's no god that holds all of us in his hands with
some design to protect us in spite of ourselves. We change and
grow and continue and come full circle again—and it's all
meaningless, it's all endless and ageless and irresolvable.
We . . . continue! And that fact that seems to give everyone else
such hope doesn't give me hope. It . . . fills me with remorse.
Humanity will always forget what it's learned; it will always
praise ignorance and deception and injustice, and claim that truth
is an uncomfortable lie. It will make saviors and heroes of the

342

greedy and the hypocrites, and it will betray everyone who has an original thought or dares to dream a new dream, or show any real courage or strength. Humanity . . . will always continue. And that fills me with remorse."

He looked at her, then—looked Orain in the eyes. Tears threatened again.

"Do you understand?" he whispered.

She closed her eyes briefly, nodded.

He confessed to her: "But I'm sitting here and looking down at that village, and I was watching you as you came up the hill. And I love you; I love you, Orain. And I like that village, in spite of itself; I like the people in it, and even the people I *don't* like— right now, I think I like them." He smiled his boyish smile; Orain tugged at his leg. "And even though I know what's going to happen, where it's all going to lead, again and again and again— until the last star, the last drop of water, the last person— Orain . . . it fills me with remorse, but even though I'm filled with remorse, I still feel excited because I'm carving some silly toy for one of those children, and because I'm in love with you. It's—so contradictory. I feel like a fool, but I feel like I'm the only one who understands what's going on, or wants to, even though there's nothing to be done about it. Nothing. I feel like I'm the only one who actually *sees* . . . and accepts what I see for what it is."

He stopped, and said no more.

He watched Orain for a long moment, then looked down at Adosia.

She whispered to him, "I do love you . . . so much. . . ."

Adred took her in his arms, held her, sat back and watched the sunset with her—and felt exhilarated and depressed in the same moment, sad and excited, happy and remorseful.

Alone.

Alone with the woman he loved, with this life and the memories that had conspired to make this his life, and the thoughts which were his and his alone.

The sun disappeared and the sky became very purple and blue, darkening.

White birds blew in from the sea, circled and squealed, floated out again and dived close to the water.

Casio and Sossian and Kedrum led the horse back toward the

village as the bell rang out, its long echoes carrying muffled up the hillside.

And out on the horizon, at the edge of the world, sea was lost to sky and the stars high above began to wink and glimmer, reflecting frostily on the expanse of the ocean.

Adred took Orain's hand and stood up, helped her to her feet; together they walked down the hillside, whispering to one another and laughing a little in the deep twilight, going home.

The Fall of the First World
THE END